The Forget-Me-Not Library

Also by Heather Webber

Midnight at the Blackbird Café
South of the Buttonwood Tree
The Lights of Sugarberry Cove
In the Middle of Hickory Lane
At the Coffee Shop of Curiosities
A Certain Kind of Starlight

The Forget-Me-Not Library

Heather Webber

ST. MARTIN'S PRESS
NEW YORK

This is a work of fiction. All of the characters, organizations, and events portrayed in this novel are either products of the author's imagination or are used fictitiously.

First published in the United States by St. Martin's Press, an imprint of St. Martin's Publishing Group

EU Representative: Macmillan Publishers Ireland Ltd, 1st Floor, The Liffey Trust Centre, 117–126 Sheriff Street Upper, Dublin 1, DO1 YC43

THE FORGET-ME-NOT LIBRARY. Copyright © 2025 by Heather Webber. All rights reserved. Printed in the United States of America. For information, address St. Martin's Publishing Group, 120 Broadway, New York, NY 10271.

www.stmartins.com

Designed by Devan Norman

The Library of Congress Cataloging-in-Publication Data is available upon request.

ISBN 978-1-250-36927-7 (hardcover)
ISBN 978-1-250-36928-4 (ebook)

The publisher of this book does not authorize the use or reproduction of any part of this book in any manner for the purpose of training artificial intelligence technologies or systems. The publisher of this book expressly reserves this book from the Text and Data Mining exception in accordance with Article 4(3) of the European Union Digital Single Market Directive 2019/790.

Our books may be purchased in bulk for specialty retail/wholesale, literacy, corporate/premium, educational, and subscription box use. Please contact MacmillanSpecialMarkets@macmillan.com.

First Edition: 2025

10 9 8 7 6 5 4 3 2 1

For the librarians.

The work you do and the support you provide are both immense and invaluable.

Thank you, thank you, thank you.

The Forget-Me-Not Library

One

A Pearl of Wisdom
from Maeve Hearnshaw
"Honey, sometimes when you're lost, the path finds you."

Juliet

On a tree-lined street in the middle of Who-Knows-Where, Alabama, fate knocked on my car window.

Later I'd learn his name was Tennyson Greenlee, age seventy-nine. He had round black eyeglasses, a long thin face lined with shallow wrinkles, a scruffy silvery-white beard, and wavy white hair that seemed to have a mind of its own.

"Don't suppose you've seen a little girl?" He spoke loudly to be heard through the closed window. "Yellow hair. Blue eyes. Purple glasses. Cute as can be?"

It wasn't what I'd been expecting him to say. Especially since I'd been parked in front of his big three-story house for a good five minutes now, cursing my luck and trying to figure out how to get where I was going. I was supposed to be in Memphis, Tennessee, by six p.m. Seven at the latest. Ahead of the stormy weather system creeping northeastward from the gulf. It was already a quarter till five, so I was definitely going to be late—if I made it there at all.

I opened the car door a crack since my windows had stopped working. "No, I haven't. Is she lost?"

"Not *lost*. Misplaced."

That sounded lost to me.

As I stepped out of the car, I asked, "Have you called the police?"

"No need. Katy never wanders far." The man didn't *sound* especially worried, but there was definitely concern darkening his blue eyes. He gestured vaguely down the street. "Last time she did this, I found her all cozied up on Vera Ingleby's porch swing. Katy had done lost herself in a book. Didn't realize an hour had passed. Couldn't hear me calling her. It was like she was in her own little world."

She most likely was. Disappearing into a book was one of my favorite things to do, too. Especially lately.

I glanced around. "How old is she and how long has she been gone?"

"Seven. And not long. An hour ago, she was tidying up her bedroom. Katy!" His voice carried down the street in heartfelt waves.

Birds scattered from the trees, squawking loudly. One, a chubby robin that had an odd splotch of white coloration at its neck, landed on an ornate sign nearby that welcomed me to the Historic Garden District. I wasn't the least bit surprised to see the bird.

I'd seen it nearly every day since I left home five weeks ago.

"Katy June!" the man shouted. "Time to come inside! It's comin' up a cloud!"

I'd never heard the phrase before, but deciphered its meaning just fine. The afternoon sky had clouded over, and the hot, humid July air had suddenly cooled. A storm was building.

This weather was *exactly* what I'd been trying to avoid by getting on the road early this morning, long before the sun came up.

My heart rate picked up as I eyed the gray clouds and absently touched the scar that sat in the hollow between my collarbones. A burn mark. There was nothing I wanted more than to get back in the car and speed off to where the skies were blue and bright and *safe*.

But two things were stopping me.

One, something was very wrong with my car.

This leg of my trip, which had started in St. Petersburg, Florida, had taken an unexpected turn after a construction detour spit me off a state highway and onto one pine tree–lined back road after another. Unable to find a cell signal amid the towering trees, my GPS failed. I kept following the empty road, longing to see any kind of detour sign, but no such luck.

Finally, I happened upon this small town. A good thing, too, because that's when all the symbols on my dashboard started flashing ominously. A few minutes later, when the engine stuttered and a plume of blue smoke puffed out from under the hood, I quickly pulled onto this residential side street and rolled to a stop. The car had shuddered, a veritable death rattle, and stalled. So far, I hadn't been able to restart it.

And the other reason I couldn't leave quite yet: I had to help find Katy. I needed to know she was safe.

"Everything okay out here, Tenn?" a woman called out from the front steps of the house next door. She was an older woman, maybe mid-sixties, wearing a simple sleeveless blue dress. A cloud of pale blond hair sat atop her head, secured with a large claw clip.

Tenn's short-sleeve button-down caught on the wind and billowed slightly as he spun around. He jammed his hands into the pockets of khaki cargo shorts. "Katy's done pulled another disappearin' act."

The woman whistled. "Best you find her soon. Tallulah will be home before you know it. Who's your new friend?"

Tenn looked at me, bushy, bristly, curious eyebrows raised in question.

"I'm Juliet. Juliet Nightingale," I said, not bothering to explain that I wasn't from around here since my Michigan license plates announced it plainly for all to see. "There was a road detour with hardly any signs. And I didn't have a cell signal. And now my car seems to have died."

I was rambling, talking too fast. I clamped my lips together and glanced at my supposedly reliable hatchback, feeling slightly betrayed. It was only a few years old and as a precaution I'd had it serviced shortly before I started this road trip. Fat lot of good it had done me.

The man scratched his beard. "Did smoke come from the engine?"

I nodded. "Blue smoke. That can't be good, right?"

His gaze softened, and he quietly said, "Not good at all."

My heart sank. I was afraid of that.

With a great flutter, the robin flew from the sign to a branch on a magnolia tree in the woman's front yard as she said, "You poor thing. I'll give my grandson, Callum, a call. He owns the local garage and will get you sorted, but I hope you didn't have somewhere to be. You'll likely be in town a spell, what with parts taking forever to get in these days and the detour of it all." Having said that, she turned and went into the house, her movements stiff but steady.

I wasn't quite sure what the detour had to do with anything, but I did have somewhere to be. I was supposed to check into the Peabody Hotel tonight, and I had a ticket to tour Graceland tomorrow in nice *sunny* Tennessee. But it wasn't as though I'd had my heart set on seeing Elvis's home. It was simply a destination. A *distraction*. One of many on this impromptu trip. Since I'd been on the road, I rarely stayed in one place for more than a day or two before moving on to the next city, following a route that had been laid out for me long ago. And, more importantly, keeping my distance from home.

"Where's *here* exactly?" I asked.

"Why, sweetheart, you're in Forget-Me-Not, Alabama."

"Forget-Me-Not—like the flower?"

"Exactly like the flower." He introduced himself, then motioned to the cottage next door. "And that there was Maeve Hearnshaw, my baby sister." He checked his digital wristwatch, and I noticed ink stains on several of his fingers. "On any other day, I'd invite you in to wait for Callum, offer something cool to drink, but it took a lot for me to convince my granddaughter, Tallulah, that I wasn't too old to keep an eye on her little girl while she was at work. She's trusting me, and I don't want to go disappointing her by telling her I misplaced Katy, so I've got to find her posthaste."

I smiled at his determined usage of the word *misplaced*. "I'm happy to help you look, if you want."

"I'd be most grateful. That's right kind of you. You can start here at my house and work your way toward the sun garden." Tenn pointed to the far end of the street, where a wrought iron arch spanned the road. "Check front porches. Check behind shrubs. Check everywhere the little sprout could curl up with a book. I'll search the other side and meet you at the end. Katy!" he yelled again, hurrying across the road, moving at an impressive clip for a man of an advanced age.

I peered down the street, enamored of its leafy canopy and mossy sidewalks. Everywhere I looked there were gorgeous pops of color in flower beds and boxes and also the houses themselves. There were at least a dozen homes, six on each side of the street, and every single one was full of charm and character and craftsmanship that spoke of days gone by.

It started sprinkling as I poked around Tenn's yard. I didn't hear any distant rumbles of thunder, but it was probably too much to hope that the storm would skirt past this town.

I hoped nonetheless.

As I looked high and low for Katy, I tried to remember if *I'd* ever sneaked out of the house when I was younger.

I couldn't recall.

Three months ago, a tragedy had stolen part of my memory, including all of my childhood recollections. Everything before I left for college was simply gone.

Sadly, it wasn't the only thing that had been lost.

Because I couldn't remember that spring day, I only knew from others what had happened. A storm had popped up while I was on a walk with my grandpa. Lightning had struck, causing chaos. Pain. Loss.

I absently touched the scar where my collarbones met. The spot was where a small bird-shaped charm had been resting when I'd been hit, melting it, burning me. *I'd* healed from all my injuries, though—physically at least.

My grandfather hadn't survived.

With a shake of my head, I snapped out of my thoughts and tried not to drown in a wave of grief. It took me a second to recall what had spun me off into the past. Right. Sneaking out.

When I had a minute, I'd text Amy, my sister. Out of my big family, she was who most often filled in the hazy parts of my life over the last few months. Well, as much as she could. Because she was ten years older—and had moved out at eighteen—there were memories she couldn't possibly fill in.

Across the street, Tenn climbed the front steps of a yellow bungalow draped in ivy, his head turning left and right, scanning. I'd just finished checking behind a hedge of flowering shrubs when a small, fluffy rusty-brown feather drifted down in front of me, swaying gracefully in the breeze. I reached out and caught it, then looked up into the oak tree, expecting to see a robin peering down. Instead, I saw a small, dirty foot sticking out from a large crook high off the ground.

"Katy?" I said loudly.

There was no answer. Not so much as a twitch of a toe.

Rain fell on the leafy canopy, a gentle pit-a-pat, as I pulled myself up onto a low branch and made my way upward. I climbed until I had the perfect view of a small girl with blond hair and purple glasses sound asleep, cradled in the strong arms of the tree. She wore a summery floral romper, its thin straps tied in bows that rested on tanned shoulders. A chapter book was open on her chest, rising and falling with her steady breaths. Her toenails were painted pink.

She was, in fact, as cute as could be.

"Did you find her?" Maeve asked from below.

In a loud whisper, I said, "She's sleeping."

"Oh, sweet thing. I'm not surprised. She's been having nightmares that've been keeping her up all hours of the night. Before you wake her, let me grab Tenn. I'll be right back."

I found her accent to be utterly endearing. She spoke slowly, the words stretched out.

When I glanced back at Katy, I was surprised to see she was now awake and watching me with sleepy blue eyes. Fortunately, she seemed more curious about my presence than disturbed.

"It's raining," she said, sitting up and turning her face toward the sky.

"It just started."

"You don't like rain."

I tipped my head. "How do you know that?"

She lifted a shoulder. "I can just tell."

It wasn't the rain I minded, actually, but it often went hand in hand with lightning, and this young girl didn't need to know my life story—or hear my grief. Especially if she was already having nightmares.

"Do you like to read?" Katy asked, clutching the book to her chest. It had a unicorn on the cover.

"I love to read," I said.

She nodded, as though I'd passed some sort of test. "Me, too. I like to read to my little sister best of all. She's just a baby, so she can't read yet. She's at Miss Edie's house. Miss Edie only keeps babies, so I get to stay with Papaw when I'm not at summer camp. Do you like babies?"

"Definitely," I said, trying to keep up with what she was saying. I suddenly wondered if this was how my family felt when I started rambling, trying to hold their attention. Then I felt a swell of sadness from thinking about them and pushed those thoughts away.

Her eyes widened behind her glasses. "Do you want to have babies?"

"That's a very personal question, don't you think?"

She blinked. "But do you? Want babies?"

If she had been one of the students at the private school where I worked, I wouldn't have answered. I'd have set a clear boundary and reinforced it. There was something about this girl, however, that told me I should be open, honest. "One day, maybe," I said. "I'm happy enough babysitting my nieces for now."

She narrowed her gaze as though she didn't quite believe me, and it suddenly made me question if *I* believed me.

Before I could stress too much about that, she asked, "Do you like trees?"

This was much safer ground. "Who doesn't?"

Her small face crinkled. "Mr. Daniels cut down two of his trees. Old ones. He said they were sick, but they weren't."

"So, we don't like him then?"

Behind her glasses, her eyes twinkled. "Mama said we shouldn't judge him because sometimes sicknesses can't be seen."

"Well, she's right about that."

Katy frowned, clearly wanting to stay mad on the felled trees' behalf, then laid a hand on a thick branch and said, "This tree's name is Bill. He's old, too. Papaw would *never* cut him down."

I looked up at the dozens of branches fanned out above our heads, then back at the crook where she sat, a wide, smooth, curved spot that seemed to have been created especially for her. "Bill seems the protective sort."

She gave the tree a loving pat, as if it were a pet. "He is. I'm seven. I'll be eight on August third. You can come to my party if you want. It's a unicorn party. How old are you?"

Honestly, I'd have guessed her to be much older. There was an old soul shining in her eyes.

"Twenty-eight, almost twenty-nine. My birthday is in September. And thank you for the invitation, but I'm not going to be in town for that long." Her birthday wasn't for another eleven days. "Did you know your great-grandfather has been looking for you?"

Quick as could be, she tucked the book into the top of her romper and scrambled forward. "I didn't mean to fall asleep. I just wanted a quiet place to read. Papaw is always playing music and likes to sing along real loud. *Real* loud."

I smiled at her dry tone and figured *Papaw* had to be what she called Tenn. "Do you need help getting down?"

"No, ma'am."

I'd been crisscrossing the South for a little more than a month now, so I was growing used to hearing *ma'am* all the time, but it still threw me a bit hearing it from a child. "You can call me Juliet if you want."

"I'm Katy June Byrd Mayfield," she said in a precious, practiced voice, scooting right past me on the branch, as if she were one with the tree. She seemed to have absolutely no fear of falling as she quickly descended. "*You* can call me Katy if you want."

Her accent wasn't as strong as Maeve's, but it was just as delightful.

I followed Katy down, taking my time, because I didn't have her bold courage. The rain picked up just as Tenn reached us, Maeve right behind him. When he saw Katy, he let out a relieved sigh. "Not a word of this to your mama, y'hear?"

She pretended to zip her lips.

With a small smile, he said, "Hurry on inside and wash up, then. Scoot!"

Katy sprinted across the yard, leaped over the line of pink flowers bordering the front walk, and ran up four wide steps to the front porch. The screen door banged behind her as she went inside the house.

"All's well that ends well!" Tenn swiped his palms against each other, as if brushing away the incident. "You'll stay for supper, Juliet? We'd be mighty pleased."

It felt like an offer too good to turn down. Especially since I didn't know when the tow truck would arrive. "Dinner sounds nice. Thank you."

He glanced at his sister. "You'll stay, too, Maeve?"

"Took you long enough to ask," she said.

He rolled his eyes, then launched forward, toward the house. "Since when do you need an invitation? You eat supper here near to every night. I'll meet y'all inside."

"Yes, yes. Go on in." She shooed him with her hands. "We'll be along in a moment."

Raindrops created polka dots on her cotton dress. Up close, I could see strands of red threading through her pale blond hair.

Taking measured, even steps, she headed up the front walk. "By the end of the day, my bad hip has had it," she said, explaining her pace. "It needs to be replaced, but I keep putting it off, delaying the inevitable."

"Why wait?" I asked, being nosy.

"Time, honey. Or the lack of it." Then she added, "I spoke with Callum, my grandson. He'll be by within the hour with the tow truck."

I supposed I should be grateful my hatchback had stopped smoking. "Thank you for calling him."

"You're quite welcome. After supper, we'll see about finding you a place to stay since you'll be in town awhile. I have an idea on that, but I need to run it by my brother."

It was the second time she'd mentioned a long stay. "Maeve? How do you know I'll be here awhile? Isn't there a chance my car repair will be an easy fix?"

"Oh, honey, I know it the same way I know it wasn't a real detour that brought you to town. Forget-Me-Not is often a landing place for those who've lost their way. That's you, isn't it?"

I rubbed goose bumps from my arms as the word *lost* echoed through my head. "But the highway construction—"

Shaking her head, she faced me. Her blue eyes were filled with kindness, empathy. "I'd venture to say you'd lost your way before you even got on the road."

I blinked away tears, feeling the weight, the pain, of the last three months.

She gently patted my arm, then pulled open the door and waved me onward. "Come now. We should help Tenn make supper. He's a man of many talents, but cooking ain't one of them."

As I followed her into the house, I realized I was still holding the robin feather. I tucked it into my pocket, finding myself suddenly wanting to tell Maeve how I *had* been feeling lost. I'd been hoping this road trip would help me remember who I was and what I wanted out of life, because my grief and fuzzy memory had made it hard to remember.

But for some reason, I had the feeling she already knew.

Two

*A Pearl of Wisdom
from Nettie Getchell*
"*Nothing, not one single thing, can carry you off
to a far-off place faster than a book.*"

Tallulah

I was being watched.

Golden eyes studied me from atop a metal bookshelf in the large-print section. A fluffy black tail dangled, swishing spines, as if dusting them. The cat's name was Deckle, and he'd been the library cat for at least five years. Maybe more. No one I'd asked had known for certain.

When I was a little girl and spent most summers here in Forget-Me-Not with my grandparents, I'd whiled away many afternoons at this library with my mamaw, who had been a librarian. In those days, there'd been a cat named Calliper, yet another black cat with golden eyes—only her fur had been short, not long like Deckle's. My younger self had delighted in finding her among the books. And in hearing the folklore explaining her presence—and that of all the library cats who'd come before her. I'd been especially intrigued to learn of the extraordinary gift the cats could bestow on patrons: returning a long-lost memory to them through the books on the shelves. Specifically, through the scent of a book, sometimes called bibliosmia. A mix of ink and paper and *life*.

My older thirty-four-year-old self, however, side-eyed the

decision to continue keeping a cat around, despite the gift of the memories.

Or, really, in *spite* of it.

I tended to hold grudges.

It seemed as though I was the only one who took issue with having Deckle here, however. Everyone else loved him. Especially Evanthe Kilburn, the library director, who typically wasn't one to display any sort of affection. She was often seen carrying him through the stacks, lovingly scratching his ears and rubbing his chin. There were even rumors of baby talk, though I didn't believe them. Evanthe would *never*.

Sunlight streamed through tall windows as I pushed the book cart toward the children's section. I'd only shelved a few titles before my gaze fell on a young boy, peacefully sleeping in a beanbag chair, his arms wrapped around a board book like it was a prized possession. Propped against the wall next to him sat his mama. She lifted her eyes from the pages of a thriller novel and gave me a conspiratorial smile.

I smiled back and tiptoed away, trying to remember the last time I'd stolen a few minutes of time to read, to escape into the pages of a book, while my little one napped.

It had been a while. Before the separation, the divorce.

These days, my life looked a whole lot different than it used to. In just eighteen months I'd gone from being happily married—well, married—to being a single mom of one, then two little girls, when a brief reconciliation resulted in the gift of Mary Joy, my seven-month-old. There had been a move and a new job and so many changes. Some good. Some not so much.

This job? That was one of the good things.

I'd been working here at the Forget-Me-Not Library for a little over a month now as a library assistant. My role meant I did a little bit of everything, floating to where I was needed most. Among other things, I helped patrons locate titles. I worked the circulation desk checking books in and out. I answered phones. Assisted with the computers. Lent a hand with programs run by other staff members, of which there were five in total.

Even though this was a small library, it had a big heart. It was a community hot spot, a meeting place, a shelter of sorts. It was a place to seek guidance, to create, to relax, to escape, to study, to learn new skills, to play board games and computer games and hear stories—and, of course, read them, too.

When I stopped to straighten a book that had fallen over, Deckle hopped onto the shelf next to my hand. I swore he narrowed his eyes before suddenly reaching out with a paw to pull a book loose. He then batted it onto the floor.

"I keep telling you," I whispered to him, picking up the book without even looking at the cover, "my memory is just fine."

I didn't need—or want—to revisit my past. Supposedly looking back was meant to help, to soothe, to console, according to the folklore. But I *knew* it could harm. It had hurt me. More than once. Every time my mama picked up a book that Calliper had knocked off the shelf and breathed in its scent, it always triggered a forgotten memory of some far-off place she'd wanted to visit. Within a matter of days, we'd be traveling again, her promises to me that we'd stay put for a while long forgotten.

I slotted the book into its empty spot as Deckle gazed at me, giving me a doleful look, his golden eyes wide and dewy.

"Nope, nope, nope," I said again, mostly to myself as fortification, because those *eyes*.

I turned my back on him and carried on with my duties. By far, shelving was my favorite thing to do.

It always had been.

In my teenage years, I'd often volunteered at libraries in the towns where my parents and I traveled, even if we never stayed in one place very long. I'd basked in the routine of shelving. In the order. Every book had its place. A specific location within the stacks, determined by alphabet and/or number. Its home *never* changed.

Unlike mine.

To me, libraries always meant comfort. Solace. This library especially, where my mamaw, June, used to roam. Working here was a dream come true for me, even if I wasn't a full-fledged librarian like she'd been. Like I always thought I'd be.

Marrying Scott Mayfield had changed those plans.

And divorcing him had altered them again, landing me here.

Did that count as a silver lining? I thought so, especially now, months after the divorce had been finalized and I could look back more clearly. I didn't regret our marriage, because it had given me Katy and Mary Joy, but I did wish Scott would take more than a passing interest in our children. His visits had become few and far between. Still a baby, Mary Joy was too young to notice, but Katy felt his absence deeply.

As I made my way toward adult fiction, I reminded myself not to dwell on things I couldn't change and focus on what had brought me to town: building a new, happy life for me and the girls. One full of friends and community and, most importantly, family. Like Papaw and Aunt Maeve and Uncle Renny and my cousin Callum.

Did I, someone who was used to being hyper-independent, have to accept Papaw's offer of help to make it happen? Yep. Did I have to force myself out of my cozy, reclusive comfort zone once we moved here? Yes. Was it worth leaving my introverted, homebody ways behind to plant deep roots? Definitely. Did I ache to be home with the girls right this minute? Absolutely.

I smiled, thinking that if the phrase *fake it till you make it* had a face, it would be mine, freckles and all. Still, I was trying. *Doing.* And I'd continue to do so. I was determined to give the girls the stability I hadn't had growing up.

As I walked through the stacks, pushing the cart along, Deckle kept pace with me. I stopped. He stopped. I gave him the most withering glance I could muster—which, I suspected, wasn't at all what I imagined it to be—and said, "Stop following me."

He only twitched his white whiskers in response.

"Please?" I asked.

His tail flicked left, then right.

It seemed to me he found amusement in reminding me of his presence, all but telling me that he wasn't going anywhere. All but insisting he would eventually accomplish his mission of returning a memory to me, despite how I felt about the matter.

I was about to pick him up and carry him to Evanthe's office when I heard Isabel Espinoza's voice coming from the opposite side of the shelf, easily recognizable with its wobbly yet ardent tone.

She was saying, "You'll need baking soda to remove those stains. Baking soda and vinegar."

Despite the shakiness of her words, nothing from her was ever spoken without conviction and sheer certainty. She was never wrong. Even when she was. She was a seventy-something retired finance attorney who'd taken a part-time job as a clerk at the library because she liked staying busy. Right now, she was supposed to be at the circulation desk, so I was curious as to what had pulled her away.

"Thank you," a man said. "I'll keep that in mind."

I didn't recognize the voice. It was deep and slightly bewildered.

I became even more curious when I heard Nettie Getchell say, "No, no. Hydrogen peroxide is best. Trust me. My mama was a midwife for more than fifty years. I've learned all the tricks. Pour it directly on the stains, let it sit a minute, then blot and rinse with cold water."

In her late fifties, Nettie was the youth librarian and had a nurturing demeanor coupled with a strong, no-nonsense, take-no-prisoners voice. The kids *adored* her.

At hearing her join in the conversation, my curiosity turned to suspicion.

You see, sometimes patrons came to the library seeking advice.

And sometimes patrons received advice even when they hadn't asked for it.

Isabel and Nettie were notorious for trapping unsuspecting

visitors and forcing unsolicited opinions upon them. When questioned about these tactics, they were always quick to point out that with age came wisdom, so why shouldn't they dispense their hard-earned lessons? After all, what better place to share knowledge than the *library*?

It was hard to argue with that logic, though in my opinion, they could be less *aggressive* in delivering the messages. I wasn't the only one who thought so. Evanthe had warned the pair against harassing the patrons—or else. So they'd taken to doing it slyly, out of Evanthe's sight—because they didn't see their method as harassment at all. They saw it only as a gift, their sharing of these shiny pearls of wisdom.

Before Evanthe caught wind of this ensnarement and fired the pair of them, I sprang into action, whipping the cart around the bookshelf. The room opened wide, revealing the center of the library, which held a spacious reading zone with a variety of seating areas. It had couches, chairs, beanbags, tables, and even a long counter with bar stool seating, where two teenagers were currently reading video game magazines.

The cart's wheel squeaked as I said in my cheeriest voice, "Hey, y'all, what's going on?"

Isabel grabbed my arm. "Tallulah Byrd."

I liked that she sometimes still used my first and middle names. She'd been a friend of my mamaw's and had known me since I was just a little bitty thing. Nettie, too.

"What better removes bloodstains?" Isabel asked. Demanded, really. "Baking soda and vinegar or hydrogen peroxide?"

For such a small woman, barely five feet tall and thin as a whittled twig, she was surprisingly strong. Her silver hair was slicked back and coiled into a tight bun at the nape of her neck, not a single strand daring to spring free. Fire burned in black eyes rimmed with delicate wrinkles. No one was more competitive. Katy had recently played a game of checkers with her, and the older woman had shown absolutely no mercy.

I glanced at Nettie, who was rolling her eyes. Then I faced their target, who was practically pinned against the shelf and nearly took a step back.

He absolutely did not look like a man who needed rescuing.

He had to be at least six foot two. Lean. Muscled. Tattooed. Short dark hair. Warm, light brown eyes. Sharp cheekbones. Stubble that didn't quite hide the dimple in his strong chin. He had on a tight white T-shirt, blue jeans, and tennis shoes. He looked to be in his mid-to-late thirties, and I definitely didn't recognize him. Because, *mercy*, I'd have remembered his face and the intelligence shimmering in his eyes.

I was a sucker for intelligence.

Isabel snapped her fingers. "*Tallulah*."

I blinked and found her staring at me.

"Well?" she asked, waiting for an answer to a question I couldn't remember.

Immediately, my cheeks started to heat, and I looked away, feeling silly, caught off guard. It had been a long time since I'd been struck dumb by a man. It was a strange feeling, uncomfortable yet . . . hopeful. As if my heart was saying, *What if him? He might be the one.*

What if no, I told it.

Besides the fact that it was a ridiculous question, given that he was a complete stranger, there were limits to me stepping outside my comfort zone. Dating was one of them. I just wasn't ready yet—and wasn't sure I ever would be again.

Nettie chuckled and said, "Seems Tallulah's a mite distracted."

I shot her a grim look.

She wiggled dark eyebrows and grinned, unoffended. "Must be the sight of the blood. Right, Lu?"

As her words sank in, I stiffened. Blood?

It was only then I noticed the man had a tissue pressed against one of his fingers, and that his shirt was dotted with a few bright red spots. "Oh!" I exclaimed. "Are you okay?"

"I'm fine," he said, his voice deep, rich. "The blood makes it look more dramatic than it really is."

"Got himself a good little slice," Nettie said, tutting. "Fingertips bleed like the dickens."

There was a puppy-training book tucked under his arm, and I stepped forward and pulled the book free, trying to keep it safe from blood-borne pathogens. "Let me put that aside for you." I set it on the cart. "What did you cut your finger on?"

Vaguely, he gestured with his chin toward the shelf behind him. "A burr, I think. On the end there."

It took a moment of searching, but I finally spotted a tiny metal spike—a defect in the shelf itself. It was a small miracle someone hadn't been injured before now.

Nettie, dressed in a short-sleeve blouse and flowy wide-legged pants, crossed dark arms over an ample chest. "You might need a tetanus shot, young man."

"You might also be eligible for compensation from the library," Isabel added. "For pain and suffering."

She obviously hadn't gotten all the lawyering out of her system.

I glanced at her. "Really, Miss Isabel? You *work* here."

She shrugged and adjusted a thin cardigan—she always had some sort of sweater on, even in the summer. "Old ways die hard."

"I'm not in pain *or* suffering," the man assured. His voice had lost some of its bewilderment and now held a hint of amusement. "I'm also up to date on my tetanus booster. But thanks."

Nettie said, "All right, then. I'll grab a Band-Aid for you. Be right back."

When Isabel was called away by a patron ready to check out a stack of books, I fought the urge to fill the sudden silence by asking the man questions like his name, how long he'd been in town, and if his car had broken down when he arrived.

Forget-Me-Not wasn't just any old quaint Southern town. It happened to be a haven for the lost. The *emotionally* lost. Whether that be the heartbroken, the confused, the angry, the hurt, the misguided. Those needing a little extra help to mend their broken spirit were often *led* here. And then were forced to stay by their car suddenly breaking down. Only when they found the right path forward, toward healing, did the town turn them loose again. Very few stayed.

I was saved from the growing awkwardness by a cool wind whistling through the room. Slowly, I turned. Evanthe Kilburn stood watching us, her thin lips pressed tightly together. Deckle sat at her feet, his fluffy black tail curled around his front paws.

"Is there a problem?" Evanthe asked in a chilly tone, looking positively regal draped in layers of cream-toned linen.

"Nope," I said, overly bright, wondering what was taking Nettie so long. "No problem at all."

Evanthe pursed her lips, which lifted high cheekbones. "Is that so?"

At eighty years old, she still stood tall, nearly five foot ten. A silvery white braid hung to her waist, but the end of the braid remained midnight black, as if the ends of her hair had been dipped in a pot of India ink. She was statuesque and lithe, active and fit. In fair weather, she often rode her red bike to work, which was a sight to behold, with Deckle sitting in the basket on the front and books strapped to the rack behind the seat.

"It is," I said, trying not to fidget.

"Interesting. How does one then explain the blood?" she asked, eyeing the drops on the man's shirt. "Are you in need of medical attention, Jake?"

Jake? She *knew* him? My gaze swung his way.

"It's just a scratch, Aunt Ev," he said. "No need to worry."

Wait. Evanthe had a *nephew*? One who called her *Ev*? She, who despised nicknames?

"Splendid." She narrowed her gaze on me. "I don't believe the books on the cart are going to shelve themselves, Tallulah."

"Yes, ma'am," I said, then winced. "I mean, no, ma'am."

Then she turned and walked away, taking the coolness with her.

Deckle stayed behind, hopping onto a shelf near my shoulder. Eye level. I did my best to ignore him.

"I didn't know Evanthe had a nephew," I said to Jake. I blurted it, really. It was the shock speaking.

He smiled. "I'm not surprised. She's not exactly an open book, is she?"

No. She wasn't.

Jake glanced over his shoulder, in the direction Nettie had gone, then shifted from foot to foot. "My finger's fine, really. I should get going. I have a puppy at home who shouldn't be left alone for too long. She's quickly developing a taste for couch cushions." His gaze landed on mine and stayed there a long second. "It was nice meeting you."

"You, too," I murmured. Being polite. That's all.

With a nod, he turned and walked away, saying goodbye to Isabel as he passed by the circ desk.

"Wait," I exclaimed, calling after him as I snagged the puppy-training book from the cart. "Your book!"

"I'll come back for it some other time," he said over his shoulder. Then he was through the doors and out of sight.

When Nettie finally returned, a Band-Aid in hand, I was fully expecting an interrogation on where the man had gone. But she was distracted by Deckle, who strolled purposefully along the shelf. In a blink, he pawed a book, sending it flying onto the floor.

We peered downward.

The Joy of Cooking stared back at us.

With a happy squeal, Nettie made a grab for the book. With glimmering eyes, she opened it, letting the pages fall at will. Then she lifted the book to her nose. Her eyes drifted closed in concentration as she breathed in the book's scent. A moment later, she blinked, then frowned. "I didn't remember a darn thing. It must be meant for you, Tallulah."

She handed the book to me.

I promptly put it back on the shelf. "No, thank you."

As determination shined in Deckle's eyes, I grabbed him and set him on the floor. "Off with you now."

He hissed, then strutted away, his tail in the air.

Nettie gasped in dismay.

I smiled at her and said, "I need to get a move on. It's almost quitting time."

As I walked away, pushing the book cart, she was still shaking her head and tutting in outrage that I'd turn down such a *gift*.

I didn't take her disapproval to heart. Not many understood why I'd decline a chance to retrieve a long-lost memory. But I knew. That's all that mattered.

Fifteen minutes later, I was almost done with shelving when I caught sight of Evanthe looking out one of the floor-to-ceiling windows that faced the back garden. Her hands were clasped behind her. Her back was ramrod straight. Her chin was lifted high. Sunlight glinted off the silver in her hair.

Once, she'd been my mamaw's closest friend in the whole world.

In fact, she was my mama's godmother.

But as I watched her now, I couldn't help but wonder why she was practically a stranger to me.

Three

A Pearl of Wisdom
from Vera Ingleby
"When baking, always measure chocolate chips and vanilla with your heart. It knows how much is needed."

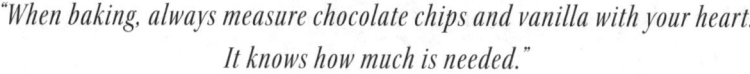

Juliet

The arrival of the flatbed tow truck had brought out the neighbors, a dozen at least, of all ages.

They streamed from their houses, scurried down the sidewalks, and gathered on Tenn's walkway and front porch, a sea of curiosity. He happily made introductions, one after another. Before I knew it, sweet tea and cookies were being handed out, and I was being interrogated in the politest way possible.

I repeated much of the same information about myself to each neighbor I met while trying not to reveal too much. My name, my age. That I was from Ann Arbor. That I worked as a nurse at a private elementary school. No, no relation to Florence Nightingale. Yes, I knew she was a nurse, too. Single. Third of five children. On a summer road trip when a detour brought me here.

One of the neighbors, Vera Ingleby, an older woman who claimed to be a retired hairdresser, but who I'd swear had once been a CIA operative, had brought the cookies with her when she arrived. Testers, she'd called them, for a big baking competition she was entering soon. It was hard to believe she was still tweaking the recipe, because the cookies were glorious. They were the size of my hand, with peaks and valleys, filled with anything and everything. I answered every single one of her queries in between chewing, but when she started asking more personal questions, about my family, I started to fidget.

That's when Maeve stepped in close and said, "My apologies for the interruption, but Callum's needing some particulars, Juliet." She angled me toward the tow truck, gave me a subtle push.

"Excuse me, please," I said to Vera.

With a big toothy smile, she said, "I'll be here when you return, sweetie."

Her and all the others. No one seemed the least bit interested in leaving, and I wouldn't be the least bit surprised if Tenn ultimately invited *everyone* for supper.

As I made my way to the flatbed, I figured Maeve must've somehow sensed I needed a minute to myself to catch my breath because currently her grandson was beneath the front end of my hatchback, attaching a cable and chains to its underside.

I was quickly growing fond of that woman.

Katy, I noted, was back in the arms of the tree, keeping an eye out for her mother and sister, who were due home any moment.

I was a bit shocked by how much I'd already learned about this family in the short time I'd been here. Names and ages and professions and relationship statuses. Hobbies and favorite books and favored foods, too. Both Katy and Maeve were talkers.

I was wishing I'd grabbed another cookie when music suddenly filled the air as Tenn made his way onto the porch, a Bluetooth speaker in hand. Playing was another song from *Pirates of Penzance*. He'd been singing along to the soundtrack in the kitchen earlier while prepping dinner, though *singing* didn't quite seem an adequate enough description. *Belting* might work better. Or *caterwauling*.

I fully understood why Katy chose to escape the house from time to time for some peace and quiet.

"Has Uncle Tenn waxed poetic about Gilbert and Sullivan

yet?" Callum asked as he walked toward me, adjusting his ball cap. Dark blond hair curled out under its red band. He was a head taller than my five foot six, slim and fit. I guessed he was around my age, give or take a year or two. He had his grandmother's blueberry-colored eyes.

I'd been so distracted by the music I hadn't heard him make his way out from under the car. "Not yet."

He wiped dirty hands on a rag, which he then stuck in the back pocket of his blue work pants. Folding his arms across his chest, he said, "It's only a matter of time. Even if you're not a fan, it's best to pretend you are or he'll go all out in trying to convert you."

I smiled. "Good to know."

We'd already talked about the car and its issues when he first arrived. He'd opened the hood and had *hmm*ed and nodded as I explained about the flashing engine lights and the puff of blue smoke. If he had a guess as to what had gone wrong, he hadn't said, but I swore I caught flashes of sympathy in his eyes a few times. That couldn't bode well for the car.

Pieces of gravel clung to the shoulder of his gray T-shirt, which was adorned with a faded blue Hearnshaw Automotive logo, as he motioned to my car with his chin. "I'm about ready to load her up. Let me give you a hand gettin' your things out of the back."

My things. One carry-on-sized suitcase and a backpack. "You don't have to do that."

He started for the back of the car and lifted the hatch. "It's included in the towing fee."

"You don't say."

"No one ever reads the fine print."

I smiled as he handed me the backpack. As I slipped it over my shoulder, I noticed the breeze had turned cool once again. The sky was darkening. I tried to ignore the increase in my heart rate as I said, "By the way, is there a hotel in town? A motel? A B&B?"

I suspected Maeve was going to suggest I stay here, at Tenn's, but I didn't want to intrude on the family any more than I already had.

Callum set the suitcase at my feet. "A hotel and a couple of rental places, but they fill up fast this time of year and stay that way straight up until the Flour Festival in a couple of weeks. That's *flour* as in *f-l-o-u-r*. You've never seen so many cakes and cobblers."

"Really? That sounds kind of amazing."

"It is. Even if your car is fixed by then, the festival is worth sticking around for."

"When is it?"

"About three and a half weeks."

I'd planned to be back in Michigan by then, but because I didn't want to go home, I started rearranging travel plans. This festival was the perfect excuse to extend my trip—and to stay in one place for a while. I had to confess my constant traveling had made me road weary. "If I can find a rental, maybe I'll stay."

When thunder rumbled in the distance, I eyed the gloomy sky, and my heart began thumping like mad.

Maeve came to stand next to me and put her hand on my arm, as if sensing that I needed comfort. "Don't you worry about looking for a place, honey. Tenn has a big ol' empty guest room in his attic just waiting for you to move on in."

"Oh, I couldn't. If I stay until the festival, I might be here for weeks, not days."

"You most certainly could," Tenn said, rushing toward me, his Velcro hiking sandals slapping against the stone walkway. "We just need to freshen up the bedding, and it'll be good to go. You can stay with us as long as you'd like."

Before I could say anything else, Katy yelled out "Mama!" and scampered down the tree.

I turned and saw a woman walking toward us, pushing a baby stroller. Tallulah was on the petite side with a softness to her that would make it hard to guess her age if Katy hadn't volunteered it earlier. Light ginger-brown hair had been pulled off her face by a fabric-covered headband, and her bold blue gaze was puzzled as she glanced around. "Hey, y'all."

Everyone called out hellos.

Once on the ground, Katy ran straight to her mother. After receiving a quick kiss on the top of her head, Katy crouched in front of the stroller to say hello to her little sister.

Mary Joy was absolutely adorable, with her big eyes, plump cheeks, and just enough fluffy, strawberry blond hair to cover her head.

"Whose car is this?" Tallulah asked, looking around until her gaze landed square on me.

I gave a little wave as the wind whistled a warning, and chill bumps rose on my skin. "Hi."

Maeve jumped in and made quick introductions and rushed explanations, going out of her way to mention the blue smoke that had billowed from my engine and the detour that led me to this town.

At that, Tallulah's eyes had gone wide, soft and sympathetic.

Katy skipped to my side and took my hand. "Juliet likes unicorns and books and babies and big ol' trees."

She surreptitiously cut her eyes toward one of the neighbors I'd met earlier, Clay Daniels, and I almost felt sorry for the sweet old man as he let out a defeated puff of air. Obviously, he'd been the one who cut down the oak trees.

Tallulah had a Forget-Me-Not Library tote bag printed with delicate blue flowers slung over one shoulder, and a smile played on her lips as she listened intently to her daughter.

"Juliet is going to be staying with us! In the attic!" Katy added as if the attic were the most wondrous place in the whole world.

The smile fell from Tallulah's face as she whipped her head toward Tenn. "What's this now?"

I eyed the darkening sky and quickly said, "I can find somewhere else. I don't want to cause any trouble."

At this point, I just wanted to get all of us inside, where we'd be safe.

Vera stepped forward. "You're welcome to my garage apartment, Juliet. It used to be my hair salon; then my late husband,

God rest his soul, turned it into his man cave when I retired. I can clean it out, quick as can be. Won't take but an hour or two."

Tenn shook his head. "You must stay with us, Juliet. I insist. We're more than happy to help a stranger in need, especially one whose car broke down in front of *our own house*. Ain't so, Tallulah?"

The wind lifted Tallulah's hair off her neck as she glanced from face to face. Worry lines deepened on her forehead. Then she glanced at my car, as if searching for some sort of answer there, and said, "That's so."

Maeve said, "Perfect! Now I hate to be the one to break up a party, but the sky's about to bust open, and I have no desire to get soaked through."

Rumbling thunder punctuated her statement, as if giving one last warning to take cover, and the crowd quickly dispersed. Katy helped her mother get the baby inside, and as soon as Callum winched my car onto the flatbed—and politely declined an offer to stay for supper—Tenn grabbed my suitcase. As Maeve and I climbed the front steps, I was beyond grateful for the hospitality I was receiving, but as I looked at the ominous sky, I was even more thankful at that moment to be out of the storm.

Later that night, I sat on my bed in the attic, looking around.

The large room appeared to be used mostly for storage. It smelled faintly of mothballs, dust, old cardboard, and freshly laundered bedding.

There was something homey about the space, though. Welcoming. The lace curtains. The colorful sheets and patchwork quilt. The mismatched handles on an old wooden dresser. The threadbare floral rug, done in pale pinks and purples, that stretched from the bed to a set of narrow steps that led down to the second floor.

A window air conditioner shook and wheezed like it was dying a slow death as rain pelted the roof and ran through the gutters. The forecast I'd seen on my phone called for another wave of storms to hit in the middle of the night, which were bound to keep me awake, tossing and turning.

Remembering things I wanted to forget and unable to recall the things I wanted to remember.

It was a cycle I'd grown used to over the past three months, since the lightning strike.

My suitcase sat on the end of the bed, unopened, as I canceled my Graceland tour and my upcoming hotel reservations. I texted my family via our group chat to let them know where I was, as I'd been doing since I hit the road. I left out any mention of car problems, however, because I didn't want them to try to fix the problem for me.

They'd become overly helpful in the last few months.

Smothering, even.

I pushed those thoughts aside and looked at the suitcase.

I decided I wouldn't unpack.

I'd sleep here tonight. That was it. Tomorrow I'd find another place to stay. I had meant it when I said I didn't want to cause trouble, and I could sense my presence bothered Tallulah a great deal, even though for the last few hours she'd been trying to hide her discomfort behind polite small talk.

I heard a gentle knock and a creak as the stairway door opened. "Juliet?" Katy whispered quite loudly. "Can I come up?"

I smiled. "Of course."

Her footfalls barely made any noise on the steps, and a second later, she was skipping over to the bed. Lamplight glinted off her glasses. She was fresh out of the bath and dressed in shortie pajamas, smelling of soap. Her damp hair still had comb lines running through it. "Mama said to ask if you needed anything."

"I don't, but thank you."

Her gaze fell on the suitcase. "I can help you unpack."

"I don't think—"

"You should unpack," she said, nodding, encouraging.

I held her gaze and wondered if she somehow knew I'd planned to leave in the morning.

"After tonight, it's probably best if I find somewhere else to stay," I said.

She perched on the edge of the bed. "Are you worried about Mama? You shouldn't be. It's just that she doesn't know you like I do yet."

I smiled at that, considering she'd just met me today; then I realized she was perfectly serious. "If I were her, I'd be worried about a stranger in the house, too."

"But you're not a stranger," Katy said. "You're Juliet."

There was something shiny and soft in her eyes that made me feel as though she really did know me. Not just what I presented to the world, but who I was deep down, even though I was still learning exactly who that person was. And, more importantly, who that person wasn't.

"Well, that's true," I finally said.

She looked at me, her eyes twinkling. "I'm glad you're here. In a few days, Mama will feel the same way. Trust me."

Strangely, I did.

"You know, I'm glad I'm here, too," I said and was slightly shocked to find that I meant it. Despite the storms, right here and now was the calmest I'd felt in months. Like I could finally take a full breath again without a twinge of pain.

"So you'll stay?" she asked, her eyes imploring, a smile blooming.

It was impossible to say no to her. I took a deep breath and allowed myself to give in. "Okay, I'll stay."

As her smile grew and grew, revealing a missing tooth, I hoped I wouldn't come to regret my decision.

After all, the last thing I wanted to do was cause any grief for this family.

I'd done that enough with my own.

Four

*A Pearl of Wisdom
from Maeve Hearnshaw*
"*Sometimes, honey, you've got to listen with your heart, not your ears.*"

Tallulah

"Lu, you hear that?" Papaw asked early the next morning from the dining room, where he was working on his latest printmaking project.

It was a quarter to nine, and I stood at the kitchen's butcher-block island eating one of Vera's monstrous cookies while busily packing lunches for Katy and me and getting Mary Joy's diaper bag ready for the day. I was due to drop Mary Joy off at Miss Edie's house in just fifteen minutes, and then I'd have another fifteen minutes to get to the library to start my shift. Papaw would drop Katy off at day camp at nine thirty and pick her up at three. Dinner was usually at six. Then it was playtime and baths and bedtime for the girls. It had taken us weeks to smooth out the wrinkles of this schedule, but it was working well now. We'd found our rhythm.

I listened for something out of the ordinary, something other than Papaw's ever-present music. Like the sound of Katy moving about upstairs as she gathered items for her backpack. Or Mary Joy in her playpen, banging one toy or another. She was in a banging phase.

"I don't hear anything," I said, taking another bite of the cookie. There was oatmeal and egg in it, so I counted it as a breakfast food.

It was good, too. Great, even. But it didn't hold a candle to the cookies my mamaw used to make. Unfortunately for us all, after she passed away, no one had been able to find her recipe box—a box she'd promised to set aside for me.

In a fit of nostalgia, I started opening cabinets, but just like all the other times I'd done the same, there was no box to be found—and it would've easily been seen on the nearly empty shelves. Papaw was a man who liked to live simply. In the years since Mamaw had been gone, he'd been slowly downsizing his belongings, giving away what he deemed to be no longer needed.

Other than his craft room, which was chock-full of supplies, one could only describe the decor of the house as minimalist. Bare-bones. He spoke often about moving to a smaller house, but so far it was only talk.

"Strange," he said. "I hear it clear as day."

I finished off the cookie, wiped crumbs from my hands, and gave another listen. Still nothing.

There wasn't even a hint that another person was here with us—a stranger. If Juliet was awake, the house didn't reveal it.

My jaw set, and I slid it side to side, to loosen it. Tried to loosen my *whole* self up. To be more open. Welcoming.

After all, Juliet seemed like a perfectly lovely person. Truly.

And I felt for her. I did. From her car troubles, I knew she was hurting. Blue smoke when a car broke down in Forget-Me-Not meant that someone had lost a loved one recently and was grieving deeply. Because that kind of pain was soul-deep, it always took the longest to heal, so I knew she'd be in town awhile.

Living here. With us.

Which was way out of my comfort zone. Miles out.

It felt all kinds of wrong to want her to stay somewhere else, but I did.

I wanted it badly, despite the fact that she was exactly where she was meant to be.

Her car had broken down here. Out front. According to

Forget-Me-Not folklore, that meant my family was supposed to help guide her toward healing.

But still. It didn't mean she had to *live* here. We could help without her being under the same roof. Yet Papaw was insistent about going above and beyond.

On the countertop, my silenced phone vibrated with an incoming message.

Uncle Renny: I heard you have a crush on the new guy in town

I sent an eye roll emoji, then typed in: You heard wrong

Uncle Renny: I'm going to need a picture

I took a quick selfie and sent it to him.

He returned an eye roll emoji and added: You know I meant of the new guy

Papaw's voice carried as he said, "How about that? Did you hear that?"

I listened. "Nope." Then I returned to the text conversation.

Me: I've got to go. Papaw's hearing imaginary noises

Uncle Renny: It was only a matter of time. I should go as well. Maeve is making me run laps.

He was joking, of course, but I could feel my chest knotting up, *wishing* he could run laps. Or even walk them. Wishing lots of things where he was concerned.

Me: Pace yourself

Uncle Renny: Always, sweetheart

Eighty-two-year-old Lorenzo "Renny" Russo wasn't really my uncle. Before retirement, he'd been a librarian alongside Mamaw and had become a close family friend. The kind of family friend who, before you knew it, simply became family. Last year, he'd been diagnosed with a lung condition, and a few months ago, he'd gone into hospice care at Juneberry Cottage, Aunt Maeve's respite house. No one knew how much time he had left, but whatever it was, it wasn't nearly long enough.

Yawning, I finished packing what was needed for the day. Last night, I'd had Katy sleep with me and Mary Joy, just to set my mind about having a stranger in the house. If there was a silver lining to that choice, it was that Katy hadn't had a nightmare. A small mercy.

The bad dreams had caught me off guard. I'd expected issues when Scott and I split up eighteen months ago. Or when he moved to Dallas. Or when the divorce was finalized. Or in May, when the school year ended and our house was finally sold—the timing was one of the terms of the divorce—and the girls and I moved to Forget-Me-Not.

Not now, though, when our turbulent life finally felt like it was settling down a little. In addition to camp, Katy had lots of time to read and play with new friends and go on nature hikes with Papaw. Life had seemed . . . if not good, then *steady*. Yet last week, Katy began having nightmares, and I wasn't sure how to help her deal with them.

The downside of having Katy in bed with me last night was that I'd barely slept a wink. I'd whiled away the time by thinking about her upcoming birthday party, which was fast approaching. I'd spent more time than I cared to admit wondering if Scott would show up.

He'd been wishy-washy about it, saying he wouldn't know until about a week before the party if he could make it. I'd done my best to prepare Katy for the fact that he might not be there. He was busy. *Blah, blah.* Lies to protect her tender heart.

Scott and I'd had more arguments in the last eighteen months about his infrequent visits than I cared to admit. He always had one excuse or another why he couldn't make the time, and I was the one left picking up the pieces of Katy's shattered hopes.

Sighing, I set the lunch boxes and diaper bag by the front door and glanced at my watch. I needed to get a move on. I had some wiggle room with Mary Joy's drop-off time, but Evanthe was a stickler about tardiness, and I didn't want to start the day by getting written up. As a new hire, I was desperately trying to make a good impression.

I'd spent some time last night thinking about Evanthe, too. And why I didn't know her well. I'd love to ask my mama, but she and my daddy were currently off the grid, somewhere in Asia, and would be for months. As travel writers, they were always on the move—and always had been. I'd traveled with them right up until I was eighteen, when I finally had a say-so about *staying put*.

Suddenly the music drifting through the downstairs cut off, and Papaw said, "Do you hear it now?"

"Hold on," I said, checking on Mary Joy, who was cooing at herself in a play mirror, her mouth glossy from the ointment I'd applied around her lips. Her endless drooling these days had given her a rash.

"Hey there, cutie." Smiling, I bent down and tickled her belly, and her blue eyes crinkled as she gave me a big gummy grin. I handed her a rattle, and she immediately started banging it against the mirror, babbling sweet sounds as she did so, as if creating her own kind of music to fill the unusual silence.

I then made my way to the dining room. The intended purpose of this space was lost. Nearly every inch of the big table was covered with carving tools, gray linoleum blocks, inks, rollers, and paper. Papaw had been carving this morning, so there were thin tendrils of gray scattered around where he sat.

For a moment, I simply looked at him, my heart full. I owed him so much, for letting the girls and me move in with him. Also for babysitting Katy this summer, which, at seventy-nine, was asking a whole lot of him, even though he insisted he could handle it. He meant the world to me, and I hoped he knew it.

Lighted magnification glasses were attached to the orange headband he wore, and tufts of white hair stuck out every which way as he said, "Might could be birds in the eaves."

I tried to ignore the hint of excitement in his voice. He'd been a field biologist most his life and loved when nature collided with his everyday living.

The eaves were a fine place for birds to nest. Great, even.

It was when the critters made their way *inside* that bothered me.

Like the time with the little brown bat, shortly after the girls and I moved in.

I shuddered at the memory and said, "I still don't hear anything. It's probably just the wind."

Papaw frowned and scratched his beard. "When's the last time you done had your hearing checked, Lu?"

I rolled my eyes. "My hearing's just fine."

He set down the block he'd been working on and took off the headlamp, which left behind red marks at his temples. His eyes danced with amusement as he said, "Not if you can't hear the scratching, it ain't."

Shaking my head, I glanced at my watch. My morning schedule was falling apart. Still, maybe I had time to ask him a question or two—about Evanthe. "Can I ask you something real quick? About Evanthe?"

His eyes grew wide and he laughed. "Anything but that." I frowned and his laugh deepened. "I'm just sassing you. What do you want to know?"

"Evanthe was Mamaw's best friend and Mama's godmother, but I barely know her. Why's that?"

He scratched his chin. "I reckon there are a few reasons. One, your mamaw's been gone a long time now or she'd probably have talked your ear off about Evanthe. They were thick as thieves, those two, ever since they were little bitty things. Except, of course, after Evanthe's husband passed. He was a good man, that Dale."

Mamaw had once told me that Evanthe had been gutted by the sudden loss of her husband and had turned into a shell of who she once was. She'd taken a leave of absence from the library. Cut herself off from everyone and everything—even Mamaw. She'd wanted only to grieve in private.

Evanthe had still been lost in her bereavement when Mamaw received her terminal diagnosis, barely six months later. Everyone had expected Evanthe to come out of her sheltered mourning, but she didn't. She dug in deeper, and speculation ran high that it was a protective measure. To save herself from experiencing more heart-wrenching grief. It wasn't until the very last week of Mamaw's life that Evanthe finally showed up at the door. Just in time to say goodbye.

I tried not to think of that time often. I didn't get a chance to say goodbye. In fact, we'd almost missed the funeral.

I'd been sixteen at the time, and my parents and I had been in Tanzania, deep in the Serengeti on a months-long excursion, with no outside contact to the world abroad. By the time we were able to check in again, we learned that Mamaw had only days left.

Papaw put his regular glasses back on and said, "Two, after your mama set off on her travels, I know Evanthe tried to keep in touch, but your mama isn't one to check in very often, is she?"

I shook my head. I was lucky if I talked to her once a month. It was probably the same for Papaw. She was just always so busy, traveling, writing, *doing*. My father, too. They were a match made in heaven.

"Three," he said, "Evanthe has always been a bit aloof. She's a private person is all, and hardly lets anyone in. After Dale and your mamaw passed so close together, it's like she closed up the doors to her heart, nailed them shut."

Which was why I didn't take her coldness personally. But oh, how I'd like to get her to open up again and maybe let *me* into her world. I wanted to know the Evanthe my mamaw had loved so dearly.

Papaw's eyes darkened. "You're not having issues with her, are you?"

"No, nothing like that," I said. "It's just that—" I cut myself off as a crackly sound filtered through the room.

Definitely scratching.

"The wind, eh?" Papaw said, raising one bushy, self-satisfied eyebrow.

"No need to gloat." I scooted around the *etching press*—I'd called it a printing press when I first saw it and had been quickly corrected by my grandfather—and headed for one of the front windows. I looked outside, searching for what might've caused the sound, but only saw the sway of hanging ferns.

"Argh! *Dagummit!*" Papaw cried out behind me.

Startled, I spun around. He was bent over, a hand pushed against his lower back. I rushed to his side. "What's wrong?"

His face twisted in pain. "Stood up too dang fast."

A fine sheen of sweat glistened on his forehead. He made like he was going to sit back down but froze up again after only descending an inch or two.

"Has this happened before?" I held his arm as panic took flight in my chest. Worry for him. And worry for me, too, though I hated to admit it, because it felt all kinds of selfish. I'd quickly become dependent on him and his help to get through the day.

"A time or two," he said through clenched teeth. "It's just a spasm. It'll pass."

The scratching intensified.

Footsteps pounded on the stairs and Katy practically bounced into the dining room. "I hear scratching! Do you think it's another bat?"

The enthusiasm in her voice was unmistakable. I blamed my

grandfather for that. Field biologists never really retired, though he'd stopped teaching at the local college nearly ten years ago. When we'd found the brown bat in the house a month ago, he'd gloved up and carefully captured the creature and taught Katy all about it. While she soaked up every second of the lesson, I stood a good distance back, questioning my life choices.

The following week, they'd constructed a bat house, which was now attached to one of the trees in the backyard. Sometimes at night, the two of them sat outside and watched the nighttime comings and goings.

Mercy.

Katy stopped in her tracks. "What happened to Papaw?"

"I've done thrown out my back, sprout," he said.

"Did you stand up too fast?" She hurried over to take his other arm.

"Indeed, I did."

She *tsk*ed, as if she'd warned him of the possibility a thousand times.

"Let's get you to the couch," I suggested.

As Katy helped me inch Papaw toward the living room, my brain was whirling. Papaw was supposed to take Katy to camp—and pick her up. Right now, there was no way he'd be able to do that. He could barely stand. Let alone drive.

He held his breath, his cheeks puffing out, as we eased him onto the sofa. Once he was settled, I put a throw pillow behind his back for a little more support.

When Mary Joy started to fuss, Katy darted over to the playpen to chat with her through the mesh. Soon Mary Joy was squealing with delight, her small voice soaring to the ceiling and floating there like a happy cloud.

I checked my watch, and my stomach dropped. I glanced between Papaw and Katy and Mary Joy and made a snap decision. Asking for help had never been my strong suit, but I knew when I was in over my head. I reached for my phone.

"Who're you calling?" Papaw asked, frowning at me.

"I'm not sure yet."

I ruled out Aunt Maeve straightaway. She'd already headed off to work—after stopping by here first for a quick cup of coffee, as she did almost every morning.

"Why're you calling *anyone*?" Papaw asked with a scowl.

"To make sure you get to the doctor and Katy gets to camp. I need to get to work or I'm going to be late."

"*Pshaw*. I'm fine. You get goin'." He braced his hands on the seat cushion and tried to lift himself up. He didn't so much as budge an inch. "Just give me a minute."

Katy ran to help him, but it was of no use.

I snapped my fingers. "I'm sure Vera will be able to lend a hand. She's the helpful type."

"No, thanks," he said, his voice tinged with alarm.

Katy glanced my way with a knowing smile.

Years ago, Vera had asked Papaw to help her fix a leaky sink, and ever since he'd been convinced that she had a crush on him and was just waiting for the right time to pounce. I wasn't sure why he was so disturbed by the idea, because she was a lovely woman, but figured it had something to do with the fact that he'd been single a long time now and had maybe grown used to being alone. "I don't think we have a choice."

"What about Juliet, Mama?" Katy asked.

"Yes! Juliet! Great idea! We can ask her," Papaw added quickly, his voice now high and hopeful.

"Ask me what?" Juliet said, stepping into the living room from the hallway.

I hadn't heard her come down the stairs, which usually squeaked at every step. She was dressed in blue shorts and a white T-shirt, and her long, light brown hair was pulled back in a French braid.

In one long drawn-out breath, Katy said, "Papaw's done hurt his back and needs to go to the doctor, and Mama is late for work, and I need to go to camp, and Aunt Maeve is at work, and

Miss Vera scares Papaw!" She gulped air and added, "Can you help us?"

Gritting my teeth, I glanced at my daughter. Sometimes she overshared. I needed to help her work on that.

"I wouldn't say *scare*," Papaw mumbled.

"Your back?" Juliet said, rushing over to him. "A spasm?"

"Yes, ma'am." He leaned forward and showed her where it hurt. "Same place as always."

"Do you usually take muscle relaxers when it happens?" Concern pulled her eyebrows down low. When he nodded, she added, "Do you have any on hand?"

"I don't believe so. Best we put in a call to Doc Cohen when his office opens at nine."

We all looked at the clock that hung above the mantel. It was five till nine. Even if I drove to work instead of walked, I was going to be cutting it close.

"Hopefully you can get in today to see him," Juliet said. "Until then, a heating pad and acetaminophen might help ease the pain a little."

"You can use my lamb!" Katy offered, running for the stairs.

Her lamb was one of those stuffed animal heating pads that was absolutely adorable and worked wonders on upset tummies. I found it terribly sweet that she was offering it to Papaw.

When Mary Joy whimpered, I walked over to the playpen, picked her up. She settled, happy in my arms. As I pressed a kiss to the top of her head, she buried her face in the soft spot under my collarbone and rubbed it back and forth against my blouse. Her sign that she was tired and ready for a nap.

Juliet stood up. "I'm happy to help out." She glanced at me. "If it's okay with you, Tallulah."

Katy sailed down the stairs and down the hallway, skipping into the kitchen. At the microwave, she stood on tiptoes and put the lamb inside. It felt all kinds of wrong to see it spinning around on the turntable.

Mary Joy was nodding off, warm and cozy in my arms, and I glanced at the clock again, willing time to stop for a second.

"Maybe it's best if I call off today," I said, hating the idea of it. But sometimes life threw wrenches into perfectly crafted schedules.

The microwave beeped, and a second later, Katy was helping tuck her lamb behind Papaw. He sighed, then said to me, "No need to do that. We've got things cover—"

It was his turn to be cut off by a scratching noise.

"That's too loud for a bat," Katy said, sounding disappointed.

"I'm of a mind to agree with you, sprout," Papaw said, his tone matching Katy's.

"A *bat*?" Juliet's concerned gaze skipped from face to face.

"They're so cute with their big ears!" Katy used her hands to mimic bat ears. "And they eat lots of bugs. Lots and lots. And Papaw says they use echoes as a way of telling how far away something is. Isn't that cool?"

"Very cool," Juliet said with a tight smile that was clearly a grimace if you looked closely.

Then came a bark.

We all turned toward the noise, and Katy quickly sprang into action, bolting down the hallway and throwing open the front door. A filthy brown puppy bounded inside, tracking mud everywhere its oversized paws touched.

Katy let out a giddy scream.

"What in tarnation!" Papaw cried, then moaned as he tried once again to stand.

Mary Joy let out a startled cry, then burst into tears. I bounced and soothed her as the dark blur raced around the kitchen island before running and jumping onto the couch to lick Papaw's face.

Right then and there, I decided I might lose my mind today.

I glanced at Juliet, whose green eyes had gone wide.

And I suddenly realized that this chaos might help her realize she'd be better off staying somewhere else, which would then give me back the tiny semblance of a comfort zone I still possessed.

"If your offer is still open," I said to her, "I accept." I smiled as sweetly as I could manage. "Obviously, we can use all the help we can get."

Five

*A Pearl of Wisdom
from Isabel Espinoza*

"Remember to ask the important questions early in new relationships. As in 'What's your credit score?'"

Juliet

My first morning in Forget-Me-Not had passed by quicker than I could've imagined. Between walking Katy to camp, driving Tenn to the doctor, and bathing the stray puppy, half the day was over.

I was currently on a mission to pick up Tenn's prescription and a few groceries. Tenn had given me use of his truck, his credit card, and directions that made no sense to me, like "Turn left at Wooly Joe's place" and "Just past the Lickety Split, you'll see the turnoff for Snug's."

So, I'd simply typed the store's address into the GPS on my phone, which now seemed to be working just fine, and let it guide me.

"Who just gives a stranger their credit card? Is he senile?"

My sister Amy's reproving voice carried clearly through my earbuds, reminding me why my brother Eric—the oldest sibling at thirty-nine—often called her a stick-in-the-mud. She questioned everything. Everyone. I wasn't sure if she'd always been that way or if it was a result of her working in the PR industry, where she'd perfected the art of spinning a lie—and spotting one, too.

I had the feeling her eleven-year-old twins, identical girls who were about to start middle school, were not going to enjoy their teenage years.

"He's perfectly normal," I said. "Adorable, even."

I'd left Tenn back at the house with the puppy, which Katy had lobbied to keep. Tallulah, however, had overruled that notion immediately. Plans were already in place to post FOUND notices with local online groups and hang posters around the neighborhood this evening.

Amy said, "Maybe he's luring you into some sort of trap. A cougar trap."

"That would be an older woman luring a much younger man."

"Same difference, really."

"Nope."

"Why are you being so argumentative, Juliet?"

Amy hated to be wrong, so she often went on the offensive to divert attention from her blatant . . . wrongness. I suspected she'd always been that way, but I could only vouch for the last ten years since I couldn't remember anything from before I started college.

"*Who's* the one being argumentative?" I asked, sweet as could be.

She huffed, but there was an air of good-naturedness to it.

The heart of the town was full of aging brick storefronts that lined both sides of the street. A hardware store, a florist, a coffee shop, a breakfast café. Many of the buildings could use a little TLC, but on the whole, the area gave off an air of lived-in charm.

Once through the main business district, I passed a fire station, the elementary school, and a large park that had a banner touting the upcoming Flour Festival. Then there was the Forget-Me-Not Library.

Perfectly inviting, it was set back from the street by an expansive lawn and elaborate flower beds. The building stretched wide and had a brick-and-stone facade, columns, and massive windows. As I imagined the rows and rows of books inside, I was sorely tempted to pull in but kept on driving.

"Oh!" I said to Amy. "There's the Lickety Split." It was an ice cream shop, built to look like a soft-serve cone, complete with a vanilla-swirl roof. "Did Mom and Dad take us out for ice cream much as kids?"

I, of course, couldn't remember. Doctors were hopeful my early memories would return one day. Given time. Given continued healing.

I was starting to have my doubts.

"Mom would be horrified you asked," Amy said. "She might actually keel over."

One good thing about never-wanted-to-be-wrong Amy was how easily she was sidetracked. She loved answering questions about my past because I couldn't question her accuracy. Who even knew if half the things she'd told me were true?

"So, no?" I asked.

"They most definitely did not take us out for ice cream."

I could have guessed that. My parents were both health nuts. The kind of people who woke up before the sun to go to the gym, kept track of macros—long before it was the trendy thing to do—and ate an all-natural diet.

"And forget buying ice cream from the grocery store. Not with all those pesky preservatives. No popsicles, no sherbet, no nothing. Every once in a while, Mom would try to make homemade oat milk ice cream, but it always turned out more like soup, so then she'd put granola and berries on it and try to call it a parfait. It was Grandpa who'd sneak us out to get cones at the Whippy Hut, then swear us to secrecy."

During the last three months, I'd been told, over and over again, that Grandpa, my mom's father, had moved in with us not too long after I'd been born. He'd been a widower for quite a while at that point, and after recuperating from a stroke caused by stress, he decided to sell his insurance business and retire early to spend more time with family. My parents had built an addition, a full in-law apartment, onto our house so he could still have separation, peace, from the rest of us. However, more often than not, in his free time he could be found alongside me or my younger twin brothers. By the time I was school age, he'd taken on the role of caregiver, babysitter, and fill-in parent—which, it seemed, had been desperately needed because my parents were workaholics.

My mom, Lydia, had a PhD in nursing and worked as a nurse scientist doing research for a cancer foundation. My dad, Chris, was a biomedical engineer who regularly worked twelve-hour days at a medical device company.

According to my family, my grandfather had been more than happy to take on his new role, and I could hardly believe it was less stressful than his career had been.

The twins had been—and still were—a handful.

Amy added, "Do you remember the Whippy Hut? It caught fire when you were in high school."

"I don't. Cute name, though."

"Oh, it was great. Before it burned down, I mean. That was tragic. You'd always get a chocolate cone with a chocolate shell."

I smiled. Apparently, I'd always loved chocolate. "What did Grandpa get?"

"He liked to get a mash-up, which was ice cream mixed with candy or cookies or brownies or sprinkles. He had a sweet tooth. Just like us."

I'd been told my grandpa and I had been especially inseparable. Yet I wouldn't even have any idea what he looked like if it weren't for all the pictures my family had shown me, trying to jog old memories loose. Amy had even taken the time to upload family albums online so I could access them anytime I wanted. There were hundreds of photos of us together, him and me. Smiling and happy. I didn't recall *any* of them.

The lightning strike had stolen *all* my memories of him, not only the ones from my childhood. Doctors couldn't quite explain the discrepancy.

Well, that wasn't quite true.

One doctor—a psychotherapist—suggested I was suppressing the memories in order to forget just how much Grandpa had meant to me in an effort to protect my heart, my mind.

Every night I studied photos of my grandfather, of us, hoping to remember *something*, and last night, for the first time since the lightning strike, I'd dreamed of him. A dream so detailed that I woke up with tears in my eyes.

"Don't tell Hunter and Jordan about the credit card," Amy advised. "They'll want to borrow it and buy something stupid."

"I won't." My twin brothers were minor league baseball players, both on the same Colorado team, and often used their sibling relationship—and good looks—for social media fodder. The boys loved the attention. Their social media numbers were astronomical.

They'd also been in my dream last night. We'd all been much younger—the twins around three years old and me around five. Grandpa had taken us on a picnic. It had felt so . . . real.

"Hey, Ames? Do you know if Grandpa ever took the boys and me on a picnic at a park? There would've been stuffed animals involved. Mine was a small, light brown polar bear, and the twins had matching blue teddy bears. The park had a merry-go-round and a splash pad and there was a big tree that was snapped in half and the boys kept crying because they felt bad that the tree was broken and—"

"Juliet!" she shrieked. "Are you remembering things?"

As I parked the truck at the far end of the Snug's lot, I winced at the high pitch of her tone. The *excitement* in it. "No, I mean, I don't think so. I dreamed it. Last night."

"That wasn't a dream. It was a *memory*. Grandpa called it a teddy bear picnic. There used to be a picture. It was of you and the boys with your bears somewhere in front of that fallen tree, but the boys destroyed it because you could tell they'd been crying. Your bear's name was—"

Milk.

"—Milk," she said. "Stupidest name for a bear in the history of bear names, by the way, but there was no swaying you. So stubborn. I mean, come on, the bear was *brown*."

My heart raced. I'd remembered the name of the bear. My voice was gravelly, filled with emotion that I was trying to keep in check as I said, "Have you not heard of chocolate milk?"

I'd *remembered*.

I wiped tears from my eyes. This was a huge moment. Enormous.

Amy adopted her smarty-pants tone. "Well, that wasn't its name, was it?"

I didn't have the energy to argue, my mind too wrapped up in the possibility the dream had been a piece of my past that had been missing for months.

"What else have you dreamed about lately?" she asked eagerly.

"Nothing. I don't usually remember my dreams."

Which was one of the reasons the dream from last night had stood out.

"Well, if you have another one, let me know."

"I will. But hey, don't tell anyone about this, okay? I don't want to get anybody's hopes up."

"O-kay," she said in a way that told me I'd soon be receiving a flurry of text messages.

I held back a sigh. From what I'd pieced together of my upbringing, I'd been a somewhat stereotypical middle child. Forgotten, mostly.

Although I couldn't remember my early years, I knew I'd jumped through hoops as an adult just to get them to notice me. Really notice me. No one had been more helpful, dependable, reliable than I was. If any of them needed something, they knew who to turn to. But that was the issue. It felt to me as though they *only* reached out when they needed my help with babysitting or dog-sitting or a ride to the airport.

It had taken a lightning strike for them to really pay me any kind of real attention.

"When do you think you'll be coming home?" Amy asked. "You've already been gone more than a month."

My family had been shocked I left at all. I'd never been one to stray far from home. Or stray at all, honestly. I'd commuted to college, and I still lived with my parents. Jaws had dropped when I told them I was taking a solo road trip, and they'd all tried to talk me out of it.

I tried for a breezy tone as I said, "There's no rush, is there? I don't have to be back to work until mid-August, so I can extend this vacation until then if I want."

"Is that what this is?" Amy asked pointedly. "A vacation?"

I turned off the truck, slipped the keys into my bag. "What else would it be?"

"Oh, I don't know. Maybe running away?"

She'd hit too close to the truth for comfort. Only I wasn't so much running away as I was *escaping*.

The thought of going back home and seeing Grandpa's empty apartment made my breath catch, my heart hurt. On top of that, there were all the ways my family had been trying to help me. Help me remember. Help me heal. Help me feel *normal* again.

It was very kind, caring, loving of them to rally around me.

But the weight of it was overwhelming. Absolutely, unequivocally crushing.

As for normal, that ship had sailed. Not only because of what I'd been through medically, emotionally, but also because over the last few months it had become clear to me that a big part of my identity had been formed by my need to be *seen* by my family.

I'd needed this trip to find out who I was *away* from everyone else.

And I was still figuring that out.

"You *are* coming back, aren't you?" she added.

"I don't know," I said, forcing a lightness to my voice. "I kind of like it here."

"Do I need to remind you that you've been in that town less than twenty-four hours?"

I smiled at the impatience in her tone. "Sometimes you just know."

She sighed dramatically.

It seemed the perfect opportunity to get off the phone, so I quickly promised I'd check in soon and hung up before she could say anything else.

I hopped out of the truck and headed for the store's front doors. A blast of air-conditioning welcomed me into the store just as I realized I'd forgotten to ask Amy if I ever sneaked out of the house when I was little.

But perhaps I didn't need to ask.

Maybe I'd remember on my own.

I was happily surprised to find that Snug's General Store was a decently sized market. People smiled or nodded as they passed by, some giving me a curious glance—as if recognizing that I was a stranger to these parts. Country music drifted through the air. The air-conditioning was *heaven*.

As I stood in line at the pharmacy, I couldn't help wondering how I'd ended up here. In Snug's, picking up a prescription for a man I'd just met yesterday but somehow felt I knew well.

I didn't quite know, but I hadn't been lying to Katy last night.

I was glad I was here. It felt . . . right. Comfortable. As if I was exactly where I needed to be.

Once I paid for the prescription, I zoomed around to pick up a few more items before finding myself in the dog food aisle, looking at the selection for puppies. I had no idea what to choose.

"Why do you look lost?" someone asked from nearby.

I turned and found Callum Hearnshaw walking toward me, his arms full of groceries.

Lost. If he only knew.

"Don't suppose you know anything about what a puppy eats?" I asked.

As he stepped up next to me, he said, "I didn't realize you had a dog."

He was dressed for work in blue pants, a gray T-shirt, and a ball cap. The faint smell of oil drifted over to me, along with something earthier. Woodsy. Cedar, maybe. I realized I didn't hate the combo. It was . . . intriguing.

I felt myself blushing slightly as I said, "I don't. Tenn does. Well, kind of. A stray puppy showed up at his house this morning, covered in mud." I eyed the loaf of bread that was being squished between his forearm and rib cage. "Do you want me to get you a basket?"

"Thanks, but no. I'm about done." He smiled. "Would you believe I only came in for one thing?"

I liked his smile. Wide, warm, friendly.

"I would, actually. I think stores should have baskets placed here and there among the aisles for people who overestimate how much they can hold. You know, if they aren't too stubborn to use one."

His lip twitched. "Are you calling me stubborn?"

I lifted my eyebrows. "Can I get you a basket?"

"Honest, I don't need one." As he said it, a can of Chef Boyardee fell from his stash and hit the floor.

I grabbed it before it rolled away and smiled as I carefully balanced it on top of his stockpile. "I rest my case."

He stared at the can accusingly. "Baskets around the store, you say?"

I laughed and gestured to all the cans of dog food displayed before me. "How am I supposed to pick?"

His eyebrows dropped low. "Was the puppy you found a girl? Brown and fluffy?"

"Well, she wasn't fluffy until *after* I gave her a bath. That was an experience."

He laughed. "I can imagine."

The sound launched butterflies in my stomach. I tried to stay focused. "Do you know who she belongs to? The puppy?"

"I don't. But someone was hanging a LOST DOG poster on the door when I came in a few minutes ago."

"Really? Katy's going to be heartbroken. She's already in love."

"I bet. That girl adores animals. Have you seen her stuffed animal collection yet?"

I shook my head.

"It's impressive. If you're lucky enough, she'll even name one after you."

I sized him up, noting the mischievous glint in his eyes. "Which one did she name after you?"

"It's a platypus. The resemblance is uncanny."

I laughed. "Platypuses are cute, so maybe she's onto something."

As soon as I said it, I wanted to snatch the words back, but instead, I died a little inside.

"That's real kind of you," he said. "I thought it was more a commentary on my big nose."

"Your nose isn't big." I almost added it was perfect but caught myself in time. Clearly it had been a while since I'd had a conversation with a handsome man. *Eons.* I hadn't been on a date since last summer—a disastrous outing involving a mud run and utter humiliation that had me swearing off men for a while.

Before I made a bigger fool of myself, I randomly grabbed several kinds of puppy food and practically threw them in the cart. "I don't suppose there's any news on my car?" I asked, seeking safer conversational ground. "I searched online for engine trouble with blue smoke and couldn't find anything."

Callum shifted the groceries in his arms. "It's pretty rare, but I've seen it before."

"So it's fixable?"

There was a softness to his blue eyes that reminded me of a morning sky, and those butterflies in my chest were mesmerized.

Nodding, he said, "It might take some time, though. I should have more information for you by tonight. I'll call."

"I'll be waiting," I said, then immediately looked around for a cliff to throw myself off of.

Our gazes locked, making those butterflies zoom every which way.

After a long beat, he said, "I should be gettin' back to work."

My whole body was buzzing, part embarrassment, part . . . hope. "And I should finish my shopping."

With a nod and a smile, he turned and walked away.

Halfway down the aisle, a bag of shredded cheese fell from his arms, and I resisted yelling out the word *stubborn*. He threw a grin over his shoulder, though, making me suspect he knew what I was thinking.

Smiling, I watched him walk round the corner, then snapped to. I quickly finished the rest of my shopping and checked out. When I saw the LOST DOG poster hanging in the store's entryway, my heart sank for Katy. It was definitely the same puppy we'd found. I pulled the sign down and decided to make a stop at the library on my way home to let Tallulah know.

Outside, I quickly loaded the groceries into the truck, then climbed in. I rolled down the windows, blasted the air-conditioning, and checked the weather radar—all clear. A few minutes later, I had the blinker on to turn left out of the lot when I finally noticed a robin's feather caught under one of the windshield wipers.

Six

A Pearl of Wisdom
from Renny Russo
"*Broken hearts are capable of loving again.*"

Tallulah

The morning at work had flown by, barely giving me any time to worry about the situation at home.

The main reason it'd gone by so fast was because the library had been gossip central where Evanthe's nephew was concerned. Word had spread about Jake's arrival in town, and everyone who came in wanted to talk about him. Nettie, Isabel, and I had fielded questions left and right.

Yet each time the doors whooshed open, I glanced up, hoping Jake himself would walk in. But only because I'd put the puppy-training book on the hold shelf, and I couldn't keep it there forever. Also because I was hoping he could tell me a little bit more about Evanthe.

I only knew a few bits and pieces that I'd collected through the years. Like how she'd been born and raised in Forget-Me-Not. And had been best friends with Mamaw. She had no siblings, which meant Jake had to be related through her marriage to Dale Kilburn. She had no children, though she often referred to the library as her baby—and treated it as such, doting and caring. She always made sure it had what it needed, fought for its budget, its upgrades. And vowed she'd never leave it willingly, so never entertained talk of retirement. Absolutely refused to consider it, and eventually the library board stopped suggesting it.

With Evanthe, one always knew when to surrender.

She'd worked here at the library for what seemed like forever and was also on the board of just about every local charitable organization around. In addition, she owned many local rental homes, all inherited from her husband when he passed away. He'd been a real estate investor. A mogul, really.

I knew from one of the many gossip sessions this morning that Jake had moved into one of those rental houses just this past Sunday. And because Evanthe's rentals were almost always long-term leases—at least a year in length—there were already plans to send the welcome wagon to his new address.

I couldn't help thinking *Better him than me* when it came to the rental because Evanthe was a stickler about rules. Since there was very little bend in her backbone, I couldn't even imagine how strict she'd be as a landlord.

When Jed Rubin, the seventy-five-year-old library custodian, had passed by Isabel, Nettie, and me without adding anything to the conversation, I narrowed my eyes on him, suspicious.

Dressed in his usual uniform of a pale blue Forget-Me-Not Library polo shirt, khaki cargo pants, and brown leather work boots, Jed was tall as a flagpole and just as thin. He kept his salt-and-pepper hair buzz cut short, and his sky blue eyes danced as he pretended to zip his lips.

Since gossiping was one of his favorite ways to pass the time, I could only think of one reason why he'd refrain from adding his two cents.

Evanthe.

He was sweet on her. Had been for years, according to Nettie and Isabel, but was too shy to act on it. No one dared ask Evanthe if she knew of his feelings.

Well, that wasn't quite true.

Shortly after I started working here, a sweet young high school volunteer had asked Evanthe if she'd ever consider going on a date with Jed. In reply, she'd received a dressing-down about appropriate workplace conversations that still rang in the rafters if you listened carefully.

Not long after, the girl found another job at the Lickety Split.

By one o'clock, Isabel had already gone home for the day—her part-time hours varied wildly. I'd finished setting up a food-related display ahead of the Flour Festival, where the library would have a vendor's booth, selling sweet treats and library-branded merchandise. And I'd also thwarted at least a half a dozen attempts by Deckle to knock a book off a shelf. He'd finally given up, kicked a cup of pencils off the circulation desk instead, and gone for a nap in a puddle of sunshine.

I was on my way to the break room to eat lunch when I heard Nettie talking to someone.

She was saying, "Perhaps suggest yoga? It might work wonders. Have you ever tried it, darlin'?"

Her bold voice carried through the stacks easily enough. Out of curiosity, I detoured, following the sound, wondering who was on the receiving end of her wisdom today.

"Not that I can remember," a woman said.

The voice sounded slightly familiar, but I couldn't quite place it.

Then I heard Vera Ingleby say, "I've been thinking about taking up yoga myself. I sat down to weed one of my flower beds last week, and it darn near took me five minutes to stand up again."

Vera didn't come here too often—she was an avid audiobook reader and checked out books via an app connected to the library so she could listen to the books on her tablet. Yet I wasn't surprised she'd shown up today. She was the biggest gossip around. No doubt she was curious about Jake as well.

Nettie said, "I'll ask Isabel if there are still spots open at the class she takes at the community center. We could sign him up and trick him into going. It would serve him right after bamboozling us into going on that bird-watching tour in the middle of a swamp that one time."

"A swamp? Really?" the unknown woman asked.

Vera sniffed. "It was a lake, not a swamp."

As I rounded a bookshelf, I stopped dead in my tracks. The person Nettie and Vera were talking to was *Juliet*.

I backed up before they saw me, though once I had, I didn't know why it had been my first instinct. Maybe because I was slightly ashamed of wanting her out of the house. Honestly, I was feeling a mite guilty about it.

Juliet cleared her throat. "I hate to rush off, but Tenn's waiting on me. Can someone give this to Tallulah?"

I was leaning as far as I dared in order to see what she was holding when I caught movement out of the corner of my eye. Deckle had wandered over and was watching me eavesdrop. If his narrowed golden gaze was any indication, he was judging me.

And I was coming up short.

I frowned at him.

His tail swished.

"You're the most annoying cat I've ever encountered," I whispered.

He flattened his ears and looked at me like I might be the most annoying person *he'd* ever encountered.

We glared at each other for a long moment before I finally gave in.

Gritting my teeth, I rounded the corner once again. "Oh, hey, y'all. Juliet? What're you doing here? Is everything okay?"

Deckle hopped up on the shelf next to me, and I swear he rolled his eyes. Why I suddenly felt like he was my conscience, I wasn't sure.

"Everything's fine," she said, eyeing the cat with a good measure of astonishment. "I wanted to give this to you. I saw it at the market just now."

She passed over a crinkled piece of paper, then held out her fingers for Deckle to sniff. He immediately pushed his head into her palm, and a wave of irrational jealousy swept through me.

Nettie and Vera leaned in for a closer look at the sheet of paper. A LOST DOG flyer.

"Poor sweet thing," Nettie said, then read aloud the description at the bottom of the page. "'Missing six-month-old Lab mix. Her name is Daisy, but she refuses to answer to it. One-hundred-dollar reward if found. Call Jake at—'"

Call Jake. The only Jake I knew around here was Evanthe's nephew.

"Isn't Evanthe's nephew named Jake?" Nettie asked, as if reading my mind. "And wasn't he in here just yesterday looking at puppy books?"

I nodded. Katy was going to be heartbroken.

Not that I'd been planning to keep the dog. Nope. No way. My hands were full enough already. But still. I hated disappointing my daughter.

"There's no such thing as a coincidence," Evanthe said, practically appearing out of nowhere without even the cool breeze as warning. She zeroed in on Juliet. "I don't believe we've met, dear. I'm Evanthe Kilburn."

"Ev-ahn-thay," Juliet said, repeating it phonetically. "What a beautiful name."

"Thank you," Evanthe said with a pleased smile.

I quickly introduced Juliet.

"Juliet's from *Michigan*," Vera added, as if it were a foreign land. "Her car broke down yesterday in front of Tenn's house. There was a puff of smoke and all."

Evanthe clasped her hands together and leveled a steely gaze on Juliet. "What color was the smoke, dear?"

She blinked like a deer in headlights. "It was blue."

Immediately, Deckle jumped into Juliet's arms and started purring softly.

"Does the *color* matter?" Juliet added, holding Deckle like he was her sanity.

Guilt washed over me. Juliet was hurting, and I should've been more welcoming.

Nettie looked like she was holding back from giving Juliet a hug. Her voice was low, gentle, when she said, "Let's just say it offers a clue as to why you're here in Forget-Me-Not."

Juliet looked at me, her eyes troubled. "I don't understand."

"It's not really comprehensible," I said, my voice thick.

I wished I were sitting in the break room eating my PB&J. Instead, here I was, wanting to swoop in, wrap an arm around her, and promise her that it'd all be okay. Those promises weren't mine to make, though—she had to realize it on her own. So I stood still. Frozen. Not sure *what* to do. Because suddenly she didn't feel like such a stranger any longer.

Evanthe reached over and plucked Deckle from Juliet's arms. "Please feel free to make use of the library's services while you're in town. There are guest passes available at the desk."

Vera snapped her fingers. "You'll have to join us for book club here on Saturday night. Six thirty, in the community room. We'd love to have you."

"I'm not sure—" Juliet began.

"No, you must," Nettie insisted.

Vera tucked a lock of pale hair behind her ear. "It's pointless to argue. We're quite persuasive."

Juliet opened her mouth, then closed it again. Confusion—no, utter *befuddlement*—flashed in her green eyes. It was no surprise when she jerked a thumb over her shoulder. "I need to get going. It was nice meeting all of you. Bye!"

With that, she turned and fast-walked to the door without looking back.

I handed the flyer to Evanthe. "By any chance, is your nephew Jake missing a dog?"

She scanned the page, her face morphing into a scowl, complete with a full lip pucker and pinched nose. "May I keep this?"

"Sure," I said, wondering at her icy tone.

With a nod, she pivoted and walked away, Deckle in her arms, linen billowing behind her.

I glanced at Nettie and Vera. They shrugged.

Then I realized I hadn't told Evanthe that we'd found the puppy so she could pass on the news and Jake could pick up the dog. *Daisy.* Oh, how Katy was going to love that name.

I didn't particularly want to run after Evanthe to let her know. Not with her current frosty mood. So, it was a good thing I'd already committed Jake's phone number to memory.

I'd simply call him myself.

Seven

*A Pearl of Wisdom
from Vera Ingleby*
"Sweetie, it's plain fact that drinks taste better when served in a mason jar."

Tallulah

Coming home after work was my favorite time of day. The utter happiness of my little family being together again puffed my heart right up, giving me a much-needed second wind.

Because the front door had been open, Mary Joy and I had been able to get inside without anyone realizing. I'd also made sure not to let the screen door slap behind me so it wouldn't upset Mary Joy, who always kicked up a fuss at loud, unexpected noises.

In the kitchen, Aunt Maeve, Katy, and Juliet were at the island. Juliet and Katy were sitting, pounding plastic-covered chicken breasts with heavy-bottomed glasses.

"Hey, y'all." I shifted Mary Joy to hold her more tightly as I set down her diaper bag.

Katy's face lit up. Behind her glasses, her eyes were sparkling with joy. "Mama! Hi! I'm cooking!"

"Not yet, little one. You're *prepping*," Aunt Maeve corrected.

Juliet looked at me, cracked a smile. "I'm not sure what I'm doing other than what Maeve tells me to do."

"If only everyone would do the same," Maeve said dryly, an amused spark in her eyes.

I smiled as she came over and drew Mary Joy out of my arms.

The baby practically fell forward into her hands. She adored Maeve.

"How're you doing, honey?" she asked Mary Joy in a melodic tone.

Mary Joy gurgled in response. She continued to coo as her chubby hands clutched Maeve's beaded necklace, the large wooden baubles too enticing to resist. She brought her mouth forward to slobber on them, and I was happy to see her rash had faded during the day.

I walked over and gave Katy a big side hug, to avoid the raw chicken of it all, and placed a kiss on her forehead. She smelled of sunshine. "Good day?" I asked her.

She nodded and smiled. A real smile, the one that showed a missing top tooth. Not the tight-lipped one she reserved for lousy days when she held in any woes, trying not to add to my worries.

My stomach twisted just thinking about her withholding to spare my feelings. We'd talked about her needing to share. Yet she continued to stifle her emotions.

Like mother, like daughter.

I glanced around. "Where's Papaw?"

Despite his back pain, I'd fully expected him to be sitting at the dining room table, his headlamp on, his focus narrowed on his current project. He was stubborn to his core, and I'd never known him to simply *rest*. It was disconcerting not to see him carving or meandering or singing or teaching Katy something about nature.

A hand shot up over the back of the sofa and gave a little wave. "Here!"

Relieved, I walked over, peered down. The puppy was sound asleep at his feet, looking fluffy and clean and quite huggable.

"How's your back?" I asked.

"I'll be right as rain by tomorrow, I know it," he said.

I smiled. "I bet so."

"Where's the munchkin?"

"Right here," Aunt Maeve said, stepping up beside me. She

pried Mary Joy's fingers off her necklace and plopped the baby on Papaw's lap.

Immediately, he started making funny sounds and faces at her. She babbled to him, then stuck her fist in her mouth, covering it quickly in drool. I grabbed a clean diaper cloth and dabbed at her face. She clutched the cloth with both hands and tried to eat it.

I wasn't sure if it was a step up—or down—from the beads.

Aunt Maeve gave me a long once-over. "Long day, darlin'?"

"Not too bad," I said. "How was your day?"

"Just fine. But Renny did tell me to give you a hug for him, and this seems like the perfect time. Come on, bring it in." She motioned me forward.

I smiled and stepped into her arms. She squeezed me so tightly that I almost lost my breath.

"Did you tell him about my back?" Papaw asked her.

She released me and leaned against the couch. "Sure did. He said that's what you get for being old."

Papaw clucked. "He's one to talk."

"He said not to worry about visiting again until you're good and ready."

He jostled a giggling Mary Joy and said, "I'm sure I'll be just fine tomorrow. Just fine."

"Oh, I'm sure." Maeve rolled her eyes.

"I heard that sarcasm," he said.

"You were meant to," she said sweetly.

It seemed to me that siblings never fully outgrew squabbling.

"How's Uncle Ren feeling today?" I asked.

"As good as can be expected," she said. "He's been sassing the nurses. Telling tall tales that he was once a big Hollywood star. You should hear him wax on about his time filming in the Sahara. You wouldn't know the man doesn't even have a passport!"

I smiled. "So the next time I visit, I should fuss and fawn and bring a picture for him to autograph?"

She laughed. "Absolutely!"

I gave Papaw another moment with Mary Joy and then scooped her up so she wouldn't wear him out. The puppy lifted her head, yawned, then put it back on Papaw's leg. He reached down and rubbed the dog's ears.

Clearly Katy wasn't going to be the only one sad to see Daisy go.

I wandered back into the kitchen and asked, "What're y'all making?"

Katy said, "Chicken picky!"

I glanced at the cookbook on the counter, open to a recipe for chicken *piccata*. Which I had little doubt would be called chicken picky from now on. I glanced at the ingredients, not seeing anything that Mary Joy couldn't sample. I'd started introducing her to solid foods about a month ago, slowly adding in new things for her to try. So far there'd been no issues.

"Sounds tasty," I said. "Need any help?"

"Nope," Maeve replied, returning to her spot at the island. "You just sit yourself down and relax for a minute."

Juliet slid off her seat, washed her hands, and grabbed a mason jar from a cabinet. She then went to the fridge, pulled out a pitcher of sweet tea, and filled the glass. I couldn't help but notice she looked perfectly at home. Being here all day hadn't scared her off in the least.

I shouldn't have been surprised.

After all, she'd been led here, to this house.

But why? That was the question I was dealing with now. What kind of grief had she suffered that we, as a family, could help her with?

I couldn't ask.

I mean, I *could*, but it wasn't usually the way it was done around here. We were supposed to wait to ask questions until she opened up about her pain, which was all part of the healing process.

Otherwise, we might scare her off by asking about things we shouldn't have a clue about. I had to be patient—which was definitely a challenge.

I about fell off my stool in shock when Juliet handed *me* the glass of tea. "You look like you could use a drink."

I glanced at Aunt Maeve, who lifted her thin eyebrows and smiled.

"Thank you," I murmured. "I sure could."

"Mama!" Katy said. "I saw a poster about a lost dog on my way home from camp. It was stuck to a light pole. I don't think it's *our* puppy, though."

Our puppy. Oh no.

"Really?" Juliet said. "I thought it looked an awful lot like her."

Bless her for trying.

"Nope." Katy shook her head.

Juliet slid back onto her stool and gave me a helpless shrug.

"I saw a poster, too," I said. "At the library. I thought it *did* look like the puppy who showed up here this morning, so I called the number listed. Because if it is her, she's probably missing her family."

Katy's brightness faded. She leaned back on the stool, folded her arms.

Papaw sat up. He wore the same displeased expression as Katy. "What's this now?"

Mary Joy reached for my glass of tea, and I let her play with the condensation gathering on its side as I said, "I talked to a man named Jake. He's actually Evanthe's nephew. Last night, his puppy wiggled out of her collar while out on a walk and ran off after a squirrel. He spent all night looking for her. His dog's name is Daisy, and he'll be stopping by later to see if the puppy we found is her."

"Why was her collar loose?" Katy asked.

Her tone was accusing, and I sighed.

Aunt Maeve said, "She has a lot of fur, sweetheart. It was probably difficult to judge how tight it needed to be."

"Humph," Katy said.

Papaw echoed it.

Mary Joy turned and buried her face in my chest. Rubbed and snuffled.

I walked over to her playpen, grabbed a rattle. I shook it, and she immediately reached for it, her tiredness momentarily forgotten. Thank heavens. If I put her down for a nap now, tonight's schedule would be all thrown off. She still needed to eat supper, have playtime, take a bath.

"But what if it isn't a *good* family?" Katy asked. "Can we keep her then?"

Lord save me from impossible questions.

As though in answer to my prayer, the doorbell rang.

At the sound, the puppy leaped off the couch and started barking.

Papaw moaned as he tried to stand up. And failed.

Startled, Mary Joy let out a wail.

"Goodness!" Aunt Maeve said, hurrying toward the front door. "I'll get it."

The puppy followed her. When her barks turned to whines, I had the feeling I knew who was here.

"Sorry, I'm a little early," I heard him say. "I'm Jake, and I think you know Daisy pretty well by now. Thanks for taking care of her."

I stood up and jiggled and cooed at Mary Joy, trying to settle her, but she was working herself into a fine frenzy.

Aunt Maeve said, "Come on inside, honey."

"Sorry for any trouble," he said loudly to be heard above all the crying, Daisy's and Mary Joy's. Maybe Papaw's, too—he was still trying to stand up.

It was pure mayhem.

I closed my eyes to block it all out and started humming and swaying, holding Mary Joy's head against my chest. Soon her wails turned to whimpers. Daisy's whines softened. And within a few minutes, all was calm. Mary Joy fell asleep, Juliet had helped Papaw off the couch, and Jake was in the kitchen, getting suspicious glances from Katy and an offer of supper from Aunt Maeve.

"Thank you, really, but I can't." He was bent low, fitting Daisy with a pink harness collar that looked brand-new. He had a Band-Aid on the finger he'd cut yesterday. "Seems I need to find a place to stay tonight."

I bit back the urge to say our inn was full up, and instead said, "I thought you were staying in one of Evanthe's rentals?" His eyebrow lifted at that, and I could feel my cheeks turning red. I shrugged. "You're kind of the talk of the library."

"Well, then you'll know soon enough that she kicked me out. It's my fault. She has a strict no-pet policy, and I didn't even think to ask before I moved in."

Papaw leaned on the island. "And she ain't one to bend rules."

"Not often, no, sir."

A loud trill suddenly filled the air, and Mary Joy fidgeted in her sleep.

"Sorry!" Juliet said, pulling a phone from her pocket. She glanced at the screen. "It's the garage. Excuse me."

She headed down the hall and out the front door, her phone at her ear, her voice fading with each step.

When I looked back at Jake, Katy was inching closer to him, her eyes narrowed. I thought she was looking at the harness, gauging its safety, but no. It was his tattoo, I realized, too late.

"This is cool." She crouched next to him, touched his arm.

He didn't flinch. A good sign. But still.

"Katy," I warned, "remember how we talked about personal space?"

"It's all right," he said. "I think it's cool, too."

"Mama, there are birds on here. Oh! And a fox. And bunnies! I love bunnies."

If she had a magnifying glass, she'd surely whip it out.

"Come look!" she added.

"*Katy June*," I said quietly so I wouldn't wake Mary Joy. It was bad enough that the baby was sleeping during suppertime. But to awaken her after only a few minutes of snoozing? That was inviting an evening of incalculable crankiness.

Katy's head snapped up to look at me. She let out a sigh and shifted her focus back to Daisy, who was belly up on the floor, practically begging for rubs. Katy obliged and said to Jake, "She's been a really good girl."

Apparently, Jake's woodland tattoo had been enough to garner Katy's forgiveness.

"She is a good girl," he said. "I need to work on my training."

I cracked a smile at that.

Aunt Maeve said to him, "You know, I might have a solution to your housing problem if you're open to it."

"Really?" he said, standing. "I'm definitely interested."

"Wonderful. Let me make a quick call."

Once again, I was taken aback by how tall, how solid he was. I caught myself glancing at his arm, looking for bunnies. I found one and smiled. Then I noticed he'd been watching me, those intelligent brown eyes filled with curiosity, as if trying to figure me out.

Under the guise of rocking Mary Joy, I spun away to hide my hot cheeks. I was quite amazed to realize that I wouldn't mind showing him who I was, deep down.

That I wouldn't mind getting to know him, either.

Nope, I wouldn't mind at all.

Not even a little bit.

Which was a problem, considering I didn't plan to date anytime soon. Opening my heart up again was simply a risk I didn't want to take. Not right now, at least.

So, I turned away from those beautiful brown eyes and tried telling myself I was making the right choice.

But I didn't quite believe it.

Eight

A Pearl of Wisdom
from Tenn Greenlee
"As much as I love Gilbert and Sullivan, the best music around is birdsong. It's a proven fact that listening to it is good for your mental health and well-being."

Juliet

I woke up the next morning to a soft tap at the door and faint light slipping under the window shade.

"Come in," I said, sitting up. I dragged the covers up to my chin, then tried to rub the sleep out of my eyes.

"Juliet!" Still in her pajamas, Katy tiptoed toward me, the movements deliberate and theatrical. She looked like a cartoon burglar sneaking through a house. "Are you awake yet?"

I closed my eyes and flopped back on the pillow. "Nope!"

Katy giggled and climbed onto the bed. Last night, Tallulah had let Katy sleep in her own room, which I took as a sign that she was starting to trust me. At least a little. Which was enough. It had also been when Katy introduced me to her stuffed animal collection, lovingly telling me about each animal. Which I took as a sign that Katy trusted me. Which was *everything*.

I'd taken particular interest in the platypus named Cal. It was, as I'd suspected, quite cute.

"Papaw's back is still throwed out," she said. "Can you walk me to camp today?"

"I sure can."

"Can we leave a little early and stop by Miss Vera's to see if Daisy is out?"

It had taken the veritable village last night to get Vera Ingleby's garage apartment whipped into shape for Jake and Daisy, but we'd gotten the job done in less than two hours.

After coming back here, I'd spent an hour or so answering texts from my family, who wanted to talk about the teddy bear picnic, because Amy, the blabbermouth, had spilled all the tea.

My sister had also told them about Tenn, which set off a string of creepy-old-man memes from the twins and safety suggestions from my mother, as though she hadn't already given them to me when I left on the road trip. After a while, I'd had enough, so I texted the family chat that Tenn was a sweet, kind man; that I hadn't recalled any other memories; and that I was tired so was going to sleep. Then I put my phone on Do Not Disturb.

I still didn't tell them about my car.

Apparently, its catalytic converter had died. When Callum called last night, he'd told me he didn't know how long the repair would take, because it depended on how soon he could get a replacement. It was a pricey fix, but necessary, and he said he'd give me the family discount.

I'd asked, "Are you allowed to do that?"

"Of course. Didn't you read your contract? It's in the fine print."

"I think I need to borrow Tenn's magnifying goggles and take a closer look at that fine print."

He'd laughed, and after we hung up, I found I was still smiling.

There was just something about him.

I wasn't worried about how long the fix would take. Not really. I already had my heart set on staying until the Flour Festival, which was weeks away.

"Sure, we can stop and see Daisy," I said, smiling, because Katy sure did love that dog.

"And can you do my hair like yours?"

I ran a hand over my braid, completely loose and falling apart at the moment from sleeping on it. "If it's okay with your mom." I didn't want to overstep.

Outside, birds were singing their dawn chorus, which I wish lasted all day long. I sat up again and glanced at the old digital clock on the wooden nightstand. Glowing red numbers told me it was a little past six in the morning. Much too early to be thinking about camp, which started at nine thirty. An eternity from now.

I must've groaned a little because Katy leaned in. "Did you have a bad dream, too?"

I searched her small heart-shaped face. "You had a bad dream?"

She nodded and stared at her toes, then began picking off their polish. "I don't like them."

Oh my heart. "I don't like bad dreams, either. Do you remember what yours was about? Sometimes it helps to talk about it."

She shook her head and adjusted her glasses, pushing them up the bridge of her nose. "Do you remember what *your* dream was about?"

I wasn't sure why she was so certain I'd had a dream at all. But she was right. I'd had one.

"Mine wasn't a *bad* dream," I said as the air conditioner rattled awake, shimmying and clanking. "It was just a dream. Or it might've been a memory. I'm not sure."

"Why aren't you sure?"

I wrinkled my nose. "My memory isn't the best. I can't really remember my childhood, and my dream was from when I was little. About your age."

In it, the twins had been sick all week and my mom had to miss work to care for them—something she didn't like to do because she hated falling behind. All her focus had been on the boys and trying to get them well. Dad had been traveling for work. Amy and Eric were away at college. I'd walked on eggshells around the house. Trying to help. Trying to stay out of the way. Feeling invisible.

Grandpa had walked me to the bus stop as usual, and I'd

dragged myself the whole way, quiet and yearning for something I didn't quite understand at that age. I hadn't been at school too long before I was called to the office, where Grandpa waited, all smiles. He was dressed in long shorts and a T-shirt that said #1 GRANDPA that stretched over a slightly rounded stomach. His silvery hair was combed back, and there was a gleam in his eyes that had me skipping toward him, not a worry in the world.

He'd told the school that I had a doctor's appointment and would be gone for a while. But we didn't go to an appointment. We'd driven to the zoo. We spent hours there, wandering from exhibit to exhibit. I ate ice cream and a warm pretzel with gooey cheese sauce and rode a carousel horse and talked his ear off. Grandpa made sure we returned before school dismissal and swore me to secrecy about our day out and about.

"School is important," he'd said as he walked me back into the building, his voice like a big hug, "but sometimes what you're supposed to do isn't what you *should* do. Some days it's more important to take care of yourself. Your heart. Your mind. Understand?"

Now, Katy tipped her head. "How do you find out if you remembered or if you just dreamed?"

Her blond hair was tousled, some of it tangled, and I hoped her nightmare hadn't led to a full night of tossing and turning. With the thought came a vague image. Of me as a little girl standing in a bathroom as someone combed my hair, gently teasing loose knots. Older hands. The tops were sprinkled in coarse hair, the knuckles slightly swollen, the skin sun-spotted and deeply lined. Grandpa's hands?

"I can ask my family," I finally said, trying to focus on the here and now. "They might know."

"I hope it was a memory." She pulled the covers around her like she planned to stay awhile.

The air conditioner cycled off, allowing the birdsong to filter through once again. "Why's that?"

"Because remembering it made you happy."

A sudden rush of emotion made my chest ache, my throat tighten, my nose sting. I nodded. "It did."

How could I have forgotten him? Why had I forgotten?

But I knew why, didn't I?

My gaze skipped over the two feathers on the nightstand as I checked the time: 6:12. "I suppose I should get up and get ready. What're you doing at camp today?"

Her face fell. Completely crumpled.

"Hey now," I said, tipping up her chin. "What's wrong?"

"I wish I could stay home today."

"Why? I thought you liked camp." When we ate dinner last night, she had excitedly told us about the scavenger hunt they'd done yesterday, culminating in a tussle over a wooden idol, *Survivor* style.

"I do. But we're canoeing today." Her lower lip twisted, and her hands balled up.

Clearly she did not want to canoe.

I nudged her with my elbow. "Afraid of paddles?"

She rolled her eyes, but the corner of her mouth lifted. "No."

"Can you swim?" I asked.

She nodded and pulled her knees to her chest, then wrapped her arms around her legs. "It's not that. I just don't want to canoe today, but Mama says sometimes we have to do things we don't want."

Somewhere below us, Mary Joy whimpered. A soft cry. Not the ticked-off screams from last night. The poor thing had just wanted a nap. I'd had many of those days myself.

With a burst of energy, Katy scooted off the bed. "I'm going to go ask Mama about my hair."

I smiled as she skipped away, then flopped back onto the pillows, which caused the feathers on the nightstand to scatter. I gathered them up, running my fingers along the soft barbs, my mind spinning.

Thinking about Katy not wanting to go to camp today.
Thinking about the dream I'd had.

And how maybe, for Katy, this was a day better spent taking care of herself. Her gentle heart. And her curious, wonderful little mind.

Nine

A Pearl of Wisdom
from Renny Russo
"If you don't ask, the answer will always be no."

Juliet

Two hours later, I stood in the kitchen, thinking that Tenn's coffee maker might be as old as I was. Big and boxy, it had once been off-white but had yellowed with age. How it still worked was beyond me, but I was grateful it did.

Once I filled a mug, I wandered into the dining room. Tenn's latest art project was on the dining table, right where he'd left it yesterday after hurting his back. I ran my fingers over the lino, feeling the ridges. He told me the carving would eventually reveal a bird, but right now it looked more like a landscape, all wiggles and squiggles. I trusted his vision, though, because around the room hung some of the beautiful prints he'd already completed. A hummingbird, an owl, a dragonfly. I loved that he used his background as a field biologist in his artwork, tying together two of his passions.

I made my way to a front window and looked out at the clear skies. I'd checked the weather radar on my phone earlier, and thankfully, no rain or storms were predicted for today. I'd had enough of those for quite a while.

A plump robin sat on the front porch railing. I took a sip from my mug and watched the bird preen, sticking its beak under a wing. My gaze went straight to the white splotch at its neck, and I absently raised a hand to the pearly scar that sat in the hollow between my collarbones. When the bird noticed me watching, it held my gaze for a long moment, and only looked away because Maeve had started up the walkway.

I hurried to the front door and pulled it open. She sailed inside with a hearty hello and dropped her big purse and lunchbox by the door, before heading for the coffeepot, travel mug in hand. "Did you get much sleep, honey?"

Her blond hair was pulled back in a loose twist and secured with a bejeweled clip. Looking ready for work, she wore a flowy blue dress, big bold jewelry, and a pair of leather slides. According to Tenn, Maeve had founded a respite house, Juneberry Cottage, fifteen years ago. It was a place that offered rest to caregivers by taking over their duties, usually for a short time, giving them a much-needed break to prevent emotional and physical burnout. I had the feeling there was a story behind the cottage because respite care wasn't just a job. It was a calling. A whole-heart, all-in, eat-sleep-breathe way of life.

I followed her into the kitchen, like a little fish caught in her wake. "A bit," I said. "You?"

She'd worked her tail off at Vera's house last night, even with her bad hip.

"About the same."

"How's the patient?" she asked, glancing out the kitchen window at Tenn and Katy in the backyard, filling bird feeders. He was moving at a glacial pace while she darted around the yard like a hummingbird, her French braid holding tight.

I took a sip of coffee. "He said on a scale of one to ten, the pain is a three."

As Maeve filled her travel mug, she smiled. "Which means it's a seven at least."

"That's what I figured. I'm going to try to get him to rest as much as possible today."

Laughing, she checked her watch. "Good luck with that. You may have noticed my brother is a stubborn man."

"Is he?" I asked with a big smile.

She laughed again as my phone buzzed. I pulled it from my pocket and saw a reminder about a hotel reservation for next week that I hadn't yet canceled.

Maeve leaned in. "I don't mean to be a nosy biddy, but I couldn't help seeing the picture on your phone. Who might that handsome gentleman be?"

She was talking about my lock-screen wallpaper. "My grandfather," I said, trying to keep my voice calm, even. "His name was Ronald. Ronald Stephens."

Sympathy filled her eyes and she pushed a hand against her heart. "Oh, honey. *Was*?"

I nodded. "He passed away a few months ago."

Rubbing my arm, she said, "I'm so sorry. I can see you two were close."

I glanced at the photo. It was of Grandpa and me about five years ago. We'd been kayaking on Lake Michigan. After the lightning strike, I'd been utterly confused in the hospital when I saw the picture on my phone and had no idea who he was.

Since then, it felt like I was slowly getting to know him through the photos, the ones in my camera roll and the ones in the albums Amy had uploaded. Through the pictures, I'd been able to study the progression of his life, from mischievous child in the '40s, earnest teen in the '50s, to a somewhat startled-looking newlywed and proud father in the '60s. It seemed to me that his thirties, forties, fifties, sixties, seventies, and right up until he passed away at eighty-five, had been spent mostly as a dedicated family man. There were many pictures with my grandma, who passed away in her forties. With my mom. With Eric and Amy and then me and Hunter and Jordan. There were hundreds of photos of birthdays and holidays and camping trips. Of apple picking and beach trips to Lake Michigan and carnivals and rides on the North Pole Express at Christmastime.

My favorite shots of him, however, were the ones taken when he was twenty-three. He'd embarked on a big solo road trip that year, six weeks long. In one of the photos, he had a beaming smile as he sat among purple sandpipers on a Tybee Island beach. In another, he posed with flamingoes in the Sunken Gardens of St. Petersburg. He'd had an ear-to-ear grin as he watched the ducks in the lobby of the Peabody Hotel in Memphis. He'd had a special fondness for birds.

Robins in particular.

"Morning," Tallulah said, shuffling into the kitchen holding Mary Joy.

The baby's hair was damp and smoothed down, but I had no doubt that once it dried, it would return to looking like downy fluff. She'd been whining until she spotted Maeve, who kissed the baby's cheek, then Tallulah's.

"I wish I could stay," Maeve said, lightly squeezing my arm and giving me a sad smile, "but I have an early meeting. I'm just going to pop out and say hello to Katy and Tenn before heading off."

Tallulah said, "Give Renny a kiss for me."

"I will, honey." Then she gathered her things and headed out the back door, through the screen room, and into the yard.

I glanced at Tallulah. "Do you want some coffee? I just made a fresh pot."

Dark shadows circled her eyes. "More than anything in the world."

I smiled at that and reached for a mug. "Rough night?"

I hadn't seen her yet this morning, because I'd been trying to stay out of the way, keeping to my room until I could deny my need for coffee no longer.

She peered out the window into the backyard, where Katy was

standing on a bucket to add seed to a finch feeder while Maeve chatted with Tenn.

The chubby robin with the white marking was now bopping around the vegetable garden.

I touched the scar at my neck. The pendant that had been melted by the lightning strike had been a robin. According to Amy, it had been a gift from my grandfather on my twenty-fifth birthday. She said it was a bit of a joke, since Grandpa was always urging me to spread my wings and fly. Apparently, he often regaled me with stories of his travels, especially of his trip to the South, and tried to talk me into going on one as well.

It was why I was here. Well, not here in Forget-Me-Not, but here in the South. I was replicating the trip I'd seen in the photo album. I'd been to Tybee Island. To St. Petersburg. And I'd have seen the ducks at the Peabody as well, if I hadn't been detoured here.

I was trying to see life through his eyes. At least a little bit of it.

And the robin with the strange white marking on its neck had been with me every step of the way.

I didn't know what to make of that. Or, at the very least, I wouldn't allow my heart to believe what it wanted so desperately to believe. It seemed too foolish. Too outlandish. Too . . . hopeful.

"The roughest," Tallulah said. "Katy had a nightmare. And Mary Joy was fussy all night. She didn't keep you awake, did she?"

"Not at all." There was no possible way to hear a fussing baby over the AC. "Cream? Sugar?"

"A little of both. Thank you."

As I set my mug on the counter, my phone dinged again. This time with a text from my mother.

Mom: Still alive?

Me: Barely—I need more coffee

Mom: Haha. Did you get your syllabus yet?

I held in a groan. I'd been trying so hard to forget that I'd enrolled in an online program to get my master's in clinical research.

Me: Nope.

Mom: Might want to check into that. Gotta run. Love you.

Me: Love you too.

As I set my phone down, I shook my head. It was so like my mom. Check in, check out. She was always busy, busy, busy.

I poured Tallulah's coffee and slid it over to her as she sat at the island. She was dressed for work in a white cotton blouse with eyelet trim, green ankle pants, and ballet flats, but her ginger-brown hair was rolled in large Velcro curlers, and her face was bare.

She nodded toward my phone. "Everything okay? You seemed . . . not *upset*, bothered, maybe?"

"Everything's fine. It was just my mom making sure Tenn didn't murder me in my sleep."

Tallulah huffed. It sounded the tiniest bit like a laugh. "You'd think she'd call for that. Anyone could be on the other end of a text. Papaw could've commandeered your phone."

I smiled at the mere thought of it. "I don't think that occurred to her, and I'm not going to tell her or she might actually call."

Tallulah cupped Mary Joy's head in her hand and kissed the top of it. She eyed me. "You don't want to talk to her. Your mom."

It wasn't a question.

I started putting away the clean dishes from the dishwasher, trying to earn my keep, since Tenn had waved off my offers to pay him for allowing me to stay here. "Not really, no."

My mom had once been a school nurse like me but hadn't loved the one-on-one care or the daily nurturing that was required of the job. So right after Amy was born, she'd gone back to school. First to get her master's, then her PhD. She'd excelled in each program.

She loved her job now, doing cancer research, and had been encouraging me to continue following her footsteps.

Strongly encouraging.

Strong-arming might be a better description.

And for some reason, I'd been letting her, even though research didn't really appeal to me. I loved the one-on-one nurturing part of my job. It was the only part I loved, if I was being honest, but there simply wasn't much need of it in school nursing. Most of my job was spent dealing with paperwork.

Mary Joy fisted Tallulah's shirt and tried to put it in her mouth. She was adorable, even when fussy. I wanted to offer to hold her, to give Tallulah a break for a moment, but I didn't think she would accept the offer.

Her gaze was full of questions as she took a sip of coffee. Hoping she wouldn't ask them, I quickly pulled more plates from the dishwasher and placed them in a cabinet that had two empty shelves. "I'm not used to all this extra space in a cabinet. Back home, ours are stuffed full."

Mary Joy started to whimper, and Tallulah stood up to walk around with her. "It didn't always used to be this way. It's happened in the years since my grandmother passed away. Papaw's become a bit of a minimalist—except when it comes to his crafting."

"He's talented. I was just admiring some of his prints." Then I held her gaze and quietly added, "How long has your grandmother been gone?"

"Eighteen years." She bounced slightly as she walked, and it seemed to be working on Mary Joy because she quieted. "She had cancer. Looked perfectly healthy until she didn't. By then, it was too late."

I recalled Katy telling me how her mother had said some sicknesses couldn't be seen at first. Now I realized the knowledge had come from experience. "I'm sorry."

"Me, too," she said. She took another sip of coffee. "Thanks again for this. It's been a long time since someone's made me a cup.

Don't suppose you have some caramel syrup hiding over there? My mornings are so rushed that fancy coffees seem to be a thing of my past."

"Sorry, fresh out."

She cracked a smile. "Next time, maybe."

As I continued unloading dishes, I tried to work up the courage to ask her about Katy staying home today.

As if sensing I was waging an internal battle, she glanced at me. "Something wrong?"

"No, not at all." I took a deep breath. "It's just that I was wondering if it would be possible for Katy to skip camp today? She can stay here with Tenn and me. I'm sure I can figure out something fun for us to do."

Clouds filled her eyes, and she shifted Mary Joy to her other hip. "I don't think—"

"She really doesn't want to canoe," I blurted, hoping Katy would forgive me for sharing.

"But she loves to— Oh." Tallulah briefly closed her eyes, then sighed. "Canoeing is something she usually does with her dad. My ex-husband, Scott. Knowing her, she probably wants to keep it that way. Something only the two of them do."

I glanced out the window. Katy was now filling a birdbath with the garden hose. "I'm not surprised to hear that. She has a tender little soul."

Tallulah turned her gaze from Katy to me. She took a deep breath, opened her mouth, then closed it again. After a long moment, she finally said, "I shouldn't really be asking you this, but I need to know before I decide about Katy. What brings you here? To Forget-Me-Not?"

I rubbed a spot on the counter with my thumb. "There was a detour . . ."

But even as I said it, I heard Maeve in my head talking about how this town was a landing place for those who'd lost their way. And how she suspected I'd been lost before I even left home.

My heart rate picked up. Lost was exactly how I'd felt since the lightning strike. Since losing part of my memory. Since losing *all* of my grandfather.

Tallulah scrunched up her whole face like she was weighing her words carefully. Her bright eyes seemed to be looking straight into my soul. "No. What *really* brings you here, Juliet? This town, it's special. Not many understand just how special. It draws in the emotionally lost. It tethers them here. It places them in the path of those who can help them heal so they can find the best way forward."

I rubbed goose bumps from my arms. *The emotionally lost.* Well. If that didn't explain exactly who I was, then I didn't know what did. "I don't understand. Why? And how does it—"

She held up a hand. "It's like I told you yesterday at the library. It's not really comprehensible. It's just the way it is. The way it's always been. You didn't end up in Forget-Me-Not by accident. You're here because you're hurting and need help healing. So, I'll ask again. What brings you here, Juliet?"

The baby lifted her head, her big blue eyes watching me intently, as if asking me, too.

My heart was now thumping wildly. This all sounded utterly unbelievable.

Then I thought about the detour, and how I'd been the only car on the road the whole way here. How my GPS had failed, yet now worked perfectly. And how my car had shuddered and died almost immediately once I made it to town—so I couldn't leave.

And I *was* hurting. There was so much pain. At times it hardly seemed bearable.

As the word *healing* wound its way around my heart, making me *want* to believe what Tallulah said was true, tears gathered. I summoned up some courage and said, "My grandfather died a few months ago, and I can't help thinking I could've—should've—prevented it."

Compassion filled her eyes, and she tipped her head. A roller bobbled but held. "I'm so sorry."

"My family tells me I couldn't have prevented it from happening. That it was a freak accident. But my heart tells me differently."

She sighed softly and said, "That explains the blue smoke."

I tipped my head. "How so?"

"Blue smoke means grief. Profound sorrow."

It took me a moment to realize what she was saying. "The smoke has meaning?"

"It gives the community a hint as to why you're here. For example, orange is a painful choice that needs to be made. A bad relationship has red smoke."

Dumbfounded, I asked, "Is my car even broken?"

She nodded. "Oh, definitely. But because fixing lost souls tends to take a while, your car won't be ready to go until you're ready to move on."

Mary Joy suddenly surged forward, her arms reaching for me. Tallulah went with the motion so the baby wouldn't fall.

"May I?" I asked, already reaching out.

Tallulah nodded, and I lifted Mary Joy from her hands, surprised at first at how heavy she was, then at how she fit so perfectly in my arms. She made a silly noise and gave me a watery smile.

"Beware of the drool," Tallulah said, handing me a diaper cloth.

I threw it over my shoulder. "I'm an elementary school nurse. Drool is not a concern. Trust me."

"I can only begin to imagine."

It seemed a good time to ask once again about Katy staying home today, but I couldn't quite let go of what Tallulah had told me. Not yet.

"You mentioned that this town can help heal. How does that happen?" I asked quietly, my hopes high, hanging in the air like bright, shiny stars.

Pulling in a deep breath, she said, "I wish I could say if you do this and that and the other thing, then you'll be good to go. Truly, though, you don't really have to do anything. Just keep on keeping on. Part of the magic of this town is that *it* guides you along. You're going to meet people who will do or say something that encourages progress in ways only you'll understand. There will be emotional connections and deep reflections. Soon you'll start to feel the sense of peace that's been missing."

Peace. I could barely remember what that felt like. It'd been gone from my life for months now. The only time I'd come close to feeling it was here. In the attic room with the noisy air-conditioning and a chatty, bighearted little girl.

Maybe, just maybe, the magic of this small town was already working.

"Does everyone know about this?" I asked.

"Most residents do, yes. Not all visitors. It's hard to explain, so most around here tend to let it unfold without saying anything at all."

"Yet you told me about it."

"I shouldn't have, really." She wrung her hands. "I just . . . I needed to know a little more about you is all. Especially with you staying here with us. I hope you understand."

I did. Her first responsibility was to her children, and I was a stranger among them. I had nothing but respect for a mama-bear attitude.

As Mary Joy grabbed my T-shirt with both hands, I let my nosiness get the better of me and said, "I know you haven't been here long, either, in Forget-Me-Not. Does that mean you're lost as well?"

She sighed. "I've actually always wanted to live here, so moving made sense after my divorce. But I'm starting to think we're all a little lost, in our own ways."

"Some are just more lost than others?"

"Exactly." She took another sip of coffee, threw a pensive look at the microwave clock, and said, "I should probably finish getting ready."

I said, "I can keep an eye on Mary Joy until you have to leave. My sister has twin girls. I've done a lot of babysitting."

Tallulah pulled her lip into her mouth. "I couldn't let you do that."

"You really could. We'll be right here wondering how we're going to get Tenn to rest instead of trying to stiff-lip his way through the day."

"That'll be just about impossible." Her gaze softened. "But with Katy here with you, you'll have better odds. You two can gang up on him. He'll *want* to go lie down."

I grinned as I realized what she was saying.

She smiled in return, picked up the mug, and headed for the hallway. After only a few steps, she stopped and turned. Her eyes were filled with bold blue sympathy. "Hearts can be big liars sometimes, Juliet. Remember that, okay?"

Soon she disappeared up the stairs, leaving me with tears in my eyes, Mary Joy in my arms, and those shiny, hopeful stars still hanging in the air.

Ten

A Pearl of Wisdom
from Maeve Hearnshaw
"When you're married, you have to grow together or you grow apart.
It's that simple and that hard."

Tallulah

It was a beautiful morning to walk to work.

The kind of morning in my old life that I would've spent puttering around the flower garden I'd lovingly planted, snipping and trimming and admiring. I would've cleaned the birdbaths—all three—and refilled them. Made sure the bird feeders were topped off. I would've skimmed any leaves or debris from the pool. Checked to see if there were any critters in the water, needing to be rescued. Katy and I would've eaten breakfast on the patio, then visited the park to soak up the morning sun before it grew too hot. We'd have stopped at the library on the way home to load up on books. An armful for her. One or two for me.

In my current life, I didn't have much free time. There was no puttering around the garden. No breakfast on the patio, but sometimes on the back porch. The birdbaths and feeders were Papaw's, and he cared for them in his own way. I couldn't remember the last time I'd read for pleasure. And I could hardly recall when I'd last taken a trip with Katy to the library. These days, it was Papaw or Aunt Maeve who brought her in.

So much had changed in the last year and a half.

I glanced down at Mary Joy, who was snapped into her stroller, her eyelids heavy as she fought sleep. We were on our way to Miss Edie's house. Right now it was in the low seventies, but temperatures were supposed to soar into the upper eighties later on with stifling humidity, which was par for the course this time of year.

It would've been the perfect day to go canoeing.

As I walked along the sidewalk, shaded under outstretched tree limbs, I tried telling myself that it wasn't Scott's fault Katy now considered canoeing something that should only be done with her father. But I couldn't quite bring myself to believe it.

Partly because blaming Scott for the messy state of our lives had become second nature. Right up there with breathing. Also because he could've called and encouraged her to go without him. Only when I texted him earlier, letting him know of the situation, he'd responded with She's sweet. I don't see any harm in letting her skip a day of camp.

Just thinking about it set my teeth on edge.

Because the text hadn't been about her missing camp.

It had been about her putting him on some sort of pedestal. One he most certainly didn't deserve, not that I could say that to her.

My grip tightened on the stroller, and I forced myself to think about something else. Anything else.

From the stroller, Mary Joy gurgled and thrust her hands in the air. She yawned, her small mouth forming a perfect pink oval. Then she caught sight of me watching her, gave me a drooly smile, and let her eyes drift closed.

My heart filled right up, fit to bust with how much I loved her.

I slowed my pace as I walked in front of Mr. Daniels's house. He was standing on his front lawn, watering patches of sparse grass that grew over the scarred earth where two majestic trees had once stood. Rainbows glittered in the mist.

"Mornin'," he said with a two-finger salute. He had rectangular black eyeglasses and a shock of white hair he always wore combed back, away from his face.

"Good morning!" I didn't stop to have a full conversation, even though I had a little extra time this morning. Katy might not forgive me if I did. She was harboring a grudge against him for taking down those oak trees.

I couldn't rightly blame her.

She'd inherited her grudge-holding tendencies from me.

I powered on, the stroller bumping along. It was only because of Juliet helping out that I was running early this morning. I even planned to stop and get a fancy coffee on my way to work.

I could hardly believe that we'd only known Juliet a couple of days. How easily she fit into our lives had taken me by surprise.

With how kind, giving, and nurturing she was, it was impossible not to care for her, and even more impossible not to hurt for her after hearing about her grandfather.

I'd wanted to ask her more questions about what had happened with him, but I hadn't wanted to push too hard. I truly shouldn't have said anything at all about the town and its ways, but sadness had been radiating from her this morning. I'd felt the melancholy the moment I stepped into the kitchen and knew I had to somehow get her to open up. Katy staying with her today had provided the perfect opening, and I'd grabbed it.

The stroller dipped into a divot, but the jostling didn't seem to bother Mary Joy in the slightest. She kept sleeping, looking like a veritable angel, completely at peace.

A bird chirped in the branches above my head, and I once again thought of the birds I'd left behind when I moved here. Were the new owners of our old house feeding the birds? We'd had two cardinals, a mated pair, who'd come by every day and eat their fill of black sunflower seeds. I'd purposely left the feeder behind, hoping that whoever bought the house would pick up where I left off. And it hurt, like a thorn deep in my soul, that I didn't know if those birds were being taken care of.

Or who was now living in my house.

My real estate agent only said it was a young couple, just married.

I hadn't wanted to know more. Or to meet them.

I simply hoped they'd have the happily-ever-after I once imagined I'd have there.

As I neared Vera's beautiful old bungalow, my gaze went immediately to what had formerly been a one-car garage, connected to the house by a breezeway. At some point in the distant past, the garage had been transformed into a two-chair hair salon, where Vera had worked for thirty-plus years. When she finally retired, her husband repurposed the salon into a man cave, essentially turning it into a studio apartment. After he passed away, the area had become a storage catchall. For holiday decorations and knickknacks and dust bunnies and cobwebs. According to Vera, the space hadn't seen a good cleaning in years.

Right up until last night, when most of the neighbors pitched in to help move Vera's belongings out and Jake Kilburn and his puppy in. I'd only stayed an hour or so before taking the girls home for baths and bedtime and a return to some semblance of a routine, even if it was later than usual.

I had to admit, though, that it had been worth our schedules going up in flames to see Jake being interrogated by the neighbors, who were so relentless with their questioning that I almost felt bad for him. Almost. Because I wanted to know the answers, too.

He was thirty-eight. An only child. He was, in fact, Evanthe's nephew by marriage—her late husband had been his mom's brother. Jake worked from home but had avoided questions about what he did for a living. He'd never been married and had no children.

Being nosy, I slowed my pace, grateful to be wearing sunglasses so I could blatantly stare at the converted garage without anyone being the wiser. It had a blue Dutch door and two tall windows adorned with wide planter boxes filled with pink petunias and orange geraniums.

Vera's front door flew open, and she came hurrying out, a coffee cup in hand. "Morning, sweetie!" Her curly white-blond hair was damp, her lipstick fresh, and her sleeveless maxi dress loose and flowy. She peeked in the stroller and *aww*ed. "What a little darlin'. I can't remember the last time I slept that soundly."

I felt the same. I'd only managed three or four restless hours last night.

"How's Tenn feeling this morning?" she asked.

Pushing my sunglasses to the top of my head, I said, "Still sore but getting around a bit better."

She cast a glance down the street. "Good to hear."

There was something wistful in her gaze that made me wonder if Papaw had been right about Vera's romantic intentions all along.

I nodded toward the garage. Parked in the driveway alongside Vera's car was an unfamiliar black truck, one with a Florida license plate. "How're things here with your new houseguest?"

"I'm about to bust from excitement! It's good seeing the garage getting used again. And that Jake? Under that tough exterior he's a softie." She sniffed. "I can tell. I can pick out a good man a mile away. It's a gift."

It was the first I'd heard of this particular gift. "But why do you think we never heard of him before? And what do you think he does for a living that he doesn't want to tell us about?"

I'd Googled him last night and had no luck whatsoever in finding anything.

Then, like the proverbial lightbulb going off, I realized why.

I'd been looking up Jake *Kilburn*, but Evanthe's husband had been his *maternal* uncle. Jake wouldn't have the same last name.

Vera laughed. "Give me time, Lu. It hasn't even been a full day yet. I do know that last night he brought in not one, not two, but *three* computer monitors. Maybe he's an online gambler?"

I smiled at her enthusiasm. "Are you going to ask?"

She pressed a hand to her heart. "Not outright! He went out for a jog about twenty minutes ago, and I've been keeping an eye out for him since. Thought I'd offer breakfast and see what I can learn. I'm making waffles."

"I don't know about him, but I'd tell you anything you wanted to know for waffles."

She laughed. "I'll remember that."

Smiling, I glanced at my watch. "I should get going. Don't want to be late for work."

"No, no, definitely not." She started for her front porch, then stopped and turned back. "Is Evanthe working today?"

"Most likely." It felt as though the woman never took a day off, though I knew she'd once taken a seven-month-long leave of absence. It was hard to imagine the library without her. Or her without the library. My heart hurt for the pain she must've been in when Dale died. Then Mamaw. For the pain that likely still lingered. After all, grief never truly went away.

She said, "Then perhaps you can get her side of what happened with Jake?"

I shook my head. "Nope. No way. I'm not treading into those waters. I don't want to be anywhere near Evanthe's bad side."

She laughed. "I have to admire a good sense of self-preservation."

With a wave, she headed up the porch steps, and I carried on, wondering why I was so curious about Jake. I told myself it was just because I had a nosy nature.

Deep within, though, I knew it was a lie.

Eleven

*A Pearl of Wisdom
from Vera Ingleby*
"There is a lid for every pot."

Tallulah

At the end of Papaw's street sat a beautiful circular garden. A wide walking path surrounded the large raised bed, then branched out, connecting to eight side streets. Three to the north, three to the south, and one each to the east and west.

From above, it looked like an illustrated sun, the paths its rays. Even though the sun garden was my favorite place in Forget-Me-Not, I barely spared the flowers a glance as I hurried along. I'd spent much more time gossiping with Vera than I'd intended, and if I wanted to grab a cup of coffee at the Bean Patch—and I most definitely did—then I needed to pick up my pace.

I veered off on the third path on my right, which led to Miss Edie's house. She'd come highly recommended to me by Nettie, one of her closest friends, and had been nothing short of a godsend. Mary Joy adored her. Usually, Edie watched over three little ones, but today she only had Mary Joy because her other two charges, siblings, were under the weather.

Despite Edie being absolutely wonderful, drop-offs at her house always tugged at my heartstrings. Today was no different, even though Mary Joy slept through the transfer. She hadn't even twitched when I kissed her downy head, said goodbye. I loved my job, I truly did, but there was a part of me that wished I could spend more time with the girls. They were only little for so long.

Heartache followed me the whole way to the Bean Patch, which was part coffee shop, part gift shop, and all kinds of quirky and quaint with its eclectic, vintage decor. As quickly as I could manage, I collected a few odds and ends for a gift basket, ordered a caramel latte and a raspberry Danish to go, and handed over my credit card.

Outside, I checked my watch and quickly zigged and zagged my way along side streets toward a tree-lined road that practically led to the staff entrance at the back of the library.

The houses on this street were a good deal smaller than the ones on Papaw's but just as charming with their pitched rooflines, picket fences, and brick walkways.

All but one, which looked like it hadn't seen love in a long time.

It sat at the end of the road, on the corner lot across from the library. A tarp covered its roof, bricks were missing from its curved chimney, and rotted fascia boards were full of woodpecker holes. The window next to the front door was broken and had plastic taped over it. The yard was overgrown, weedy, and gave me the shivers.

Amid the tall grass, I spotted a SMITH REAL ESTATE sign and smiled at the FIXER-UPPER rider perched atop it.

Fixer-upper was being generous.

It might've well said TEARDOWN.

In its heyday, however, the house probably had looked straight out of a storybook. I was still giving it a good once-over when I heard pounding footsteps behind me and the jingle of dog tags. I turned and saw Daisy and Jake jogging toward me. He was shirtless, and I tried not to gawk at his broad, muscled chest. Or how it glistened with sweat.

Mercy.

Until Daisy veered off course to say hello, Jake hadn't seemed to notice me, his face pinched, his gaze locked in the distance as he ran.

When he saw me, the tightness vanished. "Hey."

"Hello. You okay? You looked lost in thought there."

Once again, I found myself looking for bunnies in his arm tattoo, which seemed to be one large woodland scene, stretching from shoulder to wrist. It was quite elaborate, and I found it to be rather beautiful, which seemed strange only because I'd never been much of a tattoo fan before.

I didn't mind this one, however. Not even a little bit.

He smiled and ran his fingers through his damp hair, mussing it. "Just lost in general."

I wasn't sure what to make of the answer. Was it figurative? Or literal?

Figurative would make sense since he was here in Forget-Me-Not.

But so would literal, since he was new to town and it didn't appear that he had a phone on him, one with a handy-dandy GPS.

I hesitantly asked, "Do you need directions back to Vera's?"

"Now that I see the library, I should be able to find my way. But thanks." When Daisy started licking the bag holding my Danish, he pulled her back, apologized, and said, "I'm convinced her stomach is a bottomless pit. She's already had breakfast. And a second breakfast, too." He glanced at his watch. "Despite all that, she's probably counting the minutes until elevenses."

Smiling, I said, "The hobbits would approve."

"I knew I should've named her Bilbo. Or maybe Belladonna? Am I remembering that right? It's been a while since I read the book. Was Belladonna his mom's name?"

Be still, my heart.

I nodded. "Good memory. I bet you're great at trivia games."

"I hold my own in pub quizzes. Don't suppose you're putting a team together?"

Suddenly I thought it was the best idea ever. However, the

closest *pub* was a bar forty minutes away, a rowdy honky-tonk with dim lighting, sticky floors, and a cloud of cigarette smoke you could cut with a knife.

Still, I kept it as an option. "I'll keep you in mind if I do."

"I'll hold you to that."

When he smiled at me, I felt that twinge in my heart again.

What if him? There's a good chance he's the one.

I had enough common sense not to completely dismiss the idea this time around, but rather delay an answer. As in, *What if we talk about it later?*

Jake nodded to the house for sale. "Are you in the market?"

I mean, I was, kind of. But not for . . . *this*. "I'm not really looking for a fixer-upper."

I wasn't entirely sure what I was looking for, other than *newer*. This century, at least.

Again, I thought of the house I'd left behind. A new build in a family-friendly subdivision, with a stereotypical picket fence and a big sunny backyard with a rose garden and a swimming pool.

It had been my dream house, even though it had been a bribe, really.

Scott had known that I'd had my heart set on moving to Forget-Me-Not once he finally finished his master's degree. When the time came, however, he'd stubbornly insisted that we stay near Birmingham, close to his new office. I'd put up a bit of a fight, but in the end, I'd given in to his pleas, swayed when he promised me the kind of house I'd always longed for.

Back then, I'd told myself that what mattered most was that I had a wonderful husband, a beautiful daughter, a home of my own—the stable home base I'd always longed for.

In hindsight, I could see the shaky foundation of that agreement.

The resentment I felt that we were so close to Forget-Me-Not yet so far away.

His long days.

Me feeling like I was raising Katy alone.

Then, without consulting me, he lobbied for a job that required travel. Lots of it, including a possible move abroad.

It had been the beginning of the end.

"It has lots of potential, though," Jake said, nodding to the house. "Don't you think?"

I eyed him. "Are you a Realtor?"

His lip twitched. "No."

His near smile told me he was very much aware that people wanted to know what he did for a living. Also, that he enjoyed keeping it a secret.

He studied my face. "I just know something special when I see it."

I turned toward the house. For the briefest second there, it felt like he had been talking about *me*. Wishful thinking, maybe.

My cheeks were downright fiery when I said, "If it's this rough on the outside, I can only imagine the inside."

He smiled. "Can't always judge a book by its cover, right? A librarian should know that."

"Well," I said, "I'm not a librarian, am I?"

"No?"

"Just an assistant. I'd always planned to get a master's in library science but—" I cut myself off because I realized I was oversharing. No *wonder* Katy did it, too.

"But what?" he asked, curiosity blazing in his eyes.

I let out a deep breath and shrugged. "Life interrupted."

His voice was low, kind, *caring*, as he said, "Is it still interrupting? Life, I mean? Is there a reason you can't do it now?"

I was about to tell him there were a million reasons, when I happened to catch sight of my watch. I gasped. "Shoot. I need to go. I'm going to be late for work."

His eyebrows went up. "You definitely don't want that. Your boss is tough."

He almost sounded amused. But that couldn't be right, could it?

"That she is. It was good seeing you," I said before giving Daisy a quick head-pat.

I sprinted away. At the end of the lane, I looked both ways and darted across the street, bounded over the sidewalk, and practically flew over the library's lawn.

I waved my badge at the card reader on the staff door, jerked it open, and leaped into the break room. It was exactly 9:14. Talk about cutting it close.

Evanthe stood at the counter, in front of the electric kettle, slowly stirring milk into a teacup. She lifted pale eyebrows at my dramatic entrance.

"Good morning!" I said, slightly out of breath.

She deliberately looked at her watch. "I would caution you to be more mindful of the time, Tallulah. Tardiness reflects badly on employees."

I hooked a thumb over my shoulder. "I was just talking with—"

"I'm aware."

It was then that I realized she'd probably seen me talking with Jake. The break room windows had the perfect view of the house on the corner.

"Right," I said, clenching my jaw, remembering my vow to stay on Evanthe's good side. "Rules are rules."

"*Precisely.* There are rules for a reason. If not enforced, chaos would ensue. I, for one, do not enjoy chaos. Do you?"

I searched her face, looking for a hint of the woman my mamaw had loved so dearly. If she was still in there, she was well hidden behind a hard exterior. One that seemed impossible to penetrate. Suddenly it felt like a fool's mission to try to get her to open up again, let me in.

"No, ma'am."

"I didn't think so." She gave me a pointed look, then turned away. A cool breeze whispered against my ankles as she walked out of the room.

I glanced down at the floor, at Deckle's food and water bowls, and thought of the NO PETS sign on the front of the building.

Rules were rules.

But apparently, they were only meant for others to follow.

Twelve

A Pearl of Wisdom
from Isabel Espinoza
"If you make a promise, you best be keeping it."

Juliet

It was early afternoon, and Katy and I were on our way to Juneberry Cottage to see Maeve. She'd called Tenn earlier, saying she'd accidentally left her lunch bag in the front hallway that morning and was hoping Katy and I could run it over.

It was supposed to have been a quick fifteen-minute walk, but Katy was easily distracted by all things nature-related, so it was taking us much longer.

We'd had a good morning. We'd made up a goofy dance. Wrote a book called *The Sparkly Blue Dragon*. Climbed old Bill and read for a while. It had been one of the best days I'd had in a while, which just added to the evidence that what Tallulah had told me this morning was true.

That I would heal here.

Sunlight glinted off her glasses as Katy said, "Juneberry Cottage is real close to the library. Can we stop there on the way back? We can say hi to Mama. We can pick out books, too. I'm allowed to check out as many books as I can carry."

"I bet that's a lot."

She laughed and stretched her arms wide, Maeve's lunch bag swinging on her arm. "It is."

In all the time we'd spent together today, Katy hadn't said a word about her father. Because she was a chatterbox, I figured the omission had to be on purpose.

I understood. We all had things we didn't like to talk about.

She darted ahead and picked up a rock off the ground. She gave it a good once-over and then tucked it into the pocket of her yellow shorts. Then she skipped back to me, her thin arms swinging wide. "Do you know how to skip, Juliet? I can teach you if you don't."

I smiled. Skipping was definitely her preferred method of getting around. "It's been a while. Can you remind me how to do it?"

Immediately, she went bopping about and I couldn't stop grinning. I pretended to struggle before getting it right, and she clapped, then laughed, adding, "You look kind of silly."

I laughed, too. "I feel kind of silly." But I'd do it all over again in a heartbeat. It had been a long time since I laughed so freely. "I have to admit it's fun, though. Thanks for the lesson."

She skipped off again, a bundle of energy. "You're welcome."

I rushed after her and nearly stepped on a feather. I bent and picked it up. I glanced around, looking for the chubby robin with the white marking but didn't see it. Yet somehow I knew, deep down, that this feather had come from that bird.

"Juliet, look!" Katy pointed ahead to an oval sign at the mouth of a long curving gravel driveway. "There it is."

On a fuchsia background, the words *Juneberry Cottage* were written in a flowing white font atop a golden branch dotted with gold berries. Underneath the branch, in smaller print, read HOSPICE RESPITE.

My chest ached at seeing those words, my heart knowing exactly what they meant. The people who came to Juneberry, patients and caregivers alike, were facing the unimaginable.

An ending.

Katy and I headed down the tree-lined driveway, gravel crunching beneath our feet as we made our way along. When we rounded a bend, Juneberry came into view. It was larger than I'd expected for something deemed a cottage, but it had all the hallmarks of one: gables and dormers and a wide porch with wooden columns and an arched doorway.

In front of the building, the driveway circled around a small flower garden with a tree at its center. Katy carefully stepped into the flower bed and gazed up at the tree. "They're all gone."

"What are?"

"The juneberries. This tree had a mess of them the last time I was here."

"I've never heard of a juneberry. What do they look like?"

"Like blueberries! But smaller." Her face scrunched. "And pinker."

"Can you eat them?"

She nodded and tiptoed out of the garden. "But they don't taste like blueberries. They taste like cherries. And grapes. And apples. And raisins."

I laughed. "That's a lot of flavors for a little berry."

"Aunt Maeve said it's not even a berry even though it's called a juneberry. It's a *pome*." She said the word in a fancy, playful tone, the single syllable drawn out.

The only type of pome I knew off the top of my head was an apple. And I only knew that because of a language class in high school. The French word for apple was *pomme*.

I was following Katy toward the front of the cottage when I realized what had just happened.

So seamless I nearly hadn't noticed.

I'd *remembered* something from high school.

I wanted to laugh. To cry. To text Amy.

It felt a little like a miracle.

It felt a little like magic.

And just like that, I was beyond grateful for the detour that had brought me here.

A gently sloping walkway led us onto a spacious porch dotted with white rockers. Ceiling fans stirred the humid air and the leaves on potted plants.

Katy skipped ahead of me, toward the arched door, just as it swung open and Callum stepped out.

He was dressed in what I'd come to recognize as his work uniform. Dark blue pants. Gray T-shirt with the Hearnshaw Automotive logo. Dark blond hair curled out from underneath the brim of a ball cap. Once again, he smelled faintly of oil and cedar, a scent I would forevermore think of as his.

His eyes were filled with affection as he gently tugged on the end of Katy's braid. "Hey, pipsqueak."

The endearment gave me pause, knocking me a bit off-balance.

Katy gave him a half hug, squishing up close to his side. "Hi, Callum!" Then she dropped into a crouch to watch a ladybug wander across the porch.

Callum glanced at me, and I tipped my head, silently daring him to pull *my* braid.

Smiling, he kept his hands to himself. In a teasing tone, he said, "I'm starting to think you're following me, Juliet. Yesterday at Snug's, today here. People are going to start making assumptions."

Was he *flirting*? I'd been out of the dating game so long I wasn't sure. "You're the one who found *me* at the grocery store, Callum."

"Oh, that's right." His eyes twinkled.

My heart stumbled a bit, and I told it to pull itself together. I'd be leaving this town soon. Speaking of . . .

I opened my mouth, but he held up a hand, cutting me off.

"If you're about to ask about your car, I'm still on the hunt for the part. I'll let you know when I know something. I promise."

I *had* been about to ask, even after everything Tallulah had told me this morning.

"You should pinky swear," Katy said to him. "Then she'll know you're serious."

He drew in a deep breath through his nose, lifted his hand, and crooked his pinky, almost like a challenge.

Holding back a smile, I latched my pinky onto his and ignored the butterflies taking flight in my stomach.

Katy stood, the ladybug on her fingertip. She gently set it onto the leaf of a shrub and looked at Callum. "You have to *say* it."

He tightened his pinky around mine. "I pinky swear I'll let you know as soon as I get the part in."

In a loud whisper, I said to Katy, "I don't know. Do you think he's trustworthy?"

"Hey!" he said, laughing lightly.

He still hadn't let go of my pinky. And I hadn't let go of his.

She nodded solemnly. "He is."

"Thanks, pip," he said.

Pip. Pipsqueak.

I wasn't sure why the name tugged at my soul.

Though if I had to guess, I'd say it had something to do with Grandpa.

Callum finally let go of my finger, crossed his arms, and said to Katy, "Read anything good lately?"

She nodded and launched into a full report about the unicorn book, complete with hand gestures, funny voices, and dramatic reenactments.

I kept an eye on Callum while she described a plot to overthrow a villainous wizard, and he seemed to be hanging on her every word. Every so often, he chimed in with a "Really?" or a "Wow" or a "I wouldn't have seen that coming, either."

It was adorable.

They were adorable together.

"Did you come here to visit Uncle Renny?" she asked when she finally wrapped up her in-depth presentation.

"Yeah, but I need to be getting back. My lunch break is almost over. I'm sure I'll be seeing you two around." He pulled open the front door, holding it for us. "Especially since"—he nodded to me—"this one keeps following me."

"Ha-ha," I said.

But I was smiling as he let go of the door and strode off, heading for a blue truck. As I watched him go, I suddenly hoped that the part for my car would take a while to come in.

A long while.

Thirteen

A Pearl of Wisdom
from Nettie Getchell
"If you haven't found it yet, then for heaven's sakes, darlin', keep on looking."

Juliet

Maeve had told me Renny Russo used to be a big ol' bear of a man.

Now he was only a slight bear of a man, slim and sallow. Salt-and-pepper hair was slicked back, pomaded in place. A matching mustache was neatly trimmed, and the rest of his face was clean-shaven. He had high cheekbones and playful brown eyes.

He didn't look like a man who was dying.

Yet he was.

"Don't be fooled, Juliet. Renny looks sweet as can be, but he's pure trouble," Maeve said with a lilt in her voice that betrayed her fondness for him. "It's why he's here. He's been a pain in my butt for going on eight weeks now, despite the fact that Juneberry specializes in short-term care."

Currently, we stood just inside the door of Renny's room. For the last fifteen minutes, she'd been giving me a tour of the cottage, which was impressive. It was rare for a care facility to feel anything other than sterile, but Juneberry Cottage felt warm, welcoming, *cozy*.

Renny sat in a cushy wing chair pulled close to a small dining table in the center of the room, a suite that looked like a posh studio apartment—with the exception of the hospital bed. The bed was glaringly out of place, despite the fact that it was covered in pretty bedding and a fluffy down blanket. On the dining table sat a fancy wooden checkerboard, a game in progress. A small pile of dark brown wooden checkers sat in front of him, while on the opposite side there was a veritable mountain of beige checkers piled in front of Katy's empty chair. She was currently raiding the cottage's kitchen.

Grinning, Renny said, "In my opinion, rules are made for breakin'." The words were more wheezed than spoken, each one as rough as sandpaper. "And I've been a pain in your backside for much longer than eight weeks. More like thirty years."

An oxygen tank near the nightstand and a walker near where he sat were also reminders that he wasn't well. That this wasn't just a lovely room to rest and relax. As he talked, I couldn't help wondering why he wasn't using the oxygen.

"Closer to forty, actually." Maeve glanced at me. "We've been friends since Ren and Junie started working together at the library and he began showing up at Tenn's dinner table as much as I did."

Earlier, she'd told me, "Renny's practically a brother, which is why everyone calls him Uncle Renny. Back a good twenty years ago or so, we were all hoping he'd actually become family when he started dating my cousin Paul, who'd come up from Florida to visit. But it didn't work out. Renny's too picky for his own good. Which is all to say I love him with my whole heart," she said. "Then some."

"Well, we did have a falling-out that one year," Renny said now, his eyebrows lifted high.

She folded her arms, glanced at me. "He didn't approve of my choice for a husband."

I already knew she'd divorced young. And that her son and daughter-in-law lived on a farm an hour outside of town. Callum was their child, her only grandchild, and it took much effort not to pepper her with questions about him.

"And who was right about him?" Renny asked her.

She said, "We don't need to talk about that."

He laughed, which devolved into coughing.

Maeve made eye contact with him and gestured with her chin toward the oxygen tank.

He shook his head and waved her off.

It seemed to me this town wasn't lacking for stubborn men.

"Lordy, we're old," he said, still chuckling.

Maeve smiled. "*You're* ancient. I myself am just starting to mature."

As they joked, I thought about what Maeve had told me about Renny when she showed me around. About his diagnosis. His failing lungs. Two months ago, his pulmonologist predicted he had less than six months to live. Having no biological family close by, he'd immediately turned to Tenn and Maeve for guidance, for solace, for care.

Maeve had secured Renny's permission to tell me his story, of course. Which I thought was rather generous of him to share, even while I found it interesting that she'd asked him in the first place.

Why had she wanted me to know?

Maeve eyed the game board suspiciously. "You're not letting Katy win, are you, Ren?"

"No, I ain't letting her win. The girl's a shark. She should show a little mercy to an old, dyin' man." He coughed pitifully now, putting on a show. "You'd let me win, wouldn't you, Juliet?"

"Absolutely. I'd make it as easy as possible."

"I like her," he said to Maeve, nodding. "Though you know I have a soft spot for green eyes."

Her tone was dry, droll, as she said, "Yes, I've heard."

A whole lifetime stretched between them, and I wanted to pull up the empty chair and hear their stories.

"Surely," he said, "you wouldn't mind hearing it again? Perhaps Juliet would be interested as well."

I was nodding, even as Maeve was saying, "Maybe another time."

He rolled his eyes and said to me, "She's just sick of hearing the story."

Maeve said, "That's because you tell it every chance you get."

"Who doesn't like a bittersweet love story?" he protested. "But perhaps Maeve is right. Another time might be best." Then he said in a deep monotone, "What'd you think of the cottage, Juliet?"

Smiling at their give-and-take, I said, "It's wonderful."

The cottage had four suites, intended for short stays, which would allow the patient's family a break, a vacation, a breather. There were also three common rooms and day programs designed for those needing only a few hours away, to meet a friend for lunch, to go to a doctor's appointment, to not *worry*. There was always a nurse in the building along with support staff as well.

As Maeve showed me the beautiful gardens behind the cottage, she'd shared with me that it had been June, Tenn's late wife, who'd dreamed up the cottage, when she'd been ill. Tenn and Maeve had taken on most of the caregiving duties in June's final days, and even with visits from a hospice nurse a few times a week, it had taken an emotional toll. There was so little relief. Maeve, as a social worker, had done everything she could to find assistance, but there were gaps in the healthcare system. Chasms. They often wondered how people did it on their own, with no rest.

No respite.

After June passed, Maeve was determined to bring the idea of a respite cottage to life, as a place where weary folk could find a helping hand without it costing an arm and a leg.

Because of her line of work, she knew it wouldn't be easy. She had to learn about nonprofits, insurance, donations, grants, fundraisers. But she knew the community needed the kind of haven June had envisioned, so she dove in.

I added, "It's a special place."

Renny nodded. "It takes a big heart to work here."

"The biggest." I smiled at Maeve.

She looked at me, then Renny. "I like her, too."

He laughed, and Katy came skipping back into the room, her braid flying. She had a juice box in hand. "Is grape okay, Uncle Renny?"

He said, "Okay? Why, it's my favorite."

She grinned, showing off the gap where a tooth was missing, sat down, picked up a beige checker, and triple-hopped over three dark brown ones.

"*Merciless*," he muttered. "Who taught you how to play like that?"

"Miss Isabel."

Maeve laughed. "That explains some things."

I said, "We should probably get going, Katy. I don't want to leave your papaw alone too long."

Renny said, "How's his old, creaky back doing?"

I wiggled my hand back and forth. "He's not moaning every time he moves today, so better, I'd say."

Renny shook his head and muttered, "Ancient," under his breath.

As Katy said her goodbyes with big hugs, she said to him, "Don't forget about my birthday party."

He smiled. "How could I possibly forget about a sparkly-blue-dragon-themed extravaganza?"

"What's this now?" Maeve asked. "Last I heard, your mama was planning a unicorn party."

"I just thought of it today!" Katy said, not realizing she was about to throw her mother for a loop.

Maeve let out a light laugh. "Well, be sure to let your mama know, okay?"

Katy said, "Yes, ma'am."

Before I could figure out how to say goodbye to Renny, he said, "Juliet, you'll come by and see me again before you leave town, won't you? Maybe let an old man win at checkers?"

I couldn't possibly turn him down. "Of course."

"I knew I liked you."

We said our goodbyes to Maeve as well and headed for the front door. I paused as we reached it, noticing a big sign taped to the glass that hadn't been there when we'd come in.

> *VOLUNTEERS WANTED.*
> *APPLY WITHIN.*
> *ASK FOR MAEVE.*

Smiling wide, Katy pulled open the door. "Juliet, *you* should volunteer!" she said, the words sounding rehearsed. Then she added, "Even Uncle Renny thinks so. He said so when we were playing checkers."

"Did he now?" I asked, suspicious.

Solemnly, she nodded.

I shot a look over my shoulder, down the hallway toward Renny's room. I saw Maeve sneakily watching us, her head sticking out of his doorway. At being caught, she quickly ducked her head back into the room, and I swore I heard Renny laughing.

Suddenly I wondered if Maeve hadn't *accidentally* forgotten her lunch at all. I had the feeling she'd left it behind on purpose to get me to visit the cottage. Which also explained Renny's stilted tone when he asked about my feelings for this place. He'd been in on the scheme.

I glanced back at Katy, about to ask if she'd been in on the plan, too, but she was already outside, skipping down the walkway, her braid bouncing with each hop.

As I followed her out, I had to wonder why Maeve had gone to all this trouble to get me to, what? Volunteer here? If she'd simply asked, I'd have told her I was leaving soon, that it didn't make sense with such limited time.

But even as I thought it, I somehow knew that was *exactly* the reason why she'd orchestrated this visit.

She'd needed me to see the place, to meet Renny, to *feel* how comfortable I was here.

To understand that Juneberry Cottage was a place where I felt I could make a difference. A place where I could nurture to my heart's content.

Even if it was only for a short time.

Which was why I was smiling as I hurried to catch up to Katy. I knew I'd be back soon.

Fourteen

Pearls of Wisdom
from Vera Ingleby and Renny Russo
"When life gives you lemons, add sugar."
"Heavens no. When life hands you lemons, add tequila."

Tallulah

It had been a *morning* at the library.

For some reason, Fridays always brought chaos.

Isabel was off today, and the volunteer who'd been scheduled was out with a summer flu.

A leaking toilet had flooded the women's restroom.

Someone had put trash in the book drop.

The wi-fi was being sassy, which made the patrons using computers sassy, which made *everyone* sassy.

Deckle had coughed up a hair ball in the teen section, and since Jed was busy with the leaky toilet, I was the one who had to clean it up.

And if all that hadn't been enough, Tiny Tot Story Time had gone off the rails when one crying toddler created a ripple effect of crying toddlers. I'd never seen anything like it. My word, the *wailing*. It had echoed far and wide inside the building. No amount of calming or soothing from parents or Nettie could salvage the program. The session ended early, in a series of embarrassed apologies and teary goodbyes.

It was pushing one o'clock now, and it was hard to believe I was only halfway through my day. Luckily, however, things had calmed. I didn't want to say we were in a lull—in fear of jinxing it—but it was quiet. Blissfully so.

Evanthe was in her office, Deckle was napping on a chair in the reading zone, and Jed was out buying a part to fix the toilet. A volunteer was due to come in at three, and it would be nice to have an extra set of hands.

"Have you read either of these, Tallulah?" Nettie asked, picking up two cozy mystery novels from the Flour Festival display.

"I haven't yet," I said, "but Isabel has and liked them. They're quite popular."

The whole display had gone over well with our patrons and needed restocking each morning. It was fun combing the fiction catalog in search of titles that had something to do with desserts or baking. I'd been surprised by just how many book titles contained words like *cake*, *pie*, *cookies*, or *fudge*. I'd even found one with *soufflé* in the title. *Soufflé*!

Since I'd returned from my lunch break, I'd been dipping in and out of the workroom, which was located behind the circ desk, in an attempt to multitask. I was working the desk and also loading the reshelving cart. Because the books had to go on the cart in a specific order, based on section, the work soothed my frazzled nerves from the morning's mayhem.

Everything in its place.

The majority of returns today were headed for the children's section. Summer reading was coming quickly to an end since school would be starting the Monday after the Flour Festival. Now that Katy had made friends at camp, she was looking forward to going back, which was a relief, because I'd been worried about her settling into a new school.

I'd just stepped out of the workroom when I heard the automatic entry doors whoosh open and saw Georgia Smith, a local Realtor, rushing in. Once through the entryway, she took a hard left, heading straight for me, her sleeveless sundress flaring out behind her.

Georgia was about my age, had a deep tan, apple cheeks dotted with freckles, and a mass of red curls that were pulled off her face in a clip. Her daughter, Zoe, was one of Katy's campmates.

In fact, Zoe was probably in a canoe at this very moment having the time of her life.

Georgia slapped a book on the circulation desk, her eyes wide, her body practically buzzing. I tried to read her energy but couldn't quite puzzle out whether she was upset or excited.

"What's got you all fired up, Georgia Smith?" Nettie asked, coming closer.

I didn't know Georgia that well but was aware we had one big thing in common. We were both newly divorced single moms. I imagined that if we met up for coffee or a cocktail, we'd have a lot to talk about. I ought to suggest it, but right now it felt a little too far out of my comfort zone. Maybe one day, though.

Georgia jabbed a finger at the book she'd slammed down. "It's this."

I flipped the book over to look at the title, and my gaze landed on the shirtless man gracing the cover.

As I took in the muscles and tattoos, my brain immediately conjured up the image of Jake on his morning run. In my opinion, he could definitely give this cover model a run for his money.

Nettie whistled low. "Let me take a closer look at that, will you?"

I pushed the book her way and tried to ignore the heat climbing my neck as I said, "Is there a problem, Georgia?"

"Tallulah, do you know"—she paused a moment, as if searching for words—"how *spicy* this book is?"

The cover certainly hinted at the book's content. A half-naked man lying on an unmade bed. A *come hither* look in his eyes. Contrary to what Jake had said this morning, sometimes you *could* judge a book by its cover. "No, sorry, I haven't read it."

I hadn't pegged Georgia as someone who'd be opposed to a little spice, but I reminded myself I didn't know her all that well. As

I braced myself for a lecture on what constituted appropriate reading material, she fanned her face.

"It's *hot*. Beyond hot. I broke a sweat reading it. I'm *still* sweating." She leaned in. "Do you have other books by this author?"

I smiled, loving when a patron surprised me in a good way. It always made my day. "I can check."

As I tapped into the online catalog, Nettie lifted an eyebrow. "Hot, you say?"

Georgia said, "Think ghost peppers, Miss Nettie. You'll feel the burn in your *soul*."

Nettie's other eyebrow went up and both stayed there. "I see, I see. Lu, can you check if there're any holds on this? If not"—she grinned—"it's coming home with me."

And just like that, the morning's troubles evaporated. This right here was one of the reasons I loved the library so much. These little conversations. The sharing of a good book. The way it felt like the three of us were in on some sort of secret together.

Well, the four of us, if you counted Deckle. His nosy self had cut his nap short and hopped up onto the counter to watch what was going on. So help me if another hair ball was imminent. I swear he coughed up the earlier one just to get under my skin.

I gave him the stink eye to let him know I was watching him, and he looked at me with his golden eyes, as if amused that I thought I could stop him from causing mischief.

Georgia said, "I have to say, these books might just ruin dating for me. How's a man supposed to live up to this?" She gestured wildly at the cover. "I mean, come *on*."

Nettie smiled. "Ain't that the truth? And it's already slim pickings around these parts."

I slid her a wry glance. "How's your husband feel about you keeping tabs on the town's dating scene?"

She laughed. "Someone's got to be in charge of matchmaking around here."

Nettie was well-known around town for poking her nose

into other people's love lives. To be fair, she'd had a good bit of success.

She drummed her fingertips on the counter and eyed me. Sizing me up.

"No," I said, shaking my head so hard my ponytail darn near slapped my face. "Nope. No way. Not me. The ink is barely dry on my divorce."

She swung her gaze to Georgia, who laughed. "Nope, not ready, either."

Nettie shook her head. "Haven't you both heard that the best way out is through?"

"As soon as I'm ready, I'll let you know," Georgia said to her. "I promise."

Then they both looked at me.

In an attempt to change the subject, I said, "We have three more of that author's titles available to check out, Georgia." I made to come around the counter. "I can take you over to—"

She waved me off. "No need. I can find them and browse a bit, too. See what other spice I can find. Thank you, though."

As soon as she disappeared into the stacks, Nettie began to drum her fingertips on the counter again. "There's been no one since your divorce was final, darlin'?"

I cursed myself for even mentioning it earlier and shook my head.

"You know," she said in an offhand way that felt quite deliberate, "I thought I caught a spark between you and Jake the other day."

"What? No." I didn't dare even glance at the book on the counter.

"It was just the barest flicker, mind you. Sometimes that's all you need to create some mighty flames. He's newly single, you know."

I lifted an eyebrow. "How do you know that?"

"Vera texted. She wheedled it out of him over breakfast. It was a recent breakup but amicable."

"His truck didn't break down when it got to town, did it?"

"Nope."

I was happy to hear that because it meant he wasn't hurting over the relationship to the point that he'd been *led* to town. He wasn't here for healing.

Still, dating still felt way too far out of my comfort zone, and I tried to find excuses in hopes of putting an end to this discussion. "He's not even my type. Not really. I go more for a blue-eyed, blond-haired, button-down kind of guy."

She leveled me with an amused gaze. "And how'd that work out for you?"

"Hey now."

Deckle trilled like he was laughing and plopped down, folding his arms inward, curling his tail against his body, becoming one big fluffy black-cat loaf.

I rolled my eyes and moved the cup of pencils away from him, just in case he was lulling me into a false sense of security.

Smiling, Nettie reached across the counter and patted my hand. "All I'm sayin', Lu, is that if you keep doing what you've always done, you'll keep getting what you've always got. Maybe it's a good idea to give *different* a chance. Walk a different path. I'm telling you, there's something there between you and Jake. You should give it a chance."

It seemed that today *I* was the one on the receiving end of her wisdom.

I lowered my voice. "Even if I did like Jake, opening myself up, wearing my heart on my sleeve, feels . . ."

"What, darlin'?"

"It feels like I'd just be asking for heartache."

Nettie knew my history, knew why I'd become so introverted, knew why I'd closed myself off to most people. I was beyond grateful I didn't have to explain.

She gave me an encouraging smile. "I understand, I do. You're just trying to keep from getting hurt. But here's my concern, darlin'." She slid a look toward Evanthe's office and dropped her voice. "Sometimes, when you lock yourself up, all safe and protected, you forget how to let people back in. I don't want that happening to you."

As the image of Evanthe looking out the window came to mind, all stoic and unapproachable, I sighed, then tiptoed over the boundaries of my comfort zone. "Maybe it is time to date again. Test the waters."

Nettie grinned.

I groaned. "I said *maybe*."

With a laugh, she said, "I'll take a maybe. A maybe isn't a no."

Deckle took that moment to rise to his feet, yawn, and stretch. In doing so, he kicked over a pile of mail onto the floor.

I suspected it hadn't been an accident.

Bending down, I gathered the scattered mail. My gaze caught on one brochure in particular. It was from the University of Alabama, touting its MLIS program. Master of Library and Information Science. The degree I'd need if I wanted to become an official librarian here.

When the front doors slid open, I stood up. A warm breeze swept into the library, bringing with it Katy and Juliet.

Katy skipped toward the counter. "Hi, Deckle! Hi, Mama! Hi, Miss Nettie!"

It didn't escape my notice that I'd ranked second.

"Hello there!" I said, setting the collected mail down on the counter—far away from Deckle. "This is a nice surprise."

Juliet smiled. "Katy's hoping to check out some books."

"A mess of books!" Katy immediately went to Nettie for a hug, curving into her side.

Nettie squeezed Katy tight. "I swear you've done grown another inch since last week."

"I think so, too," she said. "I might be as tall as Bill one day."

"Bill?" Nettie asked.

"The oak tree in front of Papaw's house," I supplied.

"Oh, of course." Nettie nodded. "*That* Bill. He's quite magnificent. What've you been up to today?"

"Me and Juliet wrote a book and danced and we just went to Juneberry and I beat Uncle Renny in checkers."

She was glowing. It was so nice to see her excited. Just maybe she was having more fun today than she ever would've had in a canoe.

I knew I owed that to Juliet and would have to find a way to thank her.

"Why'd you go to Juneberry?" I asked.

"Aunt Maeve forgot her lunch," Katy said. "We brought it to her."

Deckle made his way to the edge of the counter, closer to Juliet. He pushed his head into her palm.

I told myself I wasn't the least bit envious.

"It's a beautiful place," Juliet said.

Nettie nodded. "It surely is."

The front doors opened again, and this time it was Miss Edie who rushed in, pushing the stroller at full speed. By the look on her face, something was terribly wrong.

"Lu! I have to— I've got—"

"What's happened?" My heart pounded as I darted around the counter, nearly tripping over my feet. As soon as I reached Edie's side, I saw Mary Joy sitting in the stroller, gumming on a frozen plastic teether. She broke into a smile when she saw me and started waving her hands. I picked her up, holding her close, until she squawked at the tightness. As soon as I loosened my grip, she dropped the teether and reached for my necklace.

"It's my mama," Edie said, the words ragged, splintered. Torn from her soul. She gulped, trying to get a little more air. She looked about ready to pass out.

Juliet stepped toward her and gently touched her arm. "Slow breaths. Lean forward a little—it helps."

Edie nodded and leaned.

I took a slow breath, too, trying to calm down, but fear still thudded against my ribs.

Juliet glanced at me. "Can we get her a cup of water?"

"I can get it," Katy said and sprinted toward the employee break room, in full helper mode.

Nettie grabbed a chair from the reading zone and, with Juliet's help, lowered Edie onto the seat. "That's it. Nice and easy like."

Katy came rushing back, her spine ramrod straight as she tried not to spill the cup of water she held. "Here you go, Miss Edie."

"Thank you, baby." She took a sip, her hand shaky, but her voice steadier.

"Now what's this about your mama?" Nettie asked her.

"She fell and hit her head bad. The hospital called me not twenty minutes ago. I need to pack and get to Roanoke straightaway."

Worry vibrated in each word she spoke, and my heart hurt for her.

"Oh no," Nettie tutted. "And you're planning to drive up to Virginia tonight?"

It's where Edie had grown up. Her mama, well into her eighties, lived in a retirement community there.

Edie nodded, and her voice was a mite bit stronger when she said, "Flying's no faster, what with the time it would take to get to the airport and the connection and all. Besides, it'll be nice to have my car up there to go back and forth to the hospital."

Nettie said, "I don't get off work till six, but let me call Vera. She can help you pack and make sure you have everything you need before you get on the road."

I knew that meant she wanted to make sure Edie was calm enough to make the trip before she drove off. And that she'd have a full tank of gas and a basket of food when she went. There was nothing like small-town compassion when a crisis arose.

Edie's eyes filled with tears, and she nodded. "I'd appreciate that." She then stood up and faced me. "I'm so sorry, Lu. I'm not sure how long I'll be gone. I reckon a week at least. I'll let you know as soon as I do."

"Take as much time as you need," I said, even though panic was seeping in. "I'm so sorry about your mama. You'll both be in my thoughts."

"Mine, too," Juliet said, empathy etched deeply in her green eyes.

Edie gave us a weak smile and set her cup on the counter. "Thank you. I should get going. There's so much to do."

Nettie put an arm around her. "I'll walk you out."

As soon as they were through the front doors, a cool wind whistled through the library. I didn't need to turn around to know who was behind me.

Katy said, "Hi, Miss Evanthe!"

"Hello, Miss Katy. And Juliet, if I recall correctly?"

Juliet nodded and said, "Hello again."

Mary Joy buried her head into my chest and rubbed her face side to side. With the motion, I guessed I had about two minutes before she started fussing. It was coming on nap time.

Evanthe gazed at the baby. "Is something amiss?"

I quickly explained about Edie. "I just need to call—"

Anxiety flooded through my veins, somehow hot and icy at the same time, as I realized that I didn't want to hand Mary Joy over to *anyone*. I just wanted to hold her and not let go. I'd been so scared. I still was, for some reason.

"I can watch her this afternoon. And while Miss Edie is away," Juliet offered with a sweet smile. "I'm going to be in town until the Flour Festival at least."

My heart was thumping. Mary Joy must've sensed my uneasiness because she let out a whimper. I didn't know how to explain what I was feeling.

Evanthe drew in a deep breath, and I swear it rattled the windowpanes. "Take your baby home, Tallulah. I will cover for you."

"But we're already short-staffed," I began.

"Go home, Tallulah." Her tone was firm. "I will see you tomorrow. Without the little ones, I trust."

I held her gaze, thoroughly confused.

She tipped her head to the side, blinked. "Do not forget to clock out."

With that, she turned around and walked away.

Juliet

The children's section of the library was sunlit, colorful, and charming. Carpet squares in rainbow colors covered the floor. In addition to the bookshelves, there were beanbags, toys, and tiny tables and chairs that made me feel a bit like a giant. The space radiated joy, and I tried to soak it in because I was on edge.

I glanced toward the STAFF ONLY door that Tallulah, with Mary Joy still in her arms, had disappeared behind a few minutes ago. She was collecting her belongings before we all headed back to Tenn's.

I wished she'd taken me up on my offer to watch Mary Joy for the rest of the day. It made me uneasy, knowing someone was in distress and I couldn't help them.

Katy had been insistent on checking out a few books before we left the library but must've understood we didn't have time to linger because she said, "I'll just get three today."

Three was definitely a step down from what she'd been envisioning.

The library was quiet this afternoon with only a half dozen other patrons here. A few people were browsing the adult section, and two were seated in study carrels not too far away. One was playing a computer game.

At the moment, Katy and I were alone in the children's area. Well, that wasn't quite true. Deckle, the fluffy black cat, had followed us. He currently sat atop a low shelf. His eyes were a pale gold, and I'd swear, hand to heaven, that there were decades of wisdom in his gaze.

"Juliet! Look!" Katy bounced up from the floor and ran over to me. She held a slim paperback in her hand. The cover illustration was of a young girl riding a dragon.

"That looks good," I said. "And it seems like it's the first in a series, too."

Her eyes widened behind her glasses. "I'll be right back."

I smiled as she practically dove onto the floor to check for sequels. I made a mental note to give Tallulah a heads-up about a dragon party in case Katy forgot to mention it. I might wait a day or two, though, to allow Tallulah's stress levels to drop a bit, or else I feared she might implode.

As I waited for Katy, I absently turned a small wooden rack, looking at titles.

The next thing I knew, Deckle was standing at my side, and with one swipe of a paw, he knocked a book off the rack, onto the floor. "Hey," I said, bending down to pick it up, noticing that it was a Berenstain Bears book.

I was about to put it back on the rack when Katy jumped up again and stopped me. "No, no! You have to sniff it."

I tipped my head. "What?"

She bounced up and down, full of excitement. "It's what Deckle does. If he knocks a book off the shelf, you need to smell it."

"You're kidding."

"You have to!"

I glanced at the cat, as if expecting him to agree with me that this was bizarre. Instead, he sat there, swishing his tail, as if . . . waiting.

I looked at the cover of the book. The bears were in their treehouse and through the window were dark skies and lightning bolts.

In a flash, I was back in a hospital bed, hearing the worst news possible—that my grandfather hadn't survived the lightning strike—and realizing I had no memory of him at all.

My hands started shaking, and my chest squeezed tight.

Suddenly I could barely pull in a breath.

I felt a hand on my arm. "Juliet? Are you okay?"

Tallulah. I faced her, and I wasn't sure what she saw, but she quickly took the book out of my hands, left it next to Deckle. "Let's go and get some fresh air. Why don't you push Mary Joy," she said, placing my hands on the stroller.

As if knowing my knees had gone weak.

"But, Mama," Katy said.

"We'll come back for your books," she said.

"But—"

"*Katy June Byrd Mayfield.*"

Katy huffed but didn't say another word.

As we made our way toward the front doors, I glanced back at the children's section. Deckle still sat on the bookshelf.

He was watching us leave, his golden eyes filled with sadness.

Fifteen

*A Pearl of Wisdom
from Nettie Getchell*

"Sure enough, love can be lost,
but always remember that it can often be found again."

Tallulah

Later that night, I said to Katy, "Now, remember, we're just dropping off the basket. It's almost Mary Joy's bedtime. We can't stay."

Katy bounded down the front steps of Papaw's house, swinging a small basket—a welcome-to-the-neighborhood gift for Jake. It held cookies from the local bakery, a gift card to the coffee shop, and a toy for Daisy. "Can I play with Daisy for just a *few* minutes? Please?"

Because I was still feeling guilty about rushing her out of the library earlier, I couldn't possibly say no. "Okay. But remember, they might not even be home."

She skipped her way to the sidewalk, looking a bit like Little Red Riding Hood, and peered down the street. "His truck is there."

I smiled. "Well, let's go see then. If he's not, we'll just leave the basket at his door."

Before we set off, I checked on Mary Joy as she banged her teether against the stroller. Even though she'd been having a rough night, she gave me a smile, and my heart melted. I bent and kissed her head, checking to feel if she felt warm as I did so. I was worried she was coming down with something. Maybe the virus that was going around.

Honestly, though, she'd seemed perfectly fine until dinnertime; then it went downhill fast. Eating had been a trial. She'd thrown more fettucine than she'd eaten. She'd whined and wiggled and cried until I picked her up, held her in my arms. An hour later, her face was still flushed, and because she still had the drool rash, she looked downright pitiful.

We started down the sidewalk, and I took a deep breath, trying to bring my stress level down a notch. It was half past seven, and the sky had a pink hue to it, hinting that the sun would soon be setting. The scent of roses swirled in the air.

I glanced back at Papaw's house, wondering if I should've asked Juliet if she wanted to come with us, but she'd been curled up on the back porch, reading one of Mamaw's old paperbacks, and I hadn't wanted to disturb her.

I wasn't sure what had caused her panic attack at the library earlier, but I had the feeling it was related to why she was here in Forget-Me-Not. I wished I could hurry her healing along or at least take away some of her pain, but I just had to be patient. It would come.

I glanced down at Mary Joy, who was watching the cloud. I'd taken Juliet up on her earlier offer, so starting tomorrow, she was going to watch Mary Joy while I was at work.

I wasn't fully confident in my decision.

But only because I was worried about the girls getting too attached to Juliet.

All of us, really.

It was going to hurt when Juliet ultimately said goodbye.

I didn't like goodbyes.

As we neared Mr. Daniels's house, I saw he was outside watering his flowers and whispered to Katy, "Be sweet."

Her small chin shot in the air.

"Evenin'!" Mr. Daniels called out. "Fine night, ain't it?"

"Hello," I said. "It's beautiful. A perfect night for a walk."

I glanced at Katy and gave a pointed cough.

Katy sniffed. "*Hi.*"

Then she started skipping at the speed of light, zooming past his yard.

I glanced at him. "Sorry. She'll come around."

He turned off the hose and pushed his glasses up his nose. "Is she still upset about the trees?"

"She's sad, is all."

He nodded. "I am, too."

Then he went back to watering, and I carried onward, the stroller bumping over cracks in the sidewalk. I wasn't sure how to get Katy to let go of the grudge she was holding, since letting go of grudges was a lesson I needed to learn as well.

I thought of Deckle and sighed. To my knowledge, he'd never chosen a book for my mama. That had been Calliper. But really, I shouldn't be holding a grudge at all. It wasn't the library cats' fault my mama had longed to travel. Or that neither of my parents had ever wanted to call one place home. Wandering was simply in their souls. They put their globe-trotting to good use as travel writers who were widely known and respected in their field.

But I didn't share their wanderlust, and the endless travel when I was younger had affected me deeply. By the time I'd reached my teen years, all I wanted was normalcy. A bedroom of my own would've been nice. A school, too. Lasting friendships would've been especially welcome.

I felt a pang just thinking about those days. The constant goodbyes. Because I'd been an inherently shy child, making friends always took a while. And it felt like every time I did, it was time to move again. Eventually, I gave up trying. I withdrew. Into books. Into myself. Until I was eighteen. That was when I decided enough was enough. I wanted stability. I chose a college close to Forget-Me-Not so I could stay with Papaw during breaks, always planning to end up here permanently one day.

Then I met Scott.

"Daisy!" Katy shouted, snapping me out of my thoughts.

The sound of barking filled the evening air, and I spotted Daisy and Jake on the sidewalk ahead. Katy gave the dog a big hug, her small fingers disappearing into chocolate-brown fur.

With a smile, Jake said, "It's like watching a love story unfolding."

I met his gaze, felt that strange flutter in my chest. "She's a lovable dog."

Katy's eyes sparkled behind her glasses as she said, "Can I walk Daisy around the yard?"

"Sure can." He handed over the leash. "If she starts pulling, just call for me."

But she didn't pull. She fell in step beside Katy, as if they'd walked together a thousand times before.

I was surreptitiously trying to find animals in Jake's tattoo as he crouched down to Mary Joy's level to pick up the teether she'd tossed out of the stroller. "Well, hi there," he said, tickling her toes. "That's quite a drool rash you've got, young lady."

She kicked her feet out at him and cooed, as if agreeing.

I said, "How do you know about drool rashes?"

Mischief glinted in his eyes. "Doesn't everyone?"

Narrowing my gaze, I took some wild guesses. "Are you a dentist? A hygienist?" I snapped my fingers. "A drool expert?"

He stood up, handed me the dirty teether, and smiled. "No, no, and definitely no."

His smile was wide, warm, and made his eyes crinkle playfully.

As I bent to pick up the basket that Katy had abandoned, I said, "Why won't you tell anyone what you do for a living?"

He folded his arms and lifted a shoulder in a half shrug. "I have my reasons, but the top one at the moment is that I'm enjoying your guessing game."

I was *beyond* curious. "Can I get a hint?"

He looked toward the sky as if searching for something among the puffy clouds. "All right. My job requires a college degree."

"Way to narrow things down." He laughed, and I spotted the image of a tawny, curled-up fawn near his elbow. It was adorable. "I don't suppose you'd tell me what you majored in?"

"Maybe next time," he said.

Next time. I liked the sound of that.

I handed Jake the basket. "This is for you. A welcome-to-the-neighborhood gift."

His whole face softened. "I've never gotten a welcome basket before."

"Just wait. You'll probably have a dozen baskets by the end of the weekend along with some casseroles and maybe a couple of loaves of banana bread, too. Perks of living in a small town."

He sifted through the gifts in the basket. "Well, clearly you know the way to my heart."

My own heart was suddenly doing a two-step. "Is it the cookies?"

He laughed. "No. The squeak toy."

He squeaked it, and Daisy's ears twitched; then she barked. She ran toward us, toting Katy along, and kept barking until Jake gave her the toy.

At all the noise, Mary Joy started crying, and I rolled her forward, then back. "That's our cue to head home. It's time to say goodbye to Daisy, Katy."

She immediately dropped to her knees to give the dog more hugs, and Daisy gave her kisses.

I glanced at Jake. "I'm sure we'll be seeing you around."

He held my gaze. "You know, most nights Daisy and I go for a walk around seven. You're welcome to join us. If you want. An open invitation."

I glanced away, unable to concentrate with him looking at me the way he was. Katy bounced up in front of me and was nodding so vigorously she was bound to have a headache later on.

I thought of Nettie and her earlier wisdom about walking a different path, then threw my perfectly crafted schedule out the window and faced him. "We might just take you up on that from time to time."

When he smiled, my chest tightened as my heart once again asked, *What if him? He seems like a keeper.*

Maybe, I told it.

As we headed back home, Katy skipped alongside the stroller and said, "Mr. Jake is nice. I like him."

I tossed a glance over my shoulder, caught him still watching us. I gave a wave and whispered to Katy, "I like him, too."

A little after nine, I was curled up on the couch with a bowl of buttery popcorn watching a movie when I heard footsteps on the stairs. The quick pace of the footfalls told me it couldn't possibly be Papaw, who'd already turned in for the night. The deep pitch of the creaking told me it couldn't possibly be Katy, since her footsteps barely made a sound—and she should be asleep by now. Juliet, then.

A moment later she appeared from the hallway, dressed for bed in an oversized T-shirt and a pair of cotton shorts. Her hair was pulled up in a sloppy bun, looking dark in the low light.

She said, "Don't mind me, I'm just grabbing a cup of water."

Pausing the movie, I smiled. "I'm not minding at all. I'm just unwinding a little before bed. I know if I try to go sleep now, I won't be able to turn off my thoughts. Today's been . . ."

"Stressful?" she supplied.

"To put it mildly." Then I took a deep breath and slipped out of my comfort zone by saying, "You're welcome to join me in the unwinding of it all. I'm watching *Pride and Prejudice*. It's my comfort movie. I've probably seen it at least a dozen times. There's more popcorn in the bag on the counter."

She tipped her head, smiled. "Maybe I will. I do love that movie, and the popcorn scent is making my stomach rumble."

Moments later, she was sitting on the couch with me and glancing at the TV screen. "This is *Pride and Prejudice*?"

I turned her way. "Don't tell me you've never seen this version." It was the BBC miniseries, the one with Colin Firth.

She shook her head. "Isn't this one like five hours long?"

"Worth every minute."

Looking doubtful, she said, "The version I love is the one with—"

I interrupted. "Don't say Keira Knightley."

"—Keira Knightley," she said with a laugh.

"I'm not sure we can be friends anymore. That movie doesn't hold a candle to this one."

"I can't believe that," she said. "It's amazing. Have you even seen it?"

"I don't need to." I gestured to the screen. "This one is perfection."

"Well, I think we need to watch my version after we finish this one, for comparison's sake. I bet afterward, you'll be converted and won't question our friendship."

I caught the lighthearted, playful look in her eyes and said, "I doubt it, but okay. I'll give it a try. But only because our friendship is on the line."

"Are we watching this whole thing tonight?" she asked.

"I was planning on taking it an hour at a time. We can pick up where we leave off tomorrow night, if that's okay with you."

She tossed a piece of popcorn in her mouth. "Sounds good to me."

And as I restarted the movie, I smiled, already looking forward to it.

Sixteen

*A Pearl of Wisdom
from Renny Russo*
"If nothing goes right, for Pete's sake, turn left."

Juliet

"Does it seem odd to you that you're remembering things in a town called Forget-Me-Not?" Amy asked.

I wasn't nearly as taken aback by her question as I should've been, because I'd been asking myself the same thing. Had I been led to Forget-Me-Not to help me *remember*? It was starting to feel like it was part of my healing.

Instead of telling that to Amy, however, I said, "I hadn't really thought about it."

It was nearly ten thirty, and I was curled up in my bed in the attic, the phone to my ear. Tallulah and I had finished the first part of the *P&P* miniseries and called it a night. So far, I wasn't swayed that it was a better production but was going to keep an open mind.

"How'd the town even get the name?" Amy asked. "Wait. I'm searching online. Huh."

The air conditioner rattled in the window. Somehow, tonight, the sound was comforting rather than annoying. "What?"

"All I can find is something about a Flour Festival. *Ohhhh*. There're pictures. Cakes and cookies and pies, oh my. It's like a dream come true! I might need to take a road trip. Especially since it might be the only way I'll see my little sister this summer."

I rolled my eyes and didn't take her bait. "Save me a cream puff."

"About that," Amy said.

"What, cream puffs?"

She sighed. "Why haven't you moved on to the next town yet? You usually only stay in a place for a day or two. This will be your third night there, and you haven't even mentioned your next destination."

"I like it here," I said.

Pipes creaked, the sound of water being turned on somewhere in the house. Probably Tallulah getting ready for bed. Katy was supposed to be asleep by now, but I suspected she might be reading instead, because I'd seen a thin thread of light under her door when I passed by on my way upstairs. I hoped that tomorrow we could find time to return to the library to check out the books she'd left behind. I was feeling guilty at how we'd rushed out of there earlier. All because an *image* of a lightning bolt on a children's book had given me a panic attack, which was something else I hadn't shared with my sister.

Mostly, because it was embarrassing. The cover art couldn't have been more benign if it had tried.

"Juliet Nightingale! Have you met a man?"

"Not everything is about a man, Amy."

She was a romantic at heart and was always trying to set me up with people she knew.

"Yeah, yeah. But have you?"

It was easy to call up a memory of Callum's face. "I've met many men here. Did I tell you about Tenn? The man I'm living with? He's super cute."

I heard a small snort of laughter, but Amy didn't drop the subject. "You're purposely being evasive."

"Am I?"

"You're worse than the girls."

The girls. Her twins. "How are they?"

"Good. Terrible. Depends on the hour. You remember that age."

I winced, then waited.

"Oh no, Juliet. Shoot! I'm so sorry. I wasn't even thinking."

"It's fine," I said.

"It isn't. It's late. I'm tired. I'm a rotten sister."

A beep sounded in my ear. I checked to see who was calling and felt my stomach knot. "I need to go, another call is coming in."

"Wait! You can't go until you tell me I'm not a rotten sister!"

I smiled. "You're not. But I do have to go. It's Mom who's calling."

"She's *calling*? Why?"

"*Amy*."

"Fine. Go. Text me after or I might die of curiosity."

And she thought *I* was as bad as her girls?

"Bye!" I said and switched over to my mom. "Hello?"

"Juliet! I was starting to think you weren't going to answer."

"I was on the other line with Amy. Everything okay?"

"Oh, yes, yes. All is good. I just thought I'd check in with you. See if you've been remembering anything else. It's so fantastic!"

"Only a little." I drew myself up into a sitting position, then adjusted the quilt around me, making myself a nest.

"Even a little is a lot."

I nodded, even though she couldn't see me.

"Your doctors will be thrilled. When's your next appointment?"

"September." I traced the design on one of the quilt squares. An eight-pointed star. Some of the points were done in a solid green fabric, the others in a colorful floral.

"Do you think you should check in before then?" Mom asked. "Considering this new development?"

I was shaking my head. "It's nothing that can't wait."

"*Mm*," she hummed.

I knew that *mm*. It was the tone of disagreement.

"When do you plan to return home?" she asked, her impatience starting to seep out in a staccato cadence.

Home.

My mind lingered on the word for a moment, thinking it didn't feel quite right.

Home was a place where you always belonged, and the house in Michigan didn't feel that way anymore. I felt out of place there now.

"Not sure yet," I said. "I'm playing it by ear."

"I see. And when does school start?"

I tugged the quilt even higher, tucking it around my chin. It smelled faintly of lavender, was super soft, lightweight, and nearly worn through in places. Right now all I wanted to do was burrow in its coziness and pretend I never had to go back to Michigan. "August eighteenth for staff."

"Not that school, Juliet."

She was talking about grad school. When I applied for the program, I had no doubts about doing so, because I'd always wanted to be just like her. Even at an early age, according to my family.

Then lightning struck.

Tragedy struck.

And I started questioning everything.

Mostly myself.

Sometime during the last few months, I'd started to feel uncomfortable following in her footsteps. Not about nursing. I loved nursing. But about research. It just didn't feel right, and I wasn't sure what to do about it.

"Online classes start at the end of August." I absently picked up one of the feathers from the growing pile on the nightstand.

"Don't you think it might be good to come home soon? To prepare?"

Gently, I blew on the feather, and it gracefully floated through the dusty attic air, drifting down onto the quilt.

"Let me rephrase that," she said. "You *should* come home. It's time, Juliet."

Clearly her patience had run out, but I still heard the undercurrent of love in her voice. It was always there. A constant thrum that ran like a mighty river beneath her expectations.

Waffling, I picked up another feather, ran my thumb along its barbs.

I understood she was worried about me and that was the driving force behind this call. I really did. Any other time in my life, I'd have bent to her will. I was tempted now. It would be so easy to let her sway me. Steer me. But the main reason I'd taken this trip was to figure out who I was without my family's influence.

"No. Not yet," I said, the words sticking in my throat. I wasn't used to being contrary. But there was no way I was going home sooner than I absolutely had to.

I had healing to do.

"What do you mean, no?"

Suddenly I had a vision of her tracking me down and giving me The Look. The one that made me feel like my heart was in a vise and she held the crank.

"Miss Edie, the woman who usually watches Mary Joy, had a family emergency and will be out of town for a while, so I offered to take care of Mary Joy until Miss Edie returns."

"*Who* is Mary Joy?"

My mother's voice wavered with weariness. As if I was testing her very last nerve. "She's the seven-month-old baby girl who lives in the house where I'm staying."

I imagined Mom rubbing the spot between her eyebrows with the pad of her thumb—the telltale action that she was at the end of her rope. "You took a job *babysitting*?"

"There's nothing wrong with babysitting."

"I didn't say there was. But you're a nurse, Juliet. Don't you think you're overqualified?"

"I think," I said, "I was in the right place at the right time to help someone who really needs it."

"I admire your generous and giving nature, Juliet, but you do not always have to offer to help people."

I squeezed my eyes shut and rubbed the spot between them. Like mother, like daughter. Finally, I said, "Be that as it may, I did offer. I start tomorrow."

"Surely they can find someone else."

"They don't have to. They have me until I need to go back to work."

"*Juliet*," she said.

I really didn't want to continue this conversation, so I knocked loudly on the nightstand. "Sorry, Mom, I have to go, someone's at my bedroom door. I'll check in soon."

"But, Juliet . . ."

"Love you, bye!" I said quickly, then hung up and put my phone on Do Not Disturb.

Then I dropped back against the pillows, let out a sigh, and started smiling.

I didn't have to leave Forget-Me-Not until August 17—a little more than three weeks from now.

Suddenly that felt like all the time in the world.

And a little bit like salvation.

Seventeen

*A Pearl of Wisdom
from Tenn Greenlee*
"*Let me tell you, in order to make the best cup of tea,
you must never ever squeeze the tea bag.*"

Tallulah

Saturday morning dawned dark and dreary and *much* too early, especially considering how little sleep I'd had.

It was just past six, and I was sitting at the kitchen island, nursing a cup of coffee and rereading the University of Alabama brochure I'd taken home from the library.

I'd stuck it in my tote bag yesterday, when I'd packed up after Evanthe ordered me to go home, though I wasn't sure why I'd taken it. There were so many reasons not to go back to school. Time, mostly. I was already spread so thin between the girls and work and *life*.

But . . . I couldn't stop thinking about a memory from when I was younger. I'd been visiting Papaw and Mamaw, and I'd gone to work with her and spent the day following her around, helping her with small tasks.

I'd been in seventh heaven.

As I helped her shelve, I'd said, "I'm going to be a librarian just like you when I grow up."

She'd cupped my cheek with her soft hand. "I have no doubt that one day, Lu, you'll be running this whole place."

This place.

The Forget-Me-Not Library.

My gaze lingered on the deadline for the MLIS application. If I wanted to start classes next spring, I had to apply by November. Which gave me plenty of time to think it over.

When I heard Papaw shuffling his way down the stairs—a sound I'd become accustomed to over the last few days—I stuffed the brochure back into my tote bag and said, "Need a hand?"

"I've got it, sweetheart. What's that delightful scent?"

"Pancakes. There's plenty."

"Just how long have you been up?"

"Awhile."

Mary Joy had a fitful night. Not waking fully, just restless. Every time she made a noise, however, my eyes popped open. Then, around four this morning, I'd woken up with a start from a dream about the little fixer-upper cottage near the library.

In it, I had seen myself inside the house, running my hand along the arched opening of the fireplace, my fingertips tracing a delicate carving, trying to figure out the pattern because the stone had been too dirty to see it clearly. It had felt so real, the dream. So much so that when I woke up, I was surprised my hands weren't filthy.

Only a few minutes after I woke up, I heard Katy crying. She'd had another nightmare that left her trembling and scared. Whispering all the soothing words I knew, I'd carried her into my bedroom and climbed back into bed, tucking her close to my side. Soon she was back to sleep.

But I had stayed wide awake. Worrying about her.

At a little after five, I finally gave up on sleep and made my way downstairs. After getting a pot of coffee on to brew, I'd made pancakes, a big batch that was currently keeping warm in the oven, letting my troubles fade into the background while I focused on measuring and mixing and cooking.

At the sound of a low groan coming from the stairway, I went to check Papaw. I about near fell over when I saw him. "Your face!"

Grinning, he carefully lowered himself down another step. "Spiffy, don't you think?"

His beard was gone. Shaved clean off.

I just kept blinking. I couldn't remember the last time I'd seen him without facial hair. Had I ever? "But *why*?"

His cheeks turned pink. "Truth be told, my hand slipped while shaving, then I got carried away trying to fix the mess. You don't like it?"

"No, no, it's not that." I *hated* it. "I just need some time to adjust, is all. It's a big change."

He chuckled. "Surely is. I almost didn't recognize my own self in the mirror. You know I'm a modest man, Lu, but I have to say, I've aged pretty darn well."

I smiled, glad he could find a silver lining in the situation. "I'd agree with that. Looks like your back is doing better, too. Another few days and you'll probably be strong enough to lead another swamp tour."

"It was a *lake*."

When he made it to the bottom of the stairs, he pressed a nonbristly kiss to my forehead, then headed for the kitchen, saying, "How's Katy doin'? She get back to sleep okay?"

I trailed behind him. "I was hoping she hadn't woken you."

He put the kettle on for tea since he wasn't a coffee drinker and pulled a tea bag from a canister. "You know me. I'm a light sleeper."

He most definitely was not. He slept like the dead.

"She fell back to sleep fairly quickly." I opened the oven door and used a fork to pull out three pancakes from the stack resting on a cookie sheet. I set them on a plate.

"Did she remember what the bad dream was about?"

I shook my head. I was going to call her pediatrician on Monday, just to get some advice on what to do next, because I felt like I was in over my head.

Papaw and I chitchatted while he ate, about anything and everything, and after he was finished, he carried his steaming mug of tea into the dining room to fuss with his carving.

Cup of coffee in hand, I headed outside to enjoy the early coolness. All down the road, sprinklers were on, misting front lawns and flower beds. The scent of wet grass filled the air as I lowered myself down onto the top porch step. I then glanced upward at Bill, in all his leafy glory, and said, "Good morning, sir."

"*Sir* is a little formal, but good morning to you, too."

I jumped, nearly spilling my coffee. Jake and Daisy were on the sidewalk. With the sprinkler noise, I hadn't heard them approach.

I smiled. "I was talking to the oak tree, but hello."

Jake tightened his grip on Daisy's leash as she strained to reach me and said, "You talk to trees? Down, Daisy. *Down.*"

Daisy paid him no attention whatsoever as she stampeded left, then zoomed right.

"Of course. Don't you?"

Ordinarily, I'd be mortified to be caught out here in my jammies, barefoot, with no makeup on, my hair piled atop my head, held in place with a bright pink scrunchie. But I wasn't. Not even a little.

"Of course," he echoed. "But I thought I was the only one."

I narrowed my gaze, trying to tell if he was joking, but he didn't seem to be. "This is Bill," I said, pointing to the old oak. "He's Katy's favorite."

"He's impressive." Daisy leaped and whined. Jake said, "Sit, Daisy."

She did not sit.

I lifted my eyebrows. "I see that puppy training is going well."

A flicker of a smile ghosted across his face. "Perhaps if I had a book on training, things would be going better."

"Perhaps"—I took a sip of my coffee—"I know where you can find one. I put the one you were looking at the other day on hold in case you were still interested in checking it out."

"Then I guess I'll have to stop by. For Daisy's sake."

Smiling, I held up my mug. "Would you like some coffee? There's plenty inside."

"Thanks, but no. I should get going."

I tipped my head. "To *work*?"

His smile stayed put this time. "As a matter of fact, yes."

"*Hmm*. Working early hours on a Saturday. Insurance?"

"No."

"Finance?"

"No."

I wrinkled my nose. "IT?"

"No."

"What was your degree in college?"

His brown eyes twinkled. "Bachelor of science."

Huh. "*Really?*"

"Why do you look shocked?" he asked, trying not to laugh.

"Because I'm just trying to think of a science job you can do from home."

"You'd be surprised."

I heard a noise behind me and glanced over my shoulder. Papaw was pushing open the screen door. "Thought I heard you talking to someone. And I'll be! Daisy's here. Doesn't this just make my day?"

Jake unclipped Daisy's leash, and she darted past me, heading straight to Papaw, who gave her lots of loving. "Who's been a good girl?"

She whined and wiggled and slurped his clean-shaven face.

Jake came up next to me and smiled. "Shameless."

"Her or him?" I asked.

He laughed. "Both?"

I thought he might be right about that.

"Can you stay for breakfast?" Papaw asked Jake. "Lu's fixed a mess of pancakes. There's enough for a whole army."

"Pancakes?" Jake said, throwing me a wry glance. "I didn't know there were pancakes at play. I'd love some. Thanks."

"Come on in then." Papaw pulled open the screen door, and Daisy raced inside ahead of him like she owned the place.

I stood up, dusted myself off, and looked at Jake. "I thought you had to get to work?"

"It can wait," he said. "Some things are more important."

The way he looked at me made my skin hot, and suddenly I could hear Nettie's voice in my head talking about sparks.

"Like pancakes?" I asked.

"Exactly."

As I slipped past him, something shifted inside me. Inside my heart. It felt a little like it was making room for him. Lots and lots of room.

Eighteen

A Pearl of Wisdom
from Maeve Hearnshaw
"Look for true friends in times of trouble, not happiness."

Tallulah

Nearly two and a half hours later, I glanced at the clock. I had to leave or I was going to be late for work.

Yet I was frozen in place, holding tightly on to Mary Joy.

Once again, I didn't want to let go of her.

Mostly because she wasn't feeling well. She'd been sick to her stomach not long after eating breakfast and had been crying on and off since then. Right now, she was whining while burrowing her face in my shoulder.

"There's a summer flu going around." I pressed my cheek to the top of Mary Joy's head, gauging her temperature. I'd taken it earlier, and it had been normal, despite her cheeks being flushed. "She's been sneezing a lot this morning."

"No coughing, though," Juliet said, trying to get a good look at Mary Joy's face.

In addition to the red cheeks, her blue eyes were teary, and the rash around her lips looked especially angry this morning. She was practically the personification of illness. "I've heard that teething can cause stomach upset."

"It can," Juliet said, "or possibly she doesn't like pancakes. Has she had them before?"

On the couch, Papaw and Katy sat at opposite ends, noses buried in books. Katy was curled up with a throw blanket, and Papaw sat tall with the lamb heating pad behind his back.

Up until Mary Joy had become ill, it had been a nice morning, even though it had been nowhere close to our normal routine.

Katy had laughed with delight at seeing Papaw's shaved face, but Mary Joy had cried her eyes out and refused to be held by him. He vowed to grow his whiskers back as soon as possible.

Thank goodness.

Jake had kept us all entertained during breakfast with tales of Daisy's adventures. Or misadventures, as the case might be. She'd already chewed through a computer cable, torn the blinds off the window, and shredded a couch cushion. He was keeping a running tab to reimburse Vera.

He'd sat next to Katy at the table, and she'd excitedly shouted out every animal she saw on his arm tattoo, all tucked secretly into the woodland design. Hedgehogs and opossums and chipmunks. She'd been beside herself with happiness, and I thought it was just what she'd needed after the night she'd had.

Jake and Daisy had stayed for a while after we ate, and Jake helped Juliet and me clean up while Papaw and Katy played with Daisy in the backyard. It wasn't until after they left that Mary Joy went downhill fast.

I drew in a breath. "No, she hasn't had pancakes before, but she only had a few bites." Mostly, she'd had her usual oatmeal and yogurt, which she had gobbled up.

Mary Joy had been good, great even, before breakfast. Despite her fitful night, she'd woken up with smiles, had cooed and gurgled and played and gnawed on a cold teething ring.

"Maybe it *was* the pancakes," I said. "Or teething. Or the flu. *Ugh.*"

Empathy flashed in Juliet's eyes.

I kissed Mary Joy's forehead again. "I wish more than anything that she could tell us what was wrong. Poor, sweet baby. I hate leaving her like this."

"I know. But she seems to be feeling better now. Sleepy but better."

I held Juliet's gaze, let her see my fear clear as day. "You'll call me if she spikes a fever or gets sick again?"

Juliet held out her arms. "I have you on speed dial."

I gave Mary Joy another kiss, then reluctantly handed her over to Juliet. Mary Joy immediately started burrowing into *her* chest, which made my heart ache.

I consoled myself with the knowledge that Saturdays were my short days at work, so I'd be home by two. Then I'd have two blissful days with the girls, since the library was closed on Sundays and Mondays.

"She's due for her nap at nine thirty, but if she needs to go down before then, just let her. There are bottles in the fridge and mashed sweet potat—"

"Tallulah"—Juliet smiled—"you told me already."

I sighed. Nodded. I'd written everything out, too. I just . . . I didn't want to leave. "And remember no sweets. I'm trying to hold off until she's one."

"No fun, you mean," Papaw called out from the couch.

I frowned. Deeply.

"I'll take good care of her," Juliet said. "I promise."

I had to let go. I *had* to.

"Okay." With tears threatening, I quickly bid my goodbyes to Papaw and Katy and rushed out the door before I could change my mind.

I'd been *off* all morning.

Just a vague feeling of unease.

I fought to shake it as I'd pulled holds, texted Juliet a billion times, restocked the Flour Festival display, wondered why I couldn't stop thinking about the storybook Tudor across the street, helped a patron fill out an online job application, and listened to the happy squeals of the children enjoying a visit from Kiki, the therapy dog—a program so popular that Nettie was lobbying for it to become a regular monthly program.

It was almost noon now, and I was currently in the workroom processing books—stamping, stickering, covering—along with Evanthe. Because this was such a small library—and she was very hands-on—she could often be found doing the same tasks as the rest of us. I honestly didn't know how she did it all. Being director came with its own set of demands and time commitments.

Sitting on a stool across the wooden worktable, she was swathed in lavender linen so pale it almost appeared gray, her hair in its usual braid. She worked efficiently, no motion wasted. From applying the Vistafoil to the book and then wielding a bone folder to eliminate bubbles like a woman on a mission.

I was tempted to take notes.

Deckle was sitting in an empty paper box on the counter near the copy machine, looking happy as could be.

He hadn't been nearly as antagonistic today as usual, and I wondered if he could sense my mood. A hair ball right now might send me over the edge.

The big workroom had a door with a window. Every once in a while, I'd see Isabel or one of the volunteers pass by and wished someone would come in and break the tension. As it was, I'd been trying to make small talk with Evanthe for half an hour now, and her one- or two-word replies were downright painful.

Yet as I carefully placed a YA sticker on a spine, I tried again.

"I've been thinking," I said.

Her gaze cut to me, an eyebrow lifted.

"I was talking with . . . a friend about trivia games recently, and one of the things that came up was pub quiz trivia, and I was thinking it would be a fun thing to do if the closest bar wasn't the Broken Wheel, which isn't ideal."

She nodded at that as if in complete agreement, then added, "And?"

As if knowing I was leading her somewhere.

"It might be nice if the library had a trivia night once a month." I set aside the book I'd been working on and picked up another. "Questions would be literature-based, of course. Prizes could come from within the community, like a gift card to the Bean Patch or Snug's or even library merchandise, like mugs or tote bags."

Slowly, she started nodding. "Can you prepare a full ten-minute proposal and present it in three weeks' time, ahead of the next board meeting?"

I stiffened just a little with panic, then smiled. She was giving me the chance to run my own program. "I can."

"Splendid."

"Thank you," I said quietly, meaning it.

Something soft flashed in her eyes. "I shall always give audience to those who take initiative."

When she went back to wrapping books and paying me little attention, I glanced around the room searching for another topic to tack onto the conversation, to keep it going.

My gaze bounced off reams of paper, art supplies, the scanner, the printer, the binding machine, the paper cutter with the guillotine arm that I called the chopping block, and, of course, Deckle, who was still watching me. Right up until his gaze shifted, looking at something over my shoulder.

I swiveled on my stool.

Jed was peeking into the room, waving, a grin on his face, cheerfulness lighting up his blue eyes. When he saw me looking, he ducked away. I threw a look at Evanthe and caught a shy smile on her face and her hand in mid-wave.

Her gaze narrowed on me, as if silently warning me not to say a word.

Outwardly, I zipped my lips. Inwardly, however, I was jumping with joy. Had I just caught a glimpse of the Evanthe my mamaw used to know? If so, this was my time to act, to wiggle my way past her walls while her defenses were down.

"Evanthe?"

"Yes?" she said sharply.

"Do you have plans for tonight?"

Her lips pursed. "Why do you ask?"

"Book club is tonight. I was hoping you'd be there."

As far as I knew, she'd never attended, though Nettie had mentioned she always extended an invitation.

Before Evanthe could say no, I rushed on. "I've only been to one meeting since moving to Forget-Me-Not and it's just plain fun. I spent the whole time thinking my mamaw would've loved to be there. Lots of food, lots of laughs, lots of book talk."

I carefully stickered another paperback and hoped I hadn't laid it on too thick.

"*Why* do you want me to attend?" she asked, clearly suspicious if the look in her eyes was any indication.

I gave a little shrug and tried to get as close to the truth as possible. "Because if Mamaw was here, she'd talk you into going with her. Since she's not, she'd want *me* to ask you, because any friend of hers is a friend of mine."

Thin lips pinched together and her hands stilled. Finally, she said, "I'll take it under consideration, but do not count on it."

Because she hadn't said no outright, I took it as a win.

Smiling, I glanced at Deckle and couldn't help thinking that he looked pleased, too.

Nineteen

A Pearl of Wisdom
from Isabel Espinoza
"You'll always be judged by the company you keep."

Juliet

"The library's not even open?" I asked Maeve as I carried a heavy box up a ramp leading to the library doors. According to the sign posted, the building had closed an hour ago.

Even though Maeve was holding a Crock-Pot, somehow she still managed to swipe a card against the reader next to the doors. They whisked open. "The community room is available after hours for private events, for a fee, of course. Everyone in the book club pitches in a few dollars a month to cover the cost. We take turns hosting."

Tonight was her turn, which was why we were here half an hour before the meeting was set to begin. The box I held was full of vegetable-themed party supplies. Cabbage-leaf-patterned paper plates, bowls, and cups. Lace tablecloths, glass candlesticks, an old wicker basket stuffed full of vegetables like cabbage, carrots, tomatoes, eggplant, artichokes. And a bouquet of wildflowers, still wrapped in florist paper.

Despite the invitation from Vera the other day, I hadn't intended to attend book club tonight. Those plans changed, however, when Maeve stopped by this morning before heading to Juneberry and volun-told me that I should meet her here at six to help set up for the meeting.

So here I was, sailing through the automatic doors, actually looking forward to tonight, even though I hadn't read the book. Even though I didn't even know the *title* of the book. "How many members are in the group?"

"Six. Me, Vera, Nettie, Isabel, Renny, and Tallulah. Sometimes Tenn sits in, but he wants to grow his whiskers back before anyone sees his naked face."

It was hard to believe that I'd been here less than a week and I already knew who all those people were.

As we made our way to the community room, late-day sunlight colored everything in a shade of gold. None of the overhead lights were on, and it was strange not to hear the faint hum of equipment, of voices, of footsteps, of pages rustling.

Strange but oddly peaceful. Part of me wanted to choose a book and curl up in one of the beanbag chairs in the children's section and stay there for a good long while.

"We've got half an hour to whip this place into shape." She flipped on the community room's lights and blinked at the sudden brightness. "I'm up for the challenge. How about you, honey?"

"Yes, ma'am," I said, then grinned when I realized what I'd said. I didn't think I'd ever called anyone *ma'am* in my whole life.

Laughing, she carried the Crock-Pot to a table pushed against a far wall. "Food will be set up here, buffet style. Everyone's bringing a dish. Can you start dressing the dining table?"

I assumed she meant the conference table in the middle of the room. "Do you always throw an elaborate dinner for book club meetings?"

This all seemed above and beyond to me. Most of the book clubs I'd been part of only served snacks and cocktails. Sometimes I enjoyed those more than the book I'd read. More often than not, we didn't even talk about the book.

"Actually, we do. It's a *cookbook* club. We each make one or two dishes from the book and serve them potluck style."

I pulled a lace tablecloth from the box. "I've never heard of a cookbook club before. It sounds fun."

"It is, though sometimes the food is iffy. We have a rule that we're not allowed to remake a dish if it doesn't turn out. It gets served as is. And," she said, walking toward me with note cards in her hand, "we stick mainly to vintage cookbooks. The older, the better. This month's book is *Practical Vegetarian Cookery*. It's from 1897. Isabel found it on the Library of Congress website. How's your penmanship?"

I placed the basket of vegetables in the middle of the table and put the candlesticks on each side of it. "Legible."

"Perfect." She passed the cards over to me, then pulled out a pen and a piece of torn notebook paper from the pocket of her dress and handed those over as well. "Can you write out the names of each of these dishes? One per card. Then put them in card holders and set them on the buffet table."

I smiled when I saw that the pen had a Hearnshaw Automotive logo on it, then glanced at the list of food being served tonight: Split pea soup. Stuffed squash. Sweet potato curry. Gingersnaps. Apple fritters. Apricot water. Italian salad. Prune whip. Corn muffins. Cottage cheese sandwiches. Asparagus pie. Spinach soufflé.

"*Prune whip?*" I hoped my tone came across as curious and not horrified, even though that's how I felt.

Laughing, she picked up the flowers. "Honestly, I'm more scared of the cottage cheese sandwiches, but Isabel was excited to try them. She's big on cottage cheese these days. Something about protein." She nodded toward one of the chairs. "Go on and sit yourself down. I'll be right back."

There was a small kitchenette off the community room, and Maeve disappeared in there for a moment before returning with three small vases of flowers. I wasn't sure where she'd conjured up the vases, but she set them on the table and said, "How was your day with the girls?"

"It went well. They're the sweetest."

After Mary Joy's morning nap, she woke up all smiles—except when she looked at Tenn, which brought about tears. She didn't seem to recognize him without his beard. We went for a walk, played in the sprinkler in the backyard, had a dance party, practiced sitting with Mary Joy, and read what felt like a zillion books. Katy tried her best to teach Mary Joy how to crawl, but the baby would only rock on her knees and then theatrically collapse onto her stomach. Katy said Mary Joy looked like a sea lion when she did it, and I couldn't disagree. Tenn had laughed and laughed. He'd spent most of the day in the dining room, carving and singing at the top of his lungs. It was nice to see him moving around more, but I made sure the girls and I spent a lot of time outside in the peace and quiet of nature.

Maeve cracked a smile. "And just how often did Tallulah check in?"

I laughed as I carefully wrote down *spinach soufflé*, making sure to spell it right. "She texted approximately a million times. Half to check on the girls, half to apologize for texting so much. She threw in a few funny memes for good measure."

"Memes? That's high praise. She doesn't send those to just anyone."

A ribbon of warmth spread through me, and I thought about what Katy had said a few days ago, about how Tallulah would soon come around and be glad I was here.

Apparently, she'd been right.

Maeve said, "Has Lu told you that her parents are travel writers? Award-winning, too. All the highest praises. They live out of backpacks and are always looking for the next adventure. They've never had a home base—they used Tenn's address for mail and packages and such. It's been go, go, go from the start. Seeing the world is an exciting career to be sure, but Tallulah really struggled with the constant change."

I glanced at her. "Tallulah traveled with them?"

Maeve nodded. "Right up until she was eighteen and decided to move in with Tenn and go to college nearby."

Until I'd landed here in Forget-Me-Not on my road trip, I'd been moving from place to place every couple of days *because* I hadn't wanted to make connections while out on the road. Hadn't wanted to get comfortable. Hadn't wanted to make friends or get to know anyone other than at a surface level.

I'd thought being alone was what I needed to figure out who I was, but all I really found was that I'd been lonely.

I couldn't even imagine if that was my *life*.

I tried to picture a young Tallulah constantly being uprooted. She with her routines and lists. "I can't imagine how hard that was for her."

"She'll be the first to tell you she saw some amazing things and met amazing people, but it definitely took its toll. It was easier not to make friends than to leave them behind. Always having to say goodbye left a lasting wound. All these years later, she hasn't really broken the habit of keeping to herself. Being back here in Forget-Me-Not is helping. But," Maeve added, "she's still has a tough time with the complexities of short-term friendships. Of opening up. Of letting people in. Especially people she knows will be leaving soon."

I met her gaze and read between the lines of what she was saying. Because I would be leaving soon, the fact that Tallulah had let me into her life, offered friendship, felt a little like she had trusted me with the moon and the stars.

At the sound of loud knocking, Maeve said, "That has to be Renny. He's a chronic early bird. I'll be right back."

A moment later, I heard Renny say, "I hope oxygen was on the list of approved dishes. I've got plenty."

Maeve laughed. "I'll be sure to add it to the menu."

I smiled and stood up as they came into the community room, Maeve first, followed by Renny and Callum, who had one hand looped through Renny's arm, while the other held a portable oxygen tank.

"Ah, it's my favorite green-eyed girl," Renny exclaimed when he spotted me. "Hi, darlin'."

"Do you know many green-eyed girls, Uncle Ren?" Callum asked, giving me a smile.

"Don't quibble, Cal," Renny said.

It was the first time I'd seen Callum out of his uniform. He was dressed in nice jeans and a royal blue T-shirt that matched his eyes. It looked like he'd tried to tame his wavy hair with some sort of product, but it seemed to have a mind of its own, curling this way and that.

I gave Renny a gentle half hug. "It's good to see you."

"Isn't it?" He pretended to fluff his hair.

Maeve smiled fondly at him. "I'm surprised your ego fit through the door."

"It simply trails behind me. Like a fabulous train."

Maeve grinned and pulled out a chair. "Come sit down."

Callum helped Renny settle in, then hitched a thumb over his shoulder. "I'll be right back. Uncle Ren bought out the liquor store."

Maeve said, "Here. You'll need this to get back inside." She handed him the access card, and a moment later, he was gone.

"A lifetime of experience has taught me that it's better to have too much than too little," Renny said, "especially since we pay extra to have booze here at all." He picked up one of the note cards I'd written out and sighed. "Is Nettie bringing prune whip because she believes we all need to loosen up?"

"Undoubtedly," Maeve said.

Renny glanced around the table. "Eight chairs? Who else is coming?"

She lifted her eyebrows high. "Tallulah invited Evanthe."

Renny whistled low. "If anyone can get her here, it's Lu." He glanced at me. "Evanthe tends to keep to herself."

Before I could question why Tallulah might hold any sway with the older woman, Callum came back inside carrying a box. The sound of bottles clanking together filled the room.

He set the box on the buffet table and said, "If you don't need anything else, I have a date and should get going or I'm going to be late and will have to hear about it all night." He looked my way. "She can hold a grudge."

I didn't like the way my heart sank at that bit of news. Like I had any right to care that he had a date. I picked up the pen again and began to write out *stuffed squash*, pretending I wasn't the least bit jealous.

"Thanks for the ride, Cal," Renny said to him.

"Anytime."

I looked up at him, forced a smile. "Have fun."

He said, "You're welcome to join us, if you want. We're going for ice cream and to the bookstore." His eyes glinted mischievously. "Unless you *want* to try the prune whip?"

I tipped my head, confused. "Go with you? On your date?"

It was then that Tallulah strode into the room, calling out a hearty hello, a pink carnival-glass pitcher of apricot water in hand. Mary Joy was nestled against her chest like a koala, wrapped in a fabric sling.

We all called out a hello; then Callum looked at me again. "Last chance, or forever hold your peace."

Maeve took him by the shoulders and pointed him toward the door. "Don't go trying to poach my guests. Out with you now."

Tallulah elbowed Callum lightly. "You best hurry. Katy's pacing the porch, waiting on you."

Then she set the pitcher on the table and gave Renny a big hug, holding on extra long until Mary Joy started protesting.

"I best hurry then," Callum said. To Renny, he added, "Just

text when you're ready to head back. And Juliet, send an SOS if you need rescuing from the prunes."

As he walked away, I realized I was smiling. Big.

His date was with *Katy*.

"So that's how it is, eh?" Renny asked, eyeing me.

I glanced at him, then realized they were all looking at me, even Mary Joy. Heat climbed my throat. "What is?"

They all smiled knowingly, and Renny wiggled his eyebrows suggestively.

I shook my head. "It's not like that. We're not . . . We barely know each other."

Renny winked. "Give it time."

Time. It was something I didn't have much of because I had to leave town in—I quickly calculated—twenty-two days.

It was funny how just yesterday that had felt like all the time in the world.

But now it didn't feel nearly long enough.

Twenty

A Pearl of Wisdom
from Renny Russo
"Having a good memory can be both a blessing and a curse."

Juliet

The prune whip wasn't half bad.

Not that I'd ever make it for myself. But with that dish I could see the beauty of a cookbook club. Trying food you might never consider otherwise.

"Who made the hockey pucks?" Renny asked, his voice breathy as he tapped a gingersnap on the table. It echoed like a hammer hitting stone.

Mary Joy, still snuggled in her wrap, was managing to sleep through the noise.

"I did the best I could with no bake time or temperature." Vera sniffed loudly as she tucked a lock of curly hair behind her ear. "The whole kitchen was filled with smoke. The alarms went off. That cutie patootie Jake came to check on me, fire extinguisher in hand."

Isabel lifted her eyebrows high. "One might think you burned them on purpose, Vera."

Tallulah looked up from pushing asparagus pie around her plate, her eyes crinkling with amusement, which was nice to see. For most of the dinner, disappointment had been written across her whole face, plain as day, as she cast glances at the eighth chair.

The empty chair.

Evanthe had never shown up.

Vera laughed. "You could never prove it, but I assure you, the hockey pucks were unintentional. But that's enough about me. I want to know more about Juliet. Did you always want to be a nurse?"

Suddenly I was suspicious that she'd only invited me here so she could find out more about me. "I believe so," I answered, circling around the fact that I couldn't quite remember. "My mom was once a school nurse, too, but eventually went back to school and got her PhD."

"Ain't that sweet," Nettie said, "you following in your mama's footsteps."

Once again, when I thought about starting grad school, my stomach churned. At this point, though, I wasn't sure I could stop that particular ball from rolling. Not without causing my family even more worry than I already had.

"Do you enjoy being a nurse?" Isabel asked, her laser-like gaze on me, as if sensing my unease.

"I love nursing. I actually wish I could do more of it. A school environment just doesn't provide that, though. Which is a good thing, right? That means the children are healthy. But . . ."

"What?" Tallulah asked.

I shrugged. "It leaves me feeling like I don't quite belong."

The lightning strike had changed so much. It had changed *me*. When I went back to work after recuperating, I had to admit to myself that I wasn't happy with my job. It just wasn't *enough*. So why was I still there? Why was I going back? I didn't quite know.

Maeve nodded, and her blond updo wobbled but didn't fall. "Perhaps another specialty would suit you better?"

"Maybe so," I said, feeling a bubble of excitement at the thought.

Then that bubble popped when I thought about what that truly meant. Quitting my job. Essentially telling my mom that no, I didn't want to be just like her. I wasn't sure I could do it. Not after everything that had happened.

"What's stopping you, darlin'?" Nettie asked.

I reached for my wine. "Life's been a little complicated recently, so I'm not sure this is the right time to be making big changes."

"Complicated?" Vera asked, leaning in. "How so?"

I rubbed the scar at my neck, felt flutters of panic. Talking about what happened was difficult, but it wasn't a secret. It had made local headlines, been on the news. My therapist had urged me to be more open, to not keep it all in, yet sadness made the words stick in my throat.

Sadness and grief.

Even though I couldn't remember my grandfather, somehow my heart knew he was gone. That a big piece of my life was no longer here.

I also carried a fair share of guilt. Because I'd been with him when he died, I couldn't help thinking I should've been able to prevent what happened. Had I been paying attention to the weather? Had I checked the radar? Had I suggested we turn back at the first rumble of thunder?

These seemed like perfectly logical things for me to have done, but I didn't know if I had or hadn't.

Because I couldn't remember.

Renny nudged me, and when I met his gaze, he held up the wine bottle, silently offering a refill. I nodded. It was impossible not to notice the empathy in his eyes, and I was reminded that I knew *his* story. Or at least some of it—and he'd offered to tell me more.

I took a big, deep breath. "A few months ago, I was on a walk in the park with my grandfather when a storm popped up. I'm not entirely sure what happened exactly because I lost part of my memory during the incident, but I was told that Grandpa and I had been walking near a tree that was struck by lightning, and we received an indirect strike called a side flash," I said, my voice so low I could barely hear myself. My throat was closing, my heart pounding. "I survived. My grandfather . . . didn't."

Before I knew what was happening, my chair was surrounded, and I was being hugged from every direction. There were murmurs of consolation, loving pats.

"I'm sorry," I said, wiping tears from my eyes. "I can never stop the tears."

"Let them flow." Nettie gave my shoulders a final squeeze before sitting back down. "Sometimes grief builds up so much it needs to find a way out."

Maeve said, "How's your memory now, honey?"

In one big breath, I told them what I'd been dealing with, then added, "But since I've been in Forget-Me-Not, I've been remembering more."

"Helping people remember what's been lost is one of the things Forget-Me-Not does best," Vera added, nodding.

"Really?" I asked.

Nettie still had a comforting hand on my back as she said, "Have you not heard the story of how the town got its name?"

I shook my head.

Renny groaned and pulled out his phone. "That's my cue to call for my ride."

Across the table, Tallulah smiled. "Uncle Renny doesn't like to admit the story tugs on his heartstrings."

"My heartstrings snapped a long time ago," he said.

"Lies," Maeve accused. "No one's a bigger romantic."

He blew a raspberry.

I smiled at them and had to admit, at least to myself, that my car breaking down on this trip might've been the best thing that could've happened to me.

Being stuck here in Forget-Me-Not had reminded me that I liked making connections.

I loved people, and I was becoming extra fond of these ones in particular.

I wasn't sure how I was ever going to tell them goodbye.

Twenty-One

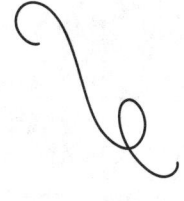

A Pearl of Wisdom
from Isabel Espinoza
"It doesn't matter how much you earn. It's how much you save that counts."

Tallulah

"I have to confess," Georgia Smith said on the following Monday afternoon, "I was surprised you wanted to see this place, Tallulah. I didn't peg you as the fixer-upper type."

She looked bright and polished today, dressed in a tailored sleeveless dress and wedge heels. Her red hair was pulled back in a twist, and her eyes sparkled in the sunlight. She carried an iPad, and the listing information for this house was pulled up on the screen.

Mary Joy, tucked into her wrap, was cooing happily as we stood staring at the neglected Tudor-style cottage. Due to its location, I'd started calling it the Library House in my mind.

I said, "That's because I'm not the fixer-upper type, but . . ."

In my head, I could hear Jake saying, *It has lots of potential*, which of course made me think of last night, when the girls and I had gone for a walk with him and Daisy. We'd strolled to the sun garden, then had taken a side street to the park where the Flour Festival would be held soon.

Our conversation hadn't strayed too far from small talk. Our childhoods—he'd grown up in Florida, and I'd grown up everywhere. Our favorite books—his was *Ender's Game*, because when he read it as a teen, it was the first book where it felt as though he were *in* the book. Time had stopped. The real world ceased to exist. Mine was *Pride and Prejudice* for much the same reason.

"But what?" Georgia encouraged, pulling me from my thoughts.

"I can't stop thinking about it."

Or dreaming about it. This house had all but plagued my dreams the last three nights. Every time I closed my eyes, I saw this house. Not even twelve hours ago, I'd dreamed of six Christmas stockings hanging from the stone mantel. Names had been stitched onto them in golden thread but had been too blurry to read.

This morning, I'd finally given in and looked the place up online, hoping to see the fireplace, but there were only a few outdoor photos posted. The listing price was suspiciously low. Eye-poppingly low. The write-up was full of phrases like *needs TLC*, *add your vision*, and *ready for your updates*. It was also being sold as is.

Alarm bells rang. Red flags waved.

When I'd bumped into Georgia earlier while dropping Katy off at camp, I impulsively asked her if she could show me the house today. I was hoping that seeing it would rid it from my thoughts. My dreams. Banish it completely.

Yet even as I stood here, faced with its disrepair, I felt a pull. A gentle tug. I could almost hear it telling me that I was home.

It was all kinds of unsettling.

"I didn't even realize you were in the market for a house," Georgia added. "I could've been keeping an eye out."

"I didn't think I was. I mean, I wasn't planning on living with my grandfather forever, but I thought I'd save for a while, maybe buy a plot of land and build something new. This"—I gestured to the house—"isn't what I'd had in mind at all."

I'd wanted a house without history so I could create one of my own. Build it from the ground up, memory by memory.

But there would always be memories, wouldn't there? Because

I couldn't imagine parting with my mamaw's sewing table or the tallboy dresser I'd refinished after finding it for a steal at a garage sale in my old neighborhood.

Those things were currently in a storage unit, on the other side of town, just waiting for me to figure out what was next. *I'd* been waiting for me to figure out what was next for a year and a half now.

Not that I'd had the money to do anything during that time. That had come only with the sale of my dream house—and the move here. Scott and I had split the profit. Because of the growth in the housing market over the last eight years, the sale price was more than double what we'd paid for it. Isabel had suggested I invest what I'd walked away with, but I hadn't gotten around to it yet.

Which meant I could pay cash for this house, then get a construction loan to fix it up.

If I wanted to buy this house.

If.

A neighbor across the street, one of the library's regulars, Mrs. Cannon, came out onto her porch with a watering can and waved. "You lookin' to buy, Tallulah?" she called out.

"Just lookin'," I shouted back and immediately regretted it when Mary Joy squawked at the loudness of my voice. I rubbed her back and whispered an apology in her ear.

Mrs. Cannon poured water onto hanging ferns. "That house has got good bones! And good neighbors!"

"*Great* neighbors," Georgia added.

I laughed, because she and her daughter lived a few doors down. "Have there been many showings?"

"Not too many. I probably shouldn't tell you this, and I'll deny it to my dying breath, but the only true interest has come from Evanthe Kilburn. She's considering it as a rental property."

My eyes widened. "Really? I didn't realize she was an active investor—I thought she only maintained what she'd inherited."

"To my knowledge, this is the first house she's ever looked at. It's a recent development. Very recent."

I glanced toward the library, fully expecting to see Evanthe's red bike tethered to the rack near the doors, even though the building was closed today. She often went in on her days off. But the bike wasn't there.

In my mind, I could easily see the empty chair at the book club meeting. Even though Evanthe had warned me she might not attend, I had set my hopes high. And when she didn't show, those hopes free-fell, crashing down.

"But she hasn't made an offer?" I asked.

Georgia shook her head. "Not yet at least. Mrs. Cannon was right, though, about the house's bones. It was built in the 1920s and is bigger than it looks. Three bedrooms upstairs, and a den downstairs that could be converted into a primary bedroom if you prefer it to be on the first floor. Did you know Bitsy Krebbs?"

The name sounded familiar, but I couldn't pull up a face to go with it. "I don't think so."

"This was her place. You'd often see her out here puttering around the yard—she loved to garden. When she took ill about two years ago, she moved in with one of her daughters near Fort Payne. It was supposed to be a temporary move, but it didn't quite work out that way. She passed away about nine months ago, and the house went on the market as soon as it was out of probate."

My chest ached with sorrow for a woman I hadn't even known.

"Don't be alarmed by the tarp on the roof," Georgia said. "It looks worse than it is."

"What happened?"

"A tree fell in a storm about a year ago. The damage was minimal, thank goodness, but it knocked off quite a few of the slate shingles."

Now that she said it, I could see where the tree had once stood, its stump just visible in the tall grass. "Shouldn't insurance have paid to fix it?"

"Bitsy had accidentally let her coverage lapse. Us neighbors pooled together and took care of the tree, at least."

"Do you think the house's condition is what's keeping buyers away?"

"Honestly, I don't think the condition is that bad. Other than the roof, most of the work it needs is cosmetic. Yes, it definitely looks like someone hasn't lived here in years, but the foundation is solid. There's no mold. No termites. It doesn't make sense to me why it hasn't already sold." Then she added, "But maybe everyone else's loss is your gain? I can definitely see you and the girls here."

I nodded. For some reason, I could, too. I blamed the dreams.

"Let's go in," she said. "So you can see for yourself what I mean."

As she pushed open the wooden gate, giving it a good shove, something rustled in the tall grass. We moved closer together, as if that would protect us from whatever it was that was making its way through the yard.

She looked back at me. "Perhaps I should've brought a lawn mower."

Smiling, I wrapped my arms around Mary Joy protectively. "We'll just have to high-step it."

"Blaze our own trail. Seems fitting somehow." She forged ahead. "Watch your footing there. One of the stones is loose."

"Thanks for doing this, by the way. Especially on such short notice."

"I'm happy to help." She freed a key from the lockbox, and before I knew it, the front door was swinging open. "Now I'm a big believer in being forewarned, so brace yourself for how dirty it is inside and try to look past it, okay? It's nothing that can't be fixed with a scrub brush and some elbow grease."

"I'll keep that in mind," I said as I followed Georgia inside. Dust motes danced in the hot, stale air of a wide foyer. There was a stairway on the right, its walls covered in sagging wallpaper. The woodwork on the staircase, however, was beautiful. And filthy—just as Georgia had warned. I ran my finger over the design on the newel post, an eight-pointed star, then wiped the grime on my shorts.

Georgia left the door open behind us. "The HVAC system needs servicing, so the air-conditioning doesn't work at the moment. The den is here on the left."

The spacious room was filled with moving boxes, making it hard to see much. I glanced past more peeling wallpaper, crown molding, and a hideous green carpet to focus on the wooden bookshelves. They stretched the length of the room and appeared to be original to the house. I tried to imagine all my books on the shelves and found I could picture it quite easily.

Georgia returned to the foyer and started down a short hallway. "You'll be happy to know there're hardwood floors underneath the carpets."

I wasn't sure why anyone had covered them up to begin with, but then I recalled how Mamaw always liked something soft underfoot and wondered if Bitsy had been the same.

"There's a half bath here on the right. You could steal some space from the dining room to expand it into a full."

Mary Joy seemed absolutely captivated. Her blue eyes were wide as she looked all around, making gurgling noises, like she was trying to tell us her opinion.

The dining room had an arched doorway and a built-in hutch that had, at some point, been painted. This room, too, was filled with boxes. As if Bitsy had packed up her life and simply left it all behind. It darn near broke my heart thinking about it.

A dark layer of grime seemed to cover everything. Floors, walls, ceiling. Cobwebs hung in every corner. Underneath the stale smell, I picked up a sweet scent. Something floral. It reminded me of Mamaw's gardenia perfume and immediately set me at ease. It was as if she were here with me, taking this tour as well.

Georgia said, "You're being awfully quiet."

"Just taking it all in."

"You haven't bolted for the front door yet, so I'm taking that as a good sign."

I smiled. "I'm definitely not as scared as I thought I'd be."

"Good, good. Let's take a look at the living room before we check out the kitchen."

The hallway spilled into a surprisingly large living room. Sheets had been thrown over couches and tables, making them look ghostly. I looked straight past it all, toward the fireplace, centered in the wall, tucked in between more built-ins, just where I knew it would be.

My breath caught, and I slowly made my way across the room.

"The fireplace is original," Georgia said. "A good cleaning will do it wonders. It looks gray now, but I bet it's off-white."

I gently touched the mantel, felt the coolness of the stone, chilly even in the sweltering heat. I saw the pointed curve of the firebox that matched the ogee-arched doorways. My heartbeat kicked up when I reached out and touched the carvings in the stone. Leaves. They were oak leaves.

It was such a déjà vu moment that I swayed a little, not understanding how I'd dreamed of something I'd never seen before.

Georgia crossed the room and opened one of the doors that led onto a back patio, letting more air into the house. The cross breeze brought in the scent of grass and sunshine.

I was still studying the fireplace when I felt my phone buzz in my back pocket. I pulled it out and frowned when I saw that it was a text from Scott. I quickly read his message and clenched my jaw.

> Working on a big project. Not going to make the party this weekend but will visit soon. I'll call Katy later.

"Everything okay?" Georgia asked.

"Not really," I said, tucking the phone away. "It's my ex-husband, Scott. He can't make Katy's birthday party."

Her eyes were filled with empathy. With *understanding*. She let out a soft sigh, then said, "Let's take a look at the kitchen."

I rubbed Mary Joy's back and told myself that Katy didn't need Scott at her party in order to enjoy it. *Did not, did not, did not.* If I said it enough, I might start believing it.

Georgia stepped into the kitchen. "What do you think about the archways?"

"I love them," I said, answering honestly.

She grinned. "Me, too. My house is open concept, and these arches make me want to start putting up walls."

My and Scott's house had been open concept, too. Because I had loved it, I thought I'd want to replicate it one day. Now, though, I was starting to wonder if a house completely the opposite of what I'd once had would be a better option. A house I could fix up from the ground up, instead of building. A house I could repair. *Heal.*

Suddenly I heard Nettie's voice in my head again, talking about new paths. I'd have to remember to tell her this story. She'd gloat for sure.

"I'm going to run upstairs," Georgia said, "and open some more windows. Be right back."

The floor squeaked as I walked around the kitchen. The 1970s brown-and-green linoleum was lifting in the corners and along the cabinet kickplates. The café curtains on the window above the kitchen sink were so dirty I couldn't tell their original color. Several pieces of the tile countertop were broken, and I noticed smudged footprints in the dust. Critter footprints. A raccoon maybe. Or a cat. Katy would've known immediately, thanks to Papaw's lessons.

The prints led to a cabinet that was missing a door, then abruptly disappeared. On one of the shelves sat a vintage Red Diamond coffee tin. My mamaw once had the exact same one, but like the recipe box, it had also gone missing after her death.

As I heard Georgia moving around upstairs, I quickly checked the other cabinets. Drawers. The coffee tin was the only item in the whole kitchen that hadn't been packed away.

Goose bumps rose on my arms.

Was it a coincidence?

It didn't feel like one.

Not the coffee can, not the gardenia scent.

Not the dreams of that fireplace.

Not the star on the stairs that looked like the one Mamaw used in her quilt designs.

Suddenly I needed air.

I slipped out onto the patio and took a deep breath.

Mary Joy pressed her head into my chest and started burrowing. Nap time had finally caught up to her. I kissed her head and started swaying. Within seconds, her eyelids fluttered closed.

I was just about to go inside when a black blur caught my eye. A cat sat on the back fence, balanced on the post cap, serene as could be. His name tag glinted in the afternoon light.

"Deckle?"

I made a kissy noise to call him to me. He wasn't an outdoor cat, and I was suddenly worried he'd gotten loose. However, at the sound of his name, he blinked his golden eyes slowly and, in one graceful leap, hopped down behind the fence line, disappearing from view.

I stared at the spot where he'd been sitting for a good minute before turning to go back inside. I couldn't shake the feeling that he'd been inside, too. That it had been his footprints that led to the coffee can. That he had been leading me to something that I didn't quite understand.

Like the possibility that this house hadn't sold yet . . . because it was destined to be mine.

Twenty-Two

A Pearl of Wisdom
from Renny Russo
"Love stories are the best stories. Don't let anyone tell you different."

Juliet

I could practically see the moisture in the hazy, humid air on Monday afternoon as I made my way to Juneberry on foot. Right now, the sky was filled with puffy white clouds, but there was rain in the forecast for the coming days, and I was trying not to worry about it.

"Why do you sound all out of breath?" Amy asked.

"I'm walking."

Today's visit to the cottage would be a short one. I only needed to fill out the necessary volunteer paperwork, go through a truncated orientation, and meet the rest of the staff. My official start day would be on Wednesday, an evening shift, fit in around Tallulah's schedule.

"Why? Is something wrong with your car?" Amy asked.

I laughed overly loud and lied through my teeth. "My car is fine. The town is small, easily walkable."

We'd been talking for a few minutes already. I'd told her how I ended up offering to watch Mary Joy and had given her a quick rundown on the cookbook club meeting. She'd made gagging noises when I mentioned the prune whip.

"Isn't it like a thousand degrees outside?"

It felt like it, honestly. "Only ninety."

"Aren't you sweaty? Why not drive?"

"Walking is good exercise." Because I knew I needed to change the subject fast, I said, "Oh! I forgot to tell you that I found out how the town got its name."

"Don't tell me. A field of sweet, beautiful, delicate forget-me-nots were plowed up and pushed asunder to build the town, and the name is a sad, ironic tribute."

I kicked a pebble as I walked along. "Wow. Having a bad day?"

"Thanks for noticing," she said.

I smiled, not the least bit bothered by her flippant attitude. "What happened?"

"Mom happened."

Why that statement made my stomach knot, I wasn't sure. "What's that mean?"

She let out a long sigh. "You know how she is when she gets something in her head."

I did. I *do*. "What's she want you to do?"

"Rearrange my whole life."

"Why?"

"Because she's Mom." She sighed again. She was a master sigher. "It's nothing I can't handle. It just gets to be a lot, you know?"

I did know. Yes.

"Tell me about the town," she said. "The flowers weren't really plowed, were they?"

"No."

"Oh, thank goodness. I wasn't sure my heart could handle that."

"There was this girl," I began. "A young woman."

"Wait. Is this a long story?"

I rolled my eyes. "Would you like the short version?"

"Yes, please. I have a meeting soon."

"A young Irish woman with black hair and golden hazel eyes from a poor family," I said, "falls for a rich guy from a nearby town. And he falls for her. His family isn't pleased and forbids any kind of relationship. They send him away to school, far, far away."

"Oh, classic."

"She's heartbroken, of course, and throws herself into her second love. Books. She scrimps and saves and starts running a little library out of her house, a homestead, really."

Amy said, "Please tell me she doesn't become a spinster cat lady. Not that there's anything wrong with that. Goals, honestly. But it's too obvious."

"I don't think we're supposed to use the word *spinster* anymore."

"Seriously?"

"And does Dave know you want to be a single cat lady?" Her husband adored her, after all.

"He's on a need-to-know basis."

"And he currently doesn't need to know?"

"That's correct. Okay, fine. He can join me and the cats."

I laughed and went on with the story. "The lady with the library does, in fact, have cats. They helped keep mice from eating the books."

"How did I know she had cats?"

A cloud crossed in front of the sun, creating sudden shade, and it was blissful. "Because you know everything."

"This is true."

"*Anyway*, the young woman's library eventually outgrows her home, mostly thanks to an anonymous benefactor who makes regular donations."

"It's him, isn't it? I know it's him."

I rounded a corner onto the street that led to Juneberry. "It's him, and she's not too proud to accept the help. She uses the funds to have a small library built. An official library. People come from all over to visit it. The cats are a hit with patrons."

"I can't get over the cats."

"Oh, just you wait. There's more to that."

"Hurry then."

I laughed and said, "One day, years later, the guy reappears."

"He still loves her, doesn't he?"

"He still loves her," I said.

"Knew it."

"He's willing to be disowned by his family to be with her—and when they do get married, he's cut off."

"But he's happy."

"Right," I said. "They run the library together. They have two children, little boys. Then, one springtime, she gets a cough."

"Oh no."

"The cough gets worse. She gets weaker. Doctors tell them she doesn't have long."

"I don't like this story anymore."

"She takes the time and energy one afternoon to plant a mess of forget-me-nots around the library."

"A mess?"

"Sorry, that's a Katy word. A *lot* of forget-me-nots. So that when they bloom every spring, he'll remember her. And also, she plants them so their story, their love story, will always be remembered."

"My heart can't take this."

"After she passes, he takes over running the library. Before long, a stray cat shows up. A black cat with golden eyes. The cat isn't a mouser. It actually starts helping patrons select books."

"Get out. A cat with black fur and golden eyes? Are we supposed to think that it's *her*?"

"I'm just telling you what I know," I said. Though everyone at the cookbook club meeting absolutely believed the cat had been her—and that part of her spirit was somehow within all the library cats that had come after her. "But don't you want to believe it's true?"

With what I'd already learned of this town, I believed it possible. Plus, I liked the theory that life somehow continued on.

As I thought so, I looked for the robin but didn't see it.

"Absolutely," she said. "You know I'm a romantic at heart."

"Dave will be glad to hear that, once he learns about your cat-lady plans."

"Yeah, yeah. So how did the town actually get its name?"

"Over the years, the forget-me-nots the librarian planted spread like crazy. They were *everywhere*. Every spring, people trekked to see them. Soon a town was built up around the library. By a unanimous vote, the community named it Forget-Me-Not."

"That is the sweetest thing I've heard, well, ever. Is her library still there?"

"Not the original one. That was destroyed by a fire about a hundred years ago. But a new one was built in its spot. One of the woman's descendants is the current library director."

"Okay, but is there a cat?"

"There is. Apparently, a new cat shows up on the library steps only days after the previous one passes away. The one that's there now is named Deckle. He's black and fluffy with big golden eyes."

"Does he pick out books?"

I thought about the book that he knocked to the ground, the one with the bears and the lightning, and goose bumps popped up on my arms. I found myself believing the library cat folklore because it couldn't possibly be coincidence that he'd chosen that specific book for *me*, especially since I now knew that the books he picked contained long-lost memories.

I had purposely withheld that information from Amy. If she knew, she'd likely leap to the same conclusion I had—that Deckle had been trying to return my memory from the day of the lightning strike. Amy would demand I haul myself straight to the library and retrieve the memory, but I just wasn't sure I wanted to remember.

"He actually does."

"That's it," she said. "I need to see the cat."

I stopped to pick up a feather and looked around. The white-throated robin sat in a maple tree not too far away, and my heartbeat quickened. "Next time I'm in the library, I'll take a picture and send it to you. Or I guess I can ask Tallulah. She works there."

"And Tallulah is Tenn's granddaughter?"

"Right."

"*Mm.*"

"That was a very Mom-sounding *mm.*"

"How very *dare* you? But now that you mention Mom, I will say she's worried."

I tucked the feather in my pocket, then rubbed the spot between my eyebrows with the pad of my thumb. "I know."

"It's just that she thinks, she *suspects*, that you're getting attached to Tenn because he's filling a Grandpa-sized hole in your life."

"How is that possible when I can't even *remember* Grandpa?"

Which was a blatant lie.

I *was* remembering him—in my dreams. Short snippets of him pulling my pigtails and calling me pipsqueak. Sitting in the audience of my school play. At my high school graduation. Parked next to me on the couch, watching reality TV. Sharing a basket of fries at the local diner. Walking with me almost every night after dinner.

It was on one of those walks that he said, "Just make sure you're doing it because *you* want to do it. Regret can be a lifelong companion."

It had been this past January, and we'd been talking about grad school. I'd just submitted my application.

I'd looked at him, his wool hat pulled low, almost covering his eyes. "Do you have regrets?"

"Everyone does, Juliet. Don't let them tell you different."

"What would you have changed?" I asked.

He'd smiled then, a soft, sad smile, as he held my gaze. "Not a thing."

I hadn't told any of this to Amy. Or anyone. Rediscovering my grandfather through my dreams felt too special to share. At least for now.

"Maybe it's a subconscious attachment?" Amy said.

"Maybe it's a ridiculous theory."

"Maybe you're ridiculous."

I couldn't help it. I cracked a smile. "There's nothing to worry about, Amy. I promise."

"*Mm*" was all she said in reply.

Twenty-Three

*A Pearl of Wisdom
from Nettie Getchell*
"Nothing changes, darlin', if nothing changes."

Tallulah

Clouds hung low that night as I pushed the stroller toward the park, Jake at my side. Katy ran ahead of us, holding on to Daisy's leash. A chance of storms was in the forecast, which made me worry about Juliet, considering what she'd been through.

Which was on top of my worrying about Katy.

She'd been sullen since Scott had called after supper. My heart had hurt at the way her face crumpled while she talked with him. With the way she blinked back tears. Held in her emotions.

I'd just wanted to gather her up, hold her tight.

I also wanted to fly to Dallas and smack Scott upside his head.

As I watched Katy veer into a patch of grass, I had to wonder if the phone call would have an effect on her sleep tonight. Would there be another nightmare? If so, it might give us a clue as to what was triggering them, but I prayed she'd sleep well.

When I called the pediatrician's office earlier today, the nurse hadn't seemed too concerned about the bad dreams. I'd scheduled an appointment anyway, for early Thursday morning. Better to be safe than sorry.

"Is Katy feeling okay?" Jake asked. "She's not skipping like usual."

We'd been walking for a while now and were nearly home.

I held back a sigh. "Physically, she's fine. She's upset that her dad isn't coming to her birthday party this weekend. He called earlier to tell her."

Scott had never been a big birthday person. He preferred to ignore them. Which was fine. For him. But I could never get through to him that Katy's birthday was about *her*. What she wanted.

Honestly, I should've known he'd bail. I should've expected it. Yet I'd been so hopeful that he'd put Katy—and her feelings—above his. Especially since he hadn't seen her in a while.

"News like that can definitely take the bounce out of you."

I glanced up at him, found sympathy in his eyes. "Definitely."

Daisy circled Katy, tying her up with the leash, and Katy laughed as she untangled herself. It was good to see her smile.

After a moment, Jake said, "Vera mentioned you were divorced. How long were you married?"

Of course Vera had mentioned it, but I couldn't be upset with her. If not her, then someone else would've brought it up. People here liked to talk. "Eleven years. We met in college and got married not too long after graduation."

"Does he see the girls much?"

"Not as much as he should. He moved to Dallas a couple of weeks after we separated."

Between here and there was a nine-hour drive Scott complained about making every time he visited, conveniently forgetting it had been his choice to move so far away. I often suggested he fly, since a nonstop flight to Birmingham was only an hour and forty minutes, but he always had one excuse or another not to.

Jake whistled low. "I can't imagine how hard that is for the girls. And you, too."

I said, "It's been tough. In eighteen months, he's only visited nine times. Mostly on big holidays."

I noticed his quick glance at Mary Joy, then practically saw the mental gymnastics taking place, trying to figure out the math of it all.

Smiling, I saved him the trouble. "A few months after we separated, he visited and we briefly considered a reconciliation, but it just wasn't meant to be. Honestly, we're much better off apart. But if not for that visit, I wouldn't have gotten the gift of Mary Joy, who arrived nine months later, so I have no regrets—about that, at least."

Slowly, he nodded, then said, "Dare I ask what those other regrets might be?"

"Oh, you know, the usual, like not buying Apple stock in the early 2000s."

He laughed. "Weren't you like ten years old then?"

"Still"—I smiled—"it haunts."

As we strolled along, Mary Joy's eyes grew heavy, and I didn't have the heart to try to keep her awake. I'd just have to give her a bath in the morning. If we continued to go on these walks with Jake and Daisy—and I hoped we would—then we might have to move up the start time.

A few moments later, we rounded the garden, the heady floral scent filling the air. Katy and Daisy led the way, and I couldn't help noticing that every few steps, Katy gave a little hop. As if she was *thinking* about skipping. Being with Daisy was helping chase away her blues.

Jake seemed to have noticed as well. "Have you ever considered getting a dog?"

"Maybe someday," I said, thinking about how happy it would make Katy. "When we have a house of our own. A big enough yard. Speaking of which . . ."

I told him about touring the Library House. And how I had a second showing scheduled with Georgia after work tomorrow. I wanted to take Katy and Papaw with me to see the place before making any decisions. If they loved it as much as I did, I was going to put in an offer.

I also told him about seeing Deckle there, so out of place.

"The library cat?"

"I swear it was him. I called Evanthe to let her know, but she didn't answer."

I left a message, but I couldn't help wondering if she was screening my call. I'd found myself often questioning whether I should abandon my mission to befriend her and just let her be—but something deep within told me to keep trying.

"I didn't think you were interested in that place," Jake said.

"I didn't think so, either, until someone mentioned its potential."

He cracked a smile. "Was it Vera?"

I laughed. "No, but now that you mention her, she may have let it slip that you, yourself, had a recent breakup. Can you confirm or deny?"

I was curious and figured it couldn't hurt to ask outright, since I'd heard the information secondhand.

His eyes lost some of their warmth as he nodded. "I, myself, can confirm. I stayed longer than I should've. Hoping," he added.

"For?"

"For her to be ready to settle down, to start a family. But you just can't make someone want something they don't. We just wanted different things in life."

"I'm sorry," I said.

I wanted to tell him I could relate, but I didn't want to share the whole story about how Scott had accepted a promotion at work that included extensive international traveling when he knew I longed for permanence, for stability.

Even thinking about it made me tense up.

Katy had been five, and I'd been at a loss as to what to do.

After much arguing, we *compromised*—he could travel, but I'd stay.

I did my best to grin and bear it when he was away. To adjust.

Then, just six months later, right after holiday decorations had been put away and the year was shiny and new, he'd told me he wanted a divorce.

Once the shock passed, I realized I wanted one, too. Life had been . . . *easier* while he was away.

"The condo we shared," Jake said, "had been hers, so at first, when I moved out, I wasn't sure where to go. Then suddenly I found myself thinking about Forget-Me-Not and how my uncle Dale's car had once broken down here and he ended up staying. That's a legendary story in my family."

Dale's car had broken down in front of the library, and Evanthe went out to tell him he couldn't park at the curb. They'd been married for close to thirty years when he passed away suddenly nineteen years ago.

"It's a legendary story around here, too. A classic love-at-first-sight story is hard to beat. Especially," I added, "considering how reserved Evanthe had always been. Your uncle must've been a special man."

"He was. I'm surprised you never met him."

"I wasn't in Forget-Me-Not very often when I was younger. I did see him from afar once, though. He and Evanthe were walking hand in hand. It was sweet."

"Talk about sweet. Look at that," Jake said, nodding ahead of us.

Katy was skipping. I smiled. "Daisy might have to become a therapy dog."

"They're good for each other, I think. Daisy's never calmer and more relaxed than after a walk with Katy. The vet assures me she'll outgrow her rowdiness, though."

"When did you adopt her?" I asked.

"I've only had her a little over a week."

It was my turn to do mental gymnastics. "Did you adopt her here, in Forget-Me-Not?"

"Funny story. I was about ten miles out of town, on my way here, when I just happened to spot a dog sitting in a patch of roadside daisies. I pulled over, pushed open the passenger door, and she hopped right into my truck, like she'd been waiting for me to pick her up all along."

"You're kidding."

He laughed. "She had no collar, no microchip. The local vet estimates she's five months old and had been on her own for at least a few weeks before I came across her. So far no one has responded to any of the notices I've posted, and I hope no one does. I've grown attached."

"I can see why. It's like she was meant to be with you."

He glanced my way. "I think so, too."

When we finally caught up to Katy in Vera's driveway, she skipped over to us, her blue eyes bright behind her purple glasses, a smile on her face. "Mama, can Mr. Jake come to my birthday party? Daisy, too?"

"A birthday?" Jake said, glancing between her and me, as if this was the first he'd heard of it. "I love birthdays."

His enthusiasm made my heart swell up, fit to burst. It was exactly the reaction Katy needed right now.

"Of course he can come." I lifted an eyebrow. "If he doesn't have to work."

"I'll make the time," he said quickly, his tone full of amusement, his smile stretching. "Don't worry about that."

I scratched Daisy's ears and tried to ignore how much I liked Jake's smile.

"The party is at Papaw's house on Sunday," Katy said. "In the backyard. At five o'clock."

"Sunday," he repeated solemnly. "I'll be there."

It was growing dark, and bedtime beckoned for the girls, so I said, "We should get going, Katy. It's getting late."

As she gave Daisy a big hug, the dog's whole body wiggled with joy. They really were good with each other. Then Katy handed the leash to Jake and skipped to my side.

Jake caught my eye. "See you tomorrow?"

I glanced at Mary Joy, who was sound asleep, her face slack, her lips pursed adorably. "Is a half hour earlier okay?"

He rubbed Daisy's head. "I think we can make that work, can't we, Daisy?"

The dog let out a sharp yip, and Katy laughed and said, "I think that means yes!"

I smiled. "I guess we'll see you then."

With a flurry of waves, we were off. Halfway home, my phone buzzed. I asked Katy to take over stroller duties while I checked the message.

Uncle Renny: I'm still waiting on a picture of your crush. It's not fair that everyone else knows what he looks like.

I glanced over my shoulder and saw Jake still standing at the end of Vera's driveway.

I flashed a smile and then typed out a message.

Me: A picture won't do him justice

Uncle Renny: Don't tease an old dying man

Me: You need to meet him in person

Uncle Renny: And when am I supposed to do that?

Me: Sunday. He'll be at Katy's party

Uncle Renny: Hot damn. I'll be sure to get there early

Me: Don't act like you weren't already planning to do that

Uncle Renny: Don't quibble, Lu. See you Sunday. Looking forward to it.

I wanted to add *Me, too* but didn't want the sassing, so I simply sent back a heart emoji and left it at that.
Truly, it was all that was needed.

Twenty-Four

A Pearl of Wisdom
from Maeve Hearnshaw
"Sometimes, honey, hope is found in the most unexpected places."

Juliet

"Are we late?" Katy asked, clutching a thin paperback book to her chest as we headed up the ramp toward the library doors. "I hope we're not late."

"We're not late," I said, smiling at Mary Joy as she slapped at a toy chain attached to the stroller handle. She looked especially adorable today in her two-piece short set patterned with dinosaurs and foliage. "The program goes until the library closes at six."

"What if they run out of books?"

She hopped over a puddle, left over from yesterday's rain. It had come, thank goodness, without a storm.

"Then we'll just borrow one instead," I said.

She made a face as though she didn't like that answer and skipped ahead of me, through the automatic doors, her pigtails bouncing.

It was coming up quickly on five o'clock, and our visit was serving two purposes.

One, I wanted to take advantage of today's library program.

And two, I was going to hand over the girls to Tallulah at five. She'd take them home with her, and I'd head off to Juneberry for my first volunteer shift. She'd promised she didn't mind starting our *Pride and Prejudice* viewing a little late tonight, since my shift went until nine. It was the last episode of the miniseries, and I had to begrudgingly admit that I was enjoying it more than I'd thought I would, considering my love of the other version—which we had yet to watch.

Time was flying by, and I wished it would slow down. Just a bit. Or, maybe, a lot. Every time I thought about leaving, going home to Michigan, I felt queasy.

As I passed through the doors, enjoying the blast of air-conditioning, I heard Katy say, "Are we late, Mama?" and I nearly laughed.

To say she was excited was putting it mildly. There was no measuring her love of books.

"Hello, hello!" Tallulah kissed the top of Katy's head and flashed me a smile as I made my way to them. "And you're not late. Not at all." Then she said to me, "How was today? Okay?"

"It was a great day. Mary Joy especially enjoyed helping her papaw weed his garden." I wiggled the baby's bare foot, which stuck out of the stroller. "Didn't you?"

She cooed, as if telling her mom that she'd barely lifted a finger, as she was snuggled up against my chest the whole time.

Katy woefully said, "They didn't find any snakes in the garden."

"Thank goodness," I put in. "My heart might not have been able to take that."

"I like snakes," Katy said, then added in a very proper tone, "They play an important role in our ecosystems."

Tallulah said, "Maybe so, but I prefer that role is undertaken in someone else's garden." She leaned down to give Mary Joy noisy kisses, and the baby squealed happily.

It was a cloudy day, yet somehow the library was still filled with light, with life. Computers hummed. Voices carried. Laughter floated along the bookshelves, coming from somewhere near the windows that faced the back garden. In the children's area, I spotted Nettie sitting at her desk, chatting animatedly with a small boy, maybe three or four years old. Jed, the building's custodian, was replacing a carpet tile in the reading area.

To Katy, Tallulah said, "Which book did you bring to swap?"

Katy held up a well-loved Pony Pals book.

"I'm sure someone will love it as much as you have. Come, come." She waved for us to follow her into the community room, where the die-cut letters placed on the windows stated today's program: NATIONAL PAPERBACK BOOK DAY SWAP!

Who even knew there was a National Paperback Book Day? I didn't, that was for sure.

Inside the room, paperbacks were scattered across three conference tables. Several patrons were browsing titles and smiled when we came in, offering hellos.

Tallulah said, "The rules are pretty simple. Bring a book, take a book. The children's books are over there." She pointed to the end of the third table, and Katy immediately darted off.

"Do you think she'll choose quickly or take her time?" I asked.

"Depends," Tallulah said. "If there's an animal book, the decision will be quick. Otherwise, it might take a while."

"Good thing the library closes at six."

She laughed. "Definitely, or we might be here all night."

It was then that Deckle sauntered into the room, his tail high in the air. In one smooth leap, he landed on the table next to Tallulah. She narrowed her gaze on him and said, "Don't you dare."

"Dare what?" I asked, amused by the stare-down going on.

"Oh, he knows." Then she added, "I'm going to grab my things. I'll meet you back here?"

"Sure," I said, just as Deckle knocked a book onto the floor. It landed at her feet.

He sat down, his tail swaying. His golden eyes glittery.

I heard Tallulah sigh deeply as she bent to retrieve the book. Without even looking at it, she set it back onto the table, then gently picked Deckle up and put him on the floor. "Go find Evanthe."

He did no such thing. His feet had barely touched the ground before he once again leaped up onto the table and sent the book flying back onto the floor.

Tallulah's jaw jutted as she picked up the paperback. This time, however, she didn't immediately put it down on the table. She simply held it, looking at its cover.

I said, "Aren't you supposed to sniff that?"

"That's what the legend says I should do."

"You don't believe the folklore?" I asked.

"Oh, I do. That's not it. It's just—" She cut herself off, shook her head. "It's just that I'm not interested in retrieving a lost memory."

Before I could ask anything else, she put the book down, scooped Deckle up, and strode off with him as he meowed indignantly.

I glanced at the book in question.

It was a vintage spiral-bound paperback church cookbook, complete with a round coffee stain on the cover.

I picked it up, flipped through it, and even, yes, sniffed it.

But whatever memory of Tallulah's it held wasn't revealed to me.

If peace were a place, it would be Juneberry Cottage.

As soon as I'd walked in the doors earlier, I'd felt it immediately.

It felt, oddly, like where I belonged.

There were four guests currently at the cottage. Two were here until the end of the day—nine p.m. One was here for the week. Then there was Renny, who would be here until . . . well, until he wasn't.

I didn't really want to think about that day. I'd already grown fond of him.

He'd been asleep when I arrived, and every so often, I popped by his room to see if he was awake yet. In between those times, I moved from guest to guest. I'd read to one, played albums for another. One of the patients was an older woman who'd asked me to take her outside to the garden, which had paved trails, wide enough for her wheelchair.

For an hour, we discovered the hidden gems of the garden like the fountain and koi pond, and we talked. Well, mostly I listened. She didn't once mention the cancer that was ravaging her body. Instead, she told me about her life. The things she loved. Her family, mostly. Kids and grandkids and great-grands. But also about sunbeams and morning glories and mimosas and bonfires.

"Juliet," she said, "the little things aren't always little. Pay attention to what makes your heart sing."

Right now my heart was singing—and was humbled—because she'd trusted me with these little pieces of her of life.

She was starting to doze off by the time we made it back to her room. I helped her into bed, pulled down the shades, and wished I could do more for her. But my role as a volunteer was limited. As I left her room, I could only hope that I would see her again, but knew in all likelihood I would not.

I supposed when you worked in a field like this, you had to learn to be grateful for the *right now*. To live in the moment.

I felt the weight of that lesson as I once again ventured down the hall toward Renny's room. As I thought about him asking me to visit, I was honored to know he wanted me to be part of his last chapter.

When I neared his room, I saw his door was wide open, and was surprised to hear voices within. I slowed as I recognized both straightaway.

Renny and Callum.

Callum was saying, "But Gran said Juliet is leaving soon. Has to get back to work."

"So what?" Renny said.

Heat immediately rose up my neck. They were talking about *me*.

"I don't do passing through," Callum said. "I'm a settle-down kind of guy. You, of all people, should understand."

"Walt might not have stayed, but he taught me what love *should* be. I wouldn't give that up for the world."

"Please don't tell me it's better to love and lose—"

"It is better to love and lose than never love at all." Renny's voice was a bit stronger than usual this evening. Probably because he'd been resting most of the day. "Good heavens, Callum. You're much too young to be so rigid. Loosen up."

"Sorry," he said, not sounding sorry at all, "but I don't like getting my heart broken."

My breath caught at that. He thought I'd break his heart?

"Does anyone?" Renny asked. "Besides, you don't know that she won't stay."

"You don't know that she will."

"Odds increase if she finds love in this town."

"It didn't work out that way for you," Callum said, not unkindly. It was spoken softly, gently, as if the words were bubble-wrapped.

"No, but I assure you, it's a risk worth taking."

"I just don't think it's a—"

"For the love of mankind, Cal. Just ask the girl out. Do it for me. A dying man's last wish."

Callum's voice was tight, as if talking through clenched teeth. "Are you seriously playing the dying card on me right now?"

"Are you kidding? It's the best card to have. Of course I'm playing it. I always say, use what you have, kid."

It seemed like a good time to interrupt. To save Callum from the guilt trip he was being subjected to. And maybe save myself from eternal embarrassment. I found, though, that I was somewhat amused—and touched—by Renny trying so hard to set us up. It was sweet, in a way.

I made a show of jingling my keys, then breezed into the room. "Oh! So sorry," I said. "I didn't mean to interrupt. I'll come back." I started to backtrack.

"Wait!" Renny widened his eyes at Callum and made a jerking motion with his chin. Then he coughed weakly.

Callum sucked in a deep breath. "Can I talk to you a sec, Juliet? In the hallway?"

It took everything in me to keep from smiling. "Sure. Something wrong?"

He glared at Renny. "*No.*"

"Attaboy," Renny said.

As I turned, I gave Renny a little wink to show him I knew what was going on, and he chuckled.

Callum followed me out to the hallway, his footsteps loud and heavy, as if he were literally dragging his feet. He smelled of oil and cedar, and I clasped my hands together because suddenly I wanted to hug him for honoring Renny's wishes, even though they were on par with emotional blackmail.

He was dressed for work in his usual uniform, his wavy hair hidden under a ball cap. Wariness filled his blue eyes, darkening them. He cleared his throat. "Juliet, have you, uh, been to the Lickety Split yet?"

I fussed with my lanyard and gazed at the word VOLUNTEER written in bold, block letters on my name badge. "No, but Katy raves about it."

He crossed his arms. "You should go before you leave town."

Loud coughing came from inside the room. Fake coughing.

"I mean," Callum said, "maybe you could go. *With. Me.*"

The last two words were spoken as if they were being ripped from the depths of his soul. Then he jerked his head toward the room and widened his eyes and did everything he could to make me aware that he was being put up to this without actually saying so.

"What do you mean?" I asked, playing dumb. "Like, on a *date*?"

A chuckle came from beyond the door. A giggle, really. Renny was enjoying this.

So was I, I realized.

"I don't think we need to label it," Callum said.

"No?" I asked.

He shook his head and again motioned toward the room with his chin.

The cedar scent filled my head and scrambled my senses. It was the only explanation for why I said, "I didn't realize you liked me that way. I, uh, like you, too. So yes, I'll go on a date with you to the Lickety Split."

What was I doing? That wasn't at all what I'd planned to say.

Then I realized I was living in the moment.

And risking heartbreak, just like Callum was. Because I *did* like him. I just hoped Renny was right—that a chance at love was worth the risk. Because I was taking a big one.

I seemed to have knocked the wind right out of Callum. He stood there, staring at me, looking slightly dumbfounded. Suddenly his gaze narrowed, studying me closely.

Then he unfolded his arms. The wariness in his eyes was replaced with something lighter, brighter. Something *amused*.

"Saturday night?" he said.

I nodded. "Sounds good."

"Seven o'clock?"

"Perfect."

Abruptly, he reached out and pulled me into a hug. I was so caught off guard that I practically toppled into him. But once I was pressed against his chest, I all but melted.

He whispered, "Thanks for playing along."

Then, after another moment, he let go and poked his head into Renny's room. "I've got to get going, Uncle Ren. I'll see you soon."

"Looking forward to it!" Renny said. "Send Juliet in, will you?"

"Sure thing." He gave me a smile. "I'll see you soon, too." Then he turned and headed for the front door.

My pulse was jumping like crazy, my knees were weak, my throat tight.

He thought I was playing along.

Just like that, my heart was already aching, before we even went on the stupid date.

And Juneberry didn't feel nearly as peaceful as it had before.

Twenty-Five

A Pearl of Wisdom
from Renny Russo
"No one ever really grows up. You just get old."

Tallulah

There was a makeover underway in the community room.

"If we lop off the horn, we can use it as the base of the tail," Vera said. A pair of reading glasses was perched atop her head, nestled snugly amid the curls.

"Sparkles," Aunt Maeve said, eyes wide with enthusiasm. "I should've brought sparkles."

Isabel pushed the sleeves of her sweater up to her bony elbows. "I'm sure we have glitter around here somewhere."

Nettie added, "Who has the box cutter?"

Two conference tables had been pushed together. Gone were the leftover paperbacks from yesterday's swap, which had been stored away, awaiting the next book sale. Now on the tables were pots of paint. Papier-mâché. Wire mesh. Newspaper. Cardboard. Wire hangers. Tissue paper. Glue guns. And the victim: a unicorn piñata.

I stood just outside the doorway, trying to stay out of sight and not butt in.

Jed stood behind me. He whispered, "What're they doing?"

"They're on a mission to transform a unicorn piñata into a dragon piñata."

"Was buying a dragon piñata not an option?"

I kept my voice low and stepped away from the door. "I suggested it, but Aunt Maeve insisted she could turn a unicorn into a dragon, no problem. On her lunch hour, no less. Vera volunteered to help. They needed space to spread out, so here they are."

Juliet had offered to lend a hand, too, but Mary Joy had other thoughts. She'd started fussing and crying not too long after they arrived, and Juliet ended up taking her outside. Every so often I'd see them pass by the window and smile.

Tonight Juliet and I would start her preferred version of *Pride and Prejudice*, which would last us two nights, since we've been watching in one-hour increments. I hoped we could find something else to watch after we were done. I'd come to enjoy our couch time each night. At some point, it had evolved from just watching the show to also talking about our lives. I'd shared with her about possibly going back to college. And she shared with me that she was thinking of withdrawing from the grad program she was enrolled in. I told her about my childhood, the traveling, and she shared with me what she'd remembered of hers so far. We found we liked many of the same things. Popcorn with extra butter. Jane Austen and Agatha Christie and thick fantasy novels. Stationery. Sunny skies. Funny memes. Cozy blankets. October leaves. And so much more.

What had started as a test of our friendship, even jokingly, seemed to have cemented it.

I tried not to think about her leaving. Tried really, really hard.

Jed motioned with his chin toward the community room. "And Isabel and Nettie? What're they doing?"

I grinned. "They're supposed to be working but couldn't help themselves."

We both glanced toward Evanthe's office. The door was closed. She was working on cataloging, which was best done without interruption.

Deckle was strutting around the Flour Festival table, probably looking for a book to drop at my feet.

I nodded that way. "Are you ready for the festival next weekend?"

Jed was a baker at heart and in years past had lured a crowd to the library's vendor booth with his legendary bourbon-pecan bars. While people waited in line, they were pitched branded tote bags, water bottles, mugs, T-shirts, all for sale, the proceeds going to a good cause: the Forget-Me-Not Library.

"As I'll ever be," he said.

"You'll save me a pecan bar, right?"

He crossed his arms, blocking the library's embroidered name on his polo shirt. "That there depends."

His response took me aback, and I gave him a good, long look. "On what?"

"On whether you'll put in a good word for me with Evanthe."

"Me?" I scoffed. "She's not going to listen to anything I have to say."

"Not true. She has a soft spot for you."

He could've knocked me over with a feather. "Are we talking about the same Evanthe?"

He chuckled. "Of course. She's one of a kind."

It was my turn to laugh. "That she is."

Behind me, I heard the doors slide open as Jed said, "All I'm saying is I can use all the help I can get. Now, if you'll excuse me, it's break time, and a cup of tea is callin' my name."

I turned to welcome whoever had come in and found Jake walking toward me. He was dressed in a button-down shirt and jeans, and I tried not to notice how handsome he looked. But have mercy. I had eyes.

I wasn't the only one to notice.

A catcall came from inside the community room, and he laughed and waved.

When I glanced into the room, all the ladies had their heads down, their hands busy. Yet I knew only one of them could whistle like that.

Isabel.

She looked up, caught me staring, and winked.

"Ma'am?" Jake said, stepping up next to me. "I heard you had a puppy-training book on hold for me?"

My heart was doing a happy dance. Sometime during this past week, it had stopped asking me, *What if him?* It was as though it knew the answer already and was simply waiting for me to get on board.

I smiled. "What'd Daisy eat now?"

He was shaking his head woefully. "The TV remote. I'm just glad she never seems to do damage to herself, only the things around her."

Deckle, the devilish little thing, hopped up on the book cart and started flapping his tail.

I knew what that meant, and I was waging an inner battle about it.

On the one hand, I didn't want the memory.

On the other, I also wanted to stop holding grudges, to set a good example for Katy.

I'd almost given in to the bibliosmia of it all yesterday when Deckle flung that cookbook at me during the paperback swap. Just one sniff was all it would take. But I couldn't bring myself to do it.

Not yet.

I tried to ignore Deckle as I led Jake to the circ desk. "Let's get you a guest pass, and the book is all yours. Well, for fourteen days. Then you'll have to renew."

"If Daisy doesn't eat it before then."

"That's a big if," I said.

"The biggest."

When Deckle hopped up onto the counter, Jake reached over to pet his head. "How'd the doctor's appointment go this morning?"

I heard purrs almost immediately. The audacity.

Jake knew about Katy's early appointment because we'd chatted about it last night, while we walked to the park and back. It was quickly becoming one of my favorite things to do. During that half hour, I'd learned his favorite foods were fresh cherries, pizza, and shortbread cookies. We also talked about my Trivia Night presentation and how I was going to put an offer on the Library House—though I didn't tell him about the dreams I'd had. The ones that kept on coming, the images a bit clearer each night.

I also didn't mention something else that was bothering me. On the second viewing of the house, the one where Papaw and Katy had come along, the coffee can in the kitchen had disappeared.

Simply vanished.

Ever since, I'd been wondering if I'd imagined it being there at all.

A trick of the mind.

A trick of the memory.

"It went okay," I said. "If the nightmares don't stop in the next month, then we'll be referred to a pediatric sleep specialist."

In the meantime, the doctor wanted us to work on a sleep routine—as if Katy hadn't had one since she began sleeping through the night as a baby. But Katy was also supposed to get plenty of relaxation. That was harder these days. I knew that missing her dad took a toll on her tender heart.

"She hasn't had a nightmare in a few days, though," I added. Not even after the phone call from Scott. "So maybe she's through the worst of it?"

"We can hope," Jake said.

With a nod, I tore my gaze away and looked at Deckle, who was rubbing his face against Jake's palm.

"He likes you." I pushed the guest pass across the counter for him to fill out.

"The feeling is mutual."

I swear the purrs got louder.

Then, in a flash, Deckle turned around and kicked a book off the counter. It fell, face up, at Jake's feet.

As Jake bent to pick it up, Deckle stared at Jake expectantly, unblinking.

There was a memory in that book for him.

I glanced around to see if anyone else was nearby who could explain the whole bibliosmia thing to Jake, but Evanthe was still in her office, and everyone else seemed to be hard at work on Frankensteining the piñata.

"I guess he doesn't like *The Wonderful Wizard of Oz*," Jake said as he put the book on the counter and reached for a pen.

I wrung my hands and Deckle meowed loudly at me.

Fine.

I reached out and put my hand on Jake's, felt a zap of electricity from my head to my toes. Sparks. A whole electrical surge. "Before you do that . . ."

His gaze lingered on my fingers. "Something wrong?"

I couldn't seem to pull my hand away—in fact, I wanted to slide my hand up his arm—so I left it where it was. "No, not wrong, necessarily." In one big breath, I told him about Deckle and book scents and long-forgotten memories. "It's supposedly always been this way. Ever since the first stray library cat showed up."

I finally, reluctantly, pulled my hand off his and then found I didn't know what to do with it. Out of desperation, I scratched Deckle's ears.

He didn't purr. Not even a rumble.

"So," Jake said, "I'm just supposed to sniff the book?"

"Open the book, let the pages fall where they will, *then* sniff."

I once again glanced toward the community room. For all their collective nosiness, the ladies were oblivious to what was going on out here. Just when I needed them the most.

"You're not making this up, right? Pranking me?"

I sighed. "I know it sounds strange, but you just have to trust the process."

I couldn't believe my own ears. Was I lobbying for Deckle now?

Jake looked like he wasn't sure he believed me; then he shook his head, chasing doubts away. "Well, I don't know about trusting the process, but I'm choosing to trust *you*, so here goes."

As he opened the book, I leaned across the counter and saw that it had fallen open to an early chapter of the story. The scene where Dorothy, in her *silver* slippers, is just starting down the yellow brick road.

Giving me an *I can't believe I'm doing this* kind of smile, Jake lifted the book upward, closed his eyes, and inhaled deeply.

I was on pins and needles as I waited and didn't realize I'd stopped scratching Deckle's head until he bumped my hand impatiently. I resumed the scritches, secretly hoping for a purr. He owed me one, I felt, after I just convinced someone to do something I wouldn't do myself.

But no. The little beast wouldn't indulge me.

Jake tipped his head, as if trying to understand something puzzling; then his eyes opened. There was curiosity there, flickering in the pale brown depths. Wonder as well.

"Did you remember something?" I asked.

Nodding, he glanced at Deckle, then me again. "How . . ."

"No one really knows. It's just part of what makes the library so enchanting."

Jake closed the book, held it to his chest. "It was a memory of my uncle Dale, talking about Forget-Me-Not. I was ten, maybe eleven, and he and Aunt Ev were on vacation, visiting us in Florida. He was telling the story of how a detour led him here, to this town, to Aunt Ev. He joked that he felt a little like Dorothy from *Wizard of Oz*. Because, like her, fate had put him on a path he'd never expected. Yet somehow it led him home."

Chill bumps rose on my arms, and a swell of emotion filled my chest, making it ache.

"I have so many questions," he said, searching my face.

"Unfortunately, I don't have any answers. No one does. Nettie always says to treat the memories as a gift. Kind of like an unexpected present."

After a moment, he nodded. "Okay then. Well, thank you"—he lifted the name tag on the golden collar—"Deckle."

Deckle blinked slowly. And now that his work here was apparently done, he meowed, then jumped down. He strutted off toward one of the couches, his tail in the air.

Jake looked toward Evanthe's office door. "Maybe I should go say hi. It's been a few days since I've talked to her."

"You're not holding a grudge? I mean, she did kick you out."

"It's hard to be mad when she might've done me a favor. I'm pretty happy with where I landed."

My heart was doing the happy-dance thing again, and I found I didn't mind its celebrating.

Not even a little.

I said, "A gift basket might be in order."

He laughed and headed for her office door. I didn't linger. Instead, I pushed the book cart into the stacks. While I went about putting books back into their proper places, I kept thinking about what Jake's uncle had said about Forget-Me-Not.

I told myself that was why, with each step I took, the word *home* echoed in my head.

Ten minutes before I was supposed to leave for the day, I found myself facing Evanthe's closed office door, an envelope in my hand.

Nervous, I shifted from foot to foot, then knocked softly.

"Enter."

Slowly, I pushed open the door. Evanthe sat in her desk chair, facing two computer monitors. A pair of glasses was perched on the tip of her nose. Today she wore beige linen, and her braid was coiled into a bun at the nape of her neck, the black tip tucked under, out of sight.

"Yes?" she said.

I practically tiptoed over to her desk and placed the envelope in front of her.

"What's this?" she asked.

"An invitation."

She suspiciously eyed the looping handwriting on the front. "To?"

"Katy's birthday party. It's on Sunday. We'd like for you to be there."

I heard her inhale, as if she didn't have the patience for this. "*Katy* wants me to be there?"

"Katy would invite the whole town if she could. But *I'd* really like for you to be there. Nettie and Isabel will be there, too. And Renny. And of course Papaw and Aunt Maeve."

She didn't open the invitation. She simply tapped the envelope against her blotter.

Instead of standing there waiting, hoping, I started backing out. "You don't need to RSVP or anything. Or even bring a gift. I just . . . I think Mamaw would want you to be part of our lives, is all. So, hopefully we'll see you. But if not, I understand. And I won't keep pestering you." Having said my piece, I gave an awkward wave and stepped out, closing the door behind me.

I leaned against it for a moment and let out a deep breath.

I'd done all I could do to establish a friendship outside of work.

Whatever happened next was now up to her.

Twenty-Six

A Pearl of Wisdom
from Isabel Espinoza
"Savings bonds are a great present for a little one.
You're never too young to learn how to manage money."

Juliet

Saturday morning, I woke up with a start, bolting upright, my heart pounding, my head aching.

Clutching the thin quilt, I took deep breaths. I'd been dreaming. I couldn't quite remember the details, but I had vague memories of a storm.

The glowing red numbers on the alarm clock told me it was almost six in the morning. The house would be waking up soon. Tallulah would be headed to work—her short day. Maeve would stop by on her way to Juneberry. Tenn would sing. The girls and I would keep busy. I had a date tonight.

A pretend date.

Groaning softly, I flopped backward, pulled the quilt over my head, and burrowed into my pillow. I did *not* want to go on that date. Not if it was just for show.

A flash of light filtered through the quilt, and I sat up again. A moment later, thunder rumbled in the distance. I cursed the forecast I'd read last night, which had made no mention of possible storms, and picked up my phone to look at the radar.

A thin, broken yellow line was inching diagonally across the state, but it was moving quickly. Thank goodness.

As rain lashed the roof, I couldn't help wondering if I'd subconsciously heard the storm while sleeping. I shivered, unable to shake the uneasiness the dream had left behind. Fear had settled deep in my soul, curled up there, as if lying in wait.

Realizing I wasn't going to be able to go back to sleep, I decided to get up for the day. I tiptoed down the stairs to the second floor and slipped into the bathroom. When I came out, I heard whimpering coming from across the hall. Katy's room.

I tapped on her door before pushing it open. A night-light threw dim light across the space. Only enough to see shapes and shadows. "Katy? Are you okay?"

She didn't answer.

I crossed the room, sat on the edge of her bed. She was hidden under her covers, just like I'd been five minutes ago. I peeled back the edge of her blanket and realized she was still sleeping. She tossed, turned, then said "Mary Joy!" in a low, frightened voice. Then she sucked in a sharp breath, sat up, and dissolved into tears.

I gathered her into my arms. She clung to me.

"It's all right," I soothed, my heart pounding. "It's just a dream. A bad dream. Should I get your mom?"

Sniffling, she shook her head.

So, I stayed where I was and rubbed her back and held her and just let her be. After a few minutes, she finally pulled away, wiped her eyes and nose. I tucked her hair behind her ears, picked up her glasses from her nightstand, and slipped them onto her face.

I cupped her soft cheeks in my palms. I wasn't at all sure what to tell her. I didn't want to tell her that dreams weren't real, because sometimes they *felt* like they were. Finally, I settled for the simple truth. "Bad dreams stink. I'm so sorry you're having them."

She nodded and hugged me again. We stayed like that for another minute until thunder rumbled, and she peeled herself away.

"It's not a bad storm," she said in a comforting tone, and I realized she was trying to soothe *me*.

"Not bad at all."

She climbed out from underneath her blankets and sat next to me on the side of her bed, her small leg pressed up close to mine. "You're not scared?"

"Only a little," I said.

She smiled at me. "A little is better than a lot."

"In this case, definitely." Then I gently asked, "Did you remember anything about your dream?"

She started to shake her head, then stopped. "Something happened to Mary Joy."

I wondered if she was able to remember because I'd asked so soon after she'd had the nightmare. It hadn't had time to hide away. "Do you remember what?"

Her face squished up as she concentrated. "No, just—" She pushed her small hands to her chest, held them there. "It scared me." She glanced quickly toward her doorway.

I said, "Do you want to go check on her?"

She nodded.

"All right, but be real quiet like, okay?"

Mary Joy's crib was in Tallulah's room, and I knew Tallulah would wake up the moment her door handle turned. She was a light sleeper. I was hoping that while Katy was in there, she'd tell her mom about the bad dream.

Leaping up, Katy tiptoed across the room, using comical, exaggerated steps, and I knew she was going to be all right. The floorboards creaked. The door handle of Tallulah's bedroom squeaked. I heard some murmurs; then Katy was back.

"Mary Joy is sleeping," Katy said. "Mama said not to wake her."

"Did you tell your mom about the dream?"

She shook her head.

"Why?"

She shrugged and grabbed one of her stuffed animals off the bed—a dog that looked remarkably like Daisy—along with a book from her overflowing shelf.

"You don't want to worry her?" I guessed.

Her chin came up, and she pulled her bottom lip into her mouth. She nodded.

"She'd rather be worried than not know. You're going to have to trust me on that. Besides, worrying is what moms do best. They're experts. It's practically an art form. It should be an Olympic event."

"Now you're being silly."

"A little," I said, standing up.

"A lot." She squeezed the poor dog, then said, "You can tell her. If you want."

I decided it was a good compromise. "Deal." I smiled and held out my hand. "How about some breakfast?"

Nodding, she slipped her hand into mine and we went downstairs. I glanced toward the TV and smiled. We'd finished the Keira version of *P&P* last night, and Tallulah and I had a heated debate about which production was better. She held firm that it was the miniseries, while I held firm that it was the two-hour movie. In the end, we agreed to disagree—and decided we'd watch *Emma*, starring Gwyneth Paltrow, next.

In the kitchen, I put on a pot of coffee and made some oatmeal for Katy, making room for the bowl—and her book—at the island. The counter was covered in birthday party items. Plates and cups and favors.

I didn't technically have a present for Katy yet. I had an idea for one, however. Something handmade. I needed to run to the store later on for supplies.

As I pulled a mug from the cabinet, I smiled at how I'd come to know—and love—little Katy after only knowing her for so short a time.

Before long, Tenn came into the kitchen, moving at a decent pace. His back was healing nicely.

"Mornin', sprout." He ruffled Katy's hair before heading to the stove to put the kettle on for tea. "Mornin', Juliet. How about a little music to drown out the noise of this storm?"

I thought I'd rather hear the thunder, which suggested that I might finally be starting to heal.

He pulled his phone from a pocket and started swiping. A moment later, music flooded the kitchen. Gilbert and Sullivan songs, of course. As he sang loudly—and off-key—about being a little buttercup, Katy looked up from her book and rolled her eyes. I tried not to laugh out loud.

I wandered into the dining room to glance out one of the front windows. The ferns swayed, and the leaves on Bill's branches fluttered wildly in the strong breeze.

The chubby robin with the white patch at its neck stood on a branch, positioned so it was sheltered from the wind. When it saw me, it lifted one of its wings, as if waving.

Emotion filled my chest and tears stung my nose. It felt silly, but I slowly lifted my hand and waved back.

The robin's happy chirp was accompanied by a squawky cry from the floor above, signaling that Mary Joy had woken up. Katy must've heard the sound, too, because she was on her feet and up the stairs in the blink of an eye.

Tenn was chuckling as he came into the room. "What's got into her, I wonder? I wasn't even singing right then."

Turning, I smiled, finding his self-awareness amusing. "I'm not sure," I said, not really wanting to talk about Katy's nightmare.

He placed a steaming mug of tea on the table, then sat down. Off came his eyeglasses, which he set aside. Then he put on his headlamp. "I'm right glad the weather's going to clear later. Do you think you'll have time to help me set up a party tent in the backyard later on? The more we get done today, the easier tomorrow will be."

"I have plenty of time."

Well, until my date tonight. Which, honestly, I was considering canceling. It just didn't feel . . . right.

He scratched his chin, which was covered with thick stubble as his beard regrew. Mary Joy could finally look at him again without breaking into tears. He said, "Katy's party is shapin' up to be quite the shindig. She's going to have herself a real good time."

I nodded, not doubting it for a minute.

When the sound of faint knocking came from outside, I glanced out the window. I first noticed that the robin had flown off. Then I spotted one of Bill's branches slapping against a porch column, like it was trying to get my attention.

I smiled, thinking about Katy's love of the tree.

Then I had the craziest, zaniest idea.

"Hey, Tenn?"

"Yes, sweetheart?"

"Do you know anything about trees?"

"Trees? Some. Why? What are you thinking?"

I told him.

He grinned. "I don't know much about that, but I know just the man you need to talk to."

Many hours later, regret followed behind me as I pushed my shopping cart through the aisles of a superstore ten miles outside of Forget-Me-Not.

It was nearing eight o'clock at night, and I was trying not to think about how instead of being here, I should be sitting with Callum at the Lickety Split, looking into his blue eyes and breathing in his cedar scent.

Except I'd canceled the date.

I just couldn't do it. *Pretending* to date felt wrong. Incredibly wrong. So, I'd texted him and said I had a headache, which wasn't a complete lie, because the one I'd woken up with still lingered. I added that I'd see him tomorrow at Katy's party and included a smiley face that I now wished I could go back and erase.

Immediately, he'd texted back, just saying, Okay.

His one-word reply had been a relief. And slightly heartbreaking at the same time.

Which seemed all kinds of silly. I tried to tell myself that I barely knew him, but my heart seemed to disagree.

Now I was steering the cart down the craft supply aisle, looking for a medium-sized loop, cord, beads, and embroidery thread for the handmade gift I had in mind for Katy's present.

The store was quiet at this time on a Saturday night, but it felt massive and overwhelming as I scanned shelves. Snug's could easily fit in here three times over, and suddenly having a variety of options felt like too many.

I enjoyed small-town life, I realized. Its coziness. Its community. I liked that the cashier at Snug's now knew my name, liked feeling as though I belonged to a bigger whole. That I was *important* to the bigger whole. And I'd only been in town for a week and a half—I couldn't imagine how it felt *living* there.

I enjoyed trying to imagine it, though.

My phone dinged as I reached for a macramé ring, which would work perfectly for the gift I had in mind. I set it onto the seat of the shopping cart and checked the text message. It was from my younger brother Jordan. A silly meme. Both twins communicated primarily by memes and GIFs. It was their love language.

The graphic he sent was an image of a skeleton sitting on a bench. ME, WAITING FOR YOU TO COME HOME was printed in block letters.

I clicked the laugh reaction.

Almost immediately, another text came in. This one from Hunter.

It was an image of Dory from *Finding Nemo*. Printed on it was ARE YOU HOME YET?

I sent back a GIF of someone shaking their head so vigorously they fell over.

As I pushed my cart along, looking for cording, I imagined the twins huddled up together—probably at a pub, since they'd had an afternoon game—searching online for memes. I smiled because I could see it easily.

However, I also had the feeling they'd been coerced to reach out in the first place. For as much as they thought alike, they didn't often text at the same time, with the same general message.

My hunch was confirmed a moment later when my oldest brother, Eric, sent a text, asking when he'd see me again.

A minute later, my dad texted as well.

Yep, this was a coordinated attack, and I had no doubt my mother was behind the ambush.

I sent a quick note to the group chat, saying I was fine and would be home soon.

Immediately, Mom texted back, asking me to define *soon*.

By August 18th, I texted along with a smiley face. Then I erased the smiley face. Then added it back and hit send. It seemed I was just a smiley face kind of person.

A series of reactions came flooding in. Most of them sad faces or thumbs-down.

Yet I couldn't help noticing that Amy hadn't chimed in. I tried to remember if she had something going on tonight or if her absence was rebellion. I wasn't sure.

I was trying to choose a color of faux suede cording when my phone buzzed once again.

Amy: Sorry about that. Mom is determined to get you home ASAP

Me: Not happening

Amy: Famous last words

Unsure if the conversation was over, I kept the phone in my hand as I added the suede to my cart and looked around for beads.

I was searching for the prettiest, most colorful beads possible. I wanted to make this homemade gift extra special because I'd abandoned my idea for a second gift—the crazy, zany one—after talking to Tenn's connection.

When my cell *rang*, I winced and checked the caller ID, fully expecting it to be my mother. I about dropped the phone when I saw the call was from Callum.

My phone kept on ringing while I debated whether to answer. Finally, I took a deep breath and said, "Hello?" But I was too late—the call had already gone to voicemail.

Should I call him right back?

Or wait for the voicemail?

Or dig a big hole, fling myself in, and bury myself alive?

The latter was appealing, but I decided to just call him back and get it over with.

I pushed the button to return the call and immediately heard ringing coming from behind me. I spun around. Callum stood at the far end of the aisle, leaning against a rack that held bolts of fabric.

He gave me a cheeky wave as he answered the call: "Hello?"

"How long have you been standing there?" I asked.

"Only a minute or so."

"Nice basket."

He held it in his other hand and playfully swung it back and forth as he walked toward me. "Thanks. Turns out they're quite handy."

He smiled and my pulse pounded.

"How's your head?" he asked in a tone that questioned whether it had ever hurt at all.

Right at this moment, I felt a little dizzy. I blamed that on the foolish way my heart was reacting. "Not too bad. I took some ibuprofen earlier."

"Good to hear." He was almost to my cart when he added, "Well, I should get a move on. I have some more shopping to do. I'm going to a birthday party tomorrow."

Jumping jacks. My heart was doing jumping jacks. "Oh? I might see you there."

"Good. You can be the one to tell Renny about our date."

Ouch.

"Sorry," I said, making crackling noises into the phone. "You're breaking up. Talk to you later, *bye*."

He hid a slight smile behind a sigh, then slid the phone into his back pocket. "You shouldn't have agreed to go on the date if you didn't want to go."

I flinched and tucked my phone back into my purse. I didn't know how to have this conversation. "It's not that."

"Then what?"

I had to look away. His blue gaze nearly did me in.

"Then what, Juliet?" he asked again, his voice gentle, quiet.

I struggled to find the words. To explain without having to put my heart on display.

"You know what?" he said. "Never mind. It doesn't matter. I'll see you tomorrow."

He spun around and walked off.

I couldn't let him leave like this. I just couldn't.

I started following and blurted, "I wasn't playing along."

As soon as the words were out of my mouth, I froze and wished I could reel them back in. It was too much. Too soon.

He turned. "What?"

I latched onto the cart, gripping the cool plastic handle for dear life. I took a deep breath. "When you asked me out, I wasn't pretending when I said yes. I wasn't playing along. I wanted to go out with you. I was too embarrassed to correct you when you thanked me for going along with Renny's idea."

He took a step toward me. Then another.

"And it was kind of mortifying. You have to see that, don't you? I thought I could do it. Just go on the date and pretend, because it was for a good cause, right? For Renny. But I just really don't want to pretend. I don't. I *can't*. Life's too short to fake your way through it."

Callum took another step toward me and set his basket down on the floor. He stood about a foot away now, and I could smell the cedar and oil, and my heart was thump-thump-thumping like mad.

I rushed on, in full ramble mode. "It wouldn't be fair. Not to me, not to you, because I'd overheard what you said about how you didn't do passing through and—"

I lost all train of thought when he reached out, cupped my face, and kissed me. I let go of the cart and leaned into him, so close I could feel his heart pounding against my chest.

Just when I thought I might die from happiness, he pulled back and rested his forehead against mine.

"What about passing through?" I whispered.

His gaze met mine, held steady. "I'll take the risk if you will."

In my head I could hear Renny saying the risk was worth it.

My heart was practically soaring when I smiled and said, "How late does the Lickety Split stay open?"

Twenty-Seven

A Pearl of Wisdom
from Nettie Getchell
"Always remember, darlin', if no one died, it can be fixed."

Tallulah

The weather was perfect for Katy's party. Warm but not too hot. Mostly clear skies with only a few puffy clouds.

Papaw and Juliet had worked tirelessly all day, doing last-minute shopping, picking up the cake, cleaning, setting up the chairs and tables. Juliet had been a godsend in the kitchen, prepping food for the grill, setting up snack trays, and creating a beautiful charcuterie board.

"I might not be able to cook," she had said with a bright smile, "but I can arrange."

Aunt Maeve—with Callum's help—had strung party lights through the trees and along the fence. Jake and Papaw had set up a croquet court in the side yard and hung the pin-the-tail-on-the-dragon on the back porch. Renny, who upon meeting Jake had said to me, "I completely understand," had parked himself next to the helium tank and filled every single balloon I'd bought.

I recognized they hadn't done all this just for Katy.

They'd done it for me as well.

My heart was full.

So full.

The only thing that would make this party better, fifteen minutes after it had started, was if Evanthe showed up.

So far, however, there was no sign of her.

As I set out trays on the food table, I glanced at Katy. She was playing a round of croquet with her friends, including Daisy, who kept trying to fetch the balls.

It was mayhem.

It was perfect.

How happy she was today was doing my heart good.

I just hoped that later, once the glow wore off, she wouldn't dwell on *who* should've been here and wasn't. Scott.

Juliet came out of the house, a big bowl of macaroni salad in hand. It seemed we had enough food to feed all of Forget-Me-Not.

"When do you think you'll tell them?" She nodded to Aunt Maeve, Isabel, Nettie, Vera, and Renny, who were sitting in a horseshoe shape of folding chairs in the shade of the tent, out of the late-day sun.

Juliet had been with me in the kitchen ten minutes ago when Georgia arrived. As soon as her daughter, Zoe, darted into the backyard to find Katy, Georgia started bouncing up and down. "You got it! You got the house."

I'd nearly cried right then and there and started bouncing with her.

"We can do all the paperwork later," Georgia said, "but I couldn't wait to tell you. I got the call on the ride over."

"Thank you," I said, feeling the sting of tears in my eyes.

"You're most welcome. It's my pleasure. Truly."

I'd looked between her and Juliet. "Let's keep this between us for now, okay? I don't want to detract from Katy's big day."

Both had promised while giving me big hugs.

"They're going to be beyond excited for you," Juliet added now, adjusting one of the battery-operated fans on the table that we were using to help keep bugs away.

I smiled at the group as they chitchatted about the Flour Festival next weekend. Aunt Maeve was currently holding Mary Joy, who was cooing at the lights strung along the canopy. She was smitten with those lights.

I said, "I'll probably tell Papaw tonight and everyone else tomorrow."

He'd been nothing but encouraging this past week about me buying the Library House, but I almost hated to tell him I was officially under contract. I'd loved my time here with him, and suddenly moving felt like a goodbye.

And I didn't like goodbyes.

I turned and looked toward the back of the yard, where Papaw, Callum, Jake, Mr. Daniels, and Georgia were standing between two maple trees, debating on how best to rig up the drago-corn, which looked very little like either creature but *was* absolutely beastly.

The blue glitter took it to a whole other level.

I adored it. So had Katy.

The appearance of Mr. Daniels had come as a bit of a surprise, but it turned out Papaw had invited him. Katy had taken the news in stride but barely spared him a glance when he said hello and wished her a happy birthday.

I was going to have to talk to her about forgiveness and grace.

Tomorrow.

Today was for celebrating.

Speaking of . . . I smiled at Juliet. Grinned, really.

"*What?*" she asked.

"You and Callum?"

Her cheeks started glowing.

I nudged her with my elbow. "I'm just saying, I noticed you two have been awfully chummy today. Are you dating?"

She threw a look his way, smiled. "I'm not really sure what we're doing, but we're determined to enjoy it for as long as we can."

I wasn't sure I could do the same if I were in her shoes, knowing I'd be leaving soon. I just couldn't risk getting hurt like that. Then

I wondered if it was possible that a relationship between them would end up keeping Juliet here, in Forget-Me-Not.

A little glimmer of hope sparked within me at the thought, because I wanted her to stay—I wanted to continue the friendship we'd begun.

"And what about you and Jake?" she asked, turning the tables. "I've noticed *you two* being awfully chummy today."

I had the grace to laugh, because she was right.

I stole a surreptitious glance at him as he tied one end of a rope around a maple trunk. He'd been such a huge help today. He'd run to the store for ice. Filled coolers. Lugged them around the backyard, trying to find the perfect shady spot. He'd arranged tables, covered them in dragon-y tablecloths. He'd charmed Renny and Aunt Maeve and, well, just about everyone he met.

"We're . . ." I shook my head. "You know, I'm not really sure what we are. Friends, I guess."

It seemed deeper than that, but I couldn't say what it was, this feeling. Maybe I'd fallen for him. No. It was too soon for that. But maybe I was *falling*.

She dropped her voice. "Would you like to be more than that?"

I stepped way outside my comfort zone by saying, "I think so."

As if sensing he was being watched, Jake looked my way. Caught me staring. He smiled, and my insides went mushy.

Juliet said, "Hmm. If I had to guess, I'd say he feels the same way."

I blew out a breath and waved her off, not wanting to get my hopes up. "I'm going to grab the platters for the grill. I'll be right back."

"Do you want some help?"

"Thanks, but I've got it."

A small, high-pitched roar came from the side yard as someone made a good croquet shot, and I was smiling as I hurried into the house.

Only to stop dead in my tracks once I reached the kitchen.

Evanthe was studying the cake on the island.

She was dressed in a ruffled blouse and flowy linen pants. Her braid was coiled in a low bun at the nape of her neck. In her hands, she held a gift that was wrapped in blue paper topped with a sparkly blue bow.

"This is beautiful," she said, eyeing the cake's details.

It was. A gold-dusted fondant 3D dragon topped a large sheet cake, its tail curling around an outer edge. The icing mimicked dragon scales, and there were gold sugar beads scattered here and there, looking like treasure.

"The bakery did an amazing job," I said, then I came to my senses. "When did you get here?"

"Only moments ago. The door was open."

I nodded. "I'm glad you're here. I saved a seat for you out—"

She cut me off. "I can't stay."

My heart fell. "No?"

She glanced around the house and offered a sad smile. "I see Tenn has embraced simplicity."

With a start, I realized she probably hadn't been inside since Mamaw passed away.

"Except for the dining room," I said.

She turned, then let out a huff that sounded like a laugh. "June would pitch a fit if she saw that."

I smiled. "Definitely."

Her gaze lingered for a little longer before she took a deep breath and turned back to me, sorrow in her eyes. "She was the best person I've ever known. She deserved so much better from me."

Swallowing hard over a sudden swell of emotion, I could almost feel her grief and suddenly understood why it might be difficult for her to be here. To be reminded of loss. To remember all the time she *hadn't* spent with Mamaw, after her diagnosis.

"Mamaw never—"

"Please give my best to Katy and thank her for the invitation."

She thrust the present at me; then, with a kick of her heel, she rushed down the hallway. As she shoved open the screen door, I hurried after her, thinking about how Nettie had once told me that the only way out was through.

I called out after her, "Are you sure you can't stay?"

She released the kickstand on her bike and looked back at me. I could tell from the lift of her chin, the set of her shoulders, and the flatness in her eyes that she had once again retreated behind her carefully crafted walls.

Her voice was toneless as she said, "I'll see you on Tuesday, Tallulah."

Baby steps, I thought as she put on her helmet and quickly pedaled away. Even though she hadn't stayed, she *had* shown up today. That was a big deal. It was, perhaps, the start of a new beginning, a new chapter, for Evanthe and me.

Which had me thinking about Mamaw. And how proud she'd be right about now.

Of both of us.

A couple of hours later, the piñata lay broken and battered on the lawn. All the candy had been scooped up, squirreled away.

Katy currently sat on a blanket on the grass, surrounded by her friends and discarded wrapping paper from the presents she'd already opened. Everyone else was fanned out around Katy, except for Daisy, who had run herself ragged and was napping underneath a table.

"This one is from Juliet," Katy said, then tore off the wrapping paper with wild abandon. When she opened the box, she simply stared for a moment, before seeking out Juliet, who was standing next to me. There was adoration in Katy's eyes, shining behind her glasses. "I love it! Thank you."

"You're welcome," Juliet said.

"What is it, sprout?" Papaw asked.

Katy carefully reached into the box and lifted up a stunning blue dream catcher, which was intricately webbed with gold thread and beaded with the colors of the rainbow. Feathers dangled from the bottom, swaying gracefully in the breeze. All of Katy's friends moved in for a closer look.

"Did you make that?" I whispered to Juliet.

She nodded.

"It's beautiful."

It was such a thoughtful gift, considering Katy's sleep troubles lately, but it was also very much Katy's aesthetic. The nature aspect, the colors, the folklore of bad dreams being caught in the webbing.

Juliet knew my daughter.

And it was obvious she cared for her.

Katy picked up the next box, a small square. Her voice went flat when she said, "It's from Mr. Daniels. Oh! And Juliet."

Juliet snapped her head to look at Mr. Daniels, who stood on the other side of Papaw. She whispered, "It was supposed to just be from you."

He came to stand next to her and whispered back, "I wouldn't have thought of it if not for you."

Katy was watching them closely, her face a picture of curiosity as she unwrapped the box. Her pale eyebrows nose-dived as she pulled out an oak leaf. She glanced at Juliet and Mr. Daniels, questions stamped all over her small face.

Mr. Daniels held up a finger. "Stay right there." He ran into the house.

I turned to Juliet. "What's all this about?"

"You'll see."

A moment later, Mr. Daniels came out with a flowerpot in his hand. It held only a scraggly stick stuck into soil. He crouched down and set it in front of Katy. "I felt terrible when my trees got sick and I had to take them down. I missed them deeply, so I knew I needed to plant new ones in honor of them. I went to a few nurseries but didn't find anything that felt right. I was being very picky because I knew the new trees would have to be just as special as the old ones. Then, in early springtime, I was walking by your papaw's house and saw his beautiful oak tree, so similar to the ones I'd taken down. Your papaw was gracious enough to let me take some cuttings from that tree, and I've been nursing them along, planning to plant them in my yard when they got big enough. Then Juliet came to me yesterday and suggested that you might like one. Another Bill for you to love. One day, hopefully, this little twig will be as big and grand as he is."

Cautiously, Katy reached out and touched the stick, let her fingers run along the thin bark. Then, in a sudden burst, she lunged forward and threw her arms around Mr. Daniels's neck. He dropped to his knees and slowly put his arms around her. My breath caught and emotions churned.

I glanced at Juliet and knew without a doubt that she didn't just care for Katy. She loved her. For her to know exactly what Katy needed most—and saw that she received it? Well, that was love, pure and simple.

Tears stung my eyes. Clenching my jaw, I told myself to pull it together. To not think about the goodbye ahead.

And how Juliet's heart was going to break as well.

It was the first time I'd considered she was going to be hurt, too, when she left, and I was ashamed I hadn't realized it before.

As Katy showed off Baby Bill, I stuffed down my feelings and checked on Mary Joy, who was nodding off in Nettie's loving arms. I checked on Renny, too. This was a long outing for him. He assured me he was just fine and didn't need a thing, so I doubled back to help with the wrapping paper cleanup, which Jake and Georgia had begun to tackle.

As I bent to collect ribbons and bows, I heard her say to Jake, "Well, if you ever do decide to move here, then I'm happy to help you find a place."

I stopped in my tracks, not sure I'd heard what I thought I heard. "Wait. What do you mean, if he decides to move here?" I faced him. "Don't you already live here?"

His brows dropped low. His voice, too. "Temporarily. Just six weeks. I thought you knew."

Georgia looked between the two of us. Her face paled, and she stepped closer to me, her shoulder bumping mine. Taking sides, as if she sensed the chasm that had just opened up between Jake and me.

I was suddenly having trouble breathing. "But Evanthe doesn't do short-term rentals."

The words came out cracked, broken. I started counting in my head, trying to figure out how long he'd already been here. Then I realized it didn't matter.

He was leaving.

"She made a family exception," he said, taking a step toward me.

I took one step back.

Georgia was talking, low and slow, and I missed half of what she said but picked up the gist of it. He'd recently bought a condo in Florida. Closing took a while. He came here to wait. He'd never intended on staying.

He was *leaving*.

Daisy was leaving.

We were going to have to say goodbye.

Katy was going to be crushed.

And any hopes I'd been harboring crashed to the ground, split open, bled into the lawn.

I felt so *stupid*, for letting my guard down, for thinking that sometimes people stayed put. For thinking that maybe one of the stockings I'd seen hanging on the fireplace in my dreams might have been *his*.

Before I made a total fool of myself, I jerked a thumb over my shoulder. "I need to get the cake."

Jake said, "I can—"

"No." I shook my head, struggled against tears. "*No.*"

Georgia said, "I—"

I shook my head again. She sighed but stepped back. I hurried into the house. I needed to be alone, even if only for a moment.

Once in the kitchen, I bent double, sucked in a breath, and tried to pull myself together.

Just get the cake, carry it outside. Sing the birthday song. After that, everyone would go home. I could give the girls a bath and tuck them in bed for the night. Then I could fall apart. Only then.

I took another deep breath, stood tall, and wiped my eyes.

I could do this.

I *could*.

My hands were shaking as I placed eight candles in front of the dragon's mouth—some of them touching a fondant flame. My hands were *still* shaking when I pulled out my phone to take a couple of quick pictures before I lit the candles. So much so that when I leaned in for a close-up, I lost my grip, and my phone nose-dived into a corner of the cake.

My breath hitched, and I flew into panic mode. I rescued my phone, then tried to fix the cake with my fingers, but it seemed the more I tried to help, the worse it looked.

Taking a step back, I stared in horror at the buttercream covering my fingers, and the damage to the perfect, beautiful cake. Slowly, all the emotions I'd been ignoring started to bubble up.

I tried to hold them in as I washed my hands. But all it took was one more look at the cake, and they spilled over.

I crumbled, sobbing.

A second later, I felt someone at my side. Rubbing my back. Tucking my hair behind my ear.

"What's wrong?" Juliet asked. "Did something happen with Jake? You two looked tense a minute ago."

Nodding, I couldn't stop crying. "And cake," I managed to say, gesturing vaguely toward the disaster. "Dropped my phone."

She stepped away. "Oh no, oh no," she said, her voice rising with each word. A moment later, she pressed tissues into my hand. "We can fix the cake."

I noticed she'd specified the cake. Jake was probably a lost cause.

He was leaving. Oh, it *hurt*.

Leaning against the counter, I sniffled and snuffled. "How?"

Juliet looked all about, as if seeking inspiration. Finally, she snapped her fingers. She turned the oven on to broil, grabbed a baking sheet, and covered it with nonstick foil. Then she found a jar of Marshmallow Fluff in one of the cabinets. In no time flat, she'd spread a thin layer of Fluff on the foil and stuck it under the broiler.

I noted that she had known exactly where to find everything she needed. She was perfectly at home here.

She was in her place.

I could see it easily, but could she?

"The only damage is on this corner," she said, pointing.

I didn't need to be reminded.

"We'll just cut it off and pile toasted marshmallow there to hide the fact that it's missing. We'll make it seem like it was done on purpose, since the dragon is facing in that direction. We'll joke that if you want a fire-breathing dragon cake, then sometimes it comes with consequences."

The kitchen was filling with the sweetest scent of toasted marshmallow, and I felt like I was falling apart, piece by piece.

Gently, Juliet put her hands on my upper arms. "Everything is going to be okay, Tallulah."

I wanted to believe her, I really did, but more tears filled my eyes, giving form to my doubts.

When she hugged me, I all but clung to her like a life raft. Right now, she was the only thing keeping me from drowning.

I managed to say, "Please stay."

She tightened her hold on me and said, "Don't be silly. I'm not going anywhere."

And for now, to carry me through the rest of this night, I pretended that she knew I meant long-term . . . and not solely for the rest of the party.

Twenty-Eight

*A Pearl of Wisdom
from Maeve Hearnshaw*
"*The heart never forgets.*"

Juliet

Please stay.

The words had been a constant companion since Katy's party, swirling and twirling in my head. I had the feeling Tallulah had meant just for the party—to not leave her side—but the plea had resonated with me, making me ask a question of myself that felt big, uncomfortable, overwhelming.

Did I have to go back to Michigan?

There were reasons to return, of course. My family was there. My job. My whole life.

But then there was here, where I felt at peace.

Where it felt like *home*.

It was early Tuesday evening, and I was volunteering at Juneberry, getting absolutely trounced in checkers by Renny. I'd already lost one game and was well on my way to losing another.

I wasn't even trying to let him win. I was simply distracted.

By Tallulah, and the heartbreak she was trying to hide from Katy. From everyone, really.

By the fact that I hadn't found a feather lately.

By how I hadn't had any dreams of my grandfather in days.

I'd started wondering if the feathers had played a role in

bringing those dreams to me. Which sounded nutty but made a strange sort of sense. When the feathers had been on my bedside table, I'd dreamed of him. Since I'd used the feathers to make Katy's dream catcher, there had been nothing. Nothing at all.

I was also preoccupied by the fact that Callum had texted this morning to let me know that the part for my car had finally arrived, and that it should be good as new in a day or two. Which of course made me remember what Tallulah had once said, about how the car wouldn't be fixed until I was ready to go.

Was I ready to go?

Grief had clouded my world for months now, but over these last couple of weeks, it had ebbed a little, letting light back in.

I wasn't fully healed, but apparently, it was enough to set me on the right path forward.

A path that I suspected would lead me right back to where I was. In Forget-Me-Not. Because it had started feeling like home.

Waning sunlight splashed across the floors of Renny's suite, creating prisms. We'd already talked about Tallulah's new house. She'd met with Georgia during her lunch break today to sign all the paperwork, and was hoping for a quick closing date so she could start repairs. Katy had already picked out a spot in the yard to plant Baby Bill when the sapling was big enough.

Renny pointed at me. His voice was strained, thready, as he said, "Is this sudden moping because of Callum? Do I need to speak with him?"

The smile came easily. "Not Callum. He's good. We're good. Getting to know each other. We went hiking yesterday."

He'd had the day off, and we spent it with Katy and Mary Joy, taking them to a nearby state park. When we initially planned the date, we hadn't intended to bring the girls along, but I thought Tallulah might like a day to herself. The fact that she didn't put up any kind of fuss when I suggested the idea told me my intuition had been spot-on.

Distant music floated down the hall and into the room. Lively notes, sparkly and bubbly. A concerto I knew but couldn't name.

"I heard you took the little ones," Renny said with a lift of his wiry eyebrows. He coughed once, twice, then added, "Hardly a romantic date."

Even as I wondered who'd told him, I thought about how Callum had carried Mary Joy in a pack on his back for hours in the heat, never complaining. More than once, I'd caught him tickling her toes, making her shriek with giggles. He'd played This or That with Katy and me, which I realized was his way of trying to get to know me better. I pictured him holding Katy's hand, to help her cross a creek. Then how he'd done the same for me. I saw him teaching Katy about the plants on the trail, pointing out poison ivy and prairie clover and wild sunflowers. I saw him on a picnic blanket, trying to spoon baby food into Mary Joy's constantly moving mouth without spilling. I saw patience. And protectiveness. And selflessness. And love.

"I wouldn't be so sure about that," I said softly, feeling warm and fuzzy.

"Really now?" Renny puffed out his chest, smoothed his mustache. "Glad to hear it. What's with the pout then?"

"Am I pouting?" I pushed my lips forward. Way forward.

"Please stop. That's disturbing. I am disturbed."

I laughed and slid a checker diagonally. "I'll have you know duck lips are quite a popular pose for taking selfies."

"How unfortunate." He double-jumped two of my pieces. "I also noticed you deflected the question. Why the pout?"

I didn't really want to bring up Tallulah's pain, and talking about the feathers would possibly make me sound bonkers, so I settled on a topic close to my heart. "I was just thinking about my grandfather. I miss him. Most of all, I miss *remembering* him. I can only recall bits and pieces."

He steepled his fingers, and his brown eyes were full of empathy as he said, "Not remembering must feel like added grief. Atop of losing him. An extra helping, so to speak."

I nodded, surprised he understood. Not many did. "A double whammy."

"As if one helping wasn't enough."

I slid another checker across the board. "Exactly."

"Life is much too hard," he said, adjusting the oxygen cannula under his nose.

I nodded. He would know.

"What kind of things have you remembered about him?" he asked.

I smiled, thinking of those fragments, as I told him about the teddy bear picnic, the unauthorized zoo trip, the way he'd gently brush my hair in the mornings.

Renny steepled his fingers, his gaze on me. There was a twinkle in his eyes. "He sounds like a man who loved you—loved his family—very much."

I nodded. "He was. I know that. I just wish I could remember more of his life. Of the time we had together."

"I can tell those moments are in your heart, even if you can't remember them. I hear the love in your voice." Then, in one smooth move, he jumped my last three checker pieces, clearing the board and chuckling. "You should ask Katy to give you lessons."

Laughing, I said, "I don't think you really want that."

"You're right. I don't." He coughed, then reached into his pocket and pulled out a handkerchief to wipe the corners of his mouth.

I'd been with him for about an hour now and could see his energy waning, so I cleaned up the game. "Can I get you a drink? Something to eat? Or are you ready for me to go so you can get some rest?"

"I'm just fine. You know, you sounded rather official right then." He stood and made his way to the bed, taking tentative, small steps. "You're enjoying volunteering?"

I hurried to help him with his oxygen tank, then pulled back his covers so he could slide in between the cool sheets. Once in bed, he leaned forward, and I fluffed his pillows behind his back, giving him support to sit up.

"Very much so," I said.

"Maeve mentioned she's going to be hiring another nurse soon."

"Oh?" I sat in the upholstered chair next to his bed and tried to pretend my heart hadn't just started bopping around.

While volunteering here, I couldn't help but notice the work done by the nurses. In addition to administering medications, managing symptoms, changing bandages, charting, they listened, they cared, they nurtured. The amount of time they were able to spend with each patient—and their family—was something I'd always wanted out of my career.

"It's not an easy job to work here. You've got to use your heart as much as your head. You've got to be compassionate. Caring. You've got to be willing to lose in checkers. Don't suppose you might know a nurse who'd be interested in applying for the job?"

"Maybe," I said, trying not to sound overeager.

Was I really thinking about staying here, in Forget-Me-Not? Like, seriously considering it? Picking up and moving my life down here? Starting fresh?

I *was*.

It made me giddy and nauseated at the same time.

But why not? I was happy here.

My family would understand that. Right?

"I'll take a maybe. Now, tell me more about your family," he said, as if knowing I'd just been thinking about them. Then he started coughing again. I jumped up and got him a glass of water.

After the fit passed and he took a few sips, I set the glass on his nightstand, next to an iPad, his cell phone, and a stack of books, most of them from the library. But atop the teetering pile was an old green book, clothbound and tattered along its edges. I bent to read the spine. *Leaves of Grass*, by Walt Whitman. It appeared well used. Well loved.

He saw me looking. "A gift from *my* Walt, way back when."

I sat down again. "I heard you talking about him last week with Callum."

A smile ghosted across his face. "Have you ever been in love, Juliet? The kind of love that's all-consuming? The kind that takes over your life, heart and soul?"

I ran a finger along the chair's trim, a thick cord of yellow velvet. "Not yet."

Though I wondered if what I was feeling for Callum was love stirring, starting, *awakening*.

"Give it time," he said.

Time. It was the one thing Callum and I didn't have.

Not unless I moved here.

My chest tight, I said, "Where did you two meet? You and your Walt?"

"Here, in Forget-Me-Not. He arrived much like you did, lost and in need of direction. His car broke down in front of my house. Orange smoke."

I knew from Tallulah that meant Walt had a painful decision to make.

Renny looked at me. "It was the early '60s. A hot June day. He came inside to use the phone, and that was that. I fell fast, I fell hard."

His voice was stronger now, as if his memories had given him a surge of energy, strength.

"He rented a room in town, and despite his car being fixed, he stayed for nearly a month. It was a different time, another era. We had to hide a lot of ourselves—at that point, neither of our families knew—but everyone with eyes could see we were inseparable." He cleared his throat. "Then he was gone, called back to where he'd come from after his father took ill. A few weeks after he left, I received that book in the mail. The inscription is a quote from one of the poems inside: 'Will you give me yourself? will you come travel with me? Shall we stick by each other as long as we live?'"

A passing cloud darkened the room. "He was asking you to come to him."

He nodded. "His father was still ill, and he felt he couldn't leave, to come back here."

"Did you go?" I asked.

"No."

I could feel his pain, his heartbreak. "Why?"

He closed his eyes. "He had another path he needed to walk."

Leaning forward, I reached for his hand. His skin was warm, soft. "I don't understand."

He blinked and looked at me. "If we were meant to be, he wouldn't have been able to leave town. I had to let him go, to live the life he'd been destined for. We exchanged letters for a while. It took a year, but his father ended up making a full recovery. But by then, he'd moved on, I moved on. The letters dwindled. Then stopped. I found love again, and I'm sure he did as well. He's a lovable guy. As hard as it is to accept sometimes, what is meant to be is meant to be, and what isn't, isn't." He pulled his hands back and clasped them on his chest. "Now, tell me more about your family. We got sidetracked."

I didn't really want to talk about my family—I wanted to know more about him and Walt and what he'd meant by saying that Walt wouldn't have been able to leave town. But I decided not to push. He was tired.

So, I leaned back in the chair and described my parents, my brothers, my sister, my nieces. I told him how I'd come to realize that my need to be noticed, seen by them, was because I hadn't felt loved by them.

And how I was realizing I'd been wrong about that.

People expressed love differently, was all.

I wasn't sure at what point he'd fallen asleep, but I stayed by his side, watching his chest rise and fall.

At some point, I heard a gentle throat-clearing behind me. Callum stood in the doorway, and at the sight of him, my breath caught, and there was a pitter-patter in my chest.

Love stirring.

As quietly as I could, I made my way over to him, nudging him into the hallway. I closed the door behind us.

There was a moment when we stood there, barely six inches apart, simply looking at each other. It should've been awkward. Goofy. But it wasn't.

He was freshly showered, his hair damp and curling around his neck. He smelled of cedar. He had on a white button-down and jeans.

"I wasn't expecting to see you here," I said.

"I was hoping I could talk you into a late supper."

I nodded. "I'd like that. Very much so."

He smiled. "Hey, pizza or Chinese food?"

It took me a moment to catch on that he was playing This or That. "Pizza." I tossed a question back. "Take out or sit down?"

"Tough one. I'll say take out."

"Me, too."

I realized we'd probably just decided our plans for the night, which sounded absolutely perfect to me.

"How's he doing?" Callum asked, nodding to Renny's room.

I lifted my hand, wiggled it side to side. "He wiped the floor with me in checkers, but he's tiring more easily these days."

Compassion flared in his blue eyes. "I know he's in the best place he can possibly be, but I hate this for him. I wish you could've known him before he got sick."

I didn't want to tell him how it felt like I'd always known Renny. Maeve and Tenn, too. Like they'd always been friends. *Family.* "I'm not sure I could handle that level of sassiness."

"Please. He'd have you under his spell in no time flat."

"Probably so." I checked the time. My shift had ended five minutes ago. I motioned for him to follow me down the hallway, so our voices wouldn't wake Renny. "He told me about Walt."

"I'm not surprised. Walt is one of his favorite topics."

We made our way toward the sunroom, my favorite space at the cottage. The fading light filtering through the windows felt magical, and the overstuffed sofas and chairs were begging to be curled up on. There were plants all about the room, large, small, and in between. It was a space that felt peaceful, and I had the feeling it had been designed that way.

We sat side by side on the love seat, and I said, "I can't help wishing that they had a different ending, but there was something he mentioned about Walt leaving that I didn't understand. I didn't want to push, because he was exhausted, but I'm wondering if you know the answer."

"About?" he asked.

"He said that if Walt was meant to stay, then he wouldn't have been able to leave."

Callum nodded. "If a lost soul finds love in Forget-Me-Not, and if that love is meant to be, their car will keep breaking down until they realize they are right where they belong." He smiled. "They won't even make it to the county line."

"You're not serious."

"Oh, but I am. It's another one of the quirks of this town, and we accept it, the same way we accept the legend of the library cat."

"But that doesn't make sense. If Walt loved Renny, doesn't that mean Walt shouldn't have been able to leave town?"

Callum leaned forward again, clasped his hands. "Based on the town folklore, yes, that should be true. But there are exceptions. Walt was needed at home. Because of his great love for his father, his family, he was allowed to go."

I frowned. "Renny must know that, right?"

Nodding, he said, "He does, but according to my gran, he was in so much pain after Walt left that the only way he could get through his grief was to tell himself over and over again that it wasn't meant to be. It became a part of the story. He ended up believing it, which is why he didn't go to Walt after the book was sent. He fully believed destiny had already made the choice. He still believes it."

I could only shake my head. Renny had once told me his and Walt's love story was bittersweet, and there wasn't a better description. I hurt for him, for Walt, and for what could have been.

I shifted, uncomfortable. This was all so much to take in, but something was bothering me more than anything else.

I absolutely hated the idea that leaving—or staying—in Forget-Me-Not might not be up to me.

That it was up to destiny.

And what was meant to be.

Twenty-Nine

A Pearl of Wisdom
from Renny Russo
"I've been alive many years, and if there's one thing I know for sure, it's this. If there's grief, there's love, plain and simple."

Tallulah

I wasn't planning to go.

Earlier, I'd even warned Katy that there was a chance we'd once again miss the evening walk with Jake and Daisy, just like last night. She'd been disappointed but hadn't pushed. It was clear to me she understood something was going on. She could see my sadness.

Yet at a little before six thirty, I found myself wandering into the dining room. I peeked out a window, toward Vera's house, and saw Jake standing at the end of the driveway, Daisy at his feet.

He was looking this way.

Waiting.

For me, and Katy, and Mary Joy.

My heartstrings were being pulled, *plucked*, even while I was silently cursing myself for looking out the window in the first place.

If I hadn't seen, I wouldn't have known.

But now I knew.

"Katy," I called out.

It was probably for the best just to get this over and done with.

Get the awkwardness out of the way. I couldn't keep avoiding him, though I wanted to.

My reaction to the news that Jake's stay here in Forget-Me-Not was temporary hadn't been his fault. He'd never led me on. He'd never been anything but friendly. Neighborly. Nice. Kind. Funny. Handsome.

Stop, I told myself. *Just stop.*

Within a few minutes, we were out the door. Katy shot ahead of me to say hi to Mr. Daniels, who was watering his shrubs. Big bold hydrangea blooms were sagging under the weight of the water, but I knew they'd perk right back up once they dried off.

I was heartened by the budding friendship growing between her and this kind man. She'd needed to understand that sometimes people would do things she might not understand. That perhaps there was a reason behind what some might deem madness. He'd taught her that lesson, and she would definitely grow from it.

Yesterday she'd brought him her sapling, so he could continue to nurse it until it was ready to plant. He promised she could visit whenever she wanted, then showed her where he planned to plant *his* tree. She had approved of the plan, as though she had a say.

Now, as I considered it, maybe she did.

As Mary Joy and I made our way slowly down the sidewalk, I tried not to look ahead. I couldn't help myself, though. Jake still waited for us, his pensive gaze unwavering.

Ordinarily, he'd smile, wave, or even start toward us.

These weren't ordinary times, however.

These were uncharted waters.

Muddy, murky waters.

Mary Joy was in her fabric carrier instead of her stroller. I was grateful she was so close, giving me someone to hold on to.

The sky was streaked with orange and red, and Mary Joy's strawberry blond hair looked like spun gold in the evening light.

A mourning dove bopped around the street, splashing in the puddles that Mr. Daniels's watering had created.

Once Katy rejoined us, she stopped to watch the bird, crouching low to get a good look.

"Mama, it looks like she's wearing makeup!"

I crouched low, too, keeping a hand on Mary Joy's back. The dove had a thin band of blue around her eyes that looked like eyeliner. "It does," I said, smiling. "She's beautiful."

"Do you know mourning doves symbolize hope and peace?" she asked in her teaching voice.

She'd been dropping these little tidbits of information ever since opening Evanthe's birthday gift: a book on bird folklore and symbolism and a stuffed owl that hooted when its belly was pressed.

"I didn't," I said, thinking I could use some hope and peace right about now.

When we stood up again, she took my hand. I saw the concern in her eyes when she looked up at me, and I smiled to reassure her that I was okay.

I was.

I *was*.

I mean, yes, I felt a bit ill when I looked at Jake, a debilitating mix of humiliation and heartache, but I was okay. I wasn't sure why this felt so much like a breakup when we hadn't even been dating.

Yet my heart hurt.

And when Daisy's tail started wagging at the sight of Katy, it actually brought tears to my eyes.

Suddenly I knew this wasn't going to go well.

I took some calming breaths and tried to arrange my features into a neutral look.

Katie skipped ahead to kneel down in front of Daisy to give her lots of love and said, "Hi, Mr. Jake!"

Jake handed her the leash, as had become custom, and said, "Hey, Katy."

"Mama, can I go ahead?"

I nodded, and the pair ran off, toward the arch at the end of the street. The sound of her tennis shoes slapping the ground and the jingle of Daisy's tags lingered behind.

Jake's dark gaze swung to me. "Hi."

"Hello," I said, looking him in the eye, then quickly away.

He reached out and took hold of Mary Joy's hand, giving it a wiggle. He smiled. "Hi there, cutie."

She kicked her legs and made happy noises.

"Is that a new tooth I see?" he asked her.

It was. It had popped through this morning, and I was hoping it meant her teething pains would let up for a while. The drool rash, too. I just couldn't seem to get rid of it for good—it kept coming back.

She grinned at him and I said, "We should catch up to Katy."

As he stepped back, nodded, I tried not to notice the sadness in his eyes.

We walked side by side, a good arm's length apart, and I tried not to think about how on our previous walks, we would stand so close that sometimes our arms would bump. Those days were over.

Mary Joy cooed along with the songs of the cicadas and crickets and frogs. As we passed under the arch and into the sun garden, Katy allowed Daisy to sniff every tree, post, and bench they came across. She had, I decided, more patience than I ever would.

As Jake and I followed the pair around the circle, he said, "I heard you signed papers on the house. Congratulations."

"Thanks," I said.

There. See? I could do this.

"When's move-in day?"

"I close in two weeks. It being a cash sale expedited things."

I assumed he had a mortgage for his new condo, which was

why his closing was taking six weeks. Or maybe the sellers needed time to pack and move. Even though I was curious, I didn't ask.

"I'm glad. I know you wanted to get in as soon as possible. Are you ready for the renovation?"

"As I'll ever be. I have the feeling I'll be scraping wallpaper for years."

We walked in silence for a moment before he said, "I'm glad you came out tonight."

I nodded, wishing I were home. "It's a nice night."

I kept telling myself to be friendlier, but I just couldn't summon up that kind of fakery.

After a moment, he said, "I really thought you knew, Tallulah. I wasn't trying to hide anything."

Oh no. I didn't want to get into this. I glanced at Katy and willed her to pick up the pace.

"I believe you," I finally said, and threw him a bone. "I was just taken by surprise. Sorry."

"Sorry for what? You didn't do anything."

For falling for you, I wanted to say, but instead said, "For overreacting. I'm actually embarrassed. I just thought—" I cut myself off, not wanting to say too much, reveal too much, though I supposed that cat was already out of the bag.

"What?"

I walked a little faster. "Nothing. It doesn't matter." I stuffed my feelings down, down, down.

"I think it does."

Tears stung my eyes, but I blinked them away before he could see them. "Jake?"

"Yeah?"

"Can we talk about something else?"

He pulled in a deep breath. "Okay. What do you want to talk about?"

I looked up at the sky, pleading with the heavens. "The weather?"

"All right."

For the rest of the walk, we chatted about different kinds of clouds and the tropical storm in the Atlantic, and how there were many different types of fog.

Well. He did most of the talking. I did a lot of *mm-hmm*-ing.

When we made it back to Vera's, I tried to joke, saying, "You seem to know a lot about the weather. Are you a forecaster?"

But my voice fell flat. My heart just wasn't in it.

He shook his head, looking as miserable as I felt.

I didn't think I could take another minute of this.

I looked over at Katy. Daisy had towed her to a fire hydrant across the street, where she was having the time of her life sniffing all the smells. "Katy, you can stay for a few minutes more, but I'm going to head home and get Mary Joy's bath ready, okay?"

She patted Daisy's back. "How many minutes?"

I hated to hurry her along. "Ten."

She smiled, and I turned to meet Jake's gaze. I wasn't sure what to say.

He shifted foot to foot. "Will I see you tomorrow night?"

I glanced at the skies again, praying. "Probably not."

I'd ask Papaw to bring Katy down to visit Daisy. I didn't want to take that away from her, since Daisy would be leaving soon.

Jake jammed his hands into his pocket. "I understand."

I took a deep breath, and it felt like my heart was cracking open. "Bye, Jake."

"Goodbye, Tallulah."

Despite how hard I was trying to keep them at bay, tears filled my eyes as I walked away.

I'd made it only a few feet when I heard him say, "If it means anything, you make me want to stay."

My knees had gone weak, but somehow I found the strength to turn around. I could barely see through the tears in my eyes. "Are you still leaving?"

It took a moment, but he nodded. "I just bought a condo . . . My friends and most of my family are in Florida."

I started walking backward, away from him, away from the hopes I'd had. "Then it doesn't mean anything at all."

Thirty

A Pearl of Wisdom
from Nettie Getchell
"Darlin', if they wanted to, they would."

Juliet

It had been a strange week.

And it was currently being made stranger by my sister. All I'd said was that I'd met someone, and Amy had gotten quiet.

"Amy? I thought you'd be squealing. Jumping up and down. Lighting off firecrackers. What happened to you being a romantic at heart?"

"Hold on," she said.

I shook a rattle in front of Mary Joy. She grabbed it and shoved it in her mouth. She had another tooth coming in, and her mouth rash was angry this morning, bright red. I'd put some ointment on it, but it didn't seem to be helping.

She'd been listless, too, and crying more than usual. Right now she was sitting on a blanket, legs wide for balance, as she played with an assortment of toys.

It was Friday morning, a little past nine. Tallulah was on her way to work. In the dining room, Tenn was singing loudly—he had his headphones on, thank goodness—while he rolled ink onto his lino block. I was sitting on the floor with Mary Joy, worrying about her.

I shifted the phone on my ear. "I'm regretting telling you."

"I said *hold on*."

"Bossy!"

She then put me on mute. Mute! I had half a mind to hang up.

There was a light rap on the front door; then it opened. "Hello!" Maeve called out. "Is the coffee hot?"

I leaned backward to see down the hallway. "Hi! There's only tea today. The coffeepot called it quits this morning."

She was dressed for work in wide-legged slacks and a floral blouse. Her hair was pulled back in a large clip. "Frankly, I'm amazed it held on so long. It's nearly as old as Lu."

I loved how Maeve dropped by in the mornings on her way to work, because I knew it had more to do with checking in on her brother, Tallulah, and the girls than getting a free cup of coffee. She was a nurturer at heart.

She put the kettle on, then stuck her head in the dining room. Tenn suddenly yelled, "Good morning!"

"Headphones, Tenn!" she said, gesturing. "Headphones."

He laughed, the sound floating from room to room, lighting the place up. "Forgot I had them on."

He was excited to have progressed to the inking part of his project, and his cheeriness was more than welcome, since it had been rather tense here this week.

Tallulah's efforts to hide her heartache continued.

Our couch time, as we'd come to call it, had been put on hold.

On Monday, I'd come downstairs at midnight for a glass of water and found her at the kitchen island, working on her Trivia Night proposal. "Couldn't sleep," she'd said sadly, her eyes red-rimmed.

On Tuesday, I spent way too much time chasing a robin around the yard, trying to see its chest. When I finally got a good look, I realized it wasn't *my* robin and had myself a good cry. I hadn't seen the robin with the white chest marking in days—or found any new feathers.

I still wasn't dreaming.

On Wednesday, day camp wrapped up, and Katy mourned, even though she'd see most of the friends she'd made next week, when she started third grade.

On Thursday, yesterday, the tide had started to turn.

I'd gotten my car back.

Vera had asked Katy if she'd like to help her prep for the Flour Festival, which was where Katy was now.

Mary Joy had mastered sitting up.

Katy continued her streak of no nightmares.

And I'd decided to stay here in Forget-Me-Not.

As soon as I made the choice, I'd sent my resignation to my boss, effective immediately, apologizing profusely for the late notice. I didn't give a reason, because I wanted to let my family know first. I could only hope they'd understand my choice.

Mary Joy heard Tenn's laugh and looked up, smiled, and then dropped the rattle so she could scratch her neck. When she kept scratching, I squinted, then leaned in, trying to get a better look at what was bothering her.

Was that a hive?

When Mary Joy reached for another toy in front of her, I tried lifting her chin, but she wasn't having it and let me know by letting out an outraged screech.

"It's okay," I said to her. "I just want to take a little look at—"

She squawked again, voicing her displeasure.

"All *right*," I said, letting her be while I formulated a plan.

Amy finally came back on the line, saying, "Juliet, you still there?"

"I grew gray hair, but yes."

"Ha-ha. Define *met someone*."

"You sound like Mom again."

She gasped, then forced a laugh, high and reedy. "Really? You're so funny!"

I pulled the phone away from my ear, stared at it, before saying, "That's it. I'm hanging up. I'll call you later."

"But—"

"Bye!"

I ended the call, then pretty much tackled Mary Joy, laying her onto her back. She giggled, thinking it was a game. I tipped her chin upward. There were several hives on her neck, raised and warm. "Oh no."

Maeve came into the living room. "What's wrong, honey?"

"Mary Joy has hives on her neck." I picked the baby up, held her close, and handed her back the rattle.

Maeve's eyes went wide. "From what?"

My brain was sliding pieces of a puzzle together, and I was kicking myself for not recognizing sooner what had been right in front of me. "I'm wondering if she might have a food allergy. I can't be sure, of course, but it makes sense with how the rash on her mouth comes and goes the way it does. It's probably not a drool rash at all."

"An allergy? Have mercy. But wouldn't she be having trouble breathing? You always see that on TV."

"With kids, most often it's a series of mild responses, like a rash and hives, before a severe reaction like anaphylactic shock. That's the breathing trouble you're thinking of."

Worry creased Maeve's forehead, drew the corners of her lips downward. "Poor little munchkin. What's she eaten today?"

With Mary Joy cuddled in my lap, I rocked side to side. "Tallulah fed her the usual breakfast of yogurt and oatmeal. Wait. Tenn made scrambled eggs. He gave her a few bites. I'm not sure she's had those before."

I brushed Mary Joy's wispy hair off her forehead. Then I recalled that she'd had a bad reaction the day she'd eaten pancakes. The pancakes that had eggs in them.

"Does she need to go to the emergency room?" Maeve asked.

As a school nurse, I'd seen more than a few children experiencing allergic reactions, and rarely did hives require medical intervention other than an oral antihistamine or steroid treatment if the hives were especially bad. "Since the hives are limited to her neck, I don't think so, but Tallulah should call the pediatrician's office to get their opinion and let them know what's going on."

I picked up my phone to call Tallulah, then decided to send a text instead so she wouldn't flat-out panic when she saw my name on her caller ID.

Me: Mary Joy is fine. Just fine. But she developed some hives after eating a few bites of Tenn's scrambled eggs. Suspect she might be allergic to eggs.

A moment later, my phone dinged with a response.

Tallulah: OMG. I'll call her doctor. Are you sure she's okay?

Me: A little itchy but otherwise good

Tallulah: I know she's due for her nap soon but can you bring her by?

I recognized her need to see for herself that Mary Joy was okay.

Me: Absolutely

Tallulah: Until we know more, no eggs!!!

Tallulah: And thank you.

I was glad she was going to call Mary Joy's doctor. And even more grateful that eggs would be cut out of her diet until further notice.

Because I was worried.

Mary Joy had only eaten one or two bites of Tenn's eggs. If that small amount had produced this kind of reaction, I shuddered to think about what might happen the next time.

Before heading to the library, I left Mary Joy with Tenn and ran over to Vera's house to make sure Katy didn't want to come along. But the minute I walked into the kitchen, I'd known she wouldn't want to leave with me. Because Daisy was there, sitting at Katy's feet, watching her adoringly.

Theirs was a mutual kind of love.

"We're dog-sitting," Vera said with an odd look in her eyes I couldn't quite identify.

Katy sullenly said, "Daisy's leaving soon."

Oh, how my heart broke for her. "I know," I said. "I'm sorry. But I'm glad you're getting this extra time with her today."

She nodded. "Me, too."

Before I left, I promised to pick out a few books for her, and when I walked back outside, I saw that Jake was packing up his truck. Suddenly I realized Katy's *soon* hadn't been referring to weeks from now.

It meant *today*.

Uh-oh.

"Hey," I said as he tucked a computer monitor into his truck's cab.

"Hi, Juliet," he said back, his voice flat, distracted.

"Going somewhere?"

"Home." He winced as he said the word, as if it were barbed and had drawn blood.

Honestly, he looked as bad as Tallulah had lately. Pale. Dark circles. Like every bone in his body hurt. Every muscle. Especially his heart.

It made no sense to me why he'd leave. It was clear he cared for her.

"Today?" I asked, even though it was fairly obvious.

He nodded. "It's just . . . I just—" He broke off, shaking his head.

"I'm sorry to hear that. I know a few other people who will be, too."

He met my gaze. "You, of all people, should understand why I can't stay. My whole life is in Florida. Just like yours is in Michigan."

A robin sang nearby, and I searched for it but couldn't find it.

I crossed my arms. "Is it, though? Isn't life where you choose to *live* it?"

I stopped myself from telling him that I'd decided to move here. I still wanted my family to be the first to know.

"It's not that simple," he said.

I wanted to tell him to stay. Beg him, really. For Tallulah's sake. But he sounded like his mind was already made up. So instead, I said, "I'd just make sure that the life you're going back to is worth leaving something so special behind. Safe travels, Jake."

I gave him a sad smile as I walked away, back to Tenn's, to pick up Mary Joy and head to the library, where I definitely would *not* be telling Tallulah that Jake was leaving today.

She'd know soon enough.

And her heart was going to break all over again.

Thirty-One

A Pearl of Wisdom
from Evanthe Kilburn
"Where better to find magic than in the pages of a book?"

Juliet

Sunlight drenched the library, filling it with brightness and a sense of happiness.

The moment Mary Joy and I had come inside, Tallulah came rushing around the front desk. She was now holding the baby and was giving her a good once-over. She lifted her arms, inspected her thighs. The hives on her neck were fading, barely visible now.

"I just got off the phone with Dr. Brown. He said to give her an antihistamine if she's still showing symptoms and recommended a specialist for allergy testing. He also warned me that it could take months to get an appointment. Months!"

I wasn't the least bit surprised to hear that. Specialist appointments were often booked well in advance.

"I hate thinking that I was feeding her something that was making her sick," she added, hugging Mary Joy so tightly the baby fussed.

"You didn't know. And we don't even know if it *is* an egg allergy. It's just a suspicion."

She wrinkled her nose. "It makes sense, though, doesn't it? Some of her fussiest times lately were after she'd eaten food with eggs in it, like fettucine and pancakes. Today was the first time she had eggs on their own, and look what happened."

I nodded. "I'm glad she'll be getting tested."

"Me, too," she said, looking at her daughter, "but no eggs for you in the meantime. I'd rather be safe than sorry." She glanced at me. "I did a quick search after you called. I can't believe how many things have eggs. Bread, mayonnaise, cookies, salad dressings, *marshmallow*! I'm so glad she didn't have any of Katy's birthday cake."

Tallulah's insistence that Mary Joy not have sweets until she was older might have protected her from a potentially terrible reaction.

"Thanks for bringing her in," she said. "I just—"

I smiled. "I know." Then I looked over my shoulder, at the children's section. "I promised Katy I'd bring her a few books."

"Anything with a touch of magic in them will be a big hit. Fantasy titles, especially. Fables. Mythical creatures. Actually, any animal"—she shuddered—"even snakes."

I shuddered along with her, then motioned toward Mary Joy, knowing how Tallulah's boss felt about the little ones being at work. "Do you want me to take her?"

"Not yet." Then she dropped her voice. "Evanthe's in a meeting. She'll never know."

"I'll hurry," I said, already walking away.

The library was busier than I'd ever seen it. People milled about, browsing. Several people were cozied up in the reading area. Someone was sleeping at a desk near the window, their head resting on an open book. Two teens were parked at the computers, earbuds in, tapping away. The muffled voices of small children vibrated in the air. Some sort of craft activity was taking place in the community room.

The children's section was quiet, probably due to the crafting going on. A woman sat with a young girl near the window, reading a book, but otherwise, I had the area to myself. As I scanned titles, I couldn't help feeling like someone was watching me.

I turned around and saw Deckle sitting on a shelf, his tail swaying. He was wearing a new pink collar. His name tag dangled, sparkling in the sunlight.

"Well, hello there."

I thought about what I'd learned of the town, its history, and couldn't help looking at him in a whole new way. It was quite the legacy he was shouldering.

I scratched behind his ears. "I like your new collar."

Purrs vibrated against my fingers.

I was still petting him when he suddenly reached out a paw and knocked a book off the shelf. It happened so fast I could hardly believe my eyes.

Yet there was a book at my feet, face down.

I swallowed hard. Deckle bumped my hand with his head and blinked, his golden eyes shimmering.

I knew what I was supposed to do, but I wasn't sure I wanted to do it.

And just then, I heard the tweet of a robin. Puzzled, I glanced around. The young girl near the window had a stuffed robin in her hand. When she squeezed it, it chirped, making my heart beat faster.

I thought of the robin that had been traveling with me, the feathers it had been giving me, and the dreams of my grandfather.

If the book contained another memory of him, didn't I want that?

Didn't I want that more than anything?

As I touched the scar at my neck, I glanced at Deckle and kept hearing in my head how it was a gift to have a book chosen by him.

"All right," I said quietly, bending down to pick up the book.

As I straightened, I flipped the book over to see the cover.

The Lightning Thief.

I narrowed my gaze at Deckle. "Seriously?"

His whiskers twitched and his tail swished.

"Fine," I said.

Unsure what I was getting myself into, I took a deep breath and let the book fall open, the pages fluttering gracefully. When they settled, I skimmed a few lines of text. In the chapter, one of the characters was dreaming about a storm. There were flashes of light. Thunder.

I broke out in a sweat.

Deckle took a step closer to me. His fur brushed my elbow.

I took it as encouragement.

My hands were shaking as I slowly lifted the book to my nose, closed my eyes, and inhaled deeply, my nose tingling with the scent of paper and ink.

In a blink, images came. They flew in quick as hummingbirds, one after another, so fast they blurred together.

Then they slowed, and I saw my grandfather and me walking side by side.

I recognized his blue spring coat, my green jacket. His gray flat cap, my ball cap, my ponytail pulled through the hole at the back.

Hats that would be blasted off our heads only moments later.

"I don't like the look of that sky," I said, eyeing the dark clouds that had blocked out all sunshine.

He glanced upward. "There was no rain in the forecast."

That was true. Only a few minutes before, the skies had been blue.

His eyes twinkled, the pale green glittering in the gloomy light, as he added, "Besides, a little rain never hurt anyone, Jules."

As if the heavens agreed with him, the clouds suddenly burst open and rain poured down.

He started laughing, his face tipped toward the sky. Then he started dancing, a pretend partner in his arms as he turned in a slow circle. "Isn't it glorious, sweetheart?"

As I put my hood up over my hat, I couldn't resist smiling. His joy was endearing, radiant. He'd always loved dancing in the rain.

He did a little shuffle toward me and held out his hand. "Care to join me?"

I figured why not—I was already soaked. I slipped my hand into his, felt his fingers fold over mine, lovingly, protectively, just like they'd been doing my whole life long.

We laughed together as he twirled me, round and round, right up until the air crackled and a luminous bolt split the sky.

The next thing I knew, I was in the hospital.

Now, here at the Forget-Me-Not Library, I remembered everything.

My eyes flew open.

Woozy, I sat down, propping myself against the bookshelf. I was having trouble pulling in enough air, and I forced myself to take even breaths.

Deckle hopped down from the shelf and climbed into my lap. He put his paws on my chest and lay down.

"I remember," I whispered, my voice shaky.

My whole *body* trembled.

Because I remembered *everything*.

Not just my grandfather, but my childhood, too. The images that had zipped by were now clear as day. Holidays and school days and every day in between. My sister, my brothers, my parents. Old memories that I thought had been lost forever were all there, waiting for me to sift through.

Tears sprang to my eyes, and my breath hitched. In my head, I could hear my grandfather's laughter, and I thought it might be the sweetest sound I'd ever heard. His last moments had been happy ones. Glorious, even.

It was a small consolation in the greater whole.

He was still gone.

But maybe, just maybe, there had been nothing I could've done to prevent it.

The storm hadn't been predicted and had popped up so fast.

It had been a freak accident. That was all.

A tragedy where there was no one to blame.

It was hard to understand, harder to accept. Nearly impossible. But I had to try.

When I heard nearby voices, I wiped my eyes and then wrapped my arms around Deckle, pretty much using him as fluffy armor. When two women rounded the corner, I thought I might be seeing things. Straight up hallucinating.

But then my sister said, "Shut. Up. There *is* a cat!"

And my mom said, "Juliet! What's wrong, baby?"

I couldn't answer because I had burst into tears.

Thirty-Two

A Pearl of Wisdom
from Isabel Espinoza
"If the past calls, you do not have to answer."

Tallulah

Fridays at the library were proving to be the day that brought out the lunacy, the absurdity, the foolishness, the madness, the shenanigans.

Needless to say, it had been quite the morning.

First the news of Mary Joy and her potential egg allergy.

Then Juliet's mom, Lydia, and sister, Amy, had shown up unexpectedly, claiming they wanted to surprise Juliet and also see the Flour Festival.

Not too long after they left, there had been a skirmish in the garden between two members of the local garden club wherein the word *hoe* had been thrown around quite a bit.

One of our regulars, Wooly Joe (I don't know the origin of his nickname), who was a devoted arachnophile, thought the little ones taking part in the "Itsy Bitsy Spider" craft program would enjoy seeing live tarantulas. He let three of them loose in the community room.

Surprisingly, the children *were* fascinated.

Their library grown-ups, however, were not.

There was much screaming. And afterward, Nettie had needed a lie-down.

One of our teenage patrons decided to start rearranging the

shelves according to color because it was "more aesthetically pleasing." Isabel was still sorting that mess.

To top it all off, one of the toilets overflowed again, and I swear I heard Jed muttering about retirement.

I didn't blame him. Not even a little. He was past the usual age for retiring, way past, plus public *toilets*. The man was a *saint*.

All those events had happened before noon, and I'd been more than ready for my lunch break. After I finished eating, I'd lingered in the break room until the last possible minute, hoping the afternoon proved less chaotic than the morning.

As I headed back to the circ desk, I heard Isabel say, "Many airlines have perk programs nowadays. Travel points add up to low-cost flights."

I smiled, thinking she sounded like a commercial.

Then Nettie said, "Don't you know that people will always remember how you made them feel? Especially children. They hold on to that. A little effort goes a long way toward a healthy relationship."

Isabel jumped in again. "You can also transfer points from your credit card so your everyday purchases go into the pot. Or, better yet, get an airline credit card. Just be sure you're paying it off every month. I cannot endorse taking on additional debt." Her voice sharpened as she added, "I do, however, suggest spending a little more money on a bouquet if you can afford it. Especially if it's being offered as an apology."

Nettie sniffed. "That there sad bouquet reads to me like you want something. It's an afterthought. A way to soften the request."

"Is that true?" Isabel demanded.

I walked a little faster, wondering what on earth was going on. Usually, their protocol was to offer harmless wisdom and advice, but this felt personal and more than a little hostile.

As I stepped into the reading zone, their backs were to me. They had someone corralled against the new materials display.

I glanced at Jed, who was headed toward Evanthe's office holding what looked like a potato, and I didn't even want to ask why. He raised his eyebrows and gave a slight shrug.

Fridays.

"Ladies," I said, "is everything okay over here?"

Nettie and Isabel parted, one to each side of the man, looking like they were considering doing him bodily harm.

"He won't say why he's here," Nettie supplied, giving the man a mean side-eye.

It took me a moment to recognize him, because he was tanned, and his blond hair was longer. When I did, I about fell over. I actually had to reach out and grab something.

That something turned out to be Isabel. She patted my hand. Comforting me.

"Tallulah! There you are," Scott Mayfield said.

"What're you doing here?" I asked my ex-husband, each word etched with pure shock.

"I told you I'd visit soon." He thrust a bouquet of flowers toward me. "These are for you."

The roses were wilted, the petals brown around their edges. Cellophane crinkled under my grip as I said, "Thanks. But you didn't tell me you'd be here this weekend." He was supposed to tell me. It was in our custody agreement.

He grinned. "I thought I'd surprise you and the girls. Surprise! I'm just here for a couple of days. Flying back out on Sunday morning."

He'd flown.

I narrowed my gaze at him. We had spent many years together, and I knew there was more to the story. For the sake of not causing a scene in the library, I let it go for now.

"Funny thing is," he added, "I can't find a vacant hotel room within thirty miles."

Nettie said, "I believe it was good ol' Ben Franklin who said something to the likes of when you fail to plan, you plan to fail. Words of wisdom, those."

Isabel nodded. "Indeed."

This trip definitely had all the earmarks of being a last-minute decision. No notice. No hotel room. Flying here instead of driving.

But *why*?

Scott sighed. "Be that as it may, I need a place to stay."

I was not going to offer up Papaw's couch. Was *not*.

"Somewhere close to the girls would be nice." He swung his gaze to me, all big puppy-dog eyes. "Can't I just stay on your couch? It's only two nights."

If he'd mentioned wanting to be with the girls, tucking them in, making them breakfast, that kind of thing, I might've given in. Thankfully for me, he didn't.

I threw a *help me* look at Isabel and Nettie.

After a long, drawn-out moment, Nettie said, "I have a spare room. You're welcome to it. For two nights only."

Scott turned a pleading glance toward me, and I pretended not to see it.

Instead, I sent veritable heart-eyes at Nettie. I owed her for this. Big-time. She was doing me a huge favor.

He cleared his throat and said, "Thank you. That's real nice of you. I accept."

I couldn't fully explain why I didn't want Scott at Papaw's. I didn't mind at all if he spent all his time here with the girls. I *wanted* him to be with them. But I didn't want to see his toothbrush on the sink near mine. It was a step too far.

He folded his arms. "I saw a sign on the front door that the library is closed tomorrow. Does that mean you have the day off, Tallulah?"

"Tomorrow is the Flour Festival, and I have to work a shift at the library's fundraising booth, but other than that, yes. I have the day off. Why?" I asked suspiciously.

"I was just hoping we'd have a chance to—"

He broke off because Isabel, Nettie, and I had collectively sucked in a breath, our gazes squarely on the front doors.

The doors that had just let Jake inside.

"Oh boy," Isabel said.

Jake carried a big rectangular bucket that had a bow stuck to its side. He took a few steps forward and blinked, as though he was trying to adjust to the change of light. Then his gaze landed on me. Zeroed in, really.

My palms started to sweat.

"Sparks," Nettie murmured.

I shot her a look.

"I call it as I see it, Lu."

Confusion was stamped all over Scott's face as Jake walked toward us, his gaze still locked on mine.

I was having palpitations.

Jake smiled at Nettie and Isabel, lifted an eyebrow at Scott, then said to me, "Hey, Tallulah. Do you have a minute?"

"Who's this?" Scott asked.

"Who's asking?" Jake said, dark eyes narrowing.

Just then, a cool wind swept through the room, signaling that Evanthe had arrived, and I eyed the front doors, suddenly wanting to make a run for it.

Scott straightened, standing tall. He was still a good four inches shorter than Jake, however. "I'm Tallulah's husband."

"Ex," I said, razor sharp. To Jake, I added, "I don't know why he's here."

"I told you—" Scott began.

"Stop," I said to him, losing my patience. "Just stop."

Amazingly, he complied.

I glanced around for somewhere private to talk to Jake. The community room was empty, but it had windows. I didn't need an audience. The break room it was, then. "Come with me," I said to Jake, not daring to look behind me at Evanthe.

Surely she'd understand.

Maybe.

I was probably going to get written up.

I held open the break room door for him, and once he was inside, I let it go. It shut with a soft *snick*, closing us in and everyone else out.

After setting the pitiful flowers on the counter, I turned to face him.

I felt sick, my stomach churning.

Jake placed the bucket on the table where I'd been eating lunch not five minutes ago. "I wanted to give you this. A housewarming present."

It was a mop bucket, I realized, and it was full of things I'd need for the new house. Cleaning supplies. Wallpaper remover. Tools. And three matching floral tool belts. Adult size, child size, and toddler size.

I stared long and hard at those tool belts until I thought I could speak without my voice breaking. "This is very sweet of you, thank you. But I don't close for a couple of weeks."

My question was clear, even though I hadn't said it aloud: Why was he giving this to me *now*?

"I know." He crossed his arms, then let them fall. "But I'm leaving today."

Oh.

Oh.

I waited for the tears, but they didn't come.

"I think it's for the best," he said.

The tears hadn't come, I realized, because I'd gone numb. I leaned, half sitting, on the table for support. I couldn't feel my fingertips. Or my toes.

I forced myself to look at him.

Sunlight was hitting his eyes just so, making them look like aged amber, dark and lovely.

"Maybe so," I whispered, the words pretty much stuck in my throat.

Before I could make sense of what he was doing, he leaned in and pressed his lips to my forehead, softly, gently.

I felt *that*. The warmth, the heartache.

Finally, he stepped back, gave me one last look, then turned and left, leaving the door open behind him.

A moment later, I heard Evanthe and Jed conversing; then she filled the doorway in all her linen-draped glory. Her hair was twisted into a fancy knot at the nape of her neck. Uneasiness darkened her eyes, and I took it to mean she hadn't been sure what she'd find in here. What kind of mess.

Jed was probably on standby right outside the door, a mop at the ready to sop up my tears.

Before she could lecture me about bringing personal problems to work, I said, "He's going home. Today."

Deckle raced in ahead of her as she stepped inside and started pushing in chairs around the table. "Is he? *Hmm*. I have the feeling we'll see him again soon."

"I'm not sure I want to." I didn't think my heart could take it. Oh, how I was going to miss him.

"Lying isn't your strong suit, Tallulah."

I tested my legs, making sure they'd hold me, before carrying the bucket across the room. I set it next to the employee lockers. Deckle came over and nudged my leg. I bent down and patted his head, scratched under his chin.

He started purring.

I suspected it was a pity purr, but I didn't even care.

I bravely picked him up and noticed he had a new collar. I was grateful for something to change the subject. "Do you worry people will think he's a girl because of the pink collar?"

Evanthe crossed her arms. "I never worry about what other people think. Pink is often undervalued for its neutrality. Besides all that, she *is* a girl. All the library cats have been girls. Have you thought *she* was a *he* all this time?"

I stared at the cat. He, *she*, stared back. Dumbly, I nodded.

"No wonder it took a while for her to warm up to you. She's quite sensitive."

I was tempted to flip the cat over, check for myself, but refrained, considering the sensitivity of it all. Deckle was a *she*. I wasn't sure why I'd thought otherwise. Maybe the name? It *was* a masculine name. No one could convince me otherwise.

I said, "I'm just going to add this to the list of strangeness that has ruled the day." I reluctantly passed Deckle over to her. "I should get back to work."

She pulled open the door. "Yes, you should."

I saw Jed lurking in the large-print section and gave him an *I'm okay* smile. He gave a stiff nod and wandered off.

Because I was in a weird headspace and the day had been *beyond*, I threw caution to the wind, risking life and limb and my job, by saying, "Can I ask you a personal question, Evanthe?"

"At work?" Her gaze narrowed. Then she sighed and allowed the door to close once again. "Fine. I'll allow it. Just this once."

A pity concession.

It was a pity kind of day.

"Why won't you date Jed?" I asked.

She hitched Deckle up a little, settling her more comfortably in her arms. "He hasn't asked."

I nearly laughed. "He's hinted. He's looking for encouragement from you. You have to know that."

He was going to owe me the *biggest* pecan bar tomorrow.

For a long, drawn-out moment, she seemed to be thinking about what to say, and I dearly hoped whatever it was wouldn't be ringing in the rafters for months to come.

Finally, she said, "His dog doesn't like cats."

I blinked, not sure I'd heard her right. "His dog?"

"I'd never dream of separating a man from his dog. They've been together twelve years now."

I let that sink in, what it truly meant.

She liked Jed. A lot. So much so that she'd imagined a future with him, one where they were all together. Him and her, his dog, her cat.

"Surely there's a compromise somewhere?" I said. "Perhaps date exclusively but live separately?"

"*Perhaps*," she said in a frosty tone, "there's a similar compromise to be found between you and Jake."

My stomach hurt just thinking about him. "He's gone. Compromise is out the window."

"He is not going very far."

"Nearly five hours and three hundred miles."

I winced, realizing I'd revealed the fact that I'd looked it up. I hoped she wouldn't notice.

The corner of her lip drifted slowly upward.

She'd noticed.

I glanced at the back door and thought again about running away.

"Tallulah, you must know that when the heart is involved, it isn't a matter of time or distance. The questions you should be asking yourself are these: Does it hurt more having him far away? Or not having him at all?"

She gave me a pointed look, then pulled open the door and sailed out, Deckle still in her arms.

She was still purring.

Thirty-Three

*A Pearl of Wisdom
from Vera Ingleby*

"In my opinion, a balanced diet is found by holding a cupcake in each hand."

Juliet

Mom was an early riser, which meant she was up super early Saturday morning, since her inner clock was still running on Michigan time. She'd texted me before sunrise, asking if I was up for a walk.

Because the replacement coffeepot Tenn ordered hadn't yet arrived, I texted back: If there's coffee involved, I'm in.

Mom: I will go to the ends of the earth to find it. See you in ten?

Me: Maybe fifteen

I took a moment to stretch my arms and rub the sleep out of my eyes. It was a little past five. Outside, the birds were just waking, and I glanced at the nightstand, missing my small pile of feathers. I didn't regret for even a moment using them for Katy's dream catcher but wished I were still finding them.

Though I supposed there was no need for them anymore. Now that my missing memories had returned.

Still. Finding a feather would mean the robin was nearby. I hadn't seen it in over a week, and I missed it.

Missed it desperately.

The air conditioner rattled to life, and I sat up, feeling slightly woozy.

I was still working through the shock of my memory returning, physically and emotionally. My head was fuzzy, foggy. As if my brain had been overwhelmed by the influx of information and decided to take a little rest. A wee snooze. Emotionally, I'd found myself welling up with tears many times yesterday.

At the memory of Jordan daring Hunter to put gum in my hair. And the resulting pixie haircut that was needed to fix the situation.

When Eric had brought me a bouquet of balloons when I had my tonsils out in high school.

When Amy took me prom dress shopping.

When my mom kissed my head every morning before heading off to work, even though she thought I was asleep.

When my dad made waffles on Sundays, always adding extra whipped cream on mine.

And my grandpa.

He'd been more than my grandparent, my caregiver. He'd been my closest friend. Fresh waves of grief crashed over me each time I recalled all the moments we'd spent together. Each remembrance knocking me down. It almost felt like he'd passed away for a second time.

I blew out a breath, threw back the quilt, and made my way downstairs.

On the second-floor landing, I paused, listening at Katy's door.

All was quiet.

Her dream catcher hung in the window next to her bed, where the beads captured any bad dreams, knitting them along the web of delicate threads.

Or at least I liked to think so.

Yesterday she'd been thrilled to see Scott. Over-the-moon excited. Bouncy and chatty and absolutely grinning ear to ear as she raced into his arms. When I was introduced to him, I smiled, trying not to judge him for not being more present in his daughters' lives, but I was finding it difficult.

Because yesterday had been a bit of a blur, I hadn't had the chance to ask Tallulah how she felt about his visit. And I couldn't tell by looking at her, either. Her emotions were locked up tight behind thin smiles and tired eyes.

Downstairs, I was surprised to find the dining room light on and Tenn sitting at the table, fussing with a frame. He was fully dressed, his hair damp. His beard was coming in nicely.

"Morning," I said quietly.

"Morning, early bird," he replied. "Couldn't sleep?"

"My mom texted. She wants to go for a walk. And she has coffee."

He chuckled. "New coffee maker should be arriving today. Gotta keep my girls happy."

I smiled again, thinking about how strange life could be. Just a few weeks ago, he didn't even know me. Now he was including me as one of his girls. The designation made my heart sing.

"What're you working on so early?" I asked.

"Gettin' this here print framed."

I walked over and felt my heart skip a beat. The print he'd been working on all this time was of a robin. I swallowed hard, looking at the bird, which seemed to be watching me with kind eyes from its perch on a gnarled branch.

"It's not perfect," he said, "but it'll do."

"It looks perfect to me."

Grinning, he pushed his glasses up his nose. "That's because you're kind. I messed up right here," he said, pointing to a spot along the bird's neck. "Looks like he done lost some chest feathers. I'll just say he's molting and leave it at that."

My skin prickled. A robin that had lost feathers. A bare white spot at its neck.

I tried for casual when I added, "What inspired you to make a robin?"

He carefully set the print on a mat, aligning it just so. "Renny asked. Figured it was the least I could do. That's why I'm wrestling with this frame. I'm planning on visitin' with him for a spell this morning before heading off to the festival."

"He'll like that," I murmured.

He tapped the frame. "I'm planning to make a print for you, too."

"Of the robin?" I asked.

He nodded. "Special request from Katy. She told me you'd want one because she read in her new symbolism book that the robin is a protector from storms and lightning—and is also a sign that you're never alone."

Happiness and grief tangled up, twisting together, as I thought of my grandfather, making my voice thick as I said, "She's right—I'd love a print."

We chatted for a few more minutes; then I was out the door, heading down the street, thinking about robins. About storms. About Renny. I was kicking myself for not telling him about the feathers I'd found because I suddenly had the feeling that he wouldn't have thought me bonkers at all.

Morning light was glowing softly on the horizon, coloring the sky in dim shades of grays and pinks. My eyes adjusted quickly, and I saw that Mom was waiting for me at the end of Vera's driveway, where Amy's SUV was parked in the spot where Jake's truck should be.

Foolish, stubborn man.

When I reached Mom, she said, "I saw Vera's kitchen light on, and she hooked us up with some coffee. She's a treasure, that woman."

Vera had welcomed her new guests into the garage apartment without even batting an eye. "Agreed."

Mom's dirty-blond hair was pulled back in a ponytail. A stub, really. When her bob was worn loose, it barely hit her chin. She had on a loose tank top, capri pants, and Birkenstocks. She'd be turning sixty-one at the end of the year and glowed with good health. She held two ceramic mugs, both steaming. She passed one over—it had scissors, a comb, and the words *Great hair doesn't happen by chance, it happens by appointment* printed on it—and gave me a kiss on my cheek.

I took a sip of coffee, sighed happily.

In companionable silence, we started walking toward the sun garden, and I was once again reminded of my grandfather. Our walks. With him, though, there was rarely silence. He was a talker.

Mom was a talker, too, which tipped me off that she was working up to what had brought her down here, to Forget-Me-Not.

Mom had explained that she and Amy had come for the Flour Festival.

But I knew that wasn't the real reason.

Amy had already told me why, with the text she'd sent last week: Mom wanted me home.

Amy hadn't told me, however, about this rescue mission, other than her cryptic rearrange-her-whole-life snippiness during one of our phone calls. Which told me that some part of her believed in Mom's campaign.

According to my sister, they planned to leave on Monday morning and make the eleven-hour trip back to Michigan in one day instead of breaking it up like they had on the way down here. I think they—*Mom*—expected I'd follow them back. A two-car Nightingale caravan.

Which wasn't going to happen.

"It's a beautiful little town," Mom said, stopping to admire the garden.

Dew glistened on petals, each small drop perfect and beautiful.

I took a sip of coffee. It was quickly growing cold. "It is."

She faced me, her green eyes looking darker than usual in the muted light. "I can see you're happy here."

I waited for the *but*.

"But—"

And there it was.

"—I worry."

I thought about what I'd told Katy once, about moms worrying. Mine was no exception.

"There's nothing to worry about," I said, noticing the spray of freckles on her shoulders.

My shoulders were the same. Just like my eyes were the same velvety green as hers.

I pulled a new-old memory out of foggy depths. Of me at six years old. It had been Halloween, and I'd dressed as a nurse. And as Mom and Grandpa had walked us younger kids around the neighborhood, I'd heard over and over again people telling my mom, "She's your mini-me!" She'd been thrilled. I remembered, too, that when I was asked if I planned to follow in my mom's footsteps when I grew up, I'd looked at her hopeful, proud eyes and said yes, even though I hadn't really understood what it meant.

Later, when Grandpa and I were sorting candy, he'd said to me, real quietly, that I didn't have to be a nurse when I grew up if I didn't want to. That I could be anything I wanted. That my life was *mine* to live.

But I'd been basking in the glow of my mother's happiness, of her pride, and I knew what I had to do. I was going to be *just like her.*

It was an unsettling memory.

Would I have chosen another career if I hadn't longed for her attention, her approval?

I wasn't sure, but I suspected no. I loved being a nurse. However, I most certainly didn't want to get a postdoctoral degree.

I had to draw the line.

As Grandpa had once so wisely said, my life was mine to live.

It wasn't going to matter to my mother what I did for a living—as long as I was happy, healthy. I wasn't sure why I hadn't understood this before, then realized that maybe I'd needed the distance between us to see it clearly.

"You're still healing," Mom said, sitting on a bench nearby. She patted the spot next to her. "You should come home, pick up where you left off with therapy. If you still want to come back here in six months, a year, then by all means, do. But take care of *you* first."

I sat. "I'm fine. Really. I didn't even check the forecast today."

Only, now that I said it, I itched to pull my phone out of the pocket of my leggings and start swiping.

She tipped her head. "Then you don't mind at all that there's a chance of storms this afternoon?"

This afternoon? When we'd be at the Flour Festival? *Outside?*

My chest squeezed. My pulse quickened. "No," I squeaked.

"Ignoring your trauma isn't going to help anything, Juliet. You can't run away from it."

"I'm not. You can't run away from something that lives in your bones, your soul."

She drew in a deep breath, blew it out. "I blame this whole trip on your grandfather, you know. This is his doing. He was always filling your head with travel talk."

He was. I couldn't even deny it.

I cracked a smile, hearing his voice in my head, saying, *If you travel, Jules, you'll discover new places, meet new people, and there's a good chance you'll find yourself along the way. If you don't want to go alone, we can go together. I'd love to show you the special places I visited when I did my big trip in my twenties.*

I knew now that it hadn't been my idea at all to retrace the path he'd taken through the South. He'd planted the seeds. And even though I'd forgotten, his encouragement to travel the same route, make the same stops, had been at work in my subconscious.

Maybe I was losing my grip on reality, but I now fully believed, without a single doubt, that the chubby robin with the white patch at its throat had been my grandfather joining me on the journey. We'd taken the trip together after all.

Mom suddenly set her mug down on the bench and jumped

up. She tucked her hands close to her armpits and started flapping her arms. Then she lifted her knees high, one at a time, running around, zagging left, then right.

I thought maybe she'd spiked her coffee until she said, mimicking Grandpa, "It's time for you to spread your wings and leave the nest, Jules."

I pulled out my phone, started filming, and laughed. "You look like a deranged chicken."

"Make like a bird and fly, Jules!" she said, still in that deep, manly voice, fully committed to the bit. "The nest will be here when you get back, Jules!"

She continued flapping and zigging and zagging, and I laughed so hard I had tears in my eyes.

Finally, she stopped, sat down again, and picked up her mug as though she hadn't just made a spectacle of herself in front of me and the birds and the dewdrops.

I wiped my eyes, and she glanced at me tenderly. "There was a time not too long ago when I thought I might never hear you laugh again."

There was a time not too long ago when I'd thought I never would. "I'm telling you, I'm doing fine. Good, even."

"Great?"

"That's an awful high standard. Is anyone great?"

"*I'm* great." She took a sip of coffee. On her mug was the image of a whisk and the words *Baking is a work of heart*. "All my kids think so."

"No need to brag," I joked.

She bumped my arm with hers. "I want you to be great."

"Being here has helped," I said.

"*Mm.* Being home would be best."

It was time to rip the Band-Aid off. "I sent in my resignation a couple of days ago."

She sighed heavily. It's where Amy learned it from. "I know," she said. "I still have friends at the school. They were concerned."

I gritted my teeth that someone had ratted me out even though it came from a place of goodness, kindness, care.

"It fueled my suspicions that you weren't planning on coming home." She faced me, lifting an eyebrow, challenging me to deny it.

"I'm happy here," I said simply, meeting her gaze, hoping she could see that it was true.

A long moment passed before she sighed again. "You really have your heart set on staying, don't you?"

I nodded.

"I'm not going to change your mind, am I?"

I shook my head.

"And what about grad school?"

I winced and tried to be brave. "I'm not sure that's the right path for me after all. I don't want to do research. I want to *nurture*. Since I've been here, I've been volunteering at a hospice respite house, and my heart is leading me in that direction."

Her eyes widened; then, slowly, she nodded. "I can see you fitting in that field quite well."

I wanted to collapse in relief that she understood.

She put her mug down and placed her hands on my cheeks. "I love you, Juliet. It might take me a while to accept you living down here, but I will if it truly makes you happy. Please remember that if you ever need anything, I'm not that far. I will fly, drive, bike, walk, crawl if I must, to get to you. And you can always come home, to your nest. Anytime. Day or night."

Only my mom would think Michigan wasn't that far. I hugged her, resting my head on her freckled shoulder. "Thanks, Mom. For everything. Always."

"Are you sure I can't change your mind about coming home?" she said into my hair.

"*Mom.*"

"Fine, fine. I'll probably keep trying, though."

"I wouldn't expect anything else from you."

She pulled back and said, "Ready for more coffee?"

"Definitely."

We took our time walking back to Vera's and found Amy sitting on the front porch, looking quite at home in her pajamas on the swing. Her auburn hair was pulled up in a sloppy bun, and she was barefoot.

As we climbed the steps, she held up a mug and a plate. Her hazel eyes danced as she said to me, "I went looking for Mom, and next thing I knew, Vera had me tucked up on this swing. Then she brought me out some coffee and a cinnamon-swirl cupcake. Are all the people around here this nice?"

"Everyone I've met, yes."

"Well," she said, taking a bite of the cupcake, "no wonder you don't want to come home."

Thirty-Four

A Pearl of Wisdom
from Tenn Greenlee
"Take notice. If bees are staying close to their hives, rain is coming."

Tallulah

I woke up early and couldn't fall back to sleep.

I wasn't the only one who was up before the sun. I'd heard Juliet moving about, then talking with Papaw downstairs, their voices just murmurs and mumbles yet somehow soothing.

I'd stayed in bed, hoping for just a little more sleep ahead of what was going to be a busy day, but it wasn't happening. My thoughts were spinning. Thinking about Mary Joy and eggs. About the new house. About Katy's nightmares and how she seemed to be through the phase. About the MLIS program and its application deadline. About Scott and how I still didn't know why he was here. About Jake. And about what Evanthe had said.

Does it hurt more having him far away?

Or not having him at all?

Well, right now it was both, so the pain was off the charts.

However, I could see the wisdom in her words. The compromise.

Long-distance dating.

I wasn't sure I could do it. I wasn't sure he'd be interested.

But maybe I wanted to try.

I wasn't sure what had happened to the person who longed

for stability, for routine. Because dating long-distance threw that right out the window. It was constant flexibility. It was *travel*.

It wasn't circling the globe, but still.

Yet I was willing to do it. For Jake. For *us*.

I fully recognized that I hadn't been willing to do the same for Scott, and it confirmed something I'd been suspecting for a while now.

My marriage had been over long before Scott and I split up.

With that thought, I threw back the covers and popped out of bed. I watched the rise and fall of Mary Joy's chest as she slept deeply in her crib. Her face was slack, her dreams peaceful if her countenance was any indication. I wanted to smooth her hair, kiss her chubby cheeks, but I also didn't want to wake her, so I backed slowly away.

I grabbed a summer robe and my laptop and headed downstairs. Where there was no sign of Juliet or Papaw. I found him easily—he was puttering around the garden. Juliet was harder. I finally spotted her down at Vera's, standing on the front porch with her mom and sister.

At a little past six in the morning.

Shaking my head, I went to make some coffee, then remembered the coffee maker was broken. Sighing, I headed out onto the back porch. The sun had just started its climb in the sky, bathing the yard in a pink glow. I'd seen in the forecast that there might be storms later on today, and I hoped the bad weather held off. For the sake of the festival. For Juliet's sake as well.

I sat on the wicker couch, pulling my legs up beneath me. I fired up my laptop and opened the PowerPoint presentation I'd been working on. The Trivia Night proposal. It was due next week, and I wanted it to be perfect.

But no sooner had I opened the file than I closed it again. I clicked open a blank document instead and quickly typed out the words, the wisdom, that had been replaying in my mind all night.

When the heart is involved, time and distance don't matter.
—Evanthe Kilburn

Then I added lines from Nettie, Isabel, Aunt Maeve, and Uncle Renny as well. All I could remember.

I didn't know what I was going to do with this collection, but sometime during the night, I had realized that these shiny pearls of wisdom should be documented so they'd never be forgotten. The philosophical and the practical and even the whimsical. There was so much to learn from those older, wiser.

My phone, in the pocket of my robe, buzzed. I pulled it free and saw a text from Scott.

You awake?

"Nope," I said, putting the phone on the table.

It was too early to be dealing with him.

He'd spent every minute he could with Katy yesterday right up until her bedtime. Mary Joy would only play with him if I was nearby, and every time he tried to hold her, she cried. He was a stranger, and the only stranger I'd ever seen her take to straightaway was Juliet.

On his way out last night, he'd given Papaw's couch the side-eye, and I didn't feel the least bit guilty waving goodbye. I'd locked the door behind him, still not knowing why he was in town. Yet knowing instinctively he had a reason for being here, beyond seeing the girls.

I told myself to stop thinking about it, because guessing what was going on with him might snap the fragile threads holding my sanity in place. He would tell me sooner or later.

As I typed out Isabel's feelings about credit card debt, I heard the front door open, then close. "Hello?" I said, just loud enough for my voice to be heard—and not wake the girls.

Footsteps neared; then Juliet appeared. She held a travel mug. "I hoped you'd sleep in but brought you coffee just in case."

I reached greedy hands toward the mug. "I could kiss you."

Stepping onto the porch, she smiled. "It's Vera we should be kissing. She's already made three pots this morning."

I took a blissful sip of the hot liquid and asked, "Your mama and sister sleep well?"

"Really well. Amy, especially, is enchanted with Forget-Me-Not. She loves it here."

"Well, it is enchanting." I smiled. "Maybe her car will break down on the way out of town."

Juliet rubbed a finger along the arm of the chair. Her eyebrows knitted together. "I thought that was just romantic love."

"I mean, yes, but who's to say rules can't be bent from time to time?" Then I opened up my heart a little, letting her inside, as I said, "Maybe *your* car will break down."

A smile spread slowly across her face. "Maybe it doesn't need to."

My eyes widened and I scooted to the edge of the couch. "Does that mean what I think it means?"

She nodded. "I'm going to stay."

I let out a squeal that was bound to wake the girls and gave her a big hug. "I know I'm not the only one who's going to be happy with this news."

And as she hugged me back, she said, "No one's happier about it than I am."

It was an odd, surreal moment to walk up to the admission gate of the Flour Festival with Scott and the girls. Like we were still a happy little family.

He'd shown up at Papaw's at seven this morning, saying Nettie had told him he was wasting daylight, moping around her kitchen. That his time would be better spent with the girls.

She'd texted me he was on his way, which I was grateful for because he hadn't.

He'd spent the time between then and now with the girls,

reading, playing. Katy had been ecstatic, Mary Joy less so, but as long as I was around, she tolerated him.

He still hadn't confessed why he was really here.

He pushed the stroller as Mary Joy watched everything go by with wide blue eyes. Katy danced to a song only she could hear as we paid the festival's entry fee and received ten tickets each that we could trade in for dessert samples.

Tents lined one side of the park pathway, tucked between trees and flower beds, their colorful canopies bright against the backdrop of cloudy skies and evergreens.

Because of my shift at the library tent, we were here earlier than Juliet and her family and even Papaw, who were all planning to arrive in the early afternoon. I hoped there'd be treats left by then because the park was already packed with people. We were barely twenty feet inside the gate, and already the path was bottlenecked as everyone oohed and aahed at displays.

As we pushed onward, Katy put her hand on Scott's arm, as if she simply needed to touch him to make sure he was really there. It made me want to yell and scream at him about priorities. Couldn't he see how much she loved him? Missed him? How was he letting this happen? Letting her grow up without him? Letting Mary Joy grow up thinking he was a stranger? It boggled my mind, hurt my heart. It was an old argument, though, and I refused to have it once again.

Katy soon came to a standstill, captivated by the macaron tent, her blue eyes shining with eagerness as I handed her a ticket to swap for a raspberry macaron.

As she skipped off, I spotted Georgia in the distance and waved. When I thought I saw another familiar face, my breath caught.

Jake?

I stepped forward, toward him, and stumbled over my feet. Once I righted myself, he was gone, and I realized it must've been a trick of the eye. The heart.

I promised myself I would text him later tonight. Send out a feeler. See how he felt about compromises.

A moment later, Katy returned and showed off her macaron, how pretty it was, before she started nibbling. We carried on, making our way along the path. It was crowded, loud, and muggy. The morning sunshine had given way to clouds. I'd stowed umbrellas in the stroller basket just in case it rained.

"Mama," Katy said, wiping crumbs from her lips, "do you know if Miss Vera won?"

"I don't think the judging is until later," I said, figuring that right about now, Vera was probably wringing her hands, worrying about her entries: two pies; her thick, gooey kitchen-sink cookies; cinnamon cupcakes; and a banana-caramel cake. I crouched and pointed. "Do you see that big white tent on the soccer field? That's where the baking competitions are taking place. Maybe your dad can take you over there while I'm at the library tent and you can look at all the entries."

Katy looked up at Scott.

He smiled. "Of course we can do that."

He was being quite amiable today, which also tipped me off that he was going to spring something big on me. What could it possibly be?

As we headed for the library tent, I cataloged the desserts I wanted to try once my shift was over. Like the churro cheesecake, toffee cookies, and a pepper jack scone.

The path split, and we went left, to the library tent, where I saw that people were lined up for Jed's bourbon-pecan bars. He was all smiles, chatting and taking tickets left and right, while Nettie was selling Forget-Me-Not Library tote bags and water bottles.

I glanced at my watch. It was time for me to take over for her.

"Please remember, no treats for Mary Joy," I said to Scott, who'd be solely in charge of the girls while I was working my shift. I'd already warned him about eggs, and he'd seemed concerned enough that I felt I didn't have to warn him again. "I packed her some snacks."

There was barely restrained impatience in his eyes when he looked at me. "I remember. You've told me three times."

I wanted to tell him a million times more. He tended to disregard what I thought in favor of what *he* thought was best. It had driven me crazy when we were married.

Instead, I clenched my jaw and said, "If you have any issues, you know where to find me."

"We'll be fine, Tallulah."

I wanted to believe it, but something was gnawing at me, deep within.

"We won't go far," he added. "We'll check out the baking competition, get some snacks, and find a picnic table not too far from you. We'll check in from time to time."

I recognized that he was giving in, just a little. "Thank you."

Trying to push aside any fears, I told the girls I'd see them soon.

As I watched them walk away, however, I was unable to shake the feeling that by letting them go, I was making a huge mistake.

Thirty-Five

A Pearl of Wisdom
from Nettie Getchell
"Maybe you're breaking down. Or maybe you're breaking through."

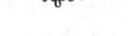

Juliet

The gray was creeping in.

"I'm in heaven. I've died and gone to heaven," Amy said, ogling desserts. "Or maybe I'm dreaming."

"Should I pinch her?" I loudly whispered to Callum. "See if she wakes up?"

"No, you should not," Amy intoned as she took a huge bite of a cupcake. "If I am dreaming, I don't *want* to wake up."

Callum smiled. Somehow he'd found us in the big crowd not too long after we arrived. I thought it quite brave of him to want to meet my mom, my sister, so soon, but he'd won them over quickly.

At one point, Amy had whispered, "Now I *really* know why you don't want to leave this town."

I'd smiled. Callum wasn't the only reason why, but he was at the top of the list.

An hour later, we were strolling along the path, making our way toward the show tent. Mom was off on the hunt for something healthy to snack on and was going to meet us there.

"I don't know how you haven't eaten anything yet," Amy said to me, finishing off the cupcake.

"I'm just not that hungry," I said.

It was an understatement. I had no appetite at all. In fact, I was a little queasy.

The clouds were darkening.

I told myself I was fine. Everything was fine. They were just *clouds*.

I was just a little thrown off by how much this park reminded me of the one my grandpa and I used visit. Narrow paths. Towering trees. No shelter.

Callum glanced at me, searching. Worry shadowed his blue eyes, and I wasn't sure what had tipped him off that something was wrong. He said, "I'm going to get a lemon donut. Can I get you one?"

Knowing he'd keep asking—or Amy would—until I ate something, I pasted on a smile. "Sure. Thanks."

"Amy?" he offered.

Her mouth was now full of red velvet cookie, so she shook her head and waved him on.

"Okay. Then I'll be right back."

We stepped off the path, out of the traffic flow, to wait for Callum as he strode toward a tent with a yellow canopy. Behind it, the leaves on a tree flapped in the breeze. The wind had definitely picked up since we arrived. I glanced at the fast-moving clouds, felt a bit dizzy, and looked down again before I tipped over.

I clasped my hands together to keep from checking the weather radar on my phone and told myself it was just *wind*.

Just clouds and wind.

That was all.

Yet my heart rate kicked up a notch, and my hand went to the scar on my neck.

Amy eyed me. "What's wrong?"

"Nothing."

"Something. The pulse is jumping in your neck."

I made like a turtle, tucking my chin to my chest. "Nope."

"*Juliet.*"

I squinted. "Is that frosting on your cheek?"

With a small *eep*, she quickly pulled a compact from her purse and swiped the smudge away. While she was at it, she reapplied her lipstick.

I'd hoped it would be enough to distract her from her line of questioning, but once she put everything away and zipped up her purse, she said, "If it's not the weather that's bothering you, what is it?"

I was saved from lying by Maeve, who came hobbling toward us, a plastic cake-slice container in one hand, a fork in the other. "Just the person I was hoping to see," she said to me. Then she promptly fell into conversation with Amy for a good two minutes, chatting about how she was liking it here, what treats she'd eaten, and what kind of lipstick she wore, because it was such a beautiful shade.

Southern charm at its finest.

Finally, she faced me and said, "Can I borrow you a minute, Juliet?"

"Sure."

Amy said, "I might try one of those donuts after all. Maybe two. Don't tell Mom."

"I promise," I said, falling in slow step with Maeve.

Once we were a few feet away, she held out the cake slice. It was pink cake with white frosting covered in what appeared to be thousands of rainbow sprinkles.

"Could you find Katy and give this to her? I promised her I'd bring it right back, but I just got a call from Juneberry and need to go."

My stomach free-fell. "Renny?"

She put her hand on my arm, shook her head. "Not Renny."

I pushed a hand to my chest, felt my heart racing, just as thunder rumbled in the distance. My head snapped up.

"What is it, honey?"

"Do you hear thunder?"

She tipped her head, listening. "I don't, no."

Strange.

"Listen," she said, checking her watch, "now's not really the time, but a little Tallulah Byrd told me you were going to be moving here, and I couldn't be happier. I'm just busting. Now, now, no need to frown. I know you asked her not to tell anyone just yet, but she can't hide things from me."

I *had* asked Tallulah to keep the news quiet for the time being, but I should've known she wouldn't be able to hide it from Maeve. Or Katy, either.

They seemed to be experts at reading people.

Maeve rushed on, talking quickly, which told me she was in a rush. Usually, she was a leisurely speaker. "I know you're used to working with littles, but I'd love to have you at Juneberry. Everyone there loves you as much as I do. Think about it, okay?"

"Think about what?" Callum asked, walking up to us, holding two donuts wrapped in waxed bakery paper.

Maeve gave him a quick kiss on his cheek, and said, "I'm trying to lure Juliet to town with a job offer."

His eyebrows went up. "Really?" The hope in his eyes brought my anxiety down a notch. "Would you consider it?"

"I definitely would."

He grinned.

"I've got to get going." Maeve nodded to the piece of cake I was holding. "Katy's at the picnic tables near the big tent. If anyone starts looking for me, tell them I'll be back as quickly as I can."

As soon as she walked away, Callum said, "What about your job in Michigan?"

"I might've already turned in my resignation." I met his gaze, let him see that I was serious. About quitting my job. About moving here. About him.

The world around us fell away. The wind died down. Sunbeams poked through the clouds. My stomach settled. My heart calmed, slowing from a jackhammer to the soft beating of delicate bee wings.

A slow smile spread across his face.

I loved that smile. His eyes. Maybe him.

I wanted to know for sure. Wanted to see where life would take me. *Us.*

Just as he was leaning in, a whistle broke the spell between us.

A catcall.

I looked over his shoulder to see Isabel giving me a thumbs-up from where she stood in the same donut line as Amy.

Callum laughed. "We're never going to hear the end of it."

"Ever," I agreed.

The wind returned, making tent flaps slap against support poles. The clouds thickened, edged in black. My feet tingled.

He nudged my arm. "Small festivals or amusement parks?"

I was trying to fight off a wave of queasiness as I said, "Festivals."

"Me, too, though I like a good roller coaster."

I searched and searched my brain for a This or That question for him, trying to ignore the light raindrops now falling. Spitting, my grandpa used to say.

In my head, I saw his kind eyes, his crooked smile.

I saw him with his face turned to the heavens, letting the rain soak him to the bone.

I saw him dancing, laughing.

My pulse throbbed in my ears.

Blinking the images of him away, I tried to find calm. I took a step closer to Callum, wanting to go back to that magical moment a minute ago, where it had been just the two of us and clear skies.

Because he was waiting for a counter-question, I looked around for inspiration and landed on the tent with strawberry cake. "Strawberries or raspberries?"

"Raspberries."

"Strawberries for me," I said, the words weak.

I gripped Katy's cake box and threw a look at Amy, wishing

the line would move faster. The sooner we could get to the big tent, the better. If I couldn't see the dark skies, feel the raindrops, maybe I could shake this feeling of impending doom.

Beyond her, farther down the path, I saw Evanthe, Tallulah's boss, walking toward us with someone who looked awful familiar. "Is that Jake?" I asked. "I thought he left town."

"His truck broke down last night, not too far from Miss Evanthe's house. It's sitting in my shop right now."

"What's wrong with it?"

"Not sure. I won't have a chance to look at it until Monday. Probably has something to do with the town's folklore, considering how close he and Tallulah became."

I looked at him, puzzled. "But he's not a lost soul. His truck didn't break down when he got here, to Forget-Me-Not. There wasn't any smoke." I knew because I'd asked Tallulah during one of our nights on the couch.

He shrugged. "Maybe it's just another of those exceptions we don't understand."

I had so many questions, but they all seemed to vanish from my mind when a roll of thunder shook the ground beneath my feet. I broke out in a sweat yet felt cold. My hands were clammy. My head ached.

Callum said, "Are you all right? You've gone pale."

"I don't like thunder," I said.

My hands started to tremble.

He tipped his head, then looked at the sky. "You hear thunder?"

I nodded. "Don't you?"

It had been loud. Powerful enough to shake the ground.

When he shook his head, I wanted to cry. Why was I the only one who could hear it?

He handed me the donuts, pulled his phone out of his pocket, and called up a weather app. "There's heavy rain to the south of us. No storms, though." He turned the screen toward me, let me see the radar.

I saw only green—rain—on the tiny map, but I knew what I'd heard.

"Do you want to leave?" he asked.

More than anything in the world.

Then my gaze fell on the cake I held. Katy was waiting for it. "I'm okay. We can stay."

He noticed me shaking when he retrieved the donuts from my hand. "How about we get you inside? Sit down for a while?"

I nodded.

Pressing a kiss to my temple, he said, "The skies will clear soon. Maybe an hour, by the look of that map. Just hold on a little bit longer."

I nodded again. It seemed to be the only thing I could do. There were no words. Only fear. Only rising panic. My chest hurt. Oh, how it hurt. Like my ribs were curling inward, trying to squeeze my heart.

Putting an arm around me, he guided me back onto the path. As we passed the donut booth, he said, "Hey, Amy, we'll meet you at the tent."

She nodded and waved.

I kept looking upward, at the clouds sinking lower, lower, lower. Their mist swirled around me, darkening the edges of my vision.

I held on to Callum.

As we reached an open field, I spotted Katy and Mary Joy and Scott. "Katy's cake," I said.

Callum steered me toward their picnic table, where treats were laid out, cookies and brownies and the remnants of strawberry cake, along with a small pot of mashed peas for Mary Joy, half eaten. She was in her father's arms, clearly unhappy. He was standing, bouncing and jostling, and she wasn't having it, emitting pitiful cries as she tried to burrow into his chest.

I heard Scott saying in a soothing, gentle tone, "It's okay, baby. Shh. Shh."

Mary Joy started to wail.

Katy saw us and ran over. "Juliet! Mary Joy threw up."

Over the crying, Scott said, "She must not like peas."

There was a giant splotch of green on his shirt.

People were starting to look, concerned about the screaming baby.

Katy looked terrified, her small hands pressed against her chest. The last time I'd seen her so frightened was right after the nightmare she'd had about her sister. At the thought, the hair rose on the back of my neck. Was it possible her dream had been a *warning*?

Since being in this town, I didn't dismiss the notion. In fact, it made me pay closer attention.

I put a hand on her head, cupping it, pulling her closer. Trying to soothe her even while struggling to hold myself together.

"Mary Joy is tired," I said to Scott. "Maybe push her in the stroller for a while? She might fall asleep."

Mary Joy lifted her head at the sound of my voice and thrust her arms out toward me. She was at the point of crying when she was losing her breath every few seconds.

I gasped when I saw her face. It was flushed, her lips swollen. The rash around her mouth was back.

I summoned strength from somewhere deep within and took her from Scott. She clung to my shirt as I carefully lifted her chin. Welts covered her neck. I pulled up the hem of her dress. They were on her thighs, too.

I looked at Callum. "Please get Tallulah." Then I noticed Katy's face, her eyes round with fear. "Take Katy with you."

He took her hand and they sprinted off.

"What did she eat?" I asked Scott, sitting down on the ground, afraid my legs might give out.

"Peas!" he said.

People were drifting closer, curious.

I shook my head. "She's fine with peas. Did she have eggs?"

"No. Of course not. Tallulah told me about the suspected allergy."

"No cake, no cookies, no nothing?" I asked. Accused, really.

He dragged a hand down his face. "No! The only sweet I let her have was some frosting. It's strawberry. She loves strawberries. It's buttercream. No eggs."

I was wondering about cross-contamination when someone in the gathering crowd said, "If it was Swiss meringue buttercream, it's made with egg whites."

I recalled seeing the strawberry cake tent and the sign boasting the silky Swiss meringue. Oh no.

Mary Joy was still crying, but her body had gone limp. This was bad. Adrenaline took over. I laid her down on the ground. "She needs epinephrine."

I barely noticed someone kneeling next to me until he said, "What's going on?"

It was Jake, and there was a look in his eyes I'd never seen before. One that said he was used to being in charge.

I pulled out my phone. My hands were shaking as I dialed 9–1–1. "She's having an allergic reaction."

He quickly leaned over Mary Joy, humming and comforting as he checked her pulse, her skin. Then he lifted her legs, resting them on his thigh.

To get better blood flow to her heart, I realized.

It became crystal clear to me that he was medically trained.

When he gestured to the phone and said, "May I?" I recognized that in my current state, it was probably better he do the talking.

I passed the phone to him just as Scott bent down to pick up Mary Joy, saying, "This doesn't concern you."

Summoning a burst of strength, I shot an arm out, stopping him, feeling murderous. "It's better she remains lying down."

Then someone must've answered the call, because Jake started talking rapid fire, his voice loud, strong, clear, yet the words tumbled together in my mind.

Dr. Jake Gallagher, life squad, Flour Festival, near the large white tent, seven-month-old female, anaphylaxis, EpiPen, *hurry*.

Someone in the crowd rushed forward, a woman. I noticed she was shaking, too, as she held something out to me. "My toddler has a nut allergy."

It was an EpiPen Jr.

I held her gaze for an extra beat. "Thank you."

She nodded solemnly.

My hands were shaking so badly as I popped the lid off the pen that I hesitated.

Jake asked, "Do you want me to do it?"

I looked at my hands, at the way they trembled, and nodded. I handed the injector to him, and he passed me the phone to talk to the 9–1–1 operator.

Then he made a fist around the injector and said to Mary Joy, "I'm so sorry, sweetheart," as he took tight hold of her leg to keep it still. Then he forcefully jabbed the injector into her thigh. Her pitiful crying stopped for a second as the pain registered; then she let out a scream. He held the pen in place for what felt like eternity but was only ten seconds—he was counting them off quietly. When he pulled the injector away, he rubbed the area on her leg, soothing, and picked her up, cradling her protectively in his arms.

He said, "She might need another dose once the paramedics get here, and will need to go to the hospital for monitoring."

He was talking to Scott, I realized.

There were sirens in the distance.

At some point, I'd dropped the phone. I didn't even know if the dispatcher was still on the line.

It had all happened so fast.

Shaking and woozy, I bent my knees, wrapped my arms around them, then lowered my head down, letting it rest on my forearms. My ribs were now squeezing my heart like an angry fist.

Something brushed against my ankle, startling me for a second before I realized it was a feather.

I looked up, searching for the robin. I spotted it flying overhead. It rose upward and upward until it disappeared into the clouds, and a tear rolled down my cheek because somehow I knew it would be the last time I'd see the bird. This was the end of our trip together.

It was the last thing I remembered before waking up in the back of an ambulance.

Thirty-Six

A Pearl of Wisdom
from Clay Daniels
"Each seed you plant today is done in hope for the future."

Tallulah

It was late by the time we got home from the hospital, past nine p.m., but Papaw had allowed Katy to stay up to wait for us. He'd been keeping watch over her all day, ever since Mary Joy had been loaded into the ambulance.

Now, as Katy hugged me and a sleeping Mary Joy tightly, I wondered if it had been the right call. Maybe it would've been better for Katy to have been there, at the hospital. To see Mary Joy starting to feel better. To hear that she would make a full recovery.

I didn't know.

I added it to the things I'd likely question for the rest of my life.

Along with letting Scott take care of the girls this morning.

He stood behind me—he'd driven us here—and Katy soon went into his arms, too.

She was much more forgiving than I was.

I could barely look at him, even though he'd been apologizing all day. Even though I could see how torn up and guilt-riddled he was. There was a part of me that recognized he hadn't meant to hurt Mary Joy. Of course not. But I'd told him no sweets, and he'd given her the frosting anyway.

Was I a stickler for not wanting her to have sweets until she was older? Maybe. That wasn't the point here, however. Scott had completely disregarded my wishes in favor of his own. Because he had, Mary Joy had suffered.

Papaw kissed the top of Mary Joy's head, then gave me a peck as well. "She scared the dickens out of me," he whispered.

Mary Joy had fallen asleep in the car on the ride home and was out cold. I suspected she would sleep through the night and maybe well into the morning. Her little body was exhausted.

I doubted I'd sleep a wink. I'd be watching her like a hawk. The doctors had warned me of a possible secondary reaction, one that could happen anytime from one hour to three days after the first. There was a name for it, but at this moment, I couldn't remember it for the life of me. I'd look it up later. We'd come home with two epinephrine injectors, just in case.

"Me, too," I said.

The emergency room's waiting area had been full of friends, of family, waiting on news, lending support by just being there. Nettie and Isabel and Vera brought snacks. Aunt Maeve and Uncle Renny came with Mary Joy's car seat. Evanthe simply paced, her linen billowing.

They weren't there just for us.

They'd come for Juliet, too.

Callum had brought Mylar balloons for Mary Joy, flowers for Juliet. I'd never seen him look so shaken.

Juliet had been released hours ago, and last I heard she'd be spending the night with her mama and sister, at Vera's.

I doubted *her* mama would get much sleep, either.

I'd tried to visit Juliet in the hospital, wanting to give her a big hug, but kept missing her as doctors ran tests, scans. Then she was gone, discharged.

Aunt Maeve had said it had been a panic attack. A bad one.

I'd sent Juliet a few texts and a couple of memes, which had gone unanswered.

I owed her so much. If she hadn't recognized the allergic reaction . . .

No.

I wasn't going there.

As I made a nest in the playpen and placed Mary Joy in it, I saw the bruises on her legs and felt nauseated. She'd needed a second injection of epinephrine at the hospital, and had been given other medications as well.

Suddenly I remembered the panic in Callum's eyes when he and Katy sprinted to find me. I'd raced to the field, my heart thundering when I saw the crowd and the way Jake was holding Mary Joy, the EpiPen on the ground, and then watched in horror as Juliet collapsed.

Giving my head a good shake, I held tears at bay and forced myself to straighten up. If I started crying now, I might never stop.

When I turned around, I found Papaw and Katy and Scott watching me.

I said to Scott, "You should go. It's late."

He nodded and bent to hug Katy, then crossed the room, leaned down, and gave Mary Joy a kiss on her forehead.

I had to clench my fists to keep from reaching out to stop him, not really wanting him anywhere near her. I'd never been so furious in my life.

He stopped in front of me. "Will you walk me out, Tallulah?"

For as much as I wanted to say no, because I couldn't stand the sight of him, I nodded. There were a few things I wanted to say. Out of earshot of anyone else. Especially Katy.

Papaw rubbed Katy's head. "We'll keep an eye on the munchkin."

Katy nodded and skipped over to the playpen, taking the job seriously.

As we walked toward the front door, I heard Katy ask Papaw, "Are they going to argue?"

"They're going to *converse*," he said.

"Is that a fancy word for argue?"

"Not really, no. But also, maybe."

She said, "I thought so."

I followed Scott out onto the porch. Moths flitted around the lights, and crickets chirped loudly. The air was warm, humid. Stars shone in the sky, giving no hint that there'd been clouds earlier.

"Tallulah," Scott said, "I'm so sorry. Please, you have to know I never meant to hurt her. It was an accident. A mistake. I love her."

I wanted to rail at him, cuss him out, but the words were stuck in my throat.

My chest ached, *burned*, as I pictured Mary Joy in the hospital, hooked up to monitors and getting treatments. I pressed my hands to my heart and bent forward, trying to ease the pain of almost losing her.

If Juliet hadn't been there. Or the woman with the EpiPen. Or Jake.

Jake, who, once he'd spoken to the paramedics, had faded into the crowd. I hadn't talked to him at all. I hadn't seen him since.

I squeezed my eyes shut. I couldn't go *there* now, either.

Scott stepped toward me, tried to hug me, console me. I pushed him back. I was crying now, unable to keep the agony inside. "She could've died!"

"I know!" He raked his fingers through his hair. Tears shimmered in his eyes. "I really did take the egg allergy seriously. I just didn't realize about the frosting. I'll learn what has eggs and doesn't. I'll research. I'll double-check. I promise I will."

He sat on the front step, hung his head.

I swiped my eyes and wrapped my arms around myself, trying to hold myself together. I took a hiccuping breath and said, "Why did you come here?"

"I've been an idiot about so many things."

I repeated the question louder this time and with less patience. "Why did you come here?"

"I came to tell you I accepted a new role in the company. Overseas. In Hong Kong. I was supposed to leave next week."

I was about to snap, *Good, go*, when it registered that he had said *was supposed to*. "What do you mean, *was*?"

He dropped his head into his hands, left it there. "I've been so stupid."

I wasn't going to argue.

"I have some decisions to make. No." He dropped his hands, looked at me. "I've made them. I'm not taking the job. I'm quitting. I'm moving back to Alabama. I'll find a job here that's closer to the girls."

I held up a hand. "Stop. This is just the guilt talking."

"Maybe some of it. Not all. I was so excited to go, right? To get on a plane and jet off? Then I saw the way Katy looked at me when I first got here, so incredibly happy just to spend a few days with me. And then how Mary Joy didn't even know me—and how I didn't know her. It hit me just how much I've been a crap father."

I wasn't going to argue that, either.

My eyes kept leaking. I kept swiping. I'd been afraid of this—being unable to stop crying once I started.

"Is my job and traveling more important than knowing Katy is in a dragon phase? Or that Mary Joy got her first tooth?" He shook his head. "I don't think so."

My head hurt, and I rubbed my temples. I was all for epiphanies, but this was too much. "This isn't the time to make hasty decisions, Scott."

He stood up. "I think it's exactly the right time. Something has to change. I'm going to do better where the girls are concerned. They *deserve* better than what I've been giving them."

They did.

Truly, I believed he wanted to be a better father, to make changes. Yet I also knew there was a big part of him that longed to fly free. If he was rooted here, he was never going to be happy.

Whisking away more tears, I said, "If you become a father who starts resenting them because he hates his job and his wings have been clipped, you won't be doing them any favors."

I could see I'd hit a nerve by the way he stiffened.

He jammed his hands into his pockets. "There has to be a middle ground. A compromise."

Suddenly I heard Evanthe's voice in my head, telling me that when the heart was involved, it wasn't a matter of time or distance. I softened. Just a little. He was *trying*. "I'm sure there is."

He said, "Maybe I can look for a job around here that has limited travel. I'd be nearby but still get to spread my wings a bit."

Blinking away moisture, I sighed, having trouble imagining him making even the smallest change. Would he follow through on any of this? Quit his job? Really?

More importantly, could I ever trust him with the girls again?

I wasn't sure. Right now, I was leaning heavily toward no.

"I know this is a lot, Tallulah, but I want you to know I'm serious. I want to be a better father. I just need to know that you'll give me the chance."

It was only because of Katy that I didn't immediately slam the proverbial door shut in his face. In my mind, I could easily see her eyes when she looked at him. All that love shining through. *She* deserved a devoted father. Mary Joy, too. Hopefully he could become one before she was old enough to notice his shortcomings.

"*Please*, Lu."

The tears had finally stopped, but my jaw ached as I said, "If you move back, I'm sure we can work something out for the girls."

There. I'd left the door open a crack. Barely a hair's width. It was up to him now, to make the changes. Make the effort.

"Thank you," he said, his voice hoarse.

"Please don't make me regret it, Scott. You're not going to get another chance."

He started down the walkway. "I won't let you down. I promise."

As I headed back inside, to my girls, I was surprised to realize I believed him.

Thirty-Seven

*A Pearl of Wisdom
from Vera Ingleby*
"Always remember that friends are the family chosen by your heart."

Tallulah

I'd been wrong about Mary Joy sleeping through the night.

She woke up around three a.m., bright-eyed and bushy-tailed, as though she hadn't had a near-death experience not even twenty-four hours ago.

The resilience of children would never cease to amaze me.

When she woke, she'd been starving. Absolutely famished.

I quickly changed her diaper, then carried her downstairs, where light glowed in the kitchen, guiding us—Papaw always left the light above the stove on at night. I'd buckled her into her high chair, warmed a bottle, then triple-checked all the ingredients on the rice cereal box. And the yogurt container, too.

When I retrieved a bowl of strawberries from the fridge, I glared angrily at the nearby carton of eggs, as if it were at fault for what had happened. I'd been researching egg allergies all night. It was going to be a whole new lifestyle for us, and I had a lot to learn, but I was more than willing. Anything to keep Mary Joy safe.

As she banged a spoon on her tray, I put on some music—*not* Gilbert and Sullivan—just to chase away the quiet. I made a big pot of coffee, grateful the new machine was set up, because I had the feeling I'd need all the caffeine I could get today.

I hadn't slept.

I'd known I wouldn't.

My eyes burned with exhaustion. I was tired to my soul.

After Mary Joy ate and played and showed off her sitting skills, I tried putting her back to bed.

At four.

At five.

At six.

She simply wasn't tired. I blamed the steroids she'd been given at the hospital.

When the sun came up, we got dressed, and I tucked her into the baby carrier, needing her near, and took her outside. I walked to the sun garden and back, hoping Juliet would see us and come out, say hi, let me hug her.

Vera's garage apartment remained dark, however. Her house, too. I couldn't remember if I'd congratulated her on her three blue ribbons yesterday, so I made a mental note to pop by later with the girls. Maybe bring some flowers from the garden.

I did stop and chat for a while with Mr. Daniels, who'd come rushing out to see Mary Joy, and to tell us how happy he was to see her and know she was going to fully recover. He was a sweet old man. I was going to miss having him as a neighbor when we moved.

On the way back to Papaw's, I'd received a text from Miss Edie, sending her love to Mary Joy. We texted back and forth for a few minutes, and she mentioned she'd be back in a few days now that her mama was on the mend and promised that Mary Joy would never be exposed to eggs while under her watch. It was a relief to know how much she cared.

After that, I walked Mary Joy around Papaw's yard for a while, pointing out birds, showing her the flowers. I mused aloud, telling her that we ought to take cuttings from his garden so we'd also have pieces of him, of Mamaw, with us at our new house. I talked about the Library House a lot, told her about her bedroom, and how I envisioned soft tangerine walls, a mural of woodland animals, and twinkle lights hung around the room, because I knew how much she loved them.

Of course talking about woodland animals reminded me of Jake's tattoo.

Which reminded me of him.

I needed to text him. Or call. Or maybe find out from Evanthe where he was staying and pay him a visit, bring him some shortbread cookies and my eternal thanks.

If he was still in town.

I was in the front yard, introducing Mary Joy properly to Bill—letting her touch his bark—when I heard a soft "Hey."

Juliet stood on the sidewalk, holding two coffee cups.

She looked a little like a zombie, with her wild light brown hair, pale face, sad green eyes. She was wearing pajamas I didn't recognize—probably her sister's.

She said, "I wasn't sure if the new coffee maker had been set up yet."

"It has, but I can always use more coffee. Thank you." I went to hug her, and did so carefully, considering the mugs and Mary Joy. "It's good to see you. I was worried."

We walked to the front steps and sat down.

"Sorry I didn't text back. I just—" She shook her head. Desolation radiated from her, making me want to cry. Again.

Mary Joy lit up at seeing her and reached her arms out of the carrier. I smiled, put down my coffee, and pulled her out. I didn't even ask Juliet if she wanted to hold her—I simply passed her over.

After setting her mug aside, Juliet wrapped her arms around the baby, held her close, swaying slightly. "I'm so glad she's okay."

"Me, too. Are you?" I asked. "Okay?"

"I don't think so," she said after a moment, her voice breaking.

I scooted closer to her. "It was a scary day. Give yourself time to sort it out, process."

She rested her cheek on Mary Joy's head, rubbed her back, and quietly told me about hearing thunder, how the park had reminded her of her grandfather, and how the panic began before she'd even seen Mary Joy was in trouble.

"I pride myself on taking care of people, on being strong, capable in an emergency. And I was barely able to dial a phone, Tallulah. I want to believe that my schooling and training would've kicked in, that it would've risen above my panic attack, but I'm just not sure. I worry that if Jake hadn't stepped in when he did, Mary Joy might've died—"

"Stop." I put my arm around her. "You were the one who saw she needed help in the first place. If not for you, then she might not have gotten *any* help until it was too late."

We sat in silence for a minute before she said, "I'm going to go home with my mom and sister. Go back to therapy. I realize now I stopped too soon—something my therapist warned me about, but I thought I had my anxiety under control. I don't want something like this to happen again. I can't be a good nurse otherwise."

My heart was breaking, falling to pieces. "But, Juliet—"

She shook her head. "I have to heal me. I don't want to live with this fear anymore."

It was really hard to argue with that, especially when I could hear her pain. Feel it.

Mary Joy had fallen asleep, her hand at her mouth, her head resting on Juliet's heart.

I held her gaze. "But you'll come back, right? One day? For good?"

Swimming in the sadness, I saw the tiniest of sparkles in her eyes as she nodded. "I promise."

Long after Juliet went back to Vera's, I still sat out front. Mary Joy was back in her carrier, still asleep. Birds were singing and chirping in the trees.

Juliet would be back later, once everyone was awake, to pack and to say goodbye to Papaw and Katy. She'd be leaving tomorrow, at first light.

I tried to pretend I wasn't crushed, because I knew therapy, picking up where she left off with her Michigan therapist, was what she needed most right now, but I was struggling with my emotions. I was going to miss her something fierce, and I knew my girls would, too.

I forced myself to remember that this wasn't a goodbye.

It was an *I'll see you soon*.

I'd been waiting to go back inside until the house woke up. It was already seven—long past when Papaw would normally be awake, puttering around. It seemed like yesterday had exhausted *everyone*.

My back rested against a column, and my legs were stretched out in front of me on the porch. I was scrolling through my phone, looking for advice on whether all egg products should be removed from the house, when I heard the jingle of dog tags.

My head came up. My heart started to thrum. I knew that sound. I swung my legs around, putting my feet on the top step.

Jake and Daisy were walking down the sidewalk.

When the puppy realized where they were, she raced ahead, straining the leash. Her backside wiggled. Her tail was a blur of motion.

I searched Jake's face for any sign, any clue, of why he was here, then realized he'd probably come to check on Mary Joy.

Daisy veered off the sidewalk, trampling flowers to get to the front steps.

I said, "I see puppy training is going well."

He cracked a smile, drew to a stop so Daisy wouldn't climb the stairs. "I'm starting to think she's training me to get used to this behavior."

I put one hand on Mary Joy's back and held out the other toward the puppy. She licked and kissed and wiggled. I rubbed her head until she settled down. "She'll learn. She's just a baby."

Jake nodded to the steps. "Mind if I—"

"Not at all."

He sat and Daisy explored. Jake smiled at Mary Joy, who had a drool bubble on her lips.

I was struggling to find the words to express what I wanted to say. How indebted I felt. The immense gratitude. Finally, I settled on, "I don't really know how to thank you."

"You just did."

"It's not enough. Not nearly."

He looked at me. "It is."

We watched Daisy trot around for a few moments before he said, "It seems Mary Joy is doing well."

"As can be. I'm still watching for a secondary reaction." Biphasic, it was called.

"So, you didn't sleep."

"Not even a wink."

"You need to take care of you, too."

"I'll nap later," I said. Maybe. I bumped him with my elbow. "So, a doctor?"

His eyes twinkled. "I was starting to think you'd never guess."

"I got a big hint yesterday."

"I don't like to tell people right off the bat. Some don't recognize boundaries and start telling me all their ailments or showing me their moles."

I made a grossed-out face.

"Exactly," he said.

The breeze rustled Mary Joy's hair, and I smoothed it back down. "How does a doctor work from home?"

"I'm a radiologist. I work for an orthopedics and sports medicine group who don't mind where I work from, just as long as I get the studies read in a timely manner."

"I was thinking that maybe you specialized in pediatrics. So many people told me how cool, calm, and collected you were while taking care of Mary Joy."

"Only on the outside," he said. "I did a sub—an internship—in pediatrics when I was in med school. I'd been thinking at the time that I wanted to go into pediatric emergency medicine, but it wasn't for me. Loved the kids, but I struggled with seeing them suffering."

His soft heart was one of the things I loved most about him.

Love.

I tried to ignore the ache in my chest as I watched Daisy sniff around Bill's trunk and said, "I was surprised you were at the festival at all. I thought you left town."

He pulled in a deep breath. "Yeah, about that. Strange story."

He looked at me and smiled, and I swallowed over the lump in my throat, felt the flutters in my heart as it said, *It's him. He's the one.*

And I told it, *I know.*

"After I saw you at the library, I only made it a couple of blocks before I started asking myself what I was doing. Where was I going? Why was I leaving town when all I've ever wanted is here?"

I could barely breathe, too afraid to believe what I was hearing.

He reached out, one hand curving over my cheek. "A chance at love. A family. *Home.* I'm sorry. Sorry for walking away, sorry for not realizing sooner."

Tears rolled down my face. With a quiver, I said, "Better late than never?"

He leaned in and kissed me softly, and I tried to soak in the moment so I'd never forget this feeling. This *joy.*

"Does this mean you're staying?" I asked, our foreheads pressed together. "Because I'm willing to try long-distance. I'd rather do that than not have you in my life at all."

I told him how it had been Evanthe who made me realize what mattered most.

"I'm staying. But it's funny you mention her," he said, pulling away but taking hold of my hand, "because she told me to ask you about something."

"About what?"

His thumb was making lazy sweeps across my skin. "It goes back to Friday, when I was leaving town. As soon as I had the big realization about you, my truck started acting up. I just barely had time to pull it off the road before it stalled and I couldn't get it started again. Aunt Ev came and picked me up. Said my truck breaking down meant I was meant to stay here and that you could tell me all about it."

I couldn't stop smiling. His truck had broken down.

But wait. That didn't make sense. Unless he *had* been a little lost after his breakup and had been led to town. Led to me.

No, it didn't quite fit with the town's folklore, but I didn't much care.

He was here.

He was *staying*.

"Well, you see, it's all about love," I began, "and how—"

Just then, I heard the soft hum of a familiar Gilbert and Sullivan song, and I cut myself off just as Papaw pushed open the screen door. His hair was damp, and he was grinning. "Daisy girl! Hello!"

Jake had the good sense to let go of the leash as Daisy bolted past us.

Papaw laughed with glee as he tried to hug the excited dog.

With a smile, Jake looked at me and quietly said, "It's like watching a love story unfolding."

My eyes once again filled with tears, remembering the first time he'd said those words, and I nodded. "I hope it has a happy-ever-after."

"It will," he said, a big, shiny promise in his gaze.

Papaw said, "Jake, you should stay for breakfast. Not sure what we're having just yet, excepting it won't be something with eggs."

"I just might. I wouldn't want to miss out on hearing the rest of a story Tallulah was telling me." He glanced my way. "You were saying something about love."

I stood and held out my hand to him. "We've got time. Loads of it."

Thirty-Eight

A Pearl of Wisdom
from Maeve Hearnshaw
"Sometimes, honey, detours lead to destiny."

Juliet

It was nearly ten in the morning, and I was sitting across from Renny, a checkers game in progress. I'd dreaded coming to Juneberry, hating to tell him I was going home, and it had hurt just as much as I thought it would.

"Leaving tomorrow, eh?" Renny said in his raspy voice after I explained. "So today is Juliet's Big Farewell Tour? What number stop am I? Tell me I'm top three at least. With my good looks alone, I think I deserve top three."

Oh gosh. I was going to miss him. "Number two. I've only told Tallulah."

Renny pumped a victorious arm.

I rolled my eyes. He pretended not to notice.

Vera was currently giving Mom and Amy a tour of Forget-Me-Not, showing them all the important places, like the Lickety Split and Snug's and here, too, though they promised to let me talk to Renny and Maeve before they arrived. They were going to stop at the Bean Patch for coffee first of all, because Vera needed to restock her bean supply after making endless pots of coffee these last couple of days. Mom had offered to buy them, Vera refused, and I knew there was going to be a battle of wills for Amy to mediate.

I had a few more stops to make after this visit. I wanted to say goodbye to Nettie and Isabel.

And to Callum.

My heart sank, just thinking about him.

He'd been amazing yesterday, so caring and understanding that I fell just a bit harder for him even thinking about it. He was never far while I'd been in the emergency room, getting oxygen, a medicated IV, blood work, heart tests, chest X-rays, and even a CT scan of my head, because of the headache.

When all the tests came back fine, the doctor had kindly talked to me about panic attacks, anxiety meds, psychologists and psychiatrists. My mom and Amy had looked on the whole time, with the same expression in their eyes, pleading with me to come home, get help. Finish healing.

My phone had been flooded with messages from my family. Text after text from my brothers checking on me. Eric sent hearts and promises of movie nights when I got back. Inappropriate hospital memes came from Jordan and Hunter. My dad had called. I'd barely been able to talk to him I'd been so choked up.

I'd been so embarrassed to have to go to the hospital for a panic attack. Ashamed, even, though it wasn't really fair of me—my heart rate had been way too high. It just felt like I should've been able to control my emotions, and clearly I couldn't.

I had to find a way to get better . . . so I could come back.

So I could be the nurse I wanted to be.

So I could be the person I wanted to be.

I reached into my pocket, felt the downy feather I'd found on the ground yesterday. Somehow it hadn't gotten lost during the trip to the hospital, the aftermath.

Last night, I'd dreamed of my grandfather. Of him holding my hand and telling me to remember the good. And let go of the rest. That he was always with me, even when he wasn't by my side.

I didn't think it had been a dream. Or even a memory. It felt more like . . . a visit.

I glanced at the robin print hanging on the wall, the one Tenn must've hung yesterday, and blinked away the tears that were building.

With a gentle push, Renny moved a checker diagonally. "You feeling better today?"

"A little," I said. "But if you don't mind, I'd rather not rehash it."

"Isn't that what therapy is about? Rehashing?"

I smiled. "Are you a therapist now?"

"I can be." He coughed, then intoned, "I'm all ears."

The game was moving slowly. I suspected it was on purpose. He was dragging it out when he could've won ten minutes ago.

"I'm going to need to see some accreditation." I slid a checker, instead of jumping over one of his pieces.

I supposed I was dragging the game out, too.

"I seem to have misplaced it. How long do you think you'll be gone?" he asked, a bushy eyebrow raised.

"I'm not sure."

I was trying not to think about being gone at all. Or even going back to Tenn's this afternoon to pack and say my goodbyes there. It might break me.

I wanted so badly to stay.

He said, "There's a chance, you know, that the town isn't going to let you go. Your car might not make it to the county line."

I'd be lying if I said I hadn't thought about that a million times since deciding to leave.

"But what if it lets me go?" I asked, my throat aching.

I fully expected him to tell me that it meant I wasn't supposed to stay.

But he surprised me by saying, "Maybe it would mean that you're not supposed to be here *right now*."

Which made me suspect that at some point in his long life, he'd come to recognize that it had been heartache that kept him and

Walt apart, not destiny. I wouldn't ask, but it did make me think about regrets, and I couldn't help thinking I was going to regret leaving this town.

"So, you don't know," I said, trying to lighten the mood.

He pressed his hands to his chest and dropped his jaw in faux outrage. "No need to call me out like that. I'm an old man. An old—"

"Don't say it."

He coughed pitifully. "—dying man."

I dropped my head, sighed heavily.

Two days with Amy and Mom and I'd already picked up the habit.

He jumped one of my checkers, gave me a smile. "I feel it in my bones that you're supposed to be here, doll."

I felt it, too.

Which was all kinds of confusing since I was leaving.

He cleared his throat, which devolved into a coughing fit. I jumped up. "Oxygen?"

"No, no. Just water," he croaked, pointing.

I darted over to his nightstand, and in my haste, I bumped my hip against it, which immediately toppled his massive pile of books. They fell one after another onto the floor.

A strange noise came from Renny, and I realized he was laughing. "Graceful."

I filled a glass of water, handed it to him. "You should've seen me take ballet when I was little. The instructor actually pulled my grandpa aside and suggested to him I try a different style of dance."

Renny sipped, then wiped his mouth with a handkerchief. "Did you?"

"No, I tried soccer instead."

"Really now. How'd that work out?"

"I broke an ankle."

He chuckled.

I started picking up books. "I know. Sometimes it takes me a while to accept the obvious. I started art lessons not long after. They went much better."

I reached for the green Whitman book and noticed an old black-and-white photograph hanging out of it, dislodged by the fall. I went to tuck it back in but stopped suddenly.

I knew that face.

Had studied it daily for nearly three months.

I tugged the photo out of the book and realized it was torn in half. The man in the image had slicked-back hair, fitted khakis, a button-down shirt.

Even though the photo was black-and-white, I knew his eyes were green.

I held up the picture.

"Oh," Renny said. "You found Walt. It's the only picture I have of him. He took the other half, the half that featured me, with him when he left."

My hands were shaking as I picked up the book and carried it, and the photo, to the table.

"Juliet? What's wrong? You're pale as a ghost."

I felt like I'd seen one.

I put the picture on the table; then I fumbled for my phone, called up the family pictures in the online cloud.

I found an old one of my grandfather. He was holding my mother, who'd been a toddler at the time. He'd been maybe twenty-four or twenty-five in the photo.

I turned the phone, put it on the table as well. "My grandfather. Ronald Stephens." As soon as I said his name, a light went on. "Ronald *Whitman* Stephens."

His breath caught. "*Walt*. I called him Walt. Ronald was much too stuffy."

His hand trembled as he reached for the phone, picked it up. He zoomed in on my grandfather's face, and a sheen of moisture filled his eyes.

My mind was spinning, counting the years. Grandpa's trip here had been before he met my grandmother, by a year or so. It had to have happened, I suddenly realized, during his big road trip. Only he hadn't told me about this stop in his journey.

My heart broke, guessing at the reason why and what had led him here in the first place. A big decision. In light of what I now knew, I suspected he'd been debating whether to keep secret this part of himself. Or let it be known.

I wanted to cry for him, that he thought he had to make a choice at all.

And that he'd ultimately kept it quiet.

A sad smile tugged at Renny's lips. "Oh, how I loved him."

I blinked and a tear fell. I opened the poetry book, read the inscription in my grandfather's hand.

WILL YOU GIVE ME YOURSELF? WILL YOU COME TRAVEL WITH ME? SHALL WE STICK BY EACH OTHER AS LONG AS WE LIVE?

I tapped the page. "He loved you, too."

His eyes were shiny as he nodded; then he suddenly laughed.

"What?" I asked, wiping my eyes.

"I should've put this together earlier. I saw that dream catcher you made for Katy and noticed the robin feathers straight off. I thought it was a coincidence. I should've known better."

Renny tugged the poetry book toward him. Every few pages, he pulled out a feather. By the time he was done, there were at least a dozen on the table.

I reached into my pocket for the feather I'd found yesterday. I pulled it out, held it in my palm, and told him all about the robin, the feathers, the dreams.

"Every time he found one, he'd give it to me," Renny said. "He told me to keep them, to remember him by, and promised me that one day he'd return and leave more feathers. I thought he meant that they'd be for me, but they were for you. He was trying to show the link between us."

I closed my fingers around the feather in my hand and could've kicked myself for not telling Renny about them earlier. I had to remind myself that the timing didn't matter. We'd made the connection. That was the important thing.

Renny chuckled. "He's a cheeky bird, isn't he? Leading you here to Forget-Me-Not to make sure I knew how much I'd meant to him—and to help you find your way again."

I said, "When I set out on this trip, I really thought I was trying to get to know myself better, but now I'm wondering if this journey had been meant for me to figure out who *he'd* been."

If you don't want to go alone, we can go together. I'd love to show you the special places I visited.

I had no doubt we would've stopped here, in Forget-Me-Not. He'd planned to reveal to me his true self, the parts he'd kept hidden all these years. He didn't want to keep it secret any longer—he'd wanted me to know.

Renny was still looking at the photo. "I think, perhaps, it was both."

"Maybe so," I said, smiling as I thought about how much I'd changed while here. How much I'd learned about myself. How much I'd healed, even though I still had some healing to do.

"You know," he said, his eyes soft, dewy, "if he'd come back to me, you might not be here."

A tear slipped out as I nodded. The what-could've-beens were almost too painful to think about.

His warm gaze settled on mine, and he gave me a smile. "I have no regrets, Juliet. No regrets. *This* is what was meant to be. *You* were meant to be."

I wiped the tears from my eyes and tried to keep my composure. Emotion was flooding me from every direction.

Renny stared at the photo on my phone awhile longer, then said, "Do you have more pictures?"

I smiled. "There are decades of albums online. You don't know what you're asking."

He ran a finger over the screen. "I think I do."

Oh gosh, the way my heart ached. "Okay then, I'll just add you to the account."

I retrieved his iPad, signed him in, and as he flipped through the photos, his gaze drew distant as he remembered another place, another time, and maybe even considered what might've been.

He peppered me with questions. About Grandpa's job—insurance. About Grandma—they'd been happy. About whether he'd stayed crazy for birds—he had. About whether he found love again—he'd dated but was tight-lipped about his love life.

Now I realized why.

I told him how Grandpa had always gushed about his trip south. I showed him the photos. He'd laughed his head off at the flamingo picture, remembering that my grandfather had told him about that visit—and how the flamingo had chased him around the garden after the picture was taken. We talked for an hour—I'd stayed longer than I planned, but I couldn't leave without answering all his questions.

Finally, he said, "First loves aren't always lasting loves, but more often than not, they leave an imprint on your heart. I hope I left that mark for him, the way he did for me."

I teared up again. "I know you did. He wouldn't have brought me here otherwise."

Slowly, he nodded, his eyes wet, a smile on his face.

I pushed back my chair, tucked away my feather, and said, "I don't know how to say goodbye."

He blinked, then looked up at me. "Juliet, you mentioned earlier how it takes you a while to see the obvious, so I'm just going to say it. You don't have to go."

I opened my mouth to explain again about therapy and healing, but he held up a hand, stopping me.

"There are therapists here. Well, one. If you'd rather a bigger selection, Birmingham is only forty minutes away."

I wrung my hands. "I wish I could, but I'm established with a therapist in Michigan, and I really need to be with my family right now."

He sighed.

I walked over to him, gave him a hug. "I'm going to miss you."

"Not as much as I'll miss you," he said. "Thank you for bringing Walt back to me."

I kissed his forehead, then walked out into the hallway, my legs a bit wobbly. I told myself not to look back, but I couldn't help it.

He was watching me, a pensive look in his eyes. "I'm rooting for the breakdown, you know."

Tears were pooling, blurring my vision. "Honestly, I kind of am, too."

It would be nice to know I was meant to be here.

That it was destined.

My heart hurting, I waved and walked away.

Outside, the sun was shining. Beating down, really, as if it were trying to make up for yesterday.

I heard a bird singing, but it wasn't a robin.

I walked slowly to my car, pretty much dragging my feet.

What Renny said was weighing on me. About there being therapists here. Would it really hurt to start over with someone new?

Yet my family . . .

I closed my eyes, sighed.

But didn't I have family here? Wasn't that what Renny and Maeve and Tallulah and Tenn had become?

I started pacing. Three steps left, three steps right.

But what about destiny?

Didn't I want to know for sure?

Suddenly I started shaking my head. Then I ran to my car,

flung open the door, and popped the hood. I looked under it, not at all sure what I was seeing. It didn't matter, though.

I wasn't leaving anything to chance.

I was making my own destiny.

I wanted to *stay*.

I reached in and started yanking on wires and hoses. I pulled off caps, covers.

I barely heard the truck pulling up next to me. Or its door opening. I didn't stop my vandalism until I heard, "Juliet, I just got the news that you're leaving—" Callum came around the hood, saw me. He blinked as if he couldn't believe his eyes, then casually said, "And what's going on here?"

My chest was heaving from exertion, and my hands were filthy as I faced him. I glanced at the car, then him. I laughed. With happiness. With *relief*. "I'm making sure I stay in Forget-Me-Not."

He glanced away for a second, as if needing to gather himself for a moment, and when he turned back, he was grinning. Rushing forward, he pulled me into a hug. "I was so scared you'd already left. I didn't want to lose you when I just found you."

I quickly told him how I didn't want to leave and that I'd find a therapist nearby. "My family will understand."

In my heart, I knew it to be true. They wanted me to be happy. *Healthy*. That was what mattered most.

I wasn't sure what to tell them about my grandfather. About his hidden chapter. I kind of wanted to keep it to myself. A secret we shared. But I wouldn't. It needed to be known. He had wanted it to be known.

I looked up at Callum. "How'd you even hear that I'd been planning to leave? And know where to find me?"

He lifted my hand, found a clean spot, and kissed it. In one big breath, he said, "It went like this. Vera told Isabel at the coffee shop. Isabel called Nettie. Nettie called my gran. Gran called me. I went to Tenn's. Tenn called Vera. Vera said you were here. I came as fast as I could. As soon as I pulled in, I got a text from Uncle

Ren, telling me to do everything in my power to keep you here even if I had to put diesel in your gas tank."

I leaned into him, laughing against his chest.

Oh, how I loved this town. Its people.

And maybe, *especially*, him, though I might keep that to myself for a while.

I glanced at the car engine. "You can tell Renny you did this, if you want."

He shook his head. "He'd be prouder knowing it was you."

Keeping one arm around me, he gestured with the other at the broken wires and loose hoses. "You know this kind of damage isn't covered in your warranty, right? It's in the fine print."

As I leaned up to kiss him, I said, "No one ever reads the fine print."

❋ The Forget-Me-Not Library ❋

Nightingale family group chat upon the debut of a video clip that would eventually go viral and produce trending hashtags such as #makelikeabird #makelikeabirdandfly #makelikeabirdandflyjules #findjules

Jordan: My best work yet

Hunter: Sweet!

Amy: Is that Mom? She looks like a deranged chicken

Juliet: That's what I said!

Mom: JULIET, YOU FILMED ME?

Amy: Was it a dare?

Dad: That's my hunny

Eric: She'll do anything to get her morning steps in

Mom: Jordan, delete this immediately!

Jordan: Too late it's already trending

Hunter: #makelikeabird

Amy: It's kind of impressive form. I score you a 9/10

Mom: Why only 9 and not 10/10?

Juliet: Isn't Mom the greatest?

To which everyone reacted with a heart, even Mom.

Thirty-Nine

*A Pearl of Wisdom
from Renny Russo*
"Memory Lane is the best place to run into people you love."

Tallulah

On Tuesday morning, a wheel on the book cart squeaked as I headed for adult nonfiction, basking in the routine of shelving. I was oddly energized for someone who'd had very little sleep over the last few days. Though in some ways the sleeplessness had been beneficial.

During the wee hours of the last few nights, I'd finished my Trivia Night proposal. I'd written down more wisdoms. I'd pinned house-decorating ideas to a Pinterest board. And I'd downloaded the application for the MLIS program.

One of the requirements was a short personal essay, and I decided that when the time came, I'd write about what the library meant to me.

How when I was younger, libraries had been my home base, my saving grace. Because at their core, they were always the same. A place of comfort. Security. *Familiarity.* They'd brought a sense of peace otherwise missing in my life and a consistency I'd craved.

Plus, they reminded me of my grandmother. Which reminded me of love.

"Do you think I'll be accepted to the program?" I asked Deckle, as if she had any clue what I was talking about.

I swore her head bobbed, and I smiled.

She'd been following me, leaping gracefully from shelf to shelf, and I found myself enjoying her company rather than being annoyed by it.

I rounded a corner, and out of the corner of my eye, I spotted Evanthe looking out the window facing the back garden. Her face was in profile, her chin lifted. Her shoulders were drawn back, her hands clasped behind her.

I watched her, wondering what she was thinking when she stared out that window. Was she remembering days long past? Old loves? Old friends?

Then I caught sight of movement in the garden. Someone coming into view. Jed, I realized. He was sweeping the patio. He didn't seem to notice she was watching him. Or see how a shy smile began to turn the corner of her lips upward.

I glanced at Deckle and grinned. "How about that?" I whispered. "She has to be thinking about compromises, right?"

However, instead of giving me a head bob or a whisker twitch to answer my question, she hopped onto the book cart. Where she promptly knocked a book onto the floor.

I stared at her.

She stared at me.

Finally, I gave in and blinked, then looked down at the book that had landed at my feet. It was a *Southern Living* cookbook titled *The Southern Cookie Book*.

I swallowed hard. It had been a while since Deckle had knocked a book in front of me—not since the day of the paperback book swap. It was as if she knew I was coming around and simply needed to give me a little more time to sort through my feelings.

That breathing room had allowed me to see that it was time to let go of this grudge once and for all.

"Trust the process?" I said to her.

Her tail swished.

I picked up the book, and for a moment, I simply stared at the pile of chocolate cookies on the cover. My heart began beating faster and faster.

Deckle meowed, as if encouraging me.

"Okay," I said, then borrowed words from Jake. "I'm choosing to trust you."

Pulling in a deep breath, I let the book fall open. Once the pages settled, I glanced down and saw a recipe for Outrageous Peanut Butter Cookies.

Deckle's golden eyes watched me closely, and I noticed a depth to them I'd never seen before that hinted at an old, wise soul. I felt a sense of calm come over me as I lifted the book upward so I could inhale deeply, pulling in the scent of ink and paper and *life*. Bibliosmia.

In a flash, I was in my grandparents' kitchen, making cookies with my mamaw. I was just a little bit, sitting on the counter next to her, my tanned legs swinging as she put cooled peanut butter cookies onto a plate.

Her dewy eyes glittered with happiness. I'd never known anyone so full of joy. "These here are your papaw's favorite. He'll gobble them all up without a second thought, so we best hide a few away for ourselves, eh?" She pulled an old coffee tin from one of the cabinets. "I call this here can my treasure chest. He doesn't like coffee, so he won't likely think to look inside. It's where I hide all my most precious things." She laughed, then added, "Sometimes, when I'm hiding something extra special from your papaw, I ask Miss Evanthe to keep this here can safe for me. So if it ever goes missing, you know where to look."

She gave me a wink and a kiss on the top of my head, and then, just as quickly as the image of her had come, it disappeared.

My knees had gone weak, and I had to lean against a bookshelf. I was taken aback by what I'd seen.

What I *felt*.

The love I had for my grandmother was all balled up in my chest, crackling, ready to break open. She'd been gone for eighteen years now, and I was so filled with happiness from seeing her once again, hearing her voice, that I could cry.

Deckle jumped off the book cart onto the floor and started bumping against my legs. I picked her up, held her close, felt the rumbles of her purrs.

"Thank you," I whispered into her fur.

We stayed that way for a good minute while I replayed the memory over and over, until I finally figured out what I'd been meant to recall.

Impulsively, I kissed Deckle's head, then put her back on the floor. Then I abandoned the book cart and went looking for Evanthe. She was no longer at the window, so I checked her office. She was sitting behind her desk, her glasses perched on her nose as she studied a computer screen.

"Yes?" she said, glancing up at me.

I wasn't sure what to say.

"Tallulah? Is something wrong? Are those tears in your eyes?"

My legs were still a little wobbly, so I sat in one of the chairs across from her. "Deckle gave me a memory."

Evanthe's eyebrows lifted, and she set her glasses on her desk. "Oh?"

"I saw Mamaw. She was baking cookies and hiding them from Papaw in her coffee tin. And I think she was telling me that—" My voice caught. "Do *you* have her coffee tin? It's been missing since she passed away, and Papaw swears he didn't get rid of it."

For a moment, she studied my face, searching, seeking. I wasn't sure for what.

Without saying a word, she stood and strode to a filing cabinet. She used a key to unlock the drawer, which squeaked when she pulled it open. She reached in and pulled out the tin, hugging it tight against her chest.

My jaw dropped.

She slowly walked over to me, her long linen dress swirling around her ankles, and sat in the chair next to mine. "I spent a lot of time with June in her final days. Reminiscing. Trying to make amends for failing her."

"You didn't fail her," I said.

"I did." She looked upward and pulled in a deep breath. "It's one of my life's greatest regrets. I foolishly convinced myself that if I didn't see her ill, then she wouldn't be. I simply did not think I could survive losing someone else I loved so immensely. I chose to live in denial until one day I woke up to Calliper knocking a book onto the floor next to my bed. A thin volume of poetry by Emily Dickinson. When I breathed in its scent, I was reminded of a time when June and I were young girls. We were here at the library, our noses in books, as they often were in those days. June had been reading Emily Dickinson that day. When she came across the poem titled 'In a Library,' she read aloud its beginning to me." Her lip quirked. "She may as well have been a Shakespearean thespian, altering her voice, gesturing wildly, as she recited, 'A precious, mouldering pleasure 'tis. To meet an antique book.' We'd dissolved into a fit of giggles and had to be shushed by Miss Primrose, the librarian."

Tears filled my eyes, my heart full as I imagined my grandmother clowning around. She'd always been one to lighten a mood or light up a room. But I was having a harder time picturing Evanthe. "I can't imagine you giggling."

"I was a different person then."

Before grief stole her joy.

"'Forever—is composed of Nows.'" She looked at me. "Those were the words written on the page I breathed in the morning I finally came to my senses. The day I realized I could spend my time hiding from what was to come or I could spend it with June, honoring our friendship. Celebrating it."

"She understood why you hadn't been there," I said softly, gently. "She never once held it against you—none of us did. She loved you and she knew you loved her. She didn't need you to be by her side. Or hear you say the words. They lived in her heart, her soul."

Tears gathered in her eyes, and she pressed a shaky hand to her chest. "You've no idea what that means to me."

I thought, maybe, I did. I suspected that in order to move on, she'd needed forgiveness. From Mamaw. Perhaps from me as well. I hoped that now that she knew how we felt, her walls would come down, once and for all.

Thumbing away tears, she glanced down at the tin. "On the last day I saw June, she gave this to me. By that time, word had arrived that you and your parents might not make it back to Forget-Me-Not for quite some time. She asked me to keep the tin safe until you came to me for it. She seemed to believe that you'd know where to find it."

I could hear the raw emotion in my words as I said, "Surely, after eighteen years, you had to realize I had no idea."

Her gaze softened as she looked me in the eyes. "Yet here you are."

Yet here I was.

With a faint smile, she stood up. "Though I will admit to growing impatient. There was even a time recently when I sought to intervene, placing the tin directly in front of you."

I tipped my head, confused. Until I remembered where I'd seen the coffee can recently. I glanced out the office window, to the storybook Tudor house across the street, its blue tarp clear as day. "The Library House."

She dipped her chin in acknowledgment. "I was behind Georgia Smith in line at the coffee shop and heard her speaking on the phone, telling someone she would be showing the house to you later that day. I concocted a plan, one that clearly failed, so I went back, collected the can once again, and knew I simply had to continue to be patient. My interference was not welcomed."

This explained why the coffee tin had been missing during the second showing. I glanced up at her, seeing her in a whole new light. "So you weren't interested in the house at all?"

"No. However, I'm unsurprised you were drawn to it. I'm not sure you're aware, but it is a house June had much admired."

Having said that, she held out the tin to me.

Chills swept down my arms as I took it from her. "Do you know what's in it?"

"I believe June called them treasures." She placed her hand on my shoulder, gave it a comforting squeeze. "Take your time."

In a swish of linen, she was gone, out the door and into the stacks.

My heart was thrumming as I carefully lifted the lid and peeked inside the large can. Immediately, I saw the recipe box stuffed full of Mamaw's treasured, handwritten recipes, and if I weren't so close to sobbing, I'd probably have squealed with glee.

Also in the tin was a square jewelry box.

I pulled it out, and the gold box felt warm in my hand, like sunshine on a cold day. A yellow sticky note attached said *Tallulah* in Mamaw's handwriting.

My gaze traced the lines of her penmanship. The loopy *l*s. The dramatic *h*.

I could barely breathe as I shimmied the top off the box, set it aside. Nestled in thin layers of white tissue paper lay a gold necklace and pendant.

As I lifted the necklace, the weight of my love for her, my grief, pushed against my chest. Crushing it. Crushing me.

I took a moment to close my eyes. Breathe.

Then I looked at the charm more closely, cupping it in my palm. It was a gold disc engraved with a beautiful compass rose, an eight-pointed star, just like the ones she used on her quilts. Just like the one carved into the newel post at the Library House. I flipped the pendant over, and my eyes filled with tears as I read the engraving.

ALWAYS FOLLOW YOUR HEART
IT KNOWS THE WAY HOME

I closed my fingers around the charm and just sat there for a minute, allowing myself to feel what needed to be felt. I didn't smother the emotions. As I pictured Mamaw picking out this necklace, choosing the engraving, my heart swelled. She'd known how I felt about having a home. A place where my heart belonged. With this gift, she was sharing a valuable pearl of wisdom.

Maybe home wasn't a place at all.

It was a feeling.

It was love.

Was it just a coincidence that I'd found love here in Forget-Me-Not? In the library, no less?

I didn't think so.

Not even a little bit.

Forty

*A Pearl of Wisdom
from Evanthe Kilburn*
"It's never too late to start a new chapter."

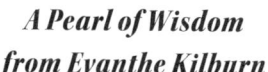

Tallulah

It had been nearly a year and a half since I moved into the Library House, and Christmas hung in the air. The scent of pine, of cinnamon, of cloves.

The tree was up in the living room, protected by a paneled baby gate. Not only to keep a toddling Mary Joy from yanking shiny bulbs off the branches, but to prevent our cat, Evie, from doing it as well. I'd just finished setting up the barrier and stood back, wondering how long it would keep them out of trouble since both were smart and clever.

Evie stared at me from the arm of the couch, her blue eyes accusing me of violating her basic feline rights. I scooped her up, cuddling her, and she allowed it, forgiving me.

She'd shown up at the back door one chilly morning *last* December, meowing pitifully, absolutely filthy. The vet estimated she was about four months old, and once she was cleaned off, she was a picture of beauty. Her fur was pure white fluff, except for the tip of her tail, which was black.

Because that dark tip reminded me of Evanthe's hair, we decided to name her Evie. Evanthe had pretended to be outraged, claiming no comparison, but she'd been smiling the whole time.

When she suggested I bring the kitten with me to work so Evie could play with Deckle, I didn't even mention how it violated regulations she'd put in place. If she was willing to break the rules, then so was I.

As I scratched Evie's chin, listened to her purr, I watched Mary Joy sleep on the other end of the couch, never tiring of seeing her so at peace.

She'd fallen asleep while watching one of her favorite TV shows, featuring a perky host who had the magical ability to captivate babies and toddlers worldwide as she performed catchy songs and taught lessons with an emphasis on language development. I hadn't the heart to move her. Not until I had to—I glanced at the clock—which was in approximately fifteen minutes.

We had a wedding to go to.

I adjusted the blanket draped over her legs. Her round cheeks were flushed from the heat of the house and the long nap. Wispy bangs had been pulled into a tiny ponytail atop her head that looked like a waterspout. She'd turn two years old next month and I could hardly believe how fast the time had gone by.

She'd had allergy testing done when she was nine months old, and in addition to eggs, she was also allergic to chickpeas and mango. The allergist was optimistic she'd outgrow some—if not all—of these, and I hoped so. Her allergic reaction that day in the park still haunted my dreams. So much so that I was often tempted to borrow the dream catcher that hung in Katy's bedroom window, because she hadn't had a nightmare since it had been gifted to her by Juliet. A miracle if I ever saw one.

Laughter came from the kitchen, and I peeked in at Katy and Zoe, who sat at the table making bracelets from the kit that Scott had given Katy the last time she'd seen him.

He'd kept his word.

He'd found a job in Birmingham and had moved into a condo near our old neighborhood, which allowed Katy to have a sense of familiarity when she visited and also allowed her to easily see old friends.

It had taken half a year of brief visitations with Mary Joy before she spent the weekend with him as well. Not only because I had trust issues, but because they didn't really know each other. They'd needed that time to form a bond.

I'd cried the first time he'd driven away with both the girls for a whole weekend visit. I was still working on being able to let them go without a knot of fear in my stomach, but I didn't know if that fear came from them being with Scott, or if it simply came from me being a mother.

I suspected the latter.

The girls were oblivious to me watching them, but Daisy had noticed. Her head came up; her tail thumped the floor. As sure as the sun rose every day, if Katy was home, Daisy was at her side.

When my phone buzzed in the pocket of my dress, I backed away from the kitchen. Balancing Evie in the crook of my arm, I pulled the phone out and saw a text from Juliet.

> Running late—hit traffic on way home! Save us seats just in case?

I sent back a quick Of course. She and Callum had gone to pick out their Christmas tree this morning. She'd wanted a living one that they could decorate, then plant, and the nearest farm that sold them was an hour away.

In the living room, I set Evie on the top tier of her cat tree so she could look out the window at the birds in the side yard. I glanced at Baby Bill, checking on him. He was still such a small thing, only three feet tall. But he was still growing. One day, I hoped, I'd see my grandchildren or great-grandchildren reading in his arms.

As I turned away, my gaze lingered on the built-in bookcase to the right of the fireplace. Specifically, on the wooden checkerboard displayed there.

My heart panged as I thought about Uncle Renny, and a fit of nostalgia spurred me down the hall toward the office. I gently pushed open the door, trying to be quiet.

But Jake heard me anyway.

He spun his desk chair toward me and took off his headphones. On his computer monitors, someone's bones were on display.

It was dark in the room, thick curtains blocking any daylight. It was easier for him to read the X-rays that way. The bookshelves were filled, mostly a mix of his books and mine. Some belonged to the girls. A few had belonged to Renny, but not his Walt Whitman book. He'd bequeathed that to Juliet.

He'd been gone now for more than a year, passing peacefully, surrounded by the people who loved him most.

Aunt Maeve. Papaw. Me. Callum. Juliet.

The first cookbook club without him had been a mix of tears and laughter. Probably just the way he would've wanted it.

"Is it time to go?" Jake asked, reaching for me, pulling me onto his lap for a kiss.

My heart gloated, saying, *I told you so.*

Technically, Jake and I were still newlyweds. We'd married this past summer at a small ceremony in the sun garden at the end of Papaw's street.

"We have a few more minutes," I said.

He gave me a look that heated me to my bones.

I laughed and pushed off him, a little weak-kneed. "Definitely not enough time for *that*." Then I stopped, thought about it, and shook my head. "The girls . . ."

It was his turn to laugh.

"I didn't mean to bother you." I crossed the room to the small secretary I used as a desk, pushed aside the textbooks for my current postgrad courses and my notes for the next Trivia Night at the library, and picked up my spiral-bound *Pearls of Wisdom* book. "I just wanted to grab this real quick."

"You're never a bother, Tallulah."

And that was just another reason why I loved him. I gave him another kiss, then backed out of the room. "I'll see you in a few."

I took the book into the living room and sat down in one of the overstuffed armchairs near the fireplace. I ran my finger over the cover. It was a limited edition, this book, sold only at this past summer's Flour Festival, with proceeds benefiting the library—a donation made in the name of my grandmother.

In it were hundreds of wisdoms I'd collected from Isabel, Vera, Nettie, Papaw, Aunt Maeve, Renny, and Evanthe, among others. I thumbed to one of Renny's wisdoms, his very last, issued a few days before he left us.

> DON'T CRY BECAUSE IT'S OVER.
> NO, WAIT. GO AHEAD AND CRY.

Then he'd added, "If there's a dry eye at my funeral, I'll haunt all y'all."

I shook my head and smiled. There'd been no dry eyes.

With tears shimmering in my eyes now, I held the book to my chest where my compass rose pendant lay near my heart and glanced up at the mantel. Hanging from individual hooks were six stockings, the names on them embroidered with golden thread. Just like I'd seen in my dreams.

Tallulah, Jake, Katy, Mary Joy, Daisy, Evie.

My heart.

My home.

Juliet

By some miracle, Callum and I made it to the wedding ceremony with a few minutes to spare.

He held my hand as we made a run for the doors, the whooshing sound familiar and welcome.

Winter sunlight spread a golden glow across bookshelves and the gathered crowd. All the couches, chairs, and tables had been cleared from the main reading area, and now it was filled with cushioned folding chairs, twenty on the bride's side, twenty on the groom's, with a satin-covered aisle dividing them.

In front of the chairs, near a flowered arch, a string trio was warming up, and a preacher was smiling at the groom, who didn't look nervous in the least.

This wedding had been a long time coming.

Nettie and Isabel had someone cornered at the front desk, a man I didn't recognize, mid-thirties, blond hair, tattooed arms. I heard Nettie say, "Are you a friend of the bride or the groom?"

"Neither," he said, looking left, looking right. "I just came inside to wait for a tow truck. My car broke down."

"Oh?" Isabel said. "Was there a plume of smoke perchance? And if so, what color was it?"

"Purple." His eyebrows dropped low. "How'd you know?"

Purple, I knew, meant his heart was lonely.

Nettie tutted. "That tow truck is probably going to take a while, considering the proprietor of the garage is attending a wedding. You should make yourself comfortable. Did you know weddings are a great place to look for love?"

Isabel added, "The reception will have an open bar. You can't beat free when asking someone if they'd like a cocktail."

I almost laughed at the man's dumbfounded expression.

Nettie turned him slightly, aiming him toward the bride's section of chairs. "See the pretty lady in the pink dress? You should go sit next to her. Her name's Georgia, and she's friendly as can be."

With a bewildered nod, he scuttled off to sit down next to Georgia, whose wide smile bloomed almost immediately.

I glanced at Nettie, and she winked.

She was matchmaking.

"Oh dear," Isabel said. "I hope we haven't traumatized him."

I didn't think so, but I knew a good therapist if he needed it. She was in Birmingham, and I saw her every other week. I was doing really well these days—leaps and bounds better—but still had a ways to go.

"I forgot to mention to him that if he does happen to find love," Nettie said, "he shouldn't drag his feet when it comes time to propose!"

She turned toward us, eyes narrowed.

"Subtle," Callum said to her. "Real subtle."

Maeve laughed as she approached from behind us. "Subtle is one thing Nettie is not, honey. Did you two have a good morning?"

She moved at a whirlwind pace these days since her hip had been replaced, healed. At work, I could barely keep up with her as we walked the halls of Juneberry.

"We had a great morning," I said. "Found the perfect tree."

"It's a Charlie Brown tree," Callum said, a hint of exasperation in his tone.

I made a face at him.

He coughed. "It's perfect."

We were going to plant it in Tenn's backyard after the holidays. *Our* backyard.

We'd bought the house from Tenn this past spring after he downsized to a one-story home that just happened to be down the street, next door to Vera's. Everyone in town was talking about how friendly the two had become. I glanced over at them now, sitting next to each other on the bride's side of the aisle, their heads nearly touching as they chatted.

Nettie must've known what I was looking at, because she bumped me with her arm, gave me a smile. "*Sparks.*"

I grinned and nodded.

As the musicians launched into a song, keeping the volume low, the preacher said, "If y'all don't mind taking a seat, we're ready to begin."

Katy came running over. She rarely skipped anymore, which broke my heart a little. "Juliet, we saved your seats!"

Callum laughed as Katy grabbed my hand, towed me along. She was nine and a half now and was growing like a weed. Her hair was longer, turning darker, and her glasses were now blue. Every so often, she stayed the night with Callum and me, and more often than not, we made time to climb into Bill's strong arms and read for a while. I'd learned you're never too old to read in the arms of a tree.

Maeve beat us to the row of chairs where Tallulah was sitting with Jake, snuggled up close together. I looked around for Mary Joy, found her on Tenn's lap in the row in front of us, pulling on his beard like she was trying to take it off. I could hear him saying, "You didn't like that so much the last time, munchkin."

I scooted in behind Katy. Callum took the last chair as the volume of the music swelled.

Katy stood on her tiptoes, looking around. "Where's Deckle? Is she here? I don't see her."

"I'm sure she is," Tallulah said, smiling. "Sit, sit."

Callum reached over, took my hand, and I laced my fingers with his. As my wrist turned, I caught sight of the small tattoos, both new, on its underside. A robin and a feather.

My family had been surprised to learn the truth about my grandfather and his trip here but not shocked—my mom, especially. I suspected she knew *all* of us better than we'd ever understand. When Amy had helped Mom clean out Grandpa's place, she'd found Renny's half of the torn picture in a Whitman poetry book and mailed it to me. I'd taped the two sides back together, and now the photo sat on the mantel in a big house on a tree-lined street that had mossy sidewalks and an abundance of charm.

Callum leaned in, and I breathed in his cedar scent as he said, "Big wedding or small?"

I smiled. "Small. Destination wedding or local?"

His eyes widened, the blue shimmering like water in the sunlight. "That's a tough one. To be determined."

When the trio started playing Canon in D, we all stood up. Katy wiggled in front of me and Callum to stand at the end of the aisle where she had a better view. "Mama," she whispered over her shoulder, "I see Deckle!"

Tallulah smiled. "Good, good, but *shh*."

I felt my eyes welling as Evanthe swept down the aisle in a stunning champagne-colored column dress, carrying Deckle in her arms instead of a bouquet. There was a rose clipped to Deckle's white collar, and it seemed to me that her knowing golden eyes were glittering with happiness as they reached Jed, who was wiping his eyes with a handkerchief.

His dog, the one who apparently didn't tolerate cats, had crossed the rainbow bridge several months before, and the next thing anyone knew, Jed and Evanthe were engaged, sending a shock wave through the community. Almost everyone had been stunned. But not Tallulah. She had seemed to know that this day would come.

Maybe not Callum, either. After all, it was Jed who had shown up in his garage early one Monday morning a year and a half ago, holding a fat cashier's check made out to Juneberry Cottage. A check offered in exchange for Callum's silence about the potato he'd found in the tailpipe of Jake's truck, which had caused it to break down. Sabotage that had been orchestrated by Evanthe and carried out by Jed. It was a transaction known only to four people: Evanthe, Jed, Callum, and me. When Callum had asked Jed *why*, all he'd said was, "Love."

A perfect explanation if I'd ever heard one.

As we sat back down, I glanced at my left hand again and couldn't help smiling as I pictured the engagement ring Callum had given to me just this morning. I'd left it at home because I didn't want my happy news to take away from Evanthe's big day. Inside, though, I was beyond excited, jumping for joy, and couldn't wait to tell Tallulah, Maeve, and Katy.

But as we sat down once again, I happened to glance to my right and saw the three of them looking at me with matching big smiles.

And suddenly I had the feeling they already knew.

Acknowledgments

I must first thank librarian—and dear friend—Shelly Franz, for giving this book an early read and for sharing her insights on library life. I'm especially thankful for her patience when teaching me the different methods used when covering paperbacks versus hardcovers.

A huge thank-you to my editor, Kristin Sevick, who is an expert at guiding me back onto the right path when I start to wander. Thank you, as well, to everyone at Forge Books, St. Martin's Press, and Macmillan Audio who helped bring this book to readers. I appreciate you so much.

Thank you to Jessica Faust and the whole BookEnds team—you're amazing.

I'm incredibly grateful to the bird nerd community, which taught me something I didn't know while writing this book: Under the Migratory Bird Treaty Act, without a permit it's prohibited to be in possession of feathers belonging to many North American birds, including American robins, even if obtained by harmless means. For the purpose of this story, I employed artistic license by choosing to keep my characters in the dark about this law but recognize its importance in keeping birds safe. For a list of protected birds, you can search the U.S. Fish and Wildlife website: FWS.gov.

For my readers, it's an honor knowing that you choose to read my stories. Thank you, thank you, thank you.

And finally, thank you to my family, who always help me remember when I forget. Much love.

About the Author

Heather Webber is a national bestselling author known for crafting stories that celebrate the power of family, friendship, and community. Her novels, including *Midnight at the Blackbird Café* and *At the Coffee Shop of Curiosities*, offer comforting tales of love, hope, and personal redemption. Heather loves to spend time with her family, read, drink too much coffee and tea, bird-watch, crochet, and bake. She currently resides in southwest Ohio.